AARON BARNES WAS ON DUTY WITH THE SONAR SYSTEM OF THE USS *MONTANA*, AN *OHIO*-CLASS SSBN BALLISTIC MISSILE SUBMARINE.

Barnes took the job seriously. He knew that if he made one mistake, they were all blind and deaf in the belly of the sea.

So when the glider, still far off, began to emit a thrumming noise as it moved through the water, it was less than a second before Barnes noticed it, and only a few seconds more before both Barnes and the sonar computer concluded, from the sound-source's course and speed, that it wasn't a fish.

Within moments, the whole crew was at battle stations. There weren't all that many countries in the world that even owned submarines, and none of them were neutral. Not at that speed, at that depth, at that time. Not in those waters.

How fast *was* it? Barnes checked again. "Sixty knots," he whispered.

"Sixty knots?" said Captain Kretschmer. His voice was calm enough—he simply didn't believe the information. "No way, Barnes. The Reds don't have anything that fast."

"Checked it twice, skipper," Barnes told him. "It's a real unique signature. No cavitation, no reactor noise. Doesn't even sound like screws." In fact, it sounded like a fish with an incredibly loud heartbeat. But sixty knots? Wasn't a fish in the sea could move that fast even if it was pissing pure rocket fuel . . .

THE
ABYSS

A Novel by
Orson Scott Card
based on an original screenplay by
James Cameron

POCKET BOOKS

New York   London   Toronto   Sydney   Tokyo

An *Original* Publication of POCKET BOOKS

POCKET BOOKS, a division of Simon & Schuster Inc.
1230 Avenue of the Americas, New York, NY 10020

ISBN: 0-671-67625-3

First Pocket Books printing June 1989

10 9 8 7 6 5 4 3 2

POCKET and colophon are trademarks of
Simon & Schuster Inc.

Printed in the U.S.A.

In memory of Ray Spencer,
who lived a life worth living
and died with love and honor
in the place he would have chosen.

Contents

Whoever fights monsters should see to it
that in the process he does not become a monster;
and when you look long into an abyss,
the abyss also looks into you.
—Friedrich Nietzsche

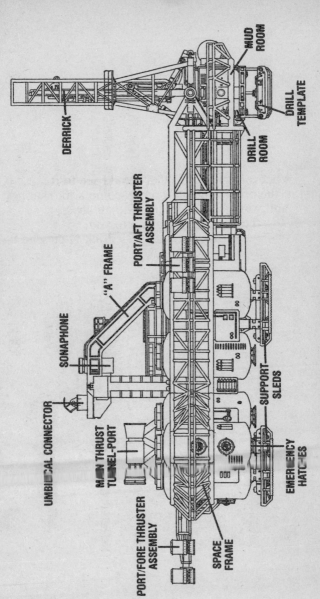

DEEPCORE II—PORT SIDE ELEVATION

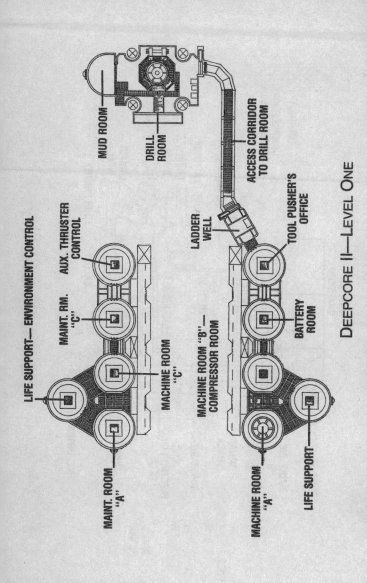

LIFE SUPPORT— ENVIRONMENT CONTROL

MAINT. ROOM "A"

MAINT. RM. "C"

AUX. THRUSTER CONTROL

MACHINE ROOM "C"

MACHINE ROOM "B"— COMPRESSOR ROOM

MACHINE ROOM "A"

LIFE SUPPORT

BATTERY ROOM

TOOL PUSHER'S OFFICE

LADDER WELL

ACCESS CORRIDOR TO DRILL ROOM

MUD ROOM

DRILL ROOM

DEEPCORE II—LEVEL ONE

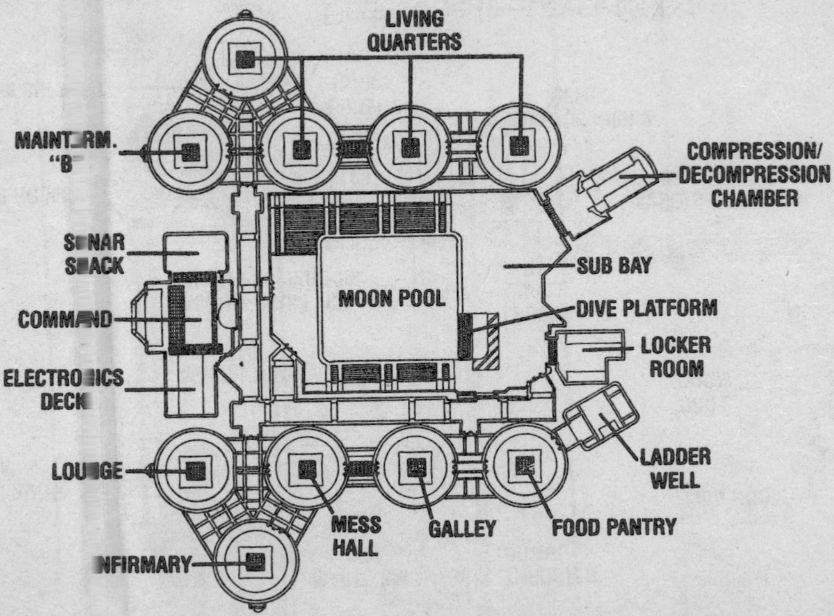

DEEPCORE II—LEVEL TWO

COMPRESSION/DECOMPRESSION CHAMBER

SUB BAY

DIVE PLATFORM

LOCKER ROOM

LADDER WELL

FOOD PANTRY

LIVING QUARTERS

MOON POOL

GALLEY

MESS HALL

MAINT. RM. "B"

SONAR SHACK

COMMAND

ELECTRONICS DECK

LOUNGE

INFIRMARY

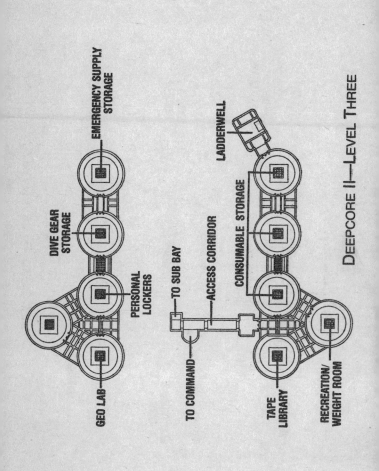

EMERGENCY SUPPLY STORAGE

DIVE GEAR STORAGE

PERSONAL LOCKERS

LADDERWELL

TO SUB BAY

ACCESS CORRIDOR

CONSUMABLE STORAGE

GEO LAB

TO COMMAND

TAPE LIBRARY

RECREATION/ WEIGHT ROOM

DEEPCORE II—LEVEL THREE

THE
ABYSS

Chapter 1

Buddy

Buddy could've written the script for that morning before it even started. His big brother Junior was asking if he could take the pickup truck down to the beach. Daddy would say no. Junior would argue. Daddy would lecture. Junior would get mad and cuss. Daddy would take off his belt and go after him. Always worked the same way. You'd think somebody besides Buddy would catch on.

"It's October. Too damn cold for the beach." Daddy said it so loud the baby got startled in the bassinet. She set to wiggling around and crying.

"Listen to that baby," said Junior. "She sounds like a mouse in heat."

On the way to picking up the baby, Mama slapped Junior lightly across his face. "Mind how you talk in this house, young man."

"Sorry, Mama." He turned back to Daddy, but Daddy was already back to reading the paper, looking for reasons to cuss out Kennedy, who was the poorest excuse for a Democrat as ever got elected President. "I got my license yesterday," said Junior. "It's Saturday. I promised my friends."

1

"You got your license on Friday the thirteenth." Daddy didn't even look up from the paper. "Proof positive that the superstition is true, because the day you got your license is the unluckiest day that ever dawned for the American driver, not to mention the poor defenseless American pedestrian."

Buddy heard all this from where he sat on the floor in front of the TV, where he was watching Saturday morning cartoons with the volume turned down low so it didn't bother anybody. So far Daddy was still joking and Junior wasn't swearing yet, but that wouldn't last long.

Unless Buddy did something.

Like always, what to do was so vague in his mind that he didn't even know what he was planning, except that he knew it would work, knew that it would make everything turn out just fine and there wouldn't be any yelling and nobody'd get hit with Daddy's belt or say terrible things that would go on stinging long after the welts from the whipping had faded. And once Buddy knew how to stop something bad from happening, he didn't wait and think about it.

Buddy spoke right up, first words that came to mind. "Daddy, couldn't I go to the beach with Junior? You never did take me that time you promised in August." Only now, when the words were said, did Buddy figure out what it was he was planning to do.

Mama called in from the kitchen, where she was nursing the baby. "You did promise him, Homer."

Junior was sharp. Junior understood right off, almost as fast as Buddy himself. Buddy liked how the two of them could figure each other out without saying a word. Like they had a pipeline pumping brains straight from one head to the other. "Come on, I don't have to take a ten-year-old along with me, do I?"

Daddy took the bait. That's what the plan depended on, Daddy and Mama acting just the way Buddy knew they would. "What is it with you, Junior?" Daddy said. "You expect to use the family pickup and family gasoline and you think you can do that without any family obligations? You think the whole world exists to serve you and you don't ever have to inconvenience yourself in return?"

Just like that, the argument had stopped being about whether Junior could go, and instead it was about whether he had to take Buddy with him. And since Buddy knew that Junior probably would have taken him anyway, they were safe on base.

"All *right,* I'll take him." Junior sullenly took the car keys when Daddy handed them to him, then stomped out to the pickup, ignoring Buddy the whole way and starting the truck moving before Buddy was inside.

Once they backed down the gravel driveway and out into the road, though, Junior whooped and stepped on the gas. "Holy *shit* but you handled the old man! I wish I *knew* how you did that!"

Buddy just grinned and tuned the radio away from Daddy's country music to a teenage station. He couldn't just push a button because Daddy got mad whenever he found one of the buttons set for that rock 'n' roll crap.

The radio started playing "Teen Angel." Junior and Buddy sang along with it, using Junior's new improved lyrics, which ended up saying, "If you're somewhere down below, unzip my pants and give a blow." Buddy didn't know exactly what this meant, but he knew it always made Junior's friends laugh their heads off. He also knew that Mama would probably cut his tongue off with the kitchen shears if he ever sang those words at home.

They stopped to pick up Todd and Dennis and Larry and Frank. Todd, who usually drove, brought firewood, Dennis had some hot dogs, Larry had a bag of marshmallows, but Frank brought beer. A whole cooler full. They used the firewood to camouflage the cooler in the back of the pickup. "Look at this," said Junior. "Beer from home, right out in the open, no arguments, no false I.D. I can't believe your parents let you do this."

"Why not?" said Frank. "They don't give a shit."

"Oh, I believe you, Frank. I can hear your mom's voice." Dennis started talking in a high voice. "Here's your beer, Frank. Don't drink it all in one place."

They all laughed. Frank's mom spent half her life whining at him about how he'd go to hell if he picked up any of his dad's filthy habits.

"They're out of town and they left the beer," said Frank. Frank looked at Buddy. "He's gonna tell."

"He won't," said Junior.

"Like hell," said Frank. "Look at him sitting there watching everything with his mouth shut."

"What's he supposed to do," said Junior, "look at the sun and sing opera?"

"I won't tell, Frank," said Buddy.

"Well you aren't drinking any," said Frank. "So don't even think about it. Don't even *breathe* near the cooler."

"OK," said Buddy. It was all fine with him, Frank could boss him all he wanted. Buddy didn't mind, because Junior had stood up for him. None of Junior's friends teased him for it, either. Junior was the kind of guy that whatever he did, the other guys knew it was OK. So Buddy ended up in the back of the truck with Dennis and Todd, watching them stick wieners into their zippers and laugh about what would happen if they stood up so other drivers could see them. Of course they stayed right down on the bed of the pickup and took the wieners out the first time they thought somebody might see, but it was funny anyway.

When they stopped at the light in Verona, Todd leaned around the cab and yelled through the window at Junior. "You drive too slow, old lady!"

"You girls in the back just keep your panties on," said Junior.

"Bite on this!" yelled Todd. He jammed a wiener into Junior's face. Junior ducked his head to the side and jerked the pickup into gear. Todd was thrown back and lost his balance, almost falling out of the truck, but as soon as he recovered he laughed and pretended he wasn't scared. "That's right!" he yelled. "Get some speed, man!" Buddy knew, though, that Junior wasn't driving any faster than before.

It took forty-five minutes to get from Jacksonville, past

Camp Lejeune, and down to the beach on Topsail Island. It was a lousy beach, as beaches go, dirty and steep and posted for no swimming, but it was close and nobody wanted to swim anyway. They had a fire going as fast as you'd expect from former Boy Scouts, and they had the beer open and flowing as fast as you'd expect from the sons of noncoms in the U.S. Marines.

Buddy'd never been at a party where everybody was drinking. At first they were funny, telling dirty jokes and funny jokes and now and then jokes that were dirty *and* funny. But after a while the stories got longer and never went anywhere, and Frank snapped at Buddy if he even breathed, and Dennis got into a shoving match with Larry that got sand into the hot dogs. Buddy took off for a walk along the beach.

It was a tricky place, where the current usually ripped across in front of the island. The sand was eaten away, so the beach was steep and the waves were higher and more violent than most other places along the North Carolina coast. Later, he'd see waves like that all the time in California, but on October 14th, 1961, Buddy thought these were the highest, most terrible waves in the world.

He couldn't take his eyes off them. He'd see a swell out on the ocean, watch it rise as it came in, and then, when it curled and broke and crashed down onto the beach, he'd imagine himself inside the wave, as if he were as small as a fish, with the slope of water behind him and the curl of the wave crashing down over his head. He felt the power of the water as if it were his own strength, his own body. It made him feel so strong that he could pound with his fists on the hard wet sand and cause an earthquake that would topple buildings in Jacksonville.

He couldn't stand not being in the water. He wasn't going to swim. He wasn't going to get anywhere close to the waves. But he had to feel the wash flowing over his feet. It was too hard to stay on the dry sand, wearing shoes. He had to root himself in the sea. Even if it was cold. Even if he got in trouble for it.

He took off his shoes carefully, untying them and laying his socks across them. The breeze was chilly on his feet, and when he got to where the sand was wet, it was even colder. His feet sank slightly into the sand, and it turned white where he stepped, as if his weight was squeezing the water out. As if he could drive the sea back from the shore just by walking toward it.

At first he stayed out where the weakest forewash only tickled and chilled him. He had always liked the way the backwash sucked sand out from around the edges of his feet, as if the ground was moving out to sea. It was a strong backwash, but the tide was ebbing, and as he walked along the beach he kept having to sidle closer to the waves in order to keep his feet wet.

He thought he heard somebody calling him. When he turned around the fire was out of sight. He had walked farther than he thought. He started running back, his feet slapping the wet sand or splashing through the forewash. "I'm coming!" Buddy yelled.

But when the fire came in sight, everything was just like it was when he left, the guys sitting on their coats around the fire. Buddy felt like a fool for yelling. Nobody called him. But now Junior was getting up, coming toward him, staggering a little. Drunk. "What is it?" called Junior.

"Nothing," said Buddy. He turned away, walked a little farther into the backwash, waving Junior off.

"What?" called Junior.

Buddy turned back to face his brother. Junior couldn't even stand up straight, he kept staggering to keep his balance. As a wave crashed behind him, Buddy yelled, "Nothing! Go on back!"

Junior yelled something and waved, but Buddy couldn't hear him. And then he felt the forewash from the wave slam into the backs of his legs. The back of his *thighs*. He'd walked too far down toward the waves. This must be a really big one, and it was above his knees. He started walking forward, a step toward the shore, but his legs moved so slowly through the water, and the backwash started before

6

he took a second step. The sand washed right out from under his feet, and he fell forward, splashing down into the water. It covered his head. He struggled to sit up, to roll over; for a moment his head was out of the water and he heard Junior yelling "Son of a bitch!" and he thought, I'm in trouble now. Then he felt his body bouncing with the turbulence inside a breaking wave, and now he was sucked under for real. He couldn't find the bottom, he couldn't remember which way was up, and he had no air in his lungs; he hadn't gotten a deep breath before he went under. His chest ached for him to open his mouth and breathe.

And then, suddenly, his feet kicked air. He'd been upside down without knowing it. He doubled over and then kicked, and his head broke the surface and he opened his mouth and breathed, a great gasp that ended with water in his mouth. He swallowed and gagged, then kicked to the surface again, trying to swim and stay on top of the water. He was a good swimmer. Daddy made sure both his boys were good swimmers.

A swell lifted him. For a moment he was high enough to see the shore, just as Junior tossed away his second shoe and splashed out into the water. That's right! thought Buddy. Junior will save me. I'll be OK.

As he slid down into the trough between waves, though, he remembered that Junior was drunk. He couldn't save anybody. Go back, he thought. Stay on the beach.

The current had already carried him so far that when the next wave lifted him, the fire was like a candle flame with the shadows of spiders jumping around in front of it. It would be stupid to try to fight the current and swim toward the fire. He couldn't even swim toward shore—the current was pulling him almost due south, along the coast and out to sea. The best he could do was swim to stay afloat and angle himself toward the west, trying to get out of the current. It was so cold. Half the time he couldn't lift himself high enough to breathe. His clothes were so heavy, it felt like big pieces of seaweed had caught hold of him, dragging him downward.

"This way!"

Buddy looked toward shore—or where he thought the shore was.

"This way, kid! Toward the boat!"

He turned in the water and saw a flash of red and blue. A fishing boat. But it was in the wrong direction. The waves were against him as he tried to swim toward it. It was even harder to breathe, and he kept getting water in his mouth. Until one time he breathed in the water and choked. You can't swim while you're choking. He went under. He coughed convulsively, against his will; he gasped more water into his lungs. It was like a hard cold fist inside his chest. Now he needed air more than ever. He tried to exhale the water, force it out. Instead his body sucked more water into his lungs in a desperate attempt to breathe.

I'm going to die.

But even as one instinctive response was killing him, another was keeping him alive. His legs kept kicking. His arms kept swimming. And that kept him close enough to the surface that the fishermen could take hold of him, pull him out, lay him on the deck and press the water out of his lungs.

He could feel the water rushing upward through his windpipe, into his throat, making him gag. It was worse than vomiting, more painful, more terrifying than the drowning had been. When the air rushed back into his lungs, it hurt. And then the huge, heavy hands of the sailor pushed again, driving more water out. He choked. He tried to cry out with the pain, and then *did* cry out. He was alive. Strong as it was, he had beaten the sea.

Then he remembered.

"Junior!" he cried.

The sailors held him down. "Just rest awhile, boy!"

"My brother!"

They let him up then, as they rushed to look. Choking, Buddy joined them, clinging to the gunnel and searching. It must be the wrong direction, because Junior wasn't there.

But Junior wasn't there no matter which way he looked, and when the sailors got him to port at Topsail Beach and a man drove him back up the coast to where the pickup truck was parked near the dying fire, Junior wasn't there either. Todd and Dennis and Larry weren't sober, but they were solemn; Frank was still raging that they shouldn't have pulled him out, he could have saved Junior and the little brat, too. Buddy didn't care about being called a little brat. He only cared about the water dripping off Frank's clothes. At least he tried.

The keys to the pickup were in Junior's pocket. They waited an hour for their parents to start coming. By then they had given statements to the police and a reporter. Nobody had sense enough to hide the beer. The reporter counted twenty-two empty beer bottles and two that still had some beer in them. The story was in the paper next day. They held a service on the base. Everybody was in their whites. Buddy used to see all those men in uniform and it made him feel safe. Now he knew that they were nothing compared to the power of the sea. Little men in little boats with little guns. They were nothing.

Two weeks after Christmas Daddy got assigned as an adviser to help train South Vietnamese soldiers. The family was going to live in Hawaii. Daddy took Buddy back to Topsail Island one more time, the last full day before they were to leave. He didn't ask Buddy and Buddy didn't ask him, but they both knew they had to go there to say good-bye. They didn't talk the whole way. Buddy kept reliving the last time he took that road. He pictured himself opening the cooler and throwing the bottles of beer out onto the road, one by one. He pictured himself sitting in the sand, putting his shoes on instead of taking them off. Walking back up the slope to the fire. He pictured them all getting back into the truck and driving home together, laughing and drunk and stupid but by God alive.

Daddy parked in the exact spot. The half-burnt wood of the fire was still there. Or maybe it was from somebody else's fire. The waves were still pounding, just like that day in October, only now it was even colder and the sky was heavy with winter clouds. But the sea moved the same, heaving under every sky as if it was trying to shrug off the whole atmosphere, to break down every scrap of land, until the whole world was just swells and currents without breakers anywhere because there was nothing solid and strong enough to break the sea.

Daddy put his hand on Buddy's shoulder. "Both my boys went into the sea," he said, "but the sea gave one back to me. I thank a merciful God every day, Virgil."

Buddy didn't thank God for anything. Buddy picked up the longest half-burnt log and walked away from his father, toward the sea. He heard his father fall in behind him, but Buddy didn't care. He walked right to the edge of the water and then stepped into it, shoes and all. Stepped in until the water was ankle deep and the backwash was sucking at his feet.

Suck all you like, you son of a bitch.

Buddy raised the firewood over his head like a club and brought it down on the first wash of water from a broken wave. The club cut through the water and struck the sand. Water splashed all over him. Then he raised the club and struck again with all his strength. Again. And again, beating the sea but leaving no scar, no mark at all, no cry of pain. The water rushed away, tugging at him, just like before.

He brought the club back again but this time Daddy took hold of it, held it.

"She always wins," said Daddy. "If she wants to."

Buddy let go of the club. It slid down to the ground, scraping along his calf as it fell. It hurt, but the pain felt good.

"Your mama's going to give us hell about your wet shoes," said Daddy.

They splashed on out of the water and drove home.

Daddy was killed in Saigon in 1965 by a hand grenade strapped to a five-year-old. Mama married an accountant and Buddy lived in their house in Modesto for two years, until he was drafted into the Army in 1968. He was stationed in Korea and never saw action. When he got out, he didn't go home to his mother and sister and half brothers. Instead he went to Texas and got work in the oil business. He figured that was as far from the ocean as he could get. But within five years he was head of a team of riggers in the Gulf, with the sea around him every day for months on end. Go figure.

Chapter 2

Lindsey

If you're going to understand anything about Lindsey Brigman, first you've got to know some things about her mother, Cathy Thomas. I guess that's true about practically everybody—I mean, either we spend our whole lives acting out all the things our parents said and did, or we spend our whole lives deliberately *not* acting like our folks. If there's one thing that matters about Lindsey Brigman, it's that she's *not* like her mother. Or so she thinks.

The last time Catherine Mary di Angeli brought a friend to her parents' house was in second grade, in 1937. Pretty Debbie Benchley stood there in the kitchen door of the di Angeli home in Queens, gaping as Catherine Mary's five brothers and three sisters and parents and grandparents wandered in and out, quarreling and jabbering in Italian. Catherine Mary couldn't understand why her friend looked so frightened, her eyes wide open, pupils darting back and forth, jaw slack; then without a word Debbie Benchley turned and fled. Catherine Mary followed her halfway down the block, demanding to know what was wrong, but Debbie only walked faster, shaking her head.

Catherine Mary walked home, sick with a sense of loss, of

failure. How did I offend her? Why wasn't I worthy? Debbie Benchley was beautiful and blond and her father was a pharmacist, prosperous by the standard of those Depression years. She wore lovely clothes and smiled shyly and everyone admired her. Catherine Mary daydreamed of waking up one morning and looking in the mirror and seeing Debbie Benchley's face.

When she got back to the house, she went straight to the kitchen door at the side of the house—as usual. Only now she tried to imagine what Debbie must have thought of this. Debbie's family certainly entered their house through the front door; Debbie's family did not have five boys sleeping in the living room.

Catherine Mary stood in the doorway, seeing the confusion through Debbie's eyes: so many people, all rushing here and there, hands chopping and waving in the air as they talked. The music of a dozen people speaking Italian, arguing, so forceful and passionate—Catherine Mary let the sound come to her as it came to Debbie, without understanding, and now it was pushy, jabbering, demanding noise, not at all like the soft way Debbie spoke.

And there was Catherine Mary's mother, tears streaming down her face from the onions she was cutting in the sink while she argued with Johnny—Giannino—about whether or not he could quit his job at the Jew grocery. Catherine Mary didn't know if Debbie Benchley had a brother, but if she did, he would certainly not be a stockboy at a grocery store, and he would never, never work for a Jew. Nor would Debbie's mother make flamboyant gestures with a knife in her hand, or roll her weeping eyes heavenward as she invoked the saints, or cross herself with an onion.

Catherine Mary was ashamed. She had seen her family through horrified Protestant eyes, and because she identified so completely with Debbie Benchley, she could never again see them any other way.

From that day on, Catherine Mary never spoke Italian, never brought another friend home, and never answered to any name but Cathy. As she grew older, she listened carefully to the radio and eliminated every trace of Italy and

New York from her speech. She learned to walk with dignity. She moved her hands only rarely, and then in delicate, ladylike gestures. She studied the covers of fashion magazines and wore her hair as the prettiest models did. After high school she attended Columbia, taking only her music and drama classes seriously, devoting the rest of her time to selecting just the right husband. In 1950, at the age of eighteen, she shocked her family by marrying a twenty-five-year-old Protestant.

To Cathy he wasn't a Protestant. Frank Thomas was an American with a brand-new engineering degree, a job offer from Kodak with a five-figure salary, and a last name that didn't end with a vowel. He was also blond and bright-faced, without the heavy brooding eyebrows and dark-shadowed whiskers that Cathy's brothers and cousins had. In short, he was exactly the sort of husband that Debbie Benchley would have married, if she hadn't died of polio in sixth grade.

Cathy proceeded to create precisely the home she imagined Debbie would have chosen. The living room was used only for company, and always looked like a picture in a magazine. Frank came home from work every day to find the table prettily set for dinner, his wife with a pert hairdo and a smile for him, and his daughters ready to greet him with a hug. Cathy was the perfect American wife.

But Cathy was always pretending. She was an imposter; she had stolen Debbie Benchley's place. In her heart she was still Catherine Mary, and in her worst dreams she spoke only Italian. She knew that none of her friends would like her if they knew who she really was.

It would be different for her five daughters. They would grow up knowing that they belonged among the best people, with never a doubt. They would have every opportunity, every grace.

It began with their names. Frank wanted to name a daughter after one of his female relatives, but they all had horrid concocted names like LaDelle and DeEsta. Nor would Cathy dream of naming any of them for a saint. She made a bargain with Frank. She would name their daughters, and he could name their sons. They never had sons.

Their daughters were Dana, Christa, Corey, Lindsey, and Gail.

She had their hair done professionally from the age of three. They took ballet almost as soon as they could walk, and studied singing before they learned to read. When it came to musical instruments, they were not utterly without choices—they could opt for piano, flute, or violin. Brass and percussion instruments were too vulgar; clarinet and cello were obscene.

Just before Christa's birth, Frank changed jobs, from Kodak to a company with an unpronounceable name that made photocopying machines. Cathy hardly noticed, except when his stock options and ever-rising salary allowed her to dress her daughters more exquisitely and take them three times a year to Manhattan, to attend operas, plays, and concerts and buy clothes that were a year ahead of any other girls in Rochester. She contributed heavily to the community theatre, and her daughters got the ingenue leads as each one came of age.

Cathy's work on her daughters was almost completely successful. Dana married a Manhattan banker and traveled all over the world with him. Christa sang opera in Europe. Corey acted in regional theatre until she won a recurring role on TV, in a situation comedy that ran six years; each of her three husbands was exactly the sort of man who was in vogue the year she married him. And little Gail wrote obscene feminist poetry under her own name, which won her a great deal of literary prestige, and a dozen historical romances under the name Angelle de Brise, which earned her an astonishing amount of money.

Four daughters out of five, living exactly the kind of life their mother dreamed of—surely any other woman would have been satisfied. But Cathy could not forgive herself for having failed with Lindsey.

Where did Lindsey go wrong? Cathy never knew, but Lindsey did. Her transformation happened, coincidentally, when Lindsey was in second grade. It was a Saturday, and her father was up in the attic rummaging around for something. Lindsey stood at the bottom of the attic stair, listening to the noises from above. It occurred to her that she had no idea what her father did at work, or what he did for fun, or even, really, who he was. She could hear him humming, and she realized she had never heard her father sing. Every morning he left early for work, with a word or two if she was up; every night was a flurry of lessons and studies, all centered around Mother. She'd trot dutifully in to kiss him good night, but they never talked.

She climbed the stairs into the attic. He must have heard her footsteps; the singing stopped. But when she got to the top, he didn't look at her. He had his back to her; he was gazing at something made of small pieces of wood, interlaced in a latticework so it seemed light and airy, even though it was about five feet long and a couple of feet high. It wasn't furniture, and it wasn't art—Lindsey had already been to enough homes and enough museums to know furniture and art when she saw them.

It was a bridge. A model of a bridge.

"My senior project," Father said. "In civil engineering."

"Do you build *real* bridges?"

"I build optical assemblies and the structures that support them and the precision machines that move them."

Lindsey didn't know what any of that meant. "Oh," she said.

"Thanks for asking."

If she had been older, she might have heard the pain in his voice, the loneliness, for he had long since realized that he was merely an unavoidable accessory in Cathy's home. There had to be a father, but no one knew what he was actually *for,* once the money was in the bank and the children were conceived. Lindsey could not know that he was in the attic this particular day brooding about his first infidelity the afternoon before, she could not know how emotionally raw he was, from guilt, from anger, from relief, from fear that it would happen again, from fear that it would not.

Lindsey was seven years old, so she saw only what mattered to *her*. Despite the seeming frailty of the bridge, she understood intuitively that it was very strong. "How does it work?"

He looked at her, saw that she was looking at the bridge, and began to explain about how the real bridge would be made of steel, and why steel was stronger than wood—but that wasn't what she wanted to know.

"There's almost nothing there. It's so light. Like it's made of air."

It shook him to have her say that. He had taken a great deal of pride in the fact that the bridge derived maximum strength from minimal materials. An untrained seven-year-old should not have noticed it. For a dizzying moment he felt as if there was a chance that one of his children might actually have inherited something from *him*. And yet, because it was an engineering question, by reflex he answered her as he answered the teams of engineers working under him. "Why do *you* think?"

Lindsey pondered for a moment. "I guess if you made it too heavy, the bridge would use all its strength holding itself up."

To her surprise, her father laughed out loud, with a delight that she had never heard from him in her entire life. He reached out and hugged her, which was very uncomfortable but also quite interesting, even *good*. This was a hug at an unscheduled moment, a nonperfunctory embrace. But she couldn't concentrate on her father, not for long. The bridge kept drawing her eye.

"Can you teach *me* how to build stuff?"

"Bridges?"

"Build things." She hadn't built anything in her life, not since piling up alphabet blocks as a toddler, and she didn't remember that. But now, seeing this bridge and knowing that somebody built it, somebody she *knew*—now she felt hungry to build something herself. She didn't even know what she wanted to make, but she knew she had to make something, *now;* she felt jittery and urgent and hurried.

"How about if I bring home these new building blocks they're importing from Europe? Legos? I've wanted to play around with them myself, I could bring some home on Monday after work. Would you like that?"

"Yes, thank you." But behind her excellent manners, she was thinking, That's two days from now, and what about today? It's *today* that I want.

He studied her face. "But Monday's a long time from now, isn't it? How about we go to the toy store right now?"

"Yes, please." She immediately turned around and ran for the stairs.

Frank Thomas got up and followed her, chuckling. Partly he laughed at himself because he knew that it wasn't *him* she was interested in, it was building. But partly he laughed in pleasure because he had just looked inside her and found a part of himself looking out. It was the part of himself that allowed him to live with a woman who didn't love him and children who didn't know him, because when he was working on a project none of that mattered, only the project, only solving the problems and making something that worked—economically, smoothly, beautifully. All else was bearable, as long as he had that. And somehow he had given that same gift to Lindsey.

Or was it a curse? It was the gift of creation; it was the curse of monomania.

They went out and bought a set of Legos. When they got home, Cathy was frantic. "How can we possibly get you to ballet if you go wandering off without telling me, Lindsey?" And to Frank: "Don't you know you can't just take the girls off any time you please?" And to Lindsey again: "Come out to the car at once, dear. I can get you there in time for the second half of your lesson, at least. Your leotard's in the back seat, you can change while we drive."

"No thank you, Mother," said Lindsey. "Daddy and I are going to build with Legos."

Cathy was furious. "That's the most absurd thing I've ever heard of, Lindsey! You'll never amount to anything if you shrug off your lessons like this! And your father knows better than to—"

Frank put a finger on her lips, leaned in close, and whispered to her in a voice he thought Lindsey could not hear. "Shove it up your ass," he said. Then he smiled, took Lindsey's hand, and together they jogged down the stairs into the den. Several decisions were made in that moment. First, Cathy could have the other four girls, but Lindsey was *his* daughter; he would take charge of her education from now on. Second, Frank would continue his affair and not feel terribly guilty about it. Cathy had the use of eighty percent of his money and eighty percent of his children; still, there was plenty of room for happiness in the other twenty percent.

Lindsey understood little of this. She only knew that from that day on, when her sisters had to go to lessons or plays or museums or deadly adult parties, all Lindsey had to do was start building something with Legos or her Erector set and she was exempt, even if Father wasn't home to intervene. Gradually she began to take charge of her whole life in a way that was simply unavailable to her sisters. In junior high she fell in love with swimming, and Father built her a pool. In high school she was so far ahead of the curriculum that Father got permission for her to attend half days at the University of Rochester, where she was taking upper-division math and engineering courses before she graduated from high school. She won the New York State Science Fair with a demand-regulated breathing apparatus for diving helmets. It was crude compared to things she later built, but she kept it and revered it the way her father had kept his model bridge. It was the foundation of all that came after.

Lindsey was hardly aware that her mother hated her and her sisters laughed at her—usually behind her back. These people just weren't very important to her, with their music and plays and books and husbands and other irrelevancies. All that mattered was that she could build what had never been built before. Anything that could help her do that was important to her—like her father, whom she adored. Anything that couldn't help her was irrelevant. And anything that got in the way had to be sidestepped or knocked down or crushed.

She ended up designing structures to withstand the pressures of the deep sea. She was the best at what she did. But

19

like all engineers, she had come to believe that it wasn't worth designing something that would never be built. So she found a big-money application for her deep-sea designs— underwater oil drilling. Sure enough, she got the development money to start work on *Deepcore*. She also got something else.

While she was working with the crew of a Gulf oil rig to learn the problems and processes of ocean drilling, she worked closely with a man named Bud Brigman. She found that when he was with her, everything went smoothly and everyone on her project got along with each other—and with her. This had never happened to her before; she had usually worked with sullen, difficult people who hated her. She had always assumed this was a problem that every engineer had to deal with. Now she realized that Bud Brigman had a skill that she utterly lacked—the ability to handle people. She studied him, tried to learn what it was he did. What little she understood, she couldn't do. Yet she needed his ability to get *Deepcore* built and working. He was the first person since her father that she had actually needed. Lacking any other definition of the word, she thought that this was love. So she married him.

Things went along all right at first. Sex was good, and that helped. They were both fascinated by the work on *Deepcore,* and that helped even more.

They both laughed about the way that the oil-company people acted. It was Lindsey's project, she designed it, she was going to build it, it was *hers*—but when the money guys came out to look at the prototype, they got as far from Lindsey as possible. She made them nervous. It wasn't that she was smarter than them—they usually worked with people who were smarter than them, and pretty much got along. It wasn't even the fact that she was speaking the language of undersea engineering. See, that sort of thing happens all the time—people who don't speak the same language, trying to understand each other. But there are ways around the problem. If both sides are men, they know how to talk the language of men, the vulgar, macho strutting and joking they all picked up when they were ten or twelve years old. If both sides are women, then they can talk the language of women, which they also learned along with all the other rituals of puberty. But when it's a woman on one side and a man on the other, then it gets tricky. Then they don't have *any* language in common.

Even so, a lot of women manage to get around this, and so do a lot of men. Not Lindsey, though. Not because she didn't know how—hadn't she watched her mother manipulate men all her life? Hadn't she watched as her sisters learned the same skills? Hadn't she seen them work even on their father, who *knew* what they were doing? But Lindsey had rejected all that from the start. She had refused to do it with her father, and she refused to do it with any other man. When these men in suits came along, she spoke to them in the language of engineering—what *Deepcore* could do for undersea oil drilling, what deep-sea drilling could do for the oil companies. The more she talked, the more nervous the guys in suits became. An hour in a closed car with Lindsey made them more jittery than a gallon of coffee. She was beautiful, she was smart, she was terrifying.

If she'd been alone there's no way anybody would've bought the project, least of all a boys' club like Benthic Petroleum. But there was Bud. They'd go with Lindsey out to the prototype, *Deepcore I,* listening to her in the car, getting more nervous all the time, and then at the pier they'd meet Bud. They looked at him like an angel come to rescue them from Hell. They stuck to Bud like he was their big brother. Which he was, in a way. These guys wore suits all the time, they had haircuts every two weeks, they played racquetball, they got their tans in a booth or on a beach. They looked at Bud and saw a guy who got his tan and his strength honestly, by working with his body out in the weather. They saw a guy who didn't go underwater in little snorkel outfits to look at the fish—he had learned to dive because guys on his rig were going down into the water, and he believed he couldn't ask any man to do something he had never done himself.

"Hey, Bud, I envy you," they all said, every one of them. "Living this close to the sea, testing yourself all the time."

Bud didn't argue with the suits. Let them get off on their macho-worship. But he always thought the same thing: Only a fool tests himself against the sea. The sea's going to win every time. No, you don't go down in that water unless you know you already got the ocean licked. You got to know every bit of your equipment is working, you got to know exactly what your equipment can do and what it can't do. You go down there knowing that it's *no* test. And then when you come up, you can look out over the water and say, I beat you, you hungry old bitch, I got in and I got out, you didn't swallow me this time.

That's what *Deepcore* meant to Bud. Going down into the water. Going deep, living there with all that pressure inside you, all around you, all those thirty or forty or fifty atmospheres poking and prying right there in your lungs, in your blood, in every cell of your body—but you're breathing, you're alive, and when it's all done, you come up and feel the sunlight on you and you won again. No contest.

Bud didn't like contests.

Which is why the marriage didn't work for long. Lindsey treated it like a contest. What bothered her most was that she always won. She'd come home raging about something that Benthic did or coldly furious about somebody's incompetence on the project, and Bud would listen patiently, sympathetically, saying little. It didn't matter—eventually he'd say *something* wrong, or not say enough at the right moment, and then Lindsey would lash out at him. Accuse him, attack him, say terrible things. And he'd answer, angry, hurt, there'd be a real fight—and then he'd go silent, he'd leave the room, and when he came back it was over, he wouldn't fight anymore. It drove her crazy, though she didn't know why.

The worst was when he "handled" her. She'd seen him in action, watched him, first with the guys on his rig, then with the test crew on *Deepcore I,* and she saw how he noticed where tension and conflict were getting out of hand, how he'd come in with the right word, separate two guys at the right time, before they even realized they were starting to hate each other. How Bud always knew how to keep a group

22

working together in the right direction. And then, when the two of them were fighting, she'd see him try to keep their marriage working, using exactly the same techniques. Giving in to her when he could, joking her out of bad tempers, being teasing or tender at just the right moments, so that she'd laugh or love him for a moment, till she caught herself.

She *hated* it when he did that. It was just like her mother—manipulating people to get them to do whatever she wanted. She was *not* going to fall for it the way her father did. What Lindsey could never see was the difference between her mom and Bud. Her mom always manipulated people to get her own way, at their expense. Bud handled people to help *them* get what they wanted. Cathy Thomas stole from people's souls, making them smaller and smaller the more she had to do with them. Bud helped people get along together, accomplish things together, and the more he worked with them, the stronger and better and more confident they got. It was the difference between a healer and a poisoner—but all Lindsey could see was the subtle way they both administered their potions.

There was only one place where Bud didn't give in to Lindsey, and that was his crew. She could snipe at him at home, and he'd go on loving her. But if she did anything to hurt morale in the crew—accusing somebody of doing a bad job, criticizing anything they did—Bud would shut her down so fast that sometimes even Lindsey was left speechless. She didn't understand it—he wouldn't fight to stand up for himself, but he'd fight to protect his people.

She convinced herself that this meant he didn't really love her. She didn't realize that Bud's crew was as important to him as *Deepcore* was to Lindsey. His crew was the one thing he had created in his life: a group of men and women who trusted each other, who liked each other, who got along well enough not to kill each other when they had to stay together for weeks on end—all without any kind of military discipline, without losing any sense of their freedom and independence. It was a delicate thing to get a bunch of individuals to work together willingly. He didn't need to have an outsider like Lindsey come in and start bossing them around like she thought she owned them. It made them defiant, and when they did go along with what she wanted, it made them feel defeated; either way, it hurt morale. Bud had to protect his crew from her or lose all he'd worked for.

It was inevitable. Since this was the one point where he'd stand up to her instead of trying to "handle" her, she kept coming back to it, again and again, criticizing his crew, blaming him in front of them for everything that went wrong. Even as she did it, Lindsey knew it was wrong, knew that if she weakened Bud's crew, got them surly and rebellious, then they'd get passed over for the first trial well. That was the worst thing she could do to Bud. He'd never forgive her.

She had married Bud because she needed him to make her project succeed. Now it wasn't working that way. The project had its funding. Now it was her turn to give Bud his chance. If being married to the project engineer would help his crew get assigned to the trial, well, then she would have stayed married to him, she was sure of that. But it wouldn't help, it would only hurt. For his own sake, she had to divorce him. Had to.

Had to get away from him, from his always being so damned decent to her. Had to get away from the fact that Bud's crew treated him better than she knew how to. Had to get away from the constant reminders that their marriage was miserable, and that it was probably her fault.

So she filed for separation just as *Deepcore II* got ready for initial tests.

It worked. No more fighting with Bud at home, because he wasn't there. A lot less tension at work because they hadn't been fighting at home. Their relationship now was all business. No more emotional involvement. Just get the job done. She even got involved with a boyfriend—a sort of recreational love affair with an ambitious young executive working in Benthic's resource-development division.

And Bud took the separation OK. Why shouldn't he? What was the marriage to him anymore, except a lot of pain, a lot of tension? What was the divorce, except the end of the fighting? A blessed relief? That's what he told himself. Glad to be rid of her. Marrying her was the stupidest mistake I ever made.

Everything was fine now. Nothing to distract him from training with his crew. Except Bud couldn't stop thinking about her, couldn't stop worrying about her, couldn't stop hating the guy who was sleeping with her now, couldn't stop longing to have her with him. He thought maybe it was just the sex that he missed. He tried to get something going with other women in Galveston, where they were testing *Deepcore II*. But when it came time to take them home, Bud couldn't do it. Didn't *want* to do it. He still wore the ring, dammit. He was still married to Lindsey. Even when he hated her, he loved her. Even when he was so damn pissed off at her that he wanted to smack her with a two-by-four, he loved her, looked out for her, wanted to make her happy.

That's the way it is sometimes. You love somebody even when you can't stand them. It made Bud really hope he'd get assigned to the first test drill. Months underwater with his crew. With his crew, and without Lindsey Brigman.

Chapter 3

Coffey

One more person you've got to meet before we go on. Lt. Hiram Coffey, U.S. Navy, SEALs.

When you see a guy in uniform, you don't see the guy at all—just the uniform. Whatever you think of the military, that's what you think about *him.* Maybe to you he's a hero. Maybe to you he's a trigger-happy killer. Maybe to you he's an unfeeling robot. But the guy inside the uniform, he isn't a hero and he isn't a killer and he isn't a robot, he's a guy. He was a kid once, and then he grew up into the kind of person who for one reason or another joined up. He saw that uniform, and he knew he had to get inside it, even though it would cost him, even though he'd give up a lot of freedom, maybe a lot of other things, too. There are as many different reasons for putting on that uniform as there are guys who wear them.

Hiram Coffey wasn't a tough kid. If he'd grown up in some "Leave It to Beaver" town, he would've played baseball and hide-and-go-seek in the neighborhood. He would've come in when his mother called and counted to ten when he got mad instead of punching anybody. The worst thing he probably ever would've done was steal a *Penthouse* magazine and share it with his best friend.

Trouble was, the neighborhood he grew up in wasn't the kind you see on TV except in cop shows. His dad walked out when Hiram was ten, and by the time he turned twelve, him and his mom were at rock bottom. The two of them lived in the second story of a crummy rundown fourplex in a neighborhood of East L.A. that needed real bad to get torn down and replaced by something better, like a freeway.

Even in hard times, though, Hiram Coffey tried to be a good kid. His definition of *good* wasn't too complicated, either. *Good* was his mom. Whatever she needed, whatever she asked for, he tried to oblige. After all, didn't she ride the bus forty-five minutes each way to get to her crummy typing job at a crummy second-rate sign company, just to buy food and clothes for him? So he didn't kneel down in his jeans if he could help it, so they wouldn't wear out and need patches, and if he scuffed up his shoes he felt like he was as low as a hammered dog turd.

It's not like his mom ran him around on the end of a stick or anything like that. She trusted him and gave him a lot of freedom. It wasn't her doing it to Hiram Coffey. It was Hiram Coffey doing it to himself. He just didn't feel like it was his right to decide what ought to happen. But once his mom said what was right and good, well then, he'd near to kill himself trying to see to it that right and good won out.

It made him a serious kid. He could laugh and joke, sure, but his face always settled right back to this firm no-nonsense look. He never clowned around in class, cause Mom said he had to take education seriously and get good grades or he'd never get into college and that's where he had to end up if he was ever going to get out of East L.A. He never just hung around on the street cause Mom said the kind of boys that did that was no good and they'd never amount to anything except maybe ending up on the post office wall with a list of phony names.

There was this kid in Hiram's neighborhood, named Darrel Woodward. He was about fifteen and big and he scared people. Not cause he was strong and dangerous. In fact he was kind of flabby and slow. What scared you was his eyes, always kind of half closed, and his mouth, which was always sort of smiling at a joke that nobody got but him. When you saw him, you knew that he'd do *anything*. Things like being fair and decent, that was for suckers. He'd beat up a baby if he felt like it. If he fought with you and got you down, he wouldn't stop, he'd go right on and poke out your eye if he wanted to.

And when you know that about somebody, it gives him power over you. As long as he leaves you alone, you don't mess with him. When he stops leaving you alone, then you try to go along with what he wants so he'll leave you alone again. Above all, you never let him know that after he touches you the first thing you got to do is go wash the place he touched you, scrub it till it bleeds, because having his mark on you makes you want to puke.

That's how Hiram felt about Darrel Woodward. Darrel Woodward hung around in the neighborhood and Hiram stayed out of his way. Now and then Darrel would notice him, though. Call him over. "Hey Folgers! Hey Maxwell House!" Hiram didn't act offended at jokes on his name. He just came over to where Darrel was standing with his cronies gathered around him. They were all of them waiting to see what kind of show Darrel was going to put on, using Hiram Coffey as the butt of the joke.

"Hey, Coffey, I hear you got your name cause your dad's really a coon."

Hiram didn't say a thing. He didn't argue, he didn't agree. The less he said, the sooner Darrel would leave him alone.

"I hear your dad's got him a big black dick, and that's why your mom ran off, cause he was nearly killing her with it all the time."

Hiram shrugged.

"Didn't she nearly choke on it, Coffey? I heard that's why she left him, cause she was sick of drinking Coffey."

Darrel's friends all laughed real loud and nasty. Hiram didn't say a thing.

"You got a big black dick, Coffey?"

Hiram shook his head.

"Come on, Hiram, don't hold out on us. Give us a look, Hiram. Come on, unzip your pants and whip it out here, give us a look at your hose."

Hiram just stood there. He wasn't going to obey, but he wasn't going to run, either. Stood there till Darrel's friends took him down and got his pants and shorts off him. He didn't wriggle around trying to get away or cover himself. He didn't argue when Darrel made a bunch of jokes about how tiny his penis was. He didn't plead when Darrel whipped out his pocket knife and made out as how he was going to cut it off. Finally Darrel said, "Shit, his dick's too small to cut off. I bet somebody already did it." When the laugh was over, he said, "Let him go."

Hiram Coffey got up from the sidewalk. He still didn't act mad or cover himself or anything. Here's the thing: He was angry, all right, but he wasn't *humiliated*. You can only be humiliated if you care what people think, but Hiram didn't care diddly-squat about what Darrel and his friends thought. The only person whose opinion mattered to Hiram Coffey was his mom. So the only thought going through his mind was: I have to get my pants back cause Mom can't afford another pair, and I have to get inside the house without her knowing what these guys did to me or she'll worry about me all the time.

Does this make Coffey sound like a mama's boy? I hope you can tell the difference. Coffey wasn't trying to *please* his mama in order to get something from her. That would mean he was thinking of himself. No, the way he pictured the world, it was his family on one side, and everybody else on the other. Mom and him, they were *us,* and everybody else was *them.* He had to do what was good for *us,* that's all, and it was Mom's job to decide what that was. Hiram's job was to help all he could, do what he was asked, and make sure she never had to worry about him, make sure he didn't add one extra burden to her shoulders.

"Get out of here," Darrel said. "What are you waiting for?"

"I need my pants back," said Hiram. His voice was as steady as if he was holding a ten-gauge shotgun.

Darrel grabbed his pants from the boy who was holding them, and held them up in the air. Darrel was about a foot taller than Hiram. "Come and get them."

Hiram just stood there.

"You must not want them real bad, then, if you won't even come get them."

"My mom can't afford to buy me another pair," said Hiram. He wasn't a bit worried about letting on how poor they were. His pride depended on getting the pants back, not pretending he wasn't poor. Everybody in this neighborhood was poor. In fact, there wasn't a one of them there who didn't know right off that Hiram was right—stripping a boy naked in the street was funny, but stealing his pants so his mom had to buy new ones, that wasn't funny.

Darrel was no fool. He could feel the boys around him kind of shifting their weight, feeling a little ashamed. The joke had gone too far.

Darrel tossed the pants in Hiram's face. Hiram saw his shorts lying on the sidewalk, and he went and picked them up. Then he turned around and walked across the street and up a few houses till he was home. He didn't stop and put his pants on. He didn't carry his pants so they'd cover him up. It's like he didn't even notice he was bare-assed. Darrel tried yelling out some ugly jokes at him as he walked away, but hardly anybody laughed. Pretty soon Hiram was up the stairs and he unlocked the door to their apartment and he went inside.

That was Hiram's pride. He got his pants back, and he got inside before Mom got home from work, so she never knew. And as for Darrel, there was nothing he could do that mattered to Hiram, as long as the family was OK. Hiram just plain didn't give a damn.

I told you about that one time because you have to realize that Hiram wasn't holding a grudge against Darrel. He didn't *care* that much about Darrel Woodward. If everything had gone on the same way, Hiram would've stayed out of Darrel's way all he could and eventually Darrel would've been drafted or addicted to some drug or killed by some punk from another neighborhood who was even meaner than him.

But things didn't go on the same way. Darrel got tired of picking on kids and started going after bigger game. He'd get his boys to knock grocery bags out of old ladies' arms and let air out of people's tires. He'd order them to steal candy and cigarettes for him. And when adults yelled at him, he'd just laugh in their faces. He didn't even try to run away. He just laughed at them. It was a new thing in those days, in that neighborhood, to have a kid show no respect at all for adults.

What brought things to a head was Mr. Ling, who ran the little corner market. He caught a couple of Darrel's boys stealing Cokes out of his cooler, and he called the cops on them. They got hauled away to the police station, and all the time Mr. Ling was saying, "About time somebody put a stop to these gangs. I won't put up with it anymore. You boys won't get away with it anymore."

It was some kind of crisis for Darrel Woodward. The cops coming into the neighborhood and taking away two of his boys—they showed who had *real* power, and it wasn't Darrel. Even though the boys' parents got them out before dark, it was a real blow to him.

Next afternoon, Darrel cut school and went into Mr. Ling's store about two in the afternoon. Didn't shoplift, didn't say anything, just stood there, watching. Finally Mr. Ling yelled at him to go outside or he'd call the cops. Darrel went outside, but he still stood there, right outside the window where Mr. Ling could see him whenever he looked up. It was driving him crazy, until along about three-thirty Mr. Ling got a phone call from his wife. He left his clerk in charge of the store and ran out the back and drove to the hospital because somebody had attacked his nine-year-old daughter on the way home from school and beat her up so bad her arm was broke and so were a couple of ribs and her face was so mashed up it took fifty stitches to pull it back together. She'd have scars all her life.

Mr. Ling told the police he knew who was responsible. It

was Darrel Woodward, getting even. But Darrel had an alibi. Mr. Ling had seen him at his store during the whole time his little girl was getting beat up.

Maybe you're thinking that I'm telling this story because Hiram heard about this and figured it was time to put a stop to Darrel Woodward and so he went out and faced him and punched his lights out and saved the neighborhood. But that isn't how it happened at all.

See, Mr. Ling and his daughter weren't *us* to Hiram Coffey. They were *them*, as surely as Darrel Woodward was. And what *they* did to *them* might be pretty sad, but it was none of Hiram's business.

A couple of days later, though, Mom stopped by Ling's grocery and found it closed. She had to go ten blocks just to get milk, and by the time she got it home it was warm. "It's a crying shame when you have to own a car just to go grocery shopping," she said. "It just stinks to high heaven when a good man like Ling can't stay in business in this neighborhood just because some vicious teenager gets out of control. The police can't do anything, even though everybody knows the Woodward boy was responsible. So what happens? Ling closes down his store, and who else is going to open up a business here? It's time for somebody to do something about Darrel Woodward. Stop him once and for all. If the law can't do it or won't do it, then it's just going to have to happen some other way, or our lives won't even be worth living." Hiram's mom got all her feelings off her chest and that was that.

What she didn't realize was that she had just given Hiram an assignment. A mission. Up till that moment, Darrel Woodward had been an annoyance. Now, though Mom had redefined the situation. Darrel Woodward was a danger to *us*, and somebody had to do something about him.

Hiram had watched TV. He knew about showdowns and gunfights where you let the other guy draw first and the hero always shot the bad guy in the hand. He also knew that shows like that were phony as a four-dollar bill. You let the bad guy draw first, he'll shoot you down. You shoot him in the hand, he'll shoot you in the head. "Playing fair" wasn't part of Hiram's plans.

Not getting caught, *that* was the important thing. Doing something decisive and final, and then not getting caught, so that the threat to *us* would be eliminated without causing Mom to worry about a thing.

It was about two weeks later. It was night. Darrel was all by himself, walking up the stairs to his apartment where his dad the drunk and his mom the screamer were having a fight. Hiram was standing partway up the next flight of stairs as Darrel came up to the landing, all alone, his back to Hiram. Hiram took two fast steps down the stairs and smashed a heavy cinder block into Darrel's head from behind. Darrel never saw it coming, never knew what hit him. Hiram went back up the stairs and out onto the roof, where he'd put the cinder block more than a week ago. Nobody saw him on the roof; nobody saw him climb down the side of the apartment building. He cut through the block, walking calm so nobody'd notice him, and went on back the long way around to his own fourplex, where he climbed up the back way into his room. It worked perfectly. He knew it would. He had rehearsed it a dozen times. He left nothing to chance.

Darrel Woodward didn't die. But his brain was damaged, and he walked and talked slow and funny. His gang broke up, of course. After he got out of the hospital, he just sort of hung around in the neighborhood, lurching along and making jokes, but nobody stuck around to listen to him. He was like a billboard saying, Don't mess with this neighborhood.

They never even had a guess who did it. They questioned Ling, but he was in Riverside working as assistant manager at a Lucky's that night and so he was in the clear. Hiram Coffey never even hinted that he was responsible, never tried to take credit even when neighbors stood there looking at Darrel lurch by and said, "Well, I'm sorry, but that boy had it coming. Whoever did that to him did the world a favor. I'd like to shake the hand of whoever it was who did that." Hiram's hand went unshook.

When Hiram was seventeen, his mom married her boss and they moved to Sherman Oaks. It didn't take Hiram long to figure out what had happened. Mom and him weren't *us* anymore. She was with her new husband, Burt. She didn't decide things anymore—she waited to find out what Burt thought they ought to do.

Maybe if Burt had liked Hiram they might have made a go of it. But Burt made it clear he didn't trust Hiram alone with his nubile daughters, age fourteen and sixteen. Burt also made it clear he didn't trust Hiram to stay out of his wallet. And Mom's feeble protests pretty soon faded away into silence.

That was the first time in his life that Hiram didn't belong to anybody, wasn't part of anything. He hardly even knew who he was anymore, if he wasn't part of that group called Mom and Hiram. He didn't have any purpose in life. His grades went down the toilet his senior year. He never had any close friends, and now he lost even the not-so-close ones, just because he never did anything with them. He hung around the new video arcades but he didn't even play all that much, just listened to the dying PacMan sounds and the music of Donkey Kong and the explosions of Asteroids. He watched the kids playing. And when he did play, I think the only thing he liked about it was that while the game was going on, he and the machine were one. The machine set up the world for him and gave him a task to do, and then he carried it out to the best of his ability. It wasn't much, but it was something.

When Hiram graduated high school he joined the Navy for reasons he didn't understand himself. But it was the right thing for Hiram Coffey to do. The Navy was something worth belonging to—it was America, wasn't it? Only it was a part of America where there was always somebody to tell you what was the right thing for Coffey to do, where there was always a purpose to fulfill.

Why are you in the Navy, Seaman Coffey?

To serve my country, *sir!*

And how can you serve your country, Seaman Coffey?

I will be the best sailor in this man's Navy, sir!

What?

I will be the best *goddam* sailor in this man's Navy, sir!

I can't hear you!

I will be the best fucking goddamn sailor in the United States Navy! Sir!

You're a good man, Coffey.

After he was in for a couple of years and did a tour of duty in the Persian Gulf, he volunteered for the SEALs. Sea, Air, and Land. He met their standards. They started him out with a group of twelve men. The training was hell on most guys. Coffey loved it.

One day early in their training their instructor led them to a twelve-foot length of telephone pole. "I want to introduce you to somebody," he said. "This is your lady. You love her with all your heart. You can't bear to be apart from her. You will carry her with you wherever you go. And I mean *all* of you, *wherever* you go. If one of you needs to piss, you all take the lady with you and stand there together while he pees. If I hear that one of you got laid then I better see him picking splinters out of his dick because this is your one and only true love, do you *understand me?*"

For weeks the twelve of them carried that pole with them wherever they went. Everything they did, they had to do with one hand on that pole. Anything they had to do that needed two hands, one of their team members had to help them do it. The twelve of them were absolutely, completely *together,* and they had to cooperate or go crazy trying.

Coffey felt like he'd come home. The twelve men holding onto that pole, they were *us* to him now. Coffey watched all the time, trying to see what was good for the team. As the pressure of training or the strain of having no privacy began to wear on the other guys, it was Coffey who was always there to help out. He didn't give any pep talks—but his hand was the one that held the knot for you. He didn't crack any jokes about the bitch—no, excuse me, I mean the *lady*—but when you felt like you were going to die you were so tired and sore, his was the voice behind you murmuring, You can do it, sailor. And when Coffey said that, you believed him, because you knew that *he* believed what he was saying, that he really believed you could do it. And you could.

He never asked you a question, never corrected you if you were wrong. If you made a mistake in something like explosives or setting a diving mask, something that really mattered, he just set it right, without a word, and when he'd fixed it, he'd look at you as if to say, Got it now? And if you had the slightest uncertainty he'd do it again, and again, until you got it. And yet through the whole thing you never felt like he was putting you down. It was like he was saying, This is a job that has to be done right, and I happen to know how, and you need to know how, so I'll help. You never felt ashamed of being taught by Hiram Coffey. But when you got it right, and he gave you that little nod, then by God you were proud.

At the end, they used their demolition training to lay a charge to blow up the pole. When it came time to set it off, the instructor handed the detonator to one of the men, a guy named Monk. Monk didn't say a word, not a single word, he just knew what they all knew without speaking. He walked over to Coffey and handed the detonator to him.

Coffey didn't smile or anything. He just looked around to make sure the whole team was safely out of the way, and then he blew that bitch to hell. Only then, with the rest of the men cheering and shouting and hugging him and each other, only then did he smile. Did he know how much they loved him in that moment? Did he know those men would die for him? I think so—but I don't think it meant that much to him, because that's just what he expected. They were a team, weren't they? When you're a team, dying for each other's just what you *do*.

You think the instructors didn't notice? This was the most perfect, smooth-functioning team that ever passed through SEAL training, and Coffey was why. When they sent Coffey's team out on assignments, they never screwed up, they never lost a man. That was unheard of. The kind of assignments SEALs got were the kind of assignments where you were damn lucky to get away with only thirty percent casualties.

SEALs never got public credit for their successes, never got public funerals when they died in the line of duty. Their work was always done by invisible hands. That got to some of them. They got hungry for recognition. But not Coffey's team. If they had his approval, that was worth more than medals. And as for Coffey, he'd settled that question long ago. He didn't work for glory. He worked for America. The Navy told him what America needed, and he and his team did it. That's what he lived for. He never wrote to his mom until an officer told him to, and then he never missed a week. He always had a supply of about thirty letters to her prewritten and sealed in envelopes, so that when he was on assignment, a SEAL from another team could mail them for him every Friday, just like clockwork. She never realized that he didn't love her anymore.

With his team, Coffey had no secrets. He told them both the stories I've told you here, about the time Darrel Woodward took his pants down, and about mashing his head in with a cinder block. Both stories, though, had an immediate point. He told the first story as he took a four-man squad with him into Beirut, on a mission where there was a good chance of getting captured. The point of his story was that you can stand any amount of torture. "Pain is nothing. What gets to you is humiliation, the sense of helplessness. But they can't humiliate you, they can't break you, if you don't care. If they cut off your balls, so what? The only reason you had those balls was to serve your country, and this is the moment when your country needs them." Maybe it sounds funny to you, in your safe, peaceful lives. But to men like Coffey and his SEALs, it was no joke. They put everything on the line, body and soul, time after time, so you could sit home and watch TV and bitch about how much you have to pay in taxes.

And that other story, the one about hitting Darrel in the head, he told that story after word got around that one ex-SEAL who ran a bar in Florida had gotten to bragging about some of the stuff he used to do and some of it got in the papers. Lieutenant Coffey didn't have to explain the point of the story. They all understood. Part of your job, he was saying, is to keep your mouth shut. Part of your job is to *never* get any glory for what you do. The papers will all talk about how the Marines landed on some dumb little Caribbean island—they'll never say a word about the team of SEALs who went in first and took out the radar installation at exactly four A.M., just before the first American ships came over the horizon. And that's right. That's what SEALs do. Marines whoop it up and say semper fi all the time. SEALs keep their mouths shut and do the job.

It was the work Coffey was born for. He made his whole team feel like they were born for it too. They were absolutely loyal to each other, absolutely obedient to their orders, the absolutely perfect team.

Except one. Funny thing is, he didn't even know it. The one who loved Coffey best, he wasn't really one of the team, not down deep, and he never guessed.

Chapter 4

Contact

The Earth isn't much as planets go, but small as it is, most of human history has taken place in a space that's smaller yet, a thin layer starting in the dirt and sticking up maybe twelve feet into the air—about as high as a man on horseback can wave a sword. Now and then a building would punch a hole in that twelve-foot ceiling. Now and then a miner's tunnel would drop down a little. But after a few years or decades or centuries, the people would abandon their works. Then the wind and rain would tear down whatever stuck up and fill in whatever went deep, until the Earth was healed again.

We could always *see* a little outside that layer—clouds rolling in, sunshine in the sky, stars at night. We could guess at what was going on under us, when the earth shook, or when big old fish swam up and beached themselves to die. But the height of the heavens and the depths of the sea, they were so far away that whole civilizations could have been going on there and we'd never have known it.

They were, and we didn't.

There's no telling how long ago they first came to Earth. No human being was capable of noticing when they arrived, but that means only that they got here sometime before high-grade telescopes and radar. *They* don't even know how long ago they got here, or how long the voyage took, because they don't measure time except the way a little child does: This happened before that, and this other happened after. Why should they keep track of years and seasons? When you live four miles under the sea, there's no spring and fall, and even the tides are like a faint daily breeze if you feel them at all. And why should they measure the passage of years? When you can't die, there's no reason to count how long you've lived.

And yet they *do* care about the past. Their name for themselves is "Builders of Memory." They cling to everything that has happened to them since their first consciousness. That vast memory is their very self. They remember their arrival on Earth, and before that their arrival on each previous world, back to their planet of origin. If we had ever mattered to them, they would have remembered all of our history, too.

They might have noticed us if we had shared the same habitat, the way we take note of ant colonies and migratory birds. But our thin layer of the Earth's crust is as hostile to them as the moon is to us. Our atmosphere is only slightly thicker than the near vacuum of space. The only part of our planet they cared about was down so deep in the ocean that the water presses like the hands of cruel giants. Only there did they feel at home, and at that depth, the human race did not matter.

Until we began to intrude. The sludge of our polluted rivers began to flow out onto the continental shelves and then seep down to the unfathomable depths, where they noticed the stink of it, the nasty taste. The fish began disappearing from the ocean, so that less and less of their detritus drifted down to where the builders were used to harvesting and using it. Torpedoes and mines made underwater explosions whose shockwaves cracked the foundations of their spindly towers.

At first, because most of their communication is chemical, they thought these things were messages, and for some time they tried to decipher them. Then, when our pollution began to make them sick, to infest and infect them like a plague, when there was a famine of skeletal remains of fish and even microscopic plankton slackened, killed by radiation passing through the depleted ozone layer—then they began to think that we, the creatures living in that thin layer between the sea and the sky, were enemies, trying to poison or starve them.

Yet they were careful. We might even say they were patient with us, though that was not their motive. For a long time they merely avoided the places where our poisons flowed, while they watched us, to try to understand who we were, what we were doing. Even though nothing we sent into the sea was a message, they finally understood that the radio waves we emitted *were* messages, if only to each other. Since they had little language, at least as we understand it, it took years for them to decipher, sorting our messages by wavelength and then gradually discovering units of meaning.

If the concept of language was hard for them, the idea that members of the same species would have *different* languages was almost unthinkable. Nations? Famines? War? All within the same species? What kind of creatures were we? Like a family whose parents have died. Like a cancer that devours the body that is its only source of life. The more they learned of us, the more alien we seemed—the more repulsive, insane, *monstrous*.

Now they regretted the many centuries they had ignored us. Instead of devoting a relatively small part of their attention to studying us, they turned all their energies in our direction. How dangerous to the builders were we? How could they stop us, if they needed to? They were not equipped for war. They had only developed the weapons needed to defend against dangerous but stupid predators. We, however, had developed weapons that could outwit and overpower enemies every bit as intelligent as we were, because our greatest danger always came from other humans. In order to learn the art of war, so they could eliminate the threat we posed to them, they had to study us.

This was not work that could be done at the bottom of the

sea, however. Our radio and television signals never reach that level. Even the sun's light means nothing to them—they take their energy from vents in the Earth's crust, the breakdown of molecules, the temperature differential between layers of seawater. To comprehend us, they had to rise up out of the sea.

They knew how to do it, of course. After all, they had crossed vast reaches of space to get here, and when their cities under the oceans of Earth reached maturity, they would build new starships and send out more colonies to other deepwater worlds. That day was still far in the future, but in the meantime their original starship still circled the Earth, out beyond the moon and perpetually behind it, where no landbound telescope could see it.

For the first time since the builders reached Earth, they released certain chemical codes among some of the porters, a related species that they had long ago domesticated. When young ones budded off the altered porters, they looked different. When they grew, they did not take the shape of bottom-crawling haulers or the small, darting messengers that were most commonly used. Instead they grew into gliders, able to hurtle through the sea at speeds we landbound creatures can't even hope for, and then to rise up into the air, taking vast energy from every ambient source—power enough to carry them over our cities and fields, over our sea lanes, through our flightpaths as the builders inside each glider watched us, listened to us, tried to understand what kind of creature we were.

Our movements were meaningless to them. They could not imagine individual people choosing to live wherever they liked, so they could not understand why we wasted incredible amounts of energy in repetitive, unproductive travel. Even our buildings were incomprehensible. Since they lived in a place without weather, the notion of shelter did not come easily to them. Building a hollow structure just to *contain* something was strange enough. But when they realized that most buildings were mostly empty most of the time, they could only conclude that we were unimaginably stupid. Everything they built was completely full and completely used; when it was no longer needed, even temporarily, it was broken down and the parts used for something else. Their contempt for us was complete.

We never saw them watching us. Oh, maybe a glint of sunlight at just the right moment of the day reflected from a smooth, normally transparent surface. Maybe, on a very dark, moonless night, the faint glow from inside a glider was visible as it soared overhead. A light in the sky, moving at unbelievable speed, then suddenly stopping, changing direction with no regard for the laws of motion. The gliders never came to rest on land. And since builders would die in seconds outside the hard-shelled gliders, no alien creature could possibly have emerged. Any such story you heard was—I was going to say it was a lie, but how do I know? It might have been a hallucination. It might have been a dream. It might have been a hope so hoped for that the mind believed it had come true. But it was *not* true. A builder could no more land and leave her glider than you could shed your skin and walk away. Almost transparent, filled to the shell with the cold spicy liquid of life; they were near us, but we never really saw them.

When we started sending up satellites, their work in understanding us leaped forward. Out in space, they could finally touch something we had made, reaching inside the metal skin to explore. They found many of our open secrets there. Electronic circuitry. The digital minds of computers.

And, the most ominous secret of all, nuclear power. To them it was brighter and more terrible than sunlight. Now they knew we were worse than a sewage-spewing race of stupid, wasteful land slugs befouling the edges of their home. We had the power to kill the world. *Their* world, too—the ocean. We were even more dangerous than they had feared.

That's why on a certain morning at the peak of hurricane season, a glider fled from the satellite it was studying and flung itself earthward. The glider easily absorbed all the heat of reentry, storing the energy in intricate structures inside itself, which could be used to speed its movement under the sea, or later to help build underwater towers, or to help another glider escape from gravity on a later outbound flight. Almost invisible to the eye, and completely invisible to radar, it glided southeastward over the Gulf of Mexico at four times the speed of sound, crossed the horn of the Yucatan, and then plunged down into the Caribbean. So smoothly did it enter the water that there wasn't even a splash. The ocean simply opened up to receive it.

Now, in the dark sea, the bright energy stored during reentry gave off a clearly visible glow as the glider skimmed along not far under the surface. Even though it was underwater, technically the glider was not wet. Not a molecule of Caribbean water physically touched the surface of the glider. Instead, it flowed around the shell as if it were repelled by a magnet. There was almost no friction. The builders were better at moving through water than they were at moving through air.

The glider seemed to be on a simple homebound flight. The oldest and greatest of all the builders' cities was here in the Caribbean, deep in the Cayman Trench, where almost no Earthborn life could penetrate. The glider's course did not vary—it was heading home.

But all these processes were carried on by the glider, by reflex. Once the homeward course had been set, there was no further intelligent guidance. The builder inside was severely injured.

The satellite she had been studying was launched into orbit only a few days before. It did what no other satellite had been able to do before: It tracked all submarines in the ocean. The exact location of every sub, in port or on maneuvers, on the surface or in its deepest dive, was detected and reported in coded messages to a series of Earth stations, hour by hour. The existence of such a sub-tracker meant that for the first time in the age of missiles, a first strike could take out land- *and* sea-based nuclear weapons. The surface of the Earth had just become a far more dangerous place.

Individual builders are often granted a great deal of intelligence and good judgment, especially if they are required to be separated from their city for long periods, doing perilous, delicate work. So this builder understood that this new satellite was the most dangerous object in space, knew that if it were allowed to remain in working order even for a single hour, it could trigger the final, terrible war. Either the nation that controlled it would use it to launch a preemptive strike, or the nations that didn't have it might find out about it and launch their own nuclear attack, fearing that if they didn't use their weapons, they'd lose them.

There was no time of safety in which she could return home, transfer the information she had learned, and let the city come to a decision. Therefore the builder made the decision herself. This satellite could not be allowed to continue to function.

Carefully she isolated her memories behind a shielded portion of the glider. Unfortunately, she could not shield her judgment and intelligence, since they were needed for the job at hand. Using the limbs and tools she had grown out of the belly of the glider, she reached into the shell of the satellite, searching for its burning nuclear heart. Her reflex was to absorb all its energy, but that would have killed her instantly. Instead, she channeled the energy flow into the satellite's most delicate computer parts. Only then did she release the power supply—rapidly, but not so rapidly as to cause a nuclear explosion. There was a burst of heat and light, visible to every tracking station on that side of the Earth. More important to the builder, the power burst included a deadly amount of radiation. The intricate molecules that comprised her intelligence were scrambled beyond repair. Except for her carefully shielded memories, she was intellectually dead.

That's why the glider's homeward course was so direct. Porters had intelligence comparable to that of a dog. Enough to carry out simple tasks—fetch, stay, go home— but not enough to do any complex maneuvering. How could the builder foresee that there would be another encounter with a human artifact on the way home? It would require only a fraction of the intelligence and judgment that she had used to make her decision about the satellite, but she lacked even that fraction, and it was completely beyond the feeble intellect of the porter. So even as surface tracking stations were trying to make sense of the burst of light and heat that had just come from a recently launched spy satellite, another encounter between human and builder, this time even more direct and fatal, was about to take place.

On that day, it happened that Hurricane Frederick was moving across the Caribbean out of the east-southeast, due to pass over that region of the sea within twenty-four hours.

Bud Brigman and his crew were twenty-two miles away, conducting the third shift of the first deep-sea trials with *Deepcore,* the underwater drilling platform that was the culmination of Lindsey's life work.

Lindsey Brigman herself was in Houston, doing the landside work and itching to get back out under the water.

Hiram Coffey was in Houston with three SEALs from his twelve-man team, preparing to go in to a certain country in the Caribbean to destroy, with surgical precision, the headquarters of a leftist guerrilla operation that posed a threat to the security interests of the United States, as defined by Coffey's superior officers.

Within an hour of the moment the glider entered the waters of the Caribbean, all would be diverted from the work they had planned to do.

What if they hadn't been there? What if Lindsey hadn't brought *Deepcore* to readiness so far ahead of schedule? What if Coffey had flown out to begin his mission the night before, breaking off radio contact so he couldn't be reassigned? What if Bud and his crew had been assigned to one of the alternate drilling sites, farther north in the Caribbean? What if Hurricane Frederick had taken the more northward course originally predicted for it, so it would dump on Cuba instead of thrashing along the north coast of Jamaica? Maybe even with changed circumstances things would have worked out to the same result, except that it wouldn't be me telling you about it.

But if things had worked out wrong, there wouldn't have been anybody much to tell it to.

Aaron Barnes was on duty with the sonar system of the USS *Montana,* an *Ohio*-class SSBN ballistic missile submarine on its way back home after a seventy-day mission. When they were running underwater, which was most of the time, Barnes was the sub's eyes and ears. He took the job seriously. He never let his concentration lapse. Because he knew that if he made one mistake, they were all blind and deaf in the belly of the sea.

So when the glider, still far off, began to emit a thrumming noise as it moved through the water, it was less than a second before Barnes noticed it, and only a few seconds more before both Barnes and the sonar computer concluded, from the sound-source's course and speed, that it wasn't a fish.

Within moments the whole crew was at battle stations; Captain Kretschmer and the Exec were both in the attack center; and Barnes was the most important man on the *Montana.* He had to identify the contact—the whatever-it-was that he was tracking—and he had to do it before it could pose a danger to the ship. There weren't all that many countries in the world that even owned submarines, and none of them were neutral. Not at that speed, not at that depth, not at this time, not in these waters.

Wait a minute. How fast *is* it? Barnes checked again. No lie. "Sixty knots," he whispered.

"Sixty knots?" said Captain Kretschmer. His voice was calm enough—he simply didn't believe the information. "No way, Barnes. The Reds don't have anything that fast."

"Checked it twice, skipper," Barnes told him. "It's a real unique signature. No cavitation, no reactor noise. Doesn't even sound like screws." In fact, it sounded like a fish with an incredibly loud heartbeat. But sixty knots? Wasn't a fish in the sea could move that fast even if it was pissing pure rocket fuel. Moving that fast, the contact should be screaming with the sound of overloaded engines. The screw or turbine or rocket or whatever was making it go that fast should be churning up the water louder than a thousand kids splashing in a swimming pool. Barnes put the signal onto a speaker so everybody could hear it. Let Captain Kretschmer make sense of it, if he could.

He couldn't. Kretschmer had never heard anything like this before. From the moment Barnes had reported the contact, he knew it was Russian. This close to Cuba it could only be theirs or ours. And if it was ours, it wouldn't sound like this. But then, neither would a Russian *Alfa*-class fast-attack sub.

Yet the electronic position board made it plain to Kretschmer that whatever it was, it was heading on a course that would put it in spitting distance in less than a minute. There weren't many options. Kretschmer ran through them in a moment: We can't possibly outrun something that fast. And it isn't like we've got a lot of maneuvering room. We've got the walls of the Cayman Trench like a canyon on both sides of us. The only choices are up or down. Go up, and we're sitting on top of the water like sharkbait—if the contact's an enemy sub, we're dead meat up there.

What Kretschmer couldn't forget, not for a moment, was that he had a full carton of unfiltered longs on board—a full load of nuclear missiles. The greatest prize any Russian ship could hope for was a boomer like his, right on the surface, ready to pluck out of the water and take home to Archangelsk for study. How did he know there wasn't a Soviet group lurking in the shadow of Cuba right now, waiting for him to show himself? The worst outcome— worse than dying, worse than losing his ship—was to let the other side get its hands on a single warhead, or the code books, or the electronics.

So Kretschmer couldn't surface to avoid the contact, couldn't turn to left or right, and there was only so far he could go downward. Maximum operating depth for his sub was officially a thousand feet down, though he knew others of its class had safely gone at least half again that depth. Go under that and you didn't necessarily reach crush depth right away, but there wasn't *much* leeway. He'd read the reports about that Russian *Golf*-class sub that went down in the Pacific about seven hundred miles west of Hawaii. When she went into an uncontrolled dive, her crew found out what her crush depth was. The sea blew in at the stern like a jackhammer into an anthill. When the Hughes *Glomar Explorer* raised a part of her, U.S. intelligence found out something about sudden violation of hull integrity. Two-thirds of the bulkheads were crushed into the first forty feet of the boat. Six-foot bunks were compressed to a foot and a half. Between the pressure and the turbulence, the bodies were broken up like egg yolks in a Cuisinart. He couldn't go very far down, no sir.

The noise kept thrumming. If it was false sonar, shouldn't it have faded by now?

"What the hell *is* it?" said Kretschmer.

"I'll tell you what it's *not*," said the Exec. "It's not one of *ours*."

Nor did he dare to call for help, giving away his position. There was still a chance that the contact didn't know he was there. There was even a chance that the contact didn't exist at all—after all, if the sonar was pegging it at sixty knots, which was ludicrous, it might be malfunctioning to such a degree that it was inventing the contact out of nothing. He could imagine the review board looking at his report. Captain Kretschmer broke radio silence because of a sonar report of an object traveling at sixty knots. That was the sort of nonsense that could end a man's career.

So what choice did that leave him? Don't pick a fight, but don't run, either. Not yet. Hold tight. Maybe by *not* running he could provoke the other guy—if he existed—into changing course, showing something of what his strange ship was capable of. If there really *was* a craft that could go sixty knots under water, then he might as well find out as much about it as he could. The Navy needed to know about this thing. If it existed.

Barnes didn't even try to guess what was going through the captain's mind. Deciding what to do—that was Captain Kretschmer's business. Making sure he was getting a true reading from the sonar was enough to keep Barnes busy. He wasn't about to let *nothing* break his concentration. Even the fact that if the Russians could actually build something that could act like this thing on his computer screen, it could sure as hell blow them out of the water, no, he didn't let that idea keep him from concentrating perfectly and completely on his work.

The moment the contact changed heading, Barnes was on top of it. Speak calmly. Convey the information. Do not ever sound upset. "Sir. Contact changing heading to two-one-six, diving. Speed eighty knots!" He wasn't sure they'd understand him. Eight knots was believable—that's what they'd hear. So he said it again: "Eighty knots!"

The captain moved away. The Exec walked along behind him, looking at Barnes's screen, as if he thought he could see something Barnes and the captain had both missed.

"Eighty knots," said the Exec. He didn't believe it. Saw it with his own eyes, but didn't believe.

Hell, neither do I, thought Barnes. But either it's true, or we're blind down here.

Kretschmer stopped at the chart table. The navigator came over, reporting their own current position. "Still diving. Depth nine hundred feet. Port clearance to cliff wall, one hundred fifty feet."

Kretschmer sketched out the *Montana*'s present depth, the contact's current angle of approach. Was the contact trying for a collision or not? It was hard to tell. It looked like he was going to skim just over the *Montana*. If the contact *wasn't* threatening a collision, then maybe it wasn't hostile, and if it wasn't hostile, maybe they should get close enough to pick up more data when it passed—enough to help the Navy figure out what in hell it was.

"It's getting tight in here," the Exec warned. That was his job. To warn the captain that maybe they shouldn't try any kind of maneuvers down here so close to the wall of the Cayman Trench. But Kretschmer knew there was still plenty of room. The contact might be going fast, but the *Montana* wasn't. Besides, it was a matter of pride. Even though standing orders said that when a boomer had a near encounter its duty was to avoid being spotted, the great powers' undersea boats played a constant game of nuclear tag with friends and enemies alike, getting as close as they could before running away. It was like counting coups among the plains Indians—tagging up on an enemy who hasn't spotted you counts as victory.

Kretschmer wasn't actually playing tag right now. He was staying silent, engine noise as low as possible. But that also meant he couldn't run, either. If the *Montana* made that much noise in the water, the enemy—if it *was* the enemy— would tag them. Or worse. Who could tell what *this* contact was after? As it was, the *Montana* might still be invisible to the contact. And if they could stay close enough they might even tag the other guy themselves—get a good identification without being spotted.

"We can still give him a haircut," said the captain. "Helm, come right two-oh-six niner, down five degrees."

The navigator didn't like it. The wall of the Cayman Trench wasn't far enough away for him to feel good about this. "Port side one hundred twenty feet narrowing to seventy-five. Sir, we have a proximity warning light."

"That's too damn close!" said the Exec. "We've got to back off."

Kretschmer got the message. This was as close to the contact as he was going to get. Was it close enough?

From back around the corner came Barnes's voice: "Range to contact, two hundred. Contact jinked to bearing two-six-oh and accelerated to—a hundred thirty knots!"

Kretschmer turned back to look at Barnes. "Nothing goes a hundred and thirty!" Kretschmer wasn't sure whether to be scared at something this strange or disappointed because it couldn't possibly be real.

In the last few seconds before the contact arrived, a line from an old movie passed through Kretschmer's mind. A child's voice. "They're *he*-ere." He almost laughed, if there had been a moment to laugh. As the contact neared to within a few hundred yards, the lights dimmed down—not just a flicker, a steady dimming that lasted maybe a full second, maybe longer. The thing hadn't *touched* them, and yet it was doing something to their power. If the Russians could drain power from a distance, then there was no stopping them. They could sit there and laugh at us when we offered to give them Alaska if they'd just promise not to blow us up.

The contact passed over them. Still sounding just the same. A smooth thrumming. Incredible that it could move so fast without making more *noise*.

What Kretschmer hadn't thought of—what no one had ever thought of because no one had ever thought of a large undersea craft moving at more than a hundred knots—was the fact that even though the contact was moving without turbulence, the regular laws of physics still applied to the *Montana*. When the smooth slipstream of water from the contact passed across the submarine, then what had been dynamically stable, a clean wave, suddenly became chaos. Turbulence. A hundred and thirty knots worth of it. Worse than you'd find in the belly of a wave in a hurricane.

The *Montana* was designed to withstand nearby explosions of serious magnitude. But turbulence like this—even if the hull could handle it, the steering mechanism couldn't. It was the equivalent of a jet fighter going into a flat spin. Jiggle that stick all you like, flyboy, you ain't going nowhere.

The deck lurched sideways under their feet. Just that fast, everybody who *had* been standing was lying down, some of them dazed from the pain of hitting metal without warning. The Exec shouted what they all knew. "Turbulence! We're in its wake!"

It didn't matter that it was the *Montana* that actually caused the turbulence, that the contact was moving on without carrying any of the chaos with it. Around the *Montana* the water was flowing in crazy, unpredictable shifting patterns. Sirens were going off everywhere. Warnings. Unstable. Too close to the cliff wall. Loss of control.

"Helm! All stop!" Kretschmer called. "Full right rudder!" By the book. The guys who wrote the book had never been in turbulence like this. He knew they were moving rapidly, but couldn't begin to guess what direction.

The helmsman echoed his command, then reported: "Hydraulic failure. Planes are not responding, sir!"

The turbulence was easing up. That was the good news. The side-scan display had the bad news. The cliff wall and the port bow were about to try to occupy the same space at the same time. Even if they got full control *this moment* it was too late. The rock was tougher than the sub.

"Hydraulics restored, sir."

Maybe they'd make it without impact, thought Kretschmer.

Then the *Montana* pranged against the cliff wall. It was a terrible sound—unbreakable metal, breaking. The whole ship flexed; joints in some internal water pipes gave way, and water sprayed into the attack room. This time the crew wasn't tossed around like dice in a cup. This time they were all thrown in one direction. Toward the cliff. A few guys had the bad luck to land wrong, trying to push their heads through a sharp corner, trying to bend their necks in ways that Mother Nature hadn't planned on. The dying had already started.

"Collision alarm!" Kretschmer clung to the ladder and shouted orders. "Collision alarm! Lighten her up, Charlie, lighten her up!"

The first impact had torn open the outer tube doors. The men in the port torpedo room at the front of the *Montana* knew it first. The inner hatches popped open like jack-in-the-boxes, only instead of a puppet, what popped out of each door was a two-foot thick column of water. Fire hoses of the gods. The men in the torpedo room who weren't killed by getting crushed between the water and the bulkhead were blinded by spray. But blind or not, somebody got to the exit hatch, somebody slammed it shut, somebody spun the wheel. The torpedo room was sealed off. Everybody inside it was as good as dead. But everybody else had a chance.

Inside the torpedo room there was a pocket of air. Two men reached it, breathed there for a moment. But the water was so cold it numbed them. The pressure was so great it hurt to breathe. And then, between the cold and the pressure and the shock and the fear, it didn't hurt to breathe anymore because nobody was breathing.

Last thoughts. I'm dying I'm dying. A whole life flashes in front of your eyes. Only you can't even be sure it's your own life, you don't remember any of this stuff actually happening to *you*, nothing in your whole life ever mattered compared to right this moment, needing to get a *breath*, needing to get warm, nice strong hands to pull you out of this water, to make this moment not be happening anymore, and then you hang on to one of those memories, one of those places in your brain where you knew you'd never die. You hold onto that feeling of immortality until you don't fear death anymore because there's nothing left of you to feel.

In the attack room, the navigator was still getting readings from the rest of the ship. "The port torpedo room is flooding!"

Kretschmer knew there was no time for anything subtle. The hull's integrity was gone. They were taking on water. They had only so much compressed air to use for flotation. At this depth, the water pressure was so great that it took ten times as much air pressure to expel the water in the flotation tanks, while the jolt of impact had loosened every seam and hatch, so that every moment they stayed this deep meant that water would burst through another barrier, crushing the air behind it, costing them what little buoyancy was left. They had to get to the surface *now*, where the pressure was less, before anything else broke open, before they took on any more water.

"Blow all tanks! Blow all tanks!"

"Blowing main tanks!"

"Blow everything!"

It wasn't working. The main forward tanks wouldn't blow—they were ruptured. They were too deep to use the auxiliary pumps, even if there'd been time. "All back full!" Kretschmer shouted, but the helmsman knew his job—with the *Montana* tilting so sharply downward, running the screws at full force backward would help the boat rise up toward the surface. But the boat wouldn't go. There was too much water on board, too little low-pressure air. The Russian *Mike*-class sub that bought it in the Norwegian Sea in April 1989 made it to the surface for a while, saved some lives. The *Montana* wouldn't.

Kretschmer and the Exec looked at each other for a moment. No time to say, Sorry, you were right, I should have got the hell out of there, I should have believed the speed the sonar was reporting, should have thought of the turbulence. No time to do anything but their duty. "We're losing her. Launch the buoy."

The Exec opened the box and pushed the button. Everyone in the attack room knew what it meant. During the whole seventy-day mission, even the Navy doesn't know where its boomers are—the captain makes up his own course, within certain broad guidelines. If the *Montana* went down without making contact at the end, it would probably never be found. So you only launched the buoy to mark your final position. It would rise to the surface and broadcast your location in one coded burst. It wasn't a cry for help. It was the marker for the *Montana* 's grave.

The helmsman was calling out the depth readings. Sixteen hundred feet. Seventeen hundred. Despite the noise of spraying water, the groaning of injured or terrified men, Kretschmer heard—or thought he could hear—the popping of each of the hatchways as the water, now at fifty atmospheres of pressure, burst through, probing ever deeper into the ship. Maybe the Russians had it better when that earlier sub went down in the Pacific. One burst and they were crushed into pulp. We're getting it pop by pop, and we have time to know we're dying, time to drown or freeze to death or feel ourselves getting crushed or battered to death. Time to savor the last terrible moments of life.

Before the aft tanks ruptured, they provided enough buoyancy to make the sub slope sharply downward toward the bow. Barnes found a toe-hold on the equipment that had once been to his left, and now was below him. With the bow sonar dome smashed in the first impact, his sonar equipment was useless now—but he could reach the planesman's yoke, maybe do something to help. Where was the planesman? Didn't matter. Barnes struggled to get control, to right the ship, but how? The only way to bring the sub back to level was to flood the aft section to balance the bow. Either that or hit bottom. *Then* they might level out, if they hit bottom. But where was the bottom in the Cayman Trench? It was an old submariner's joke that this was the asshole of the Earth. A sub goes in here like a suppository, it ain't never coming out.

Barnes heard the captain give the order, saw the Exec launch the emergency buoy. They were giving up. Not Barnes. His hands were working so hard that his arms and shoulders ached with the exertion, but his brain was hardly connected to it anymore. It was the craziest thing. He knew he was going to die, his body was working to the breaking point trying to do what couldn't be done, and yet he was thinking about something so far away that it might have happened to somebody else. But no, that wasn't it. *This* was happening to somebody else. The real Barnes wasn't here.

The real Barnes was back in Gaffney, South Carolina, in a big old ramshackle white house on Floyd Baker Boulevard, where Deena had her T-shirt up with Junior sucking his brains out and making milk bubbles all white against the mahogany brown of his face, the deep chocolate brown of her breast. He saw that picture clear in his mind, and if he just looked up a little, turned his head, there'd be Deena's mama in the kitchen, dropping gobs of batter into the oil in the frying pan, backing away and muttering her nastiest blessings when the oil spat back and stung her. Outside, the sound of kids yelling and fighting each other in the shade of the trees, as if the day wasn't hot enough already.

Last spring Barnes came this close to losing all of it, and he knew it. You stay there in Gaffney, he told Deena on the phone. I'm only in port a couple of days. You just stay there. And all the time he's talking, there's Moter's sister, her hand on his waist, her fingers scooping down into his pants, finding the crease of his buttocks, sliding along the sweat. Don't come down this time, he says. But then he hangs up the phone and Moter's sister gives him a kiss like her tongue's a hook and he's a wide-mouth bass. This can't be happening to me, he says to himself. And then he says, That's right. This can't be happening to me. It's somebody else. And he blows off like Moter's sister wasn't even there, just says No thanks goodbye and gets him a bus ticket and five hours later there he is in that living room of that big old white house and Deena's telling him she's so glad he came home, look at your papa, Junior, he just couldn't stay away from you.

That's right, can't stay away. Not like *my* papa who blew mama off the second her ass didn't look cute in tight jeans no more. Not like Deena's papa who drunk himself into the Oakland Cemetery before she was six years old and never put one dime's worth of dinner on the kitchen table. Nobody there even to show me what a papa *was,* I'm going to have to make it up as I go along, but I'll be there, that's who I am, I won't be no filling-station self-serve pump to every twitching ass that goes by like half these guys, I'm going home on leave, my boy's going to know my face and my voice and when *he* gets older he'll know all about what a papa does cause I'll still be there, doing it. Not lying in the cemetery so pickled up with booze that they don't even have to embalm me.

And sure as hell not in a tin can lying on the bottom of the Cayman Trench.

He got his wish. The *Montana* didn't make that terrible free-fall miles down to the bottom of the Cayman Trench. It ran onto a rock outcropping maybe sixteen hundred feet deep. Slammed down on it like a football getting spiked in the end zone. Only the *Montana* didn't bounce. It crumpled, it tore, and then it rolled like a log down the canyon wall until it came to rest on a narrow ledge at twenty-one hundred feet. A huge bubble of air belched out of it. The last gasp of the *Montana.*

Long before it reached the ledge, the crew was dead. The freezing water squirted right through the sub from bow to stern. The men that weren't killed by repeated impacts as the sub rolled down the canyon wall either died by drowning or froze in the water as they sucked desperately at the last of the air—air under so much pressure that breathing it in was like inhaling fire.

Only they didn't die completely dead, not at first, anyway. The human body doesn't switch itself off that fast. Especially at deep-ocean temperatures. Everything just slows down in the cold. You're dying, sure, but the breakdown of cells in your brain gets slowed down enough that for a while—an hour maybe, or ten minutes, or two hours, or thirty seconds —you're hanging there in the water, unconscious, your heart stopped, your lungs not doing any more of the old in-and-out, but your brain's still alive, your thoughts are still hanging there, your memories are still locked away in that time-release safe, waiting for death to lock them up for good.

That was how the crew was, some of them, anyway, when the builders came to look at the sub. The glider whose wake had destroyed the *Montana* made it home almost as soon as the *Montana* stopped its descent on the ledge of the canyon wall. It took only moments for the city to realize that the builder inside was mostly dead. They found and swallowed her memories, and so learned about the new satellite and what she had meant to do about it. Then they tasted the glider's much more primitive memories to make sure the job had been carried out. They learned that it had. They also learned about the near collision with the *Montana*.

The city was so near, the builders so quick, that when they got to the *Montana* there was still life, still memory locked in the brains of the near-frozen men. All were beyond reviving, but the builders wouldn't have tried to revive them anyway. To them, all that was necessary was to preserve the memories of the dead and build them into the city. They were doing for the crew of the *Montana* exactly what they would do for each other.

The only difference was that they hardly knew how to begin trying to comprehend human memory. It was stored differently, organized strangely. They passed through the *Montana* like archaeologists trying to salvage strange new writings from a long-buried civilization, only they couldn't even be sure which artifacts were writing and which were garbage. So they took a record of everything—electrical and chemical patterns, and where each cell of each brain was in relation to all the others. Though twenty-one hundred feet was quite shallow to them, as dangerous as it is for us to climb a four-mile mountain without oxygen, they persisted.

They worked with unimaginable speed—at the molecular level they were as quick as blood, as quick as chemistry. Each builder would enfold the head of a newly-dead man inside her own body, and then reach into the brain with microscopically small fluid tentacles, probing like slender fingers between and around and *into* the cells of the brain. Yet they did this delicate operation, not with one or two or five fingers at a time, but with ten thousand fingers; they did it by reflex, no more noticing or planning the movement of each tendril than we notice the individual sensations carried by each neuron from our retinas. They got a perfect three-dimensional image of the human brain at a molecular level as easily as we memorize a melody after hearing it only once. Long before they could suffer irreversible damage from the low pressure at the shallow depth of twenty-one hundred feet, they had finished their work and dropped back down into the trench, down to the depths where they were comfortable, back to the city. Not one builder was injured.

Even if some had died, though, it would have been worth the attempt. They knew that if they gathered *enough* information, then perhaps they could decode it, compare it to the information they'd already collected, and eventually learn how to taste our memories the way they tasted each others' —pure and strong and clear. If they succeeded, they would know us better than we knew each other. They would see our lives from the inside out, see all that we had seen, exactly as we saw it. And, knowing us at last, they could then discover how to stop us from destroying the Earth.

Not for our sakes. For their own. If they could not stop us, they would be forced to abandon this world. And their life cycle on this world wasn't half complete, none of the cities was finished yet. They would be a failed colony, with nothing to do but return to their mother world empty-handed, in shame. It would be worse than death.

They would send other builders to the *Montana,* of course, to study the structures, the guidance and control systems, the torpedoes, the missiles, the warheads that could destroy the world. But this was secondary work. They had already discovered the principles of our machinery and electronics.

The most vital information was the data collected by the first wave of builders. And included in that original data was the mind of a certain sonarman named Aaron Barnes, who wasn't really inside his body when he died, who was in fact alive in a house on Floyd Baker Boulevard in Gaffney, South Carolina, where a baby nursed and a woman smiled at him and said, Good thing you come home, Ary, cause I was about to tell Junior his papa was Kareem. Good thing you come home cause supper be almost ready and no way all us can finish this mess Mama's cooking without you sucking down your share, you hear me?

Does that make any sense to you, me telling you that Aaron Barnes wasn't really there? I tell you this—it made a hell of a lot of sense to the builders, once they figured out how to understand the way our brains worked. A person's body being in one place, while he thinks his real self is back home where his best memories are kept, why, that was the natural way of life to them. If all they'd found were minds full of thoughts of struggling to stay alive—or filled with despair and self-blame, like Captain Kretschmer's—if all they'd found were thoughts of here and now, then to them we would have been mere animals, nothing more. They would have dealt with us like animals.

But they found Aaron Barnes, a man who had put himself in another place, outside his own body. It wasn't all that clear to them. They couldn't watch our thoughts unfold like a movie or a book, they couldn't be *sure* of what they found. But Aaron Barnes, dead, gave them a glimmer that human beings might be alive in the sense that the builders themselves were alive. Barnes never knew it, but his being on that sub and dying there, thinking the way he did, it was just enough to give the builders hope that perhaps they could share this planet with us.

On the surface of the Caribbean Sea, the *Montana*'s emergency buoy bobbed up and began sending out radio signals.

Chapter 5

Civilian Asset

When the Pentagon finds out that an emergency buoy from a nuclear sub is singing its heart out somewhere, the bureaucracy shakes itself and discovers, like a bear coming out of hibernation, that it's actually capable of moving fast. This is partly in the hope that by acting quickly, the men might be saved. But in the cold reality of nuclear strategy, the loss of the men would not be half so damaging to the United States as loss of the code books and electronic intelligence, the warheads and guidance systems. Even a dead sub is a prize the presumed enemy would give a lot to get their hands on. So whether the crew is breathing or not, the sub has to be found and protected while the situation is sized up and further decisions are made.

Within fifteen minutes of the buoy's signal, a ship with bottom-scanning capability was sent out from GITMO—the base at Guantanamo—along with enough escort vessels to secure the site from enemy observation and interference. It took a while to get to the *Montana,* since the group had to pretend to be heading somewhere else, to avoid Cuban reconnaissance. Once they got there, though, they did their work quickly and well. The scanning ship made several

62

passes, towing a camera and side-scan sonar; when it was finished, the military was able to put together a mosaic photograph of the *Montana*.

The sub was located at twenty-one hundred feet, resting nearly on its side on a narrow shelf in the wall of the Cayman Trench. The hull had obviously been breached; the military knew that there was no chance at that depth for anyone to have survived more than a few minutes. They didn't tell that to any of the civilians, of course— government officials would move much more quickly if they thought there might be lives to save, even though the codebooks and warheads required even more urgency.

Immediately there was talk of bringing the old *Glomar Explorer* out of mothballs. The Hughes Corporation's huge floating crane had lifted a piece of a Soviet sub out of the Pacific more than a decade before. Since then the government hadn't been able to use it—the operation's cover as a commercial gig was blown in the press, so that now whenever the *Glomar* moved, everybody assumed it was really on a CIA or military operation. But cover or no cover, the *Glomar* could do the job. Trouble was, she was on the West Coast. It would take months to outfit her and bring her around. The Russians couldn't be expected to sit there and wait politely until the U.S. had finished all its efforts to raise the *Montana*. Something had to be done immediately to secure the most sensitive contents of the sub.

The Navy had deep-submergence rescue vehicles— DSRVs—designed for the job. The trouble was, the composite pictures showed that the *Montana* had rolled, and now was tilted more than forty-five degrees, which would keep a DSRV from locking onto the hull properly. Even if the Navy could improvise some way to use them, the DSRVs simply weren't available. The one in Norfolk was in drydock undergoing repairs from a minor training accident. The one in San Diego couldn't possibly get there in time, not with Hurricane Frederick bearing down on the spot where the *Montana* lay. Within twenty-four hours the Navy group protecting the site would have to disperse for the duration of the storm—taking any DSRV with them.

Complicating everything was the fact that no one could guess *why* the sub had sunk. Was it an enemy attack? No enemy sub was known to be in the area—but there had been a flash of light and heat from the newest Russian spy satellite only a few minutes before the *Montana*'s buoy sent out its signal. Could there possibly be a connection? The satellite was in a polar orbit, and at the moment it flashed, it had been directly over Venezuela—close enough, in global terms, that it might well have done something to the *Montana.*

"Done what?" demanded the President. "A sub-killing satellite? If such a thing is possible, why don't we have one in development? I hope I don't sound combative, but Senator Nunn is going to ask me that question and I'd better know the answer."

"We don't think it's possible," said the Chairman of the Joint Chiefs. "But we don't know it's *im*possible, either."

"It's coincidence," said the CIA chief. "There's no plausible connection between the burst from SL-420 and the *Montana* going down."

"You don't know any more than we do," said the Secretary of Defense. "For all you know the Russians are watching us and laughing. They could have timed it so the hurricane would sweep us out of there tomorrow."

"If they did it," said the President, "it means they have the ability to track our subs from space." That remark was followed by heavy silence. They all knew that would be an intolerable situation, leading to the toughest decision for a President since Harry Truman had to decide about dropping the A-bomb on Japan. Only this time, the other side wouldn't roll over and play dead.

"What matters *now,*" said the Navy chief, "is that we don't have the capability to get anything in there that will help us accomplish damage minimalization before the storm."

"Damage minimalization consists of what?" asked the President.

"In Phase One," said the Navy chief, "we extract codebooks, electronic intelligence, guidance systems, and any information about what caused the sub's loss."

"And of course rescue survivors," said the President.

"That goes without saying," said the Navy chief. "When we've cleared the sub, we either secure the area until we can raise it, or, if it looks like the Russians have figured out what we're doing and plan to interfere in a major way, we go on to Phase Two, Three if necessary."

"Which is?"

"Prepare to blow it off the shelf and let the Cayman Trench take care of security on what's left."

"But we can't do any of that, is that what you're telling me?"

"I'm telling you we can't get our own assets in there before the storm."

"Whose assets do you have in mind?" asked the CIA chief. *He* didn't know of any foreign power in the area that had equipment that would do the job, and it would be a real slap in the face if military intelligence had uncovered such information when the CIA hadn't.

"American," said the Navy chief, easing his mind. "A civilian asset, of course. Benthic Petroleum is running an experimental underwater drilling operation twenty-two miles away from the site. We could bring them in under the storm, put a team of SEALs on board, and they could have the *Montana* secured and stripped before the hurricane's gone."

"I thought *Deepcore* required an umbilical," said the CIA chief. It was his way of letting everyone know that *he* knew all about Benthic's experimental underwater drilling station. "The *Benthic Explorer* is the mother ship, isn't it? We can't expect them to ride out a hurricane, can we?"

"The umbilical is flexible and far stronger than it would ordinarily need to be," said the Navy chief. "And the *Benthic Explorer* is designed to withstand some pretty bad seas. But—"

"Nothing can stand still in the water during a hurricane," said the President. He had served on a carrier in his youth, and went sailing every summer all his life—he knew what could and could not be done on the water.

"Right," said the Navy chief. He was about to make that very point, but so much the better if the President realized it himself first. "The designer allowed for that. If it gets really bad, *Deepcore* can cut loose from the umbilical and survive on its own for four days while the *Explorer* moves out of the hurricane's way and then comes back in behind it. Not that any of us would enjoy being on board the *Explorer* tomorrow, with the heavy seas she'll have to navigate, but these oil companies wouldn't let their profits depend on rigs that can't deal with hurricane season in the Gulf."

"The real question," said the Secretary of Defense, "is whether Benthic will let us use their rig."

"They will," said the President. "I'll see to that."

"You think these oil-company bastards are so patriotic they'll respond to their nation's call?" asked the CIA chief.

"I think they wouldn't want the publicity if word got out that Benthic had refused to help us rescue an American submarine crew," said the President. "If there's anybody the American people love to hate more than politicians, it's corporations." They all laughed. The Navy might know the sea, but the President knew politics, and from Washington, at least, politics looked far more dangerous.

"That asshole told the President *what?*" It didn't occur to Lindsey that she was talking to the president of the resource development division of Benthic Petroleum, and that the asshole she was referring to—the CEO—had the power to cut off her whole *Deepcore* project whenever he felt like it. "You can't just stop drilling like that and take off on some wild goose chase!"

"Yes we can," said Deeter. "It's the best P.R. Benthic could possibly get. Big oil company is still a loyal American enterprise, always at our nation's beck and call."

"Why don't they use their own goddamn divers?"

"I don't know." Deeter was trying to be patient. "I don't know anything about it."

"You break off the drilling just as we're about to get to contract depth, and you *don't know anything about it?*" Her tone of voice was full of withering contempt, as if she thought Deeter was the most spineless fool ever to head a division of a major international corporation. Of course he wasn't. You don't get to the division-president level of a company like Benthic unless you've got a steel rod of ambition up your ass. But Lindsey measured people by a much simpler measure. If they were helping her get her work done, they were bright and good. If they were getting in the way, they were slime.

The secretaries listened, marveling. No one ever spoke to Deeter except in the most respectful tones, as if he were God. And here was this *project engineer,* for heaven's sake, talking to him as if he were a third-grader who just wet his pants on the playground. "There goes her Christmas bonus," whispered one of them.

But Deeter wasn't the sort of person to let his pride get offended when it wasn't helpful. "The Navy asked if we had somebody who knew *Deepcore* inside out—how it's made, what kind of pressures it can stand. I told them that McBride has the specs on the *Explorer,* but our project engineer—"

"I hope you don't think I'm going to get on the phone and give some Navy pinhead all the information I sweat blood over for the last five years."

"No," said Deeter. "I think you're going to get in the fastest helicopter the Navy has here in Houston and go out to the *Benthic Explorer,* at which time you will give some Navy pinhead anything he asks for, up to and including your pretty little head."

That was different. She was going out there. She'd be on the spot. Maybe she could even stop them from making some half-wit mistake that would destroy *Deepcore.* "All right," she said. "When do I go?"

"You're already gone," said Deeter. Then, because he couldn't resist cutting her down to size, just a little, he added, "If you're on your period, you'd better borrow tampons from the secretaries, because the helicopter's on the roof and they've already waited longer than they said they would."

It wasn't until she was sitting inside the Navy chopper that she realized how Deeter had insulted her. Pretty little head my ass, she thought. And he no doubt meant the sexual innuendo as well. Not to mention the insulting remark about tampons. She assumed that Deeter must talk this way to all women. It never occurred to her that he never did; that her arrogant attitude had goaded him beyond endurance.

Fuming inwardly, she looked around at the others in the chopper with her. There were a couple of chopper crewmen, keeping to themselves when they weren't busy with something. The only other passengers were four soldiers. Or sailors, who could tell? What were *they* doing here, anyway? Her escort? They wore an insignia she didn't recognize—a trident on their left breast pockets. They weren't young kids, either. They looked older. Almost ageless, and their faces were hard. No, not hard. Just empty. They didn't seem to show any emotion at all. It made Lindsey extremely uncomfortable whenever she was in a situation that she didn't understand completely. Were they part of this secret operation? Were they there to control *her?* Or did they just happen to be on this helicopter? She had to know who they were, so she'd know what to expect from them.

They had sidearms. "What are you, Marines?" she asked.

"SEALs," said one. And then, because she obviously didn't recognize the term, he explained. "It's an acronym. Sea, Air, and Land. Navy. *Not* Marines. I'm Monk."

"Are you going to the *Benthic Explorer,* too?" she asked.

Monk said nothing. Nor did he look around for someone else to answer her, or for permission to answer her. It was eerie, the way none of them so much as flinched in such a way as to tell her who was in command.

Then a man who had been facing away from her turned on the bench to face her. *"We're* going to the *Benthic Explorer. You* are the one who's going to the *Benthic Explorer* 'too.' You are not essential to this mission. You've already cost us eight minutes in unnecessary delay."

That was all. He made no threats, he did not raise his voice, and yet she felt as though she had just been whipped. She almost apologized, almost started explaining about how bad the traffic was in Houston today and she got to the Benthic Building as soon as it was humanly impossible. But she caught herself in time. This walrus or seal or whatever he was might think he was in command, but no one was ever in command of Lindsey but herself.

Kirkhill was loving it. He made damn sure he was the one to talk with Commodore DeMarco, overall commander of the naval operation, when he made radio contact from his approaching helicopter. Kirkhill didn't want anybody else talking to the Navy. It's my job to make sure everybody cooperates, Kirkhill told himself. I've got to get the word directly, so I can pass it along without screw-ups. Damn lucky thing I happened to be doing an on-site management audit of the *Benthic Explorer* this week.

The fact was Kirkhill just plain loved being in the center of something that actually mattered. Sure, searching for oil and testing the new underwater drilling platform mattered, but he knew—and so did everyone else—that the real work was going on down in *Deepcore II,* at the bottom of the Caribbean. Up here in the mother ship, all they had to do was caretaker work. He was on the fringes, close enough to see what was going on, but too far off to have any effect on it.

It wasn't that Kirkhill wanted glory. He suspected, as most men do, that if it came right down to it, if a hero was called for, he wouldn't be able to find any hero-stuff inside himself. Even now, the Navy wasn't here for the *Benthic Explorer* itself, it was here for *Deepcore,* at the other end of the lifeline. But for a few minutes an important military operation was being funneled right through Kirkhill's hands. He was damn well going to get as many of his own fingerprints on it as he could.

Of course, the secrecy was so thick that Kirkhill didn't know much more than the fact that Benthic had ordered him to put his vessel completely at the disposal of the Navy, as long as it did not compromise the safety of the crew. He had his guesses, though, and they weren't far off. There aren't all that many reasons the Navy could need a deep-water undersea craft on an emergency basis. If *he* could guess on the basis of what he knew, he'd better make sure his people knew even less. So the men who actually ran the topside part of *Deepcore*'s work—McBride, the drilling operations supervisor, and Bendix, the crew chief—were told only to stand by and wait for further developments. "And above all, don't talk about this to *anyone.*"

Only a moment ago, Bendix had cleared the choppers to land on the *Explorer*'s deck. In an hour, maybe less, the approaching hurricane would make such heavy seas that no helicopter could possibly land, but these had gotten here with such perfect timing that the choppers from GITMO and the one from Houston arrived almost at once.

Now Bendix and McBride stood on the bridge of the *Benthic Explorer,* watching as the Navy helicopters spewed out armed invaders and mysterious equipment. Kirkhill was down there greeting everybody as if they were all coming to a party and he were the host.

"Pretty easy not to talk about this to anybody," said Bendix, "since I don't know anything to talk about." Seeing the way the military seemed to be taking over the deck, shoving the *Explorer*'s crew out of the way, Bendix foresaw a lot of problems he'd have to deal with right away. Doubtless with that asshole Kirkhill looking over his shoulder the whole time. "This could be ugly."

McBride didn't like it either. He'd come out of the Army a good many years back with a low opinion of the military, and he was pretty sure that whatever else happened, this test well and all the time and effort invested in drilling it were pretty much screwed. "Does not look at all good," he said.

That was when Bendix saw a woman get off one of the choppers, along with four military guys who didn't look Navy. For a moment he wondered why the military had a woman along on an operation like this. Then he realized that this was the helicopter from Houston and the woman was from Benthic.

"Oh, no, look who's with them."

It was Lindsey Brigman. Didn't he already have enough shit to deal with today? Was somebody at Benthic trying to get him to take early retirement or something?

A few minutes later, Kirkhill was on the bridge with Commodore DeMarco and the SEALs from the Houston chopper. Sure enough, all they wanted to know about was *Deepcore*. Practical things. How far divers working out of *Deepcore* could range. How long they could stay away. Above all, how fast *Benthic Explorer* could tow *Deepcore* without bringing it to the surface, and how soon they could start moving it.

"As you can see," said Kirkhill, "you can follow everything they're doing down there from up here. It allows us as much information about actual drilling operations as we get on a surface rig."

DeMarco didn't pick up on Kirkhill's enthusiasm. He just stared into the video screen, which showed divers on the bottom, working in total blackness except for a few pools of artificial light.

"No light from the surface," said DeMarco. So the boy knew underwater work well enough to recognize conditions through a video. "How deep are they?"

A question that Kirkhill couldn't answer. No problem— he could pluck answers out of the crew at will. "McBride?" he said.

"Seventeen hundred feet," said McBride. *The dickhead doesn't even know how deep our rig is, and he still acts like he's in charge.* But McBride didn't let his contempt show. *What's the point? If he didn't work for Benthic, he'd work for some other company that would put dickheads in charge.*

"I need them to go below two thousand," said DeMarco.

"No problem," said Kirkhill. "They can do that."

Yeah, right, thought McBride, *but how* much *over two thousand? Trust Kirkhill to promise the moon before bothering to find out if our boys can actually do it.*

But if McBride was keeping his objections to himself, Lindsey wasn't. She'd been listening, none too patiently, as everybody stood around saying yes sir to DeMarco. Men didn't need to enlist. They all thought they were soldiers. It was like some secret cult among men, that when an officer says, I need your balls, they all unzip and reach for a pocketknife.

Well, I'm not one of the secret regiment, thought Lindsey. I'm not going to let Kirkhill give away my project without a squeak. "So that's it? You just turn the whole thing over to the goon squad?"

Kirkhill was all aggrieved innocence, of course. "Look, I was told to cooperate. I'm cooperating." Hey, none of this is *my* fault. Just following orders. Go take your shower.

Lindsey wasn't actually too worried, not yet. There was at least *one* man who didn't kiss any ass that wore a uniform. Bud would put a stop to all this nonsense. All he had to do was say no, and the whole thing was over. *Deepcore* would stay where it was, and the military could take their choppers and fly back to wherever they came from. They were still Americans. The military was *not* supreme. Still, Kirkhill had caved in so easily. Lindsey was never good at hiding her scorn, but this time she didn't even try. "Kirkhill, you're pathetic." She walked away.

McBride almost felt sorry for Kirkhill—after all, getting publicly castrated by Lindsey Brigman was an experience most of the men on this ship had experienced. At the same time, he knew how Lindsey felt. He didn't *like* having these guys who knew nothing about the *Deepcore* project come on board and act like they owned the world. Especially he didn't like having all their work go down the toilet, just when they were close to succeeding.

"Get Brigman on the line," said Kirkhill.

Dundla got on the horn and started calling. *"Deepcore, Deepcore."* While he was waiting for *Deepcore* to answer, he turned to McBride and said exactly what McBride was already thinking. "Oh, man, if Bud goes along with this, they're going to have to shoot her with a tranquilizer gun."

McBride could only raise his eyebrows in agreement.

Somebody was on the line. "Hippy," said Bendix. "Get me Bud."

Down in *Deepcore* itself, things were going on as usual. Bud Brigman sat at the dome port window of the mud room, talking to Catfish and Finler, who were working outside today. He could see them sometimes, and he liked what he saw. Catfish might be a hard-drinking foul-mouthed skirt-chaser on land, but put him in a hat and a drysuit and give him something to do underwater, and he did as sweet a job as you could ask for—quick, but never so quick you had to worry he wasn't doing it right. And Finler was right with him. They were a good team.

Catfish swam near the window, looked in at Bud. "Hey," Bud said. His headset picked up his voice and carried it to the divers by UQC. That was the Navy's designation for high-frequency sound transceivers. Radio was no good in the water, but close to *Deepcore* they could use UQC, which translated their voices into high-frequency sound, which could keep its coherence for a little way in the water, and then translated it back on the other end. It made it a lot less lonely underwater when you could chatter a little bit. So even though you didn't keep the UQC so busy that somebody with an emergency couldn't break in, it was a good thing every now and then to give a reminder that somebody else was still alive in the world. It wasn't just you and the hissing of the breathing regulator in your hat. "You guys are milking that job," said Bud.

A joke, of course. If they thought even for a second that Bud meant it as serious criticism, Catfish would blow up and Finler would go into a slow burn that would last for days. But Bud knew how to say things so they knew he was joking. Or maybe it's that they knew Bud so well that it didn't occur to them that he might mean it. They knew that if he had a real criticism, he'd say it to them in private, and unless it was an emergency he'd find a way to bring it up without it feeling like a criticism at all.

But it wasn't "just" a joke. Down here in *Deepcore* every word counted, everything you said had meaning whether you wanted it to or not. These guys were doing boring, tedious maintenance and safety checking. A joke would help break it up, keep them alert. More important, though, was that it meant Bud was there, he was watching them. Not watching them like a zealous supervisor, hoping to catch them goofing off. Watching them more like a mother hen. They knew that if anything went wrong, Bud would see it right away. They weren't alone. And out in the cold and darkness, it didn't matter how grown-up you were, how good a diver you were, how brave you were. It felt good to know somebody was watching. That's what Bud's joke was for—to let them feel his gaze on them like a pat on the back, like a caress.

But you don't say all that right out. You keep it light. So when Catfish answered, he didn't sound grateful. "That's cause we love freezin' our nuts off out here for you so much."

Catfish turned away, swam off toward where Bird-Dog Finler was already closing down and cleaning up. "Come on, Finler," said Catfish. "Let's get it done, I'm tired."

You'd think, listening to him, that Catfish was beat, but it wasn't true. Or if it was, it didn't matter much to him. Bud knew that if he needed it, Catfish would stay at the job another hour, two more, whatever it took. But then, Catfish also knew that Bud would never ask for such a thing if it wasn't safe or necessary.

Working on a drilling platform is no job for weak men, even when the platform is rooted solidly in Mother Earth and sticks up several hundred feet above the sea. There's real danger in it. The ocean doesn't care whether you're a first-time tourist dipping your toes at the beach or a rigger drilling for oil day after day. Make the wrong mistake, and you're just as dead. And on a rig there's a lot more can go wrong than on your average tourist beach.

But what separates platform riggers from flatfoot land crews isn't just the danger. It's the isolation. A guy on a rig in Oklahoma can get in his pickup and drive somewhere that sells beer or *Hustler,* a place with people you don't know who say things you didn't know they were going to say. People, in other words, who are not crew. Fellow riggers always say exactly what you know they'll say, because they've said it ten thousand times already, till you want to ram a screwdriver through their ear just to give them something new to talk about later.

Now take that platform, wrap it up in a metal cocoon, and plunge it seventeen hundred feet under the water, and you've got *Deepcore,* the world's first working underwater drilling platform. Far more dangerous if anything goes wrong, and a hell of a lot more isolated. At least on a surface platform you can see an occasional bird or passing ship. You can see the *sky*. But in *Deepcore* all you can see is the same walls around you, and that small part of the sea floor that's within range of the lights.

And if you should decide you can't stand it anymore and you want to leave, well, it isn't just a jaunt in a boat or a helicopter. First you've got to decompress. Working at these depths has got your body so full of nitrogen that if you don't take your time in the chamber, decompressing the equivalent of rising through the water three to four feet an hour, you die of the bends. There's no quick trip home. If you feel like you have to get out of this tin can right this second, all you can do is climb into an even tinier can and spend three weeks all by yourself decompressing.

Just knowing that makes most people just a little bit crazy in the back of their minds. Like they got this little teeny scream going on all the time, not so bad that they notice it's there, but droning on and on so that all of a sudden one day something happens, you let go just *this* much, and suddenly you've gone completely bugfuck and they take you up in a straitjacket. If they don't take you up in a sack. Most of the time, most people keep that scream under control. But it's there, and you know it, and everybody else knows it, and you watch each other to make sure nobody's losing it.

You want variety? You're in the wrong job. Everything you're going to eat for the whole time you're underwater is already there in the galley—the stuff in storage is more of the same. No Big Mac or beer on tap for you, sorry to say. And everything you breathe comes down the lifeline from the *Benthic Explorer,* the mother ship floating above you on the surface. Everything's the same, day after day, hour after hour, minute after minute. And yet you can't let the boredom distract you. If you fail to concentrate just once, at the wrong time, you can die real quick.

It's not like an office, where it's OK to have a couple of people you can't stand or just ignore, because what the hell, you're going home at five anyway. Down here, if you even suspect one of the guys you're with is stupid or careless, it poisons everything, because you're never sure he isn't going to get you killed. It's no place for polite hypocrisy. If you don't trust him, you just don't work with him. And when he notices you won't ever work with him—which is immediately, the first time you refuse—that's the worst insult you can pay him. He hates you worse than anything in the world, because you've told all the other guys on the crew that you think he's no damn good. And if he's no good in the eyes of his crew, then he knows, right down in his most secret soul, that he is truly worthless. He's so ashamed he wants to die, and he can't *leave.*

So picking a crew for *Deepcore* wasn't just a matter of drawing names out of a hat or seeing who volunteered. They had to take a crew that already trusted each other to the edge of death, that had already worked out all their personality quirks so they didn't piss each other off just by breathing, and, above all, a crew in which all the members were absolutely competent and careful at every job they'd ever have to do.

There were six crews that started at the same time, training as deep-sea saturation divers, not just the penny-ante shallow-depth hat stuff they had to learn for quick underwater work on surface rigs. Three of them finished training and qualified. Two of them would go into permanent rotation, one month under, three weeks coming up, one week of shore time, and back down into the water. And when it came time to pick the prime crew, the one that would go out to start sinking the first deepwater test drill, Bud Brigman's crew got the nod because they were the smoothest, quickest, happiest, *readiest* bunch that ever volunteered to live all but six weeks of every year in tin cans at the bottom of the sea or in even smaller tin cans coming up.

Catfish must have caught Finler doing something not exactly perfect. "What you think you're doing here, buddy?" A little annoyed-sounding. Other guys got pissed off when Catfish talked to them that way. But Finler usually didn't mind getting corrected by Catfish, and when he *did* mind, Catfish didn't mind getting sassed by Finler. That was why Bud kept them together.

Now that he was sure Catfish and Finler were wrapping up OK, Bud moved away from the window and started checking gauges. He could hear the pounding from the drill crew tending the turntable about twenty feet away. This was the working heart of the rig. Because of some first-rate semi-automated equipment, it only took a crew of five to tend to the actual drilling. All the rest of the people in *Deepcore* were there to keep that drill crew alive at the bottom of the sea.

In a lot of ways *Deepcore* resembled a spaceship out of the movies. The white metal framework holding together the trimodules around the central bay, all neat and clean and sterile and cold. But here on the drilling floor, you knew that you weren't out in space. This was a hardhat area, as sure as any topside drilling rig, and the men who worked it were covered with mud and chewed-up bits of rock and sludge the drill had brought back from deep in the hole. So much for clean.

"Hey Bud!"

He looked around, trying to see who had called his name. It was Jammer, the big guy, standing a full head taller than anybody else on the rig. *Deepcore* wasn't designed for a basketball team—Jammer only had about ten places on the rig where he could stand up straight. Bud walked over to him so he could hear.

"Hippy's on the bitch-box. It's a call from topside. That new company man."

Bud had to think a moment to remember his name. Guys with ties came and went. "Kirkhill?"

"Yeah."

"That guy doesn't know his butt from a rathole." Lindsey's boyfriend probably looked just like Kirkhill. A guy who wore a tie all the time. They were a bunch of weasels. They all went to college and came out with an MBA, which as far as Bud could tell stood for My Bleeding Ass. He liked to say it after their name. Meet your new manager, Mr. Gerard Kirkhill, My Bleeding Ass.

Bud chattered at the drill crew on his way to his office. "Hey, Perry!"

"Yo!"

"Do me a favor, will you? Square away that mud hose and these empty sacks? This place is starting to look like my apartment."

It wasn't all that funny, but Perry chuckled. Bud had learned how to give orders without sounding like he thought it was all that hot being in charge. And yet his joking never sounded like he was apologizing, either. Nobody ever doubted that Bud was in charge down here. Nobody ever doubted that Bud *should* be in charge, either.

Bud ducked through the hatch and tramped through the corridor, the steel grating under his boots making a noise like out-of-tune church bells reverberating down the tube. Now, away from the drill, he could hear Hippy's voice over the P.A. "Bud, topside line, urgent."

"I'm coming, I'm coming. Jeez, keep your pantyhose on." Not that anybody could hear him yet. It just felt good to answer.

He ducked into his office, which was just small enough to feel cramped and just large enough that nobody would listen if he complained about it. There were stacks of paperwork all over the place. Stuff that the guys with ties insisted he look at or fill out or obey. He'd got to it all real soon now. But till then it was part of his office decor.

He picked up the phone, punched down the button that was blinking.

"Brigman here. Yeah, Kirkhill, what's going on?"

Kirkhill was full of importance and urgency, so of course he couldn't just say what he had to say. He had to set it up.

He had to make sure Bud knew exactly *how* important this was.

Yeah, yeah, right, Bud said silently. Get on with it. "Yeah, I'm calm. I'm a calm person. Is there some reason why I shouldn't be calm?"

So Kirkhill told him. "The Navy's here. Benthic Petroleum has agreed to cooperate fully with an operation they've got going. It means moving the rig."

Bud practically climbed down into the phone. "What!"

Hippy Carnes was in the control module of *Deepcore*, watching through a viewport as Little Geek obeyed his commands, dancing a little as he listened to his cassette player. This was the part of his work that Hippy loved most, controlling an ROV—remotely operated vehicle—so smoothly that it might have been his own body out there, only infinitely tougher than his own flesh would ever be. Yet even though his own hands controlled everything it did, he still thought of Little Geek almost as a living creature. Another person, but one who always did what Hippy expected. A true friend. A second self.

He had Little Geek out on flashlight duty—the ROV's lights helped the diver by filling in shadows. But Little Geek, like his big brother Big Geek, was a flashlight with eyes. Hippy had to watch the monitor with absolute concentration because a diver, Sonny, was depending on him to warn him of unseen obstacles, tangles, fouling—any kind of danger—and if Hippy missed anything, it was Sonny who'd pay. Also in the back of his mind was some awareness that One Night was out in Flatbed, the manned deepwater submersible, so that if he got clumsy or lazy, she'd see. Not that he had the hots for One Night or anything, not that he even thought she was particularly attractive, but Hippy just naturally got extra careful, extra sharp when there was a woman watching. As a kid he always got his best videogame scores when he had an audience, and he never got a top score unless it was a girl watching him play. One time playing Galaga it felt like he could go on forever, shooting down wave after wave. He doubled the last high score. Some poor fool had thought that total was the ultimate, but Hippy left him in the cold. He only let his turn end because the girl had started running her hand along the seat of his jeans and down between his thighs and he figured if he quit playing now he could get two high scores tonight. Funny thing, though. He couldn't remember the girl's name or even her face or even whether it was particularly good or not. But he remembered how it felt, that game of Galaga.

As he brought Little Geek around, One Night manipulated Flatbed's right arm to give Sonny the brace he was about to install. "Heads up, hon."

"Perfect timing, sweetie," said Sonny. It was true, too. Lisa "One Night" Standing was always paying attention, always knew just what you needed and when.

Of course, she *knew* she was that good. "Don't I always?" she said. But nobody minded her being a little cocky about it. There's nothing wrong with knowing when you're good.

This was something Hippy knew about himself: He concentrated best when there was a steady, unpredictable distraction going on. Like that girl's wandering hand. Like dancing a little to the music. Like his white rat, Beany, who right now was crawling along his shoulders, along his neck, little feet pressing here and there, the delicate brush of whiskers, the faint wet press of Beany's nose and breath on his neck. He'd had bosses who didn't understand how Beany helped him, how Beany's unpredictability kept him alive and on edge. He'd lost jobs over Beany. But Bud Brigman never made a big deal about Beany. It was like he understood that Hippy needed Beany the way some guys had to chew gum or cuss or something. It was part of being yourself.

OK, that part of the job was done. Hippy checked both the window and the video display from the camera mounted in the front of Little Geek—the same video they were watching topside. When he was sure he wasn't tangled up with anything, he backed Little Geek out of the work area a little bit so that Sonny could move on to the next job.

That was the moment when Bud burst into the control module, slamming the hatch open as he came, knocking something over. Hippy might have cussed at Bud for surprising him like that, distracting him—only the look on Bud's face told him that wasn't the world's best idea.

Bud didn't say a word, but he slammed the top of the cassette player with his fist, turning off the music.

Yeah, he was *not* calm. Hippy watched as Bud reached out and slammed his palm down on the recall switch. Outside *Deepcore* the hydrophone loudspeaker started blaring a siren. Diver recall. And just in case anybody missed the point, Bud picked up a headset and barked, "All divers, drop what you're doing. Everybody out of the pool."

Hippy immediately began pulling Little Geek out of the way so they could all come back in. He could hear One Night and Sonny talking on the headphones.

"Dammit, we just got out here," said One Night.

Sonny just sighed. "There was a time when I would have asked why." Right. As if Sonny was as old as the hills, as if he'd seen it all.

Hippy happened to notice that as Sonny swam past Flatbed's manipulator arm, One Night made the arm grab at Sonny's butt. Sonny saw it, twisted out of the way. "Oh, hey!" said Sonny.

The thought passed through Hippy's mind: One Night's in heat, and Sonny's number just came up. Not a speck of jealousy, though. Any such emotion Hippy might have felt drained away, as if each of Beany's footprints on his shoulders was a tiny hole that let feelings seep right out.

Sonny got on top of Flatbed and hung on as One Night piloted it between *Deepcore*'s legs. She was skimming only a few feet above the sea floor. Hippy brought Little Geek along right behind her, for all the world like a faithful puppy. Hippy saw Flatbed slip into the lighted area under the moonpool, then rise up into the light.

"Deepcore, Deepcore," said One Night, "this is Flatbed, preparing to surface."

Hippy checked out Flatbed's position, especially in back, where she was blind. "Roger, Flatbed, you're clear."

"Thank you much."

Catfish and Finler caught one of the lines dangling there

and pulled themselves up hand over hand. Sonny caught a ride on Flatbed's back as One Night brought the craft directly under the pool. Hippy brought Little Geek along right after. Just chasing your little ass up into heaven, baby.

Flatbed rose to the surface of the moonpool as Jammer and Perry and a couple of other drill-room boys were helping the other divers out of the water. The water at this depth was only about six degrees above freezing, and despite their heated drysuits, the divers were all cold and stiff and not too good at little things like pulling off their helmets and getting the rubber neck-dam off without ripping all their hair off at the roots. No fun, but it was part of the job.

They weren't thinking about it that much, anyway. Their minds were all on something else—wondering why they'd been called in. Anything out of the ordinary like this smelled like a problem, and any problem at this depth could get pretty bad in no time. They were worried, they were annoyed, they were curious.

"What the hell's going on?" asked Finler. "Why'd they recall us?"

"Hell if I know," said Sonny. His tone of voice sounded like he didn't care, either. Nobody was fooled for a second.

The moonpool looked like a swimming pool at an indoor gym. The difference was that in here, it wasn't gravity holding the water in the pool. It was air pressure. Like when you push a glass upside down into dishwater. There's still air in the glass, so the water stays down at the bottom. But if the air seal ever broke, the water from the moonpool would erupt and fill all of *Deepcore,* if it could. Just one of the little things that could kill them if something went wrong.

Finler was as nervous as a cat, and as often as he could find somebody to listen to him, he was asking questions that nobody could answer. "So what's the drift, partner? Why're we up?"

Catfish pulled his neck-dam off, dragging past his sweat-soaked beard. It hurt every time. You have to be some kind of masochist to wear a beard as a diver. But because Catfish had one, Finler had one. "Just follow standard procedure, will ya?" Catfish said. "Flog your dog till somebody tells us what's happening."

That was what they needed to break the tension— somebody talking crude. "Hey, Catfish," said Jammer, on the deck a few feet away. "I'll sell you my October *Penthouse,* with the letters, for twenty bucks, what do you say?"

By this time One Night was climbing out of Flatbed. Dry as a bone, so she was the only one not shivering with the cold. Jammer tossed her a line.

"Save your money," One Night said to Catfish. "The pages are all stuck together by now."

Bud came in just as Jammer pulled Catfish out of the water. Everybody looked to Bud. He'd have the answers, and they knew he'd tell them all he could.

"Hey Bud, what's the deal, huh?" asked Jammer.

Bud shook his head. "Folks, listen up. We've just been told to shut down the hole and prepare to move the rig."

Move. "Shee-it," said Sonny. They all knew that moving was the end. The project was cut off. Benthic had lost its nerve and was getting out of the underwater experiment business. Chickenshit accountants somewhere decided they weren't cost-effective. It was over.

Or maybe not. Bud knew what they were all assuming— that their project was a victim of corporate politics or the bottom line or pure stupidity or something—and he dispelled that idea as fast as he could. "We've received an invitation to cooperate in a matter of national security. Now you know as much as I do. So get your gear off and get to control. We've got a briefing in ten minutes."

There were some groans. Bud clapped his hands together a couple of times. Like a coach encouraging his team. "Let's move it," he said. What they heard was: I don't like it either but we've got to do it, and what the hell, it probably won't be so bad.

Somehow the whole crew fit into the command module for the briefing. It was sweaty and the air stank, but nobody wanted to get the news secondhand. There was a Navy guy on the monitor from the *Benthic Explorer*—Commodore DeMarco, he said. Kirkhill was visible in the background. If *he'd* been talking, Bud wouldn't've believed him for a second. Guys with ties tell you what they think will get you to do what they want. Whereas Bud knew—wasn't his dad a Marine?—that guys in uniform will leave stuff out for national security reasons, but by and large they'll tell you what you need to know in order to do a good job. The difference was trust. Corporation types, they expected everybody to use whatever they knew to stab everybody else in the back so they could get ahead. They couldn't tell anybody the truth because they couldn't trust anybody not to use it against them. Whereas military types expected you to obey orders, period, so it was OK to tell you the truth. A lot of civilians didn't understand that. Bud did.

"At 0922 local time this morning," DeMarco was saying, "an American nuclear submarine, the USS *Montana,* with a hundred and fifty-six men aboard, went down twenty-two miles from here."

"Damn," said Bud. Civilians could hear of a couple of hundred servicemen missing, probably dead, and they'd think, well, that's what they're for, to die for their country. But people in the military—and their families—they always felt it like a part of their own family dying. Because it could have been. Bud knew. One of those numbers they read over the TV news during Vietnam, one of those "forty-two casualties" or even "light losses" was his dad. That was why DeMarco paused, why Bud swore. It was a moment of silence. It was all the mourning they had time for right now.

"There has been no contact with the sub since then. The cause of the incident is not known. Your company has authorized the Navy's use of this facility for a rescue operation. The code name is Operation Salvor."

It was a two-way connection, and One Night had a question. "You want us to search for the sub?"

"No. We know where it is. But she's in two thousand feet of water and we can't reach her. We need divers to enter the sub and search for survivors, if any."

This was the part that Bud didn't like. His people were

trained to work with *Deepcore*. With drilling equipment that they knew, stuff that was all in the right place. Inside a wrecked sub they might find anything. Bud flashed on a picture of twisted wreckage snagging on an air hose or tangling in something. He saw one of his own crew coming back dead. "Don't you guys have your own stuff for this kind of thing?" he asked.

DeMarco knew it was a fair question, and he gave it a fair answer. "By the time we get our rescue submersibles here the storm front will be right on us. But you can get your rig in under the storm and be on-site in fifteen hours. That makes you our best option right now."

Bud knew the urgency the Navy felt—it was their men in that sub, and if any of them were alive, they had to get them out. Had to do *anything* to get them out, if they could, because that's what they'd expect the Navy to do for *them,* if they were in trouble.

Bud's crew didn't necessarily feel that way. "Why should we risk our butts for something like this?" asked Hippy.

DeMarco didn't have an answer. Poor guy, thought Bud. He still hasn't learned that civilians don't give a shit about military lives. Yes sir, Commodore, this is the guy you're supposed to die for, if we get in a war. Makes you proud, right? For just a moment, Bud was ashamed to be part of this crew, though he knew that he wasn't being fair, that civilians were *supposed* to regard the military as expendable.

The silence didn't go on long, though. This sort of question was right up Kirkhill's alley—this was something a guy with a tie could understand. Hippy was speaking his language. Kirkhill thrust his face toward the screen. "I have been authorized to offer you all special-duty bonuses equivalent to three times normal dive pay."

There were whistles and hoots of appreciation. "Yes sir," said Finler, pointing at the screen. "Yes sir!"

Catfish plucked Beany off Hippy's shoulder. "Hell," said Catfish, "for triple time I'd eat Beany."

"No!" said Hippy. Catfish gave the rat back without looking.

Finler was getting into the spirit of this. Just how eager

was he for triple pay? "I'm here to tell you, you could set me on fire and put me out with horse piss."

It really annoyed Bud, Kirkhill bribing the crew like this. Triple pay was dead man's pay, and Bud knew it. He didn't want any part of this. It was Commodore DeMarco he spoke to, though. He knew better than to try to talk sense to a suit. "Look, I don't care what kind of deal you guys made with the company, but my people are not qualified for this. They're oil workers."

That was military language, a military way of thinking; Bud had learned it from his father. You never put your men in a situation beyond their training. And if an officer orders you to do so, you inform him of their limitations.

DeMarco understood at once. "This is Lieutenant Coffey. His SEAL team will transfer down to you to supervise the operation."

That was a help. They'd have somebody there who knew how to do the job. But that brought up another danger. Bud had never known a SEAL, but he assumed they were gung-ho Rambo types, Green Berets with flippers. "You can send down whoever you like, but I'm the toolpusher on this rig, and when it comes to the safety of these people, there's me, and then there's God. Understand? If things get dicey, I'm pulling the plug."

DeMarco gave him a short nod. It was all according to the book—you rescue your men if you can do it without unacceptable losses.

Kirkhill, though, was obviously embarrassed that his toolpusher was talking back to the Navy. Bud sounded so—so *uncooperative*. Smooth this over, make everybody feel good, that was Kirkhill's job, right? "I think we're all on the same wavelength, Brigman," he said. "So relax. Now let's get the wellhead uncoupled, shall we?"

Silently Bud answered, Let's get our head out of our ass, shall we? But he didn't say anything out loud. No point in it. He and DeMarco understood each other, and that's all that mattered. He'd have the authority to keep his crew safe, and he couldn't ask for more.

Bud started out of the room. Nobody else was moving. "Let's get to work, gang," he said.

They caught on. The meeting was over. Bud stood near the hatchway as the others filed out, heading for their tasks. They all knew what was at stake. They had to uncouple the wellhead in such a way that it could be recoupled later. That was their only chance to make this project work. Even so, once *Deepcore* was unhooked from the well, it would be only too easy for one of the opponents of the project—which included everyone in the corporation who wasn't in position to claim credit if it succeeded—to use this as an excuse to cancel the whole thing. They had to make it as easy and cheap as possible to get everything back like it was.

The only good thing about this, Bud thought, is that Lindsey isn't here. And when she finds out, I want to be on another continent for about a year. Because somehow, God knows how, she's going to find a way to make this all my fault.

Chapter 6

High-Pressure Nervous Syndrome

They got the wellhead uncoupled with no problems, except the problem that they didn't want to do it in the first place. All the triple-pay enthusiasm was gone by the time everybody got back inside. They'd thought through the difference between a couple of days at triple pay and having a job at regular pay for three months. Even the slow ones knew enough arithmetic to figure it out. Besides, they were about four days from the end of their four-week shift. Counting decompression time, just over halfway to getting back topside. Who knew how long this detour would slow things down?

Bud sat at the controls of *Deepcore*, using a joystick to pilot it through the water like an airplane, except that *Deepcore* didn't make much better than a knot and a half under water. The rig was meant for going down to the bottom and staying in one place—it was only supposed to be maneuverable enough to choose the best resting place, within a few hundred yards. *Deepcore* was equipped with thrusters powerful enough to get its five thousand tons of mass moving, but it took Flatbed on tow cables to steer it with any kind of precision. That's part of the reason why *Deepcore* needed as powerful a submersible as Flatbed.

So Bud had One Night piloting Flatbed, the mobile platform, out in front, picking a safe course as Bud did the coarse steering that kept *Deepcore* lined up behind her. *Plus Deepcore* was still attached to the *Benthic Explorer* on the surface by the long umbilical. He figured *Deepcore* looked about as silly as a randy doberman straining against a leash, trying to catch up with a chihuahua in heat.

"Hey, One Night, how you doing?"

"I got white line fever, baby." As well she should. It was at least a twelve-hour trip, and there was no time to unhook the tow cables, bring Flatbed back, and change drivers.

Bud read off a slight course correction from the *Explorer.* "Why don't you take her about five degrees left?"

"Five degrees left, roger."

Hippy came in, checked out a couple of things. McBride, in the meantime, came onto the topside monitor with the latest news. "Well, it's official, sportsfans. They're calling it Hurricane Frederick, and it's going to be making our lives real interesting in a few hours."

Hippy walked out again just as a new face appeared on the topside monitor. It was just about the last person Bud was hoping to see.

Lindsey didn't even try to build up to things gently. "I can't believe you let them do this."

It was as bad as his worst fears. All his fault, of course. And Lindsey was using her you-are-screwed voice. But he was determined not to let her get under his skin. He smiled. In fact, he couldn't help it. He was glad to see her, even when she was pissed off, even when he knew she was here to cause him trouble, here to punish him for every sin she could pin on him. He was glad, and not just because she was sure to make life unbearable for Kirkhill.

"Hi, Lins. I thought you were in Houston." Actually I wish to hell you were in Houston, sweetheart. Don't I have enough trouble without you being up there in the *Explorer,* griping at me?

"I was, now I'm here. Only *here* isn't where I left it, is it, Bud?"

"It wasn't up to me." He tried to laugh at the idea, help her see how ridiculous it was to blame him.

"We were *that close* to proving a submersible drilling platform could work. I can't believe you let them grab my rig!"

"*Your* rig?"

"*My* rig. I designed the damn thing."

"Yeah, and Benthic Petroleum paid for it. So as long as they're holding the pink slip, I go where they tell me." But the pink slip didn't rule him, and she knew it. She was maybe a little bit right to blame him. He *could* have stopped the whole thing. Why didn't he? It wasn't the triple pay. It was—duty, maybe. There was a sub down. What was he supposed to do, ignore it? Forget he was a citizen? Forget he grew up in a Marine family?

He couldn't explain *that,* not to Lindsey. Couldn't explain that sometimes you just don't have a choice.

"I had a lot riding on this. They *bought* you. More like rented you cheap."

Hippy came back into the control room. Bud had no intention of letting Lindsey rake him over the coals in front of an audience. Not this time. "I'm turning you off now," he said cheerfully.

She still managed to get in a lick before he could reach the switch. "Oh, Virgil, you're such a wiener! You never—"

"Bye bye," said Bud. Still trying to sound cheerful, so Hippy wouldn't see how it bothered him.

But Hippy was off on a brand new discovery. "Virgil?"

So the kid hadn't known Bud's real name. So what? So that was one more way Lindsey had found to undercut him with his crew. "God, I hate that bitch," he muttered. Trying to make it sound like a joke.

Hippy took it at face value. "You probably never should have married her, then."

You think I never thought of that, Hippy? You think it never crossed my mind?

Hippy must've read something in Bud's expression. He turned to the monitors and got back to work.

Talking to Bud had been as useless as ever. He didn't even seem to *mind* when she called him names. She was so *angry* and all he did was smile, never losing his cool, always with that damned *smile.*

And the worst thing was there wasn't a damn thing she could do about it up here on the *Explorer.* Nothing to do but watch Kirkhill strutting around acting important while the Navy cut his balls off and fed them to him with a spoon—didn't the idiot even know when he was being bullied? Nothing to do but sweat it out till they got *Deepcore* into place. And then the *Explorer* would have to cut loose and sail away for a couple of days or else get bounced around like a beanbag in the middle of the hurricane. She wouldn't even *know* what was going on, she'd just have to sit out in the Caribbean somewhere with nothing to do but wait while Coffey's goons went down to *Deepcore* and took it to the edge of the Cayman Trench, of all places, where the mission would either succeed, in which case the Navy would probably keep *Deepcore* and classify all her designs so she could never build another, or else the mission would fail, no doubt getting *Deepcore* banged up, not to say *wrecked,* in which case the Navy would throw *Deepcore* away like a used tissue. Benthic would never pay to repair it. The project's enemies —and with Lindsey as designer, they were legion—would say that *Deepcore* obviously wasn't tough enough to make it. Nobody else would take it on if Benthic abandoned it as a failure. The project would *die,* just like that.

The more she thought of that smartass Coffey going down into *her* rig while she was trapped up here, the angrier she got.

Then she remembered how they were going to get there. One of the Cabs, of course. Only no way would the SEALs be piloting it themselves. *She* knew how to drive them. Why shouldn't *she* be the one to take them down? They wanted the project engineer on hand to take care of problems, didn't they? Well, she'd be even *more* on hand if she was downstairs in *Deepcore*.

She was lucky. Lots of service crewmen were standing around. Cab Three was the submersible they'd have to use to transfer anything or anyone down to *Deepcore*. It must already be prepped or they'd be busy. So—what were they waiting for?

A driver. The driver wasn't down there. Good. She wouldn't have to argue with anybody. Yet.

The SEALs were ready to go—Coffey and Schoenick were outside Cab Three, handing the last of the gear bags in to Wilhite and Monk. The submersible slammed violently each time the *Explorer* rolled in the heavy seas, but that didn't seem to slow down the SEALs. Cab Three was completely prepped; it was only in its steel cradle for loading, and the lifting cable was already attached.

Lindsey walked straight to the SEALs, determined to take charge and bluff it out. "Let's go, gentlemen! We either launch now or we don't launch."

Coffey looked at her in surprise, but she didn't wait around for his questions. She climbed up the side of Cab Three, grabbed the lifting shackle, and circled her raised hand to signal the crane man. "Take her up, Byron!"

Byron was quick. Byron was a good man. Coffey and Schoenick only had time to slide in the last of their heavy equipment cases before the cable tautened and Cab Three rose into the air. A minute later it was swinging directly over the launch well as Lindsey clambered over and dropped down into the upper hatch. She closed it over her head with one hand while she picked up the headset with the other. "This is Cab Three. Clear me for launch, McBride."

"Roger, Cab Three, you're clear to launch."

She could hear somebody—Kirkhill—in the background. "What do you mean, cleared for launch? Who's taking her down?"

And Bendix's voice. "Bates, isn't it?"

"Bates is right here!"

"Then who's in Cab Three?"

Me, thought Lindsey. The only person who has a *right* to be heading down to *Deepcore*. Plus four rambos in the back. She glanced back over her shoulder to see that all four of them were in place on the cramped little benches in back, with the top hatch sealed and the rear lockout hatch secure. They were ready for Byron to lower them down into the water.

Instead, Byron held them swinging fifteen feet above the pool. Each roll and pitch of the ship took them too far to one side or the other, and in the ship's chaotic movement pattern, Byron no doubt felt it was impossible to lower them without grave risk of smashing Cab Three into the edge of the pool. Still, it had to be done. What did he think, that if he waited long enough the seas would kindly hold still and allow them to make a textbook descent? Besides, the longer they hung over the pool, the better the chance that Kirkhill or somebody would try to stop them, would give orders to swing them back into the launch bay and get that goddamn woman out of there.

Every spider knew that there was a time to gently descend holding onto a thread, and a time to cut loose and drop. What Byron couldn't do by lowering Cab Three on the end of a string, Lindsey could do by pulling the red shackle-release lever. She reached out and took hold of it, watching out the window for a moment when it looked like Cab Three was directly over the pool.

"Hang on, gentlemen," she said. Act confident and Coffey won't think something's wrong and decide to interfere. But then it wasn't acting—she *was* confident. She knew how to do this job better than anybody else. Bates? What would Bates have been good for down here? He'd have waited until Byron was sure. He'd have waited until it was perfectly safe. He'd have waited until hell froze over.

She pulled the lever. Cab Three fell fifteen feet into the water. The falling wasn't bad. But the landing rattled them from ass to elbow, giving a good solid toss to the boys in back and all their gear.

"Touchdown," Lindsey said. "The crowd goes wild." She

had missed the edge of the pool by about two feet. Very complicated geometry, making a straight drop inside a randomly moving ship. "How're you boys doing back there?"

They were pissed off at the rough landing, but they didn't say anything. Just glared at her. Glare all day, Coffey. We didn't hit the edge, we aren't still hanging on a cable, and I've got my ride down to *Deepcore.*

Lindsey flooded the trim tanks and Cab Three sank quickly under the water, down between the twin hulls of the *Benthic Explorer. "Explorer,* this is Cab Three," she said. "We are styling."

"Roger, Cab Three," said McBride.

Bless the man, he wasn't doing a thing to stop her.

Then Kirkhill came on the wire. Gone was the mild-mannered executive, the make - no - waves can't - we - all - handle - this - in - a - reasonable - manner bullshit. "Lindsey, what the hell are you doing?"

This wasn't a conversation she wanted to have. Nor did it matter anymore. As usual, Kirkhill had got here a day late and a dollar short. She flipped the switch and turned off his voice. Then she turned on her floodlights and maneuvered Cab Three until she could see the umbilical cable a few feet ahead of her front port. That's all she needed—she could follow it down and it would lead her right to *Deepcore.*

One Night was staying alert in Flatbed by singing at the top of her voice. The song was "Willing," a great old truck-driving song.

"I've been rocked by the rain," she sang, "driven by the snow. I'm drunk and dirty, don't you know. I'm still willin'. Out on the road late last night, I've seen my pretty Alice in every headlight. Alice. Dallas Alice."

Bud and Hippy were in the control room, hearing the song on their headsets. Hippy couldn't help himself. He joined in singing, and so did Bud. It was a lonely song, but there was nothing lonely about singing it together.

"And I been from Tucson to Tucumcari, Tehachapi to Tonapah, driven every kind of rig that's ever been made."

Yeah, that was their theme song now, wasn't it? This was sure no rig you'd ever see going down I-40 through Oklahoma. "Driven the back road so I wouldn't get weighed. And if you give me weed, whites and wine, and you show me a sign, I'll be willin' to be movin'."

One Night was feeling so good—and so tired—she couldn't keep from laughing, and Bud was smiling too. This was the good life. Bud and his people, doing their jobs, the rest of the world cut off by an ocean and a hurricane. Drifting over the ocean bottom like a lazy manta ray.

"I've been kicked by the wind, robbed by the sleet, I've had my head stove in but I'm still on my feet, and I'm still—"

A voice cut in on the headset. *"Deepcore, Deepcore.* This is Cab Three on final approach."

"Yeah, roger, Cab Three," said Hippy. How many times had they heard that voice during training? "That you, Lins?"

"None other," she said.

"Oh no," said Bud. "No, you gotta be kidding me."

Hippy was grinning his face off. Didn't the kid have any compassion? It was all right for *him* to think the fireworks would be fun. But it wouldn't be fun for Bud. He was supposed to keep things running smoothly and safely down here, while a bunch of SEALs carried out a mission that *Deepcore* wasn't designed for. Now they were sending Lindsey down, Lindsey who'd try to take charge of things, Lindsey who wouldn't have anything but criticism and second-guessing for every decision Bud made. So much for feeling good.

Lindsey handled Cab Three perfectly, following the umbilical down, yet never getting close enough to risk contact with it. Near the surface, the umbilical had flexed with the movements of the *Explorer* as it rolled and pitched in the heavy seas. Farther down, the movements traveled down the umbilical in languid waves. The surface of the ocean sends few messages into the deep.

As they neared *Deepcore,* Lindsey couldn't resist passing

through the A-frame that supported the umbilical and making a sweep around the rig. She told herself that she had to inspect it for damage—but of course there was no damage. Why should there be? It was as beautiful as ever, a structure graceful in its raw utility, no wasted space, no line or beam or tube or tank that did not have a function vital to *Deepcore*'s work. This rig was born in her mind, and now it was real at the bottom of the sea. She never wearied of seeing it; she wanted, without knowing it, to make sure Coffey and the other SEALs saw it, too. She never quite let this idea rise into consciousness, but whenever she looked at *Deepcore* she saw the shadow of her father's model bridge on it. Look at this, Father—not just a model in the attic, to gaze at and wish for what might have been. This is real. I made this. This is mine.

Yet, because she was Lindsey, that single pass around the rig was all the self-admiration she indulged in; immediately she brought Cab Three into place to couple with the compression chamber. She heard the clunk as the flange of Cab Three's lockout hatch settled over the pressure collar on the back of *Deepcore*. When the instruments confirmed that the mating was set, she went back and opened the hatch.

None of the SEALs made a move to help her. Lindsey was used to men thinking that because she looked so frail, she needed their strong arms all the time. Maybe these SEALs had a keener eye for what a woman was made of. Or maybe Coffey guessed that she had just hijacked the cab, and he was hoping to make her pay for it in sweat. Didn't matter. Love me or hate me, I'm here and that's all I care about.

She dropped through the hatch into the compression chamber. The SEALs came down after her, handing down equipment. They weren't particularly quiet, but they weren't particularly noisy, either. Just as much noise as went along with doing the most efficient job possible.

The compression chamber was a cylindrical room, designed to be as boring and uncomfortable as possible—steel benches, a folding card table, breathing masks, medical supplies. A tiny fish-eye porthole at one end, so they could catch a glimpse of what was going on in *Deepcore* itself. Or rather, so that the *Deepcore* crew could keep an eye on *them*.

She recognized Catfish peering in at them. "Howdy, boys," he said. Then he realized she was there. "Hey, Lindsey! I'll be damned! You shouldn't be down here, sweet thing, y'all might run your stockings."

Lindsey genuinely liked Catfish, and she was willing to believe he was glad to see her. "Couldn't stay away, Cat. You running mixture for us?"

"Yeah."

"Good. Couldn't get any better." The breathing mix had to be adjusted constantly throughout pressurization. Less and less nitrogen, since it stopped being an inert gas and turned into a poison under pressure. In shallow dives people still used trimix, in which the nitrogen was replaced by helium, so that everybody talked like a duck the whole time underwater. You got used to it after a while, or at least you stopped laughing at each other, but it was still disturbing to forget what your own voice sounded like. It was better now with tetramix, which used argon to replace most of the helium. As for oxygen, it was down to two percent of the mixture. At that depth, the topside norm of twenty-one percent oxygen would be fatal. You'd die of convulsions.

At this depth it was going to take eight hours to get pressurized, all the time getting used to a new breathing mix. It used to take twenty-four hours before they started using argon. Even so, eight hours was a hell of a long time to sit and do nothing. But it was a lot faster than *de*compression, because once your body's completely saturated, it takes a long time for the gases to seep back out of your cells, into your blood, and then out through your lungs and your kidneys and your sweat. Lindsey heard a story once about a couple of guys cooped up together for three days of decompression. One of them went plain crazy—or the other guy drove him nuts. Anyway, the one guy killed the other. And the support crew had to stand outside the chamber and *watch* and there wasn't a damn thing they could do, because if they opened the chamber too soon then *both* guys would die. She'd been through decompression often enough to believe it.

The SEALs had settled themselves on their benches. Benches that existed because Lindsey had drawn them in on her original plans. She felt like the host, welcoming guests into her new house. "OK, fellows, make yourselves comfortable. The bad news is we got eight hours in this can, blowing down. The worse news is it's going to take us three weeks to decompress later." It didn't occur to her that she might sound patronizing.

Coffey looked at her coldly. "We've all been fully briefed, Mrs. Brigman."

So much for being friendly. "Just don't call me that, OK? I hate that."

Usually people backed off when she used that tone of voice. Coffey just stared back at her and said, "OK, what would you like us to call you? 'Sir'?"

One of the SEALs laughed under his breath. It was Coffey's way of letting his men know exactly how seriously to take her. Which is to say, not seriously at all. In Coffey's eyes, she was exactly as important to their mission as, say, Kirkhill, and twice as likely to try to interfere. Coffey was right. Her whole purpose in coming down was to interfere with the mission—to try to protect *Deepcore* by resisting anything the SEALs proposed that she thought might be too risky. It wouldn't do to let her think, even for an instant, that the SEALs were willing to concede her any authority. Not even the authority of a genial host. *Deepcore* might be "her" rig, but as long as the SEALs were using it to accomplish their assignment with the *Montana,* they intended to regard it as *their* rig, and the people on it as either tools or problems. Tools they could use. Problems they would solve.

Catfish finished setting the mixture and adjusting the pressure. Their stay in the pressure chamber would be the equivalent of a slow, eight-hour descent, steadily building up pressure as their bodies adjusted. The pressure chamber allowed them to come directly down, skipping the eight hours of traveling time; but nothing could speed up the actual process of pressurization. When Catfish's voice cut in over the loudspeaker, it shut down the awkward conversation. "There we go! Y'all start equalizing—*now.*"

They heard the hiss of inrushing gas, and immediately they all held their noses and started yawning, making faces, moaning, opening their ears so they didn't get a relative vacuum inside and burst their eardrums.

Whatever message Coffey intended to send, Lindsey didn't get it. She still felt responsible for anybody coming onto *Deepcore,* even if she didn't particularly like them. "Let's watch each other closely for signs of HPNS—high pressure—"

"High-pressure nervous syndrome," said Monk, reciting verbatim from the passages they had all memorized in training with the Submarine Development Group years before. Coffey had already made them recite the relevant passages several times before Lindsey joined them. SEALs didn't wait for civilians to teach them things at the last minute. "Muscle tremors," Monk continued. "Usually in the hands first. Nausea, increased excitability . . ."

The other SEALs joined in. "Disorientation, delusions."

And Coffey finished it up by singing, "And a partridge in a pear tree." We know this stuff, lady. Don't imagine for a moment that you can teach us *anything.*

"Very good," she said. But Lindsey did not take hints easily. They might *think* they knew it all, but she knew they didn't. They may know this by the book, but did they know the reality of it? HPNS wasn't funny. It could kill. Why did they think a minute proportion of nitrogen was retained in the breathing mix? Because it was a narcotic to counter HPNS. Because *everybody* got HPNS. Without the nitrogen, everybody'd get the jitters, get paranoid, scream or kill people or curl up and whimper in a corner. Even with the nitrogen, some people went over the edge. Maybe a little, maybe a lot. And just because you had no problems the first time—the first thirty times—you went down, that didn't mean you couldn't have problems the next time. So she didn't take the hint and drop the subject. If these guys thought there was no problem, that was all the more reason to remind them. "About one person in twenty can't handle it. They just go buggo."

"Look," said Coffey, "they've all made runs at this depth. They're checked out."

"No, I understand that. What I'm saying is that it's impossible to predict just who's susceptible."

"They're checked out." The discussion was over. Coffey didn't have to give an order. His men knew that it was time to go over their assignments inside the sub. They had been through all the floorplans and diagrams, planning alternate routes through the sub, depending on damage, making sure they all knew every item that had to be picked up. They knew it—but they went over it again. It was their answer to Lindsey: If they said they were prepared, they were *prepared*. These men didn't leave anything to chance.

"Fine," Lindsey said. They ignored her. "Fine." She sat back, trying to make herself comfortable on the bench. These guys obviously didn't have as much experience doing time in a chamber as she had. Even with people you dislike, you could still help each other, read, tell stories, something. You never had to be *alone*. But these military goons were going to make her go through this like solitary confinement. Maybe she shouldn't have pushed them, but why did they have to get so annoyed? Didn't they know it's better to be safe than sorry? So now they were going to punish her for trying to help, for trying to be a decent person.

It really bothered her to see them all working together. It was obvious they knew each other so well they hardly even had to complete sentences. Coffey didn't have to give orders, either. Just lead them through a review. They all knew exactly what part to play. Lindsey couldn't have put it into words, but this was what bothered her most of all. She'd never been part of a group like that. The only time she ever came close was when she spent time with crews on *Deepcore* —especially Bud's crew. She knew she didn't really belong, but there was the illusion, especially during those hours locked up together in the compression chamber. Singing, talking, laughing, playing cards—even if she didn't really belong with them, she caught a glimpse of what it felt like.

But most of her life had been like this. Watching a family from outside. For the longest time she had believed "closeness" was a myth—like her own family, her mother and sisters, the only way they were "close" was that her sisters allowed Mother to run them like trained chimps. Her dad, *he* knew that these group things were all fake. All pep club and locker room fakery.

Except that Bud's crew was real—she knew that. Maybe that was one of the reasons she couldn't stop harping at him in front of them—she wanted in, and couldn't forgive him for the fact that she never really *was* in. Always a stranger, always a visitor. And now these SEALs. They weren't just faceless military robots. They were individuals, different from each other, she could see that. But despite their differences, somehow they were really together, they were one. And she wasn't part of it.

"You guys know any songs?" she asked. They didn't answer her—probably didn't hear her. It was her little joke, for an audience of one.

One of the bad things about life in *Deepcore* was that sometimes you just had to sit around and do nothing. Up top, the *Benthic Explorer* was having a terrible time making way through the heavy seas ahead of Hurricane Frederick, but down below *Deepcore* was moving along calmly and steadily, Flatbed leading the way. Except for the handful of people on duty at any given moment, driving Flatbed and piloting *Deepcore,* everybody else had to find ways to entertain themselves.

And there weren't all that many ways. They only piped down TV from the *Explorer* when there was nothing else more important to send over the video lines—which is to say, never. Listening to cassettes is fine, but you get through forty albums in about three days, and then you repeat, repeat, repeat. You can lift weights till your muscles burn, but your brain doesn't do much more than count to ten a lot. And on *Deepcore* there aren't enough people off duty at the same time for a decent game of basketball—even if the ceilings were tall enough for a hook shot.

Which is why rig crews are about the most literate people in the world. Not lit*erary,* mind you. But they do read. They read everything, and then they read it again, and then they read it to *each other.*

Catfish, Jammer, and Hippy were keeping each other company outside the pressure chamber. Catfish was tending the mixture for the pressure chamber—he actually had a real job at the moment. Hippy was playing with Beany and eating Cap'n Crunch out of the box. Jammer was doing occasional oral readings from a Louis L'Amour paperback everybody had already read at least once.

Between checks on the gauges, Catfish watched Hippy play with Beany. It wasn't like Hippy was so crazy he thought Beany was a person or anything. It was more like Hippy was so nervous he needed to keep touching the rat, needed to have the rat keep touching him. "Hey, Hippy. Why'd you name that little turdmaker Beany, anyway?" asked Catfish.

Hippy grinned. It was one of his favorite stories, and he thought he'd already told it to everybody in *Deepcore* twice each. Somehow he'd missed Catfish.

"God, not that again," said Jammer. "It was the TV show 'Beany and Cecil.'"

Hippy was annoyed. Jammer didn't have a right to shut down his story, especially when Catfish *asked* for it. "That's not even half of the story anyway, Jammer," he said.

Jammer knew he'd been out of line. He pulled the book up in front of his face more and pretended not to be listening.

"I had this snake, see, named Cecil," said Hippy. "Big old buck snake, *not* poisonous, but it made people shit bricks when they saw him cause everybody thinks all snakes are deadly."

"Whereas in your case it's only the snake's *owner,*" said Jammer.

"If I brought a girl over and she wasn't treating me like she ought to, I'd let Cecil out of the closet. Used to freak 'em to see me pick him up and kiss him right on the mouth. His tongue flicking out on my lips."

"What I always wanted to know," said Jammer, "is did the snake give head?"

Catfish slapped Jammer's leg. "Not everybody can fit his dick between a snake's teeth like you, Jammer." Once again the book went up in front of Jammer's face.

"The best thing," said Hippy, "was when I fed Cecil in front of some girl. All Cecil ever ate was live white rats. I must've kept Furry Friends Pet Store in business all by myself, buying rats."

"You mean like Beany?" asked Catfish. The way Hippy babied that rat, it was plain crazy to think of him ever letting some snake swallow it whole.

"I never got to *know* any of those rats then," said Hippy. "Anyway I had this one girlfriend that I liked enough that she kind of moved in, only when I was gone on the rig I was working then, she had friends over to visit."

"Men friends," said Catfish.

"Man, if you ever saw that babe, you'd know there's no way she ever had a *girl* friend in her life. She had king-size pillows on a twin-size bed."

"So she had a friend over."

"I don't know if it was an accident or she did it on purpose, the way I always used to," said Hippy, "but somehow Cecil got out of the closet where he stayed all day. Only this guy she's humping, he gets scared all right, but he doesn't run out screaming, he jumps down off the bed and stomps on Cecil. Squished his head like an egg."

"With his bare feet?" asked Catfish.

"With his boots, of course."

"He stopped to put his boots on?"

"He already *had* his boots on. This girl, you didn't stop to take your shoes off when she was ready for you. Anyway, I come home and the girl's gone and there's bloody footprints all over my floor and Cecil's brains are spattered all over in my bedroom. I admit it, I cried like a baby."

"Did the girl ever come back?"

"I would've strangled her with the snakeskin. One of the girls where she worked told me what happened. Said she puked for three days straight. Anyway I had this one rat left over. He was meant for that day's feeding. He was the only living thing I had to remind me of Cecil. So I named him Beany."

"You mean this rat watched Cecil die?" asked Catfish. "No wonder he's psycho."

"Not *this* rat. This one's Beany the Fourth. Rats don't live all that long."

"Neither do snakes," suggested Jammer. "And you can't make a belt out of a dead rat."

"That's a real lousy thing to say, Jammer," said Catfish.

"But he did it," said Jammer. "Made a belt out of Cecil."

"Well what was I supposed to do?" said Hippy. "Bury him? Stuff him? Bronze him?"

"I hope I don't ever die around you," said Catfish. "Probably make a jacket out of my skin."

"I'd probably make you into a two-man pup tent," said Hippy. He stuffed a handful of Cap'n Crunch in his mouth.

At that moment Jammer found a libidinous double meaning in one of the sentences in the western he was reading. "He was a tough man, born of hard days when men were hard."

"And sheep were nervous," said Catfish.

Nobody laughed. Not at that, not at anything in Hippy's saga of the death of Cecil. You didn't have to laugh out loud after a few weeks together. You could hear something funny and just appreciate it. Hippy got up and walked over to the window into the pressure chamber.

Hippy was the only one who couldn't keep himself from peeking in at the SEALs, but he wasn't the only one thinking about them. Lindsey was trouble, but they knew exactly how much trouble and she didn't worry them. But the SEALs— they had a reputation. Jammer had been Navy once, and he told them about SEALs, about them being the toughest bastards in the U.S. military and therefore probably the toughest in the whole world. Of course, a lot of military groups thought they were tough. Green Berets, Airborne, the U.S. Marines. The SEALs thought of Marines as pussies, but the Marines—and everybody else—thought of the SEALs as a bunch of psychos, always going on suicide missions. "If the tough guys think you're insane," said Jammer, "then that's true toughness."

But the SEALs weren't the *meanest* in the world—that was reserved for the KGB, because they didn't have to follow any rules. For instance, the KGB could kill pop-ups during gun battles, no questions asked. But SEALs followed rules. They didn't go around wasting civilians just because they happened to panic and stand up in your line of fire.

But if you happened to be the enemy a SEAL group was assigned to destroy, you might as well make out your will and put it in a safe place. Jammer had a friend who was a Marine in Beirut, and he said that the people there didn't really hate Americans in general, not even the Marines. Even when they blew up the Marine barracks there, it wasn't that they hated the individual Marines, just what they represented as a group. But SEALs now, that was different. SEALs had done real damage in Beirut, and they hated them. "You know that Navy diver those hijackers killed on that plane back then?" Jammer had told them. "Kicked him and beat him to death?"

"You mean he was a SEAL?"

"I don't know," Jammer told them. "But two things tell me he *was*. First thing—the government only identified him as a Navy diver. That's the closest the government ever comes to identifying a SEAL when he's caught on a mission. Now there really are Navy divers in the world, but I just don't believe a regular Navy diver would have been on that plane at that time. And the second thing—the way they killed him. It was mean. It was personal. They killed him with their own hands and feet. Not a bullet. Not a bomb. Not tossing him out of the plane. They wanted him to die *at their hands*. And a third thing—"

"You said there was two."

"There's three. They said he didn't make a sound when the Shi'ites were killing him. Didn't make a sound except when they kicked him in the chest and *forced* air out of his lungs. That's a SEAL. That's how tough they are. You can't torture them, you can't make them whine, because nothing you can do to them short of killing them is as bad as what they already went through during training. That's what they say."

Well, that kind of talk made the four SEALs inside that pressure chamber seem like they were bigger than life, like if they wanted to they could tear open the pressure door with their bare hands. Hippy was the most intrigued by them. Couldn't help himself. He had to go look at them through the window. And then he had to say something stupid about them afterward.

"Those are the SEALs?"

Catfish knew better than to say something like, No, they're meter readers. Hippy could be just a little bit paranoid, so you had to be careful about making him feel like you were making fun of him. That's just one of the things everybody knew about Hippy without having to say it. So Catfish didn't make fun of the stupid question. But he also didn't leave it alone—there's such a thing as being *too* nice. "Yeah," said Catfish. "Those guys ain't so tough. I fought guys plenty tougher'n them."

Hippy didn't know people were always careful about teasing him—he had no such restrictions about teasing back. "Now we get to hear about how you could've been a contender?" He pulled back the neck of Catfish's shirt and poured some Cap'n Crunch down his back.

That was too much for Catfish. Bad enough to pour cereal down his back, but to make fun of his old boxing days was going too far. He whirled around and slapped Hippy a couple of times with his cap. Then he held up his fist. "You see this? They used to call this the Hammer." Catfish was mostly demanding that Hippy take him seriously as an ex-boxer. But he was also, just a little bit, warning Hippy not to go too far.

Jammer spoke up. "Hippy wasn't born then." You're an old guy, Catfish, and Hippy's a dumb kid. Don't take him seriously.

Catfish got the message. He unclenched a little. "Hippy never *was* born." He pulled some Cap'n Crunch out of the bottom of his shirt and threw it at the boy. "Here, eat some of this."

Hippy still didn't get the idea that Catfish was really annoyed at him. He threw more Cap'n Crunch, hitting Catfish in the back of the head. But Catfish ignored him and went back to work. That's part of the reason Catfish made a good crew member—even when he really was pissed, he didn't do more than growl; if that didn't work, he withdrew and ignored the other guy. He might've been a boxer once, but he didn't throw punches now, not down here, anyway.

And when Catfish just ignored the last salvo of Cap'n Crunch, Hippy finally understood that Catfish wasn't going to play. That's why Hippy made a good crew member, too. He might be a little bit paranoid, might be a little bit insensitive, but then you have to be crazy and antisocial to want to live on the bottom of the sea. But another kid, a topside kid, a kid who didn't belong on a rig crew, he might have *kept* throwing cereal until Catfish finally *did* blow up, until there really *was* a fight. Topside people can do that, because after the fight they can go away somewhere. Not on a Gulf rig or down in *Deepcore*. You get in a fight, you still got to eat with the guy and work with him and cover his ass and trust him to cover yours. Crazy or dumb about people he might be, but Hippy still knew how to stop before the joke went too far.

Lindsey was bored beyond belief. Coming on impulse as she had, she hadn't brought anything of her own with her—no books, no papers, nothing. The SEALs didn't have that problem. They managed to keep busy—in shifts. Right now Monk and Wilhite were asleep, while Coffey and Schoenick were intent on reading documents.

No doubt top-secret reports, thought Lindsey. That was what bothered her most about this business of turning over *Deepcore* to the government. They'd be expected to tell these SEALs everything, but in return the SEALs would say nothing. After all, nobody on *Deepcore* had security clearance. Didn't they realize how dangerous that was? How easy it would be for one of the crew to make some trivial mistake because they didn't know the consequences? It was even more likely that the crew would fail to do something, fail to give some warning because it never occurred to them what these top-secret, eyes-only boys were about to do. Somebody's going to die because of your secrecy.

She shook off the idea. Pure paranoia on her part. Nobody was going to die, beyond the kids on the sub. *They* were certainly dead. Lindsey knew that, even if people like Kirkhill still thought there was a chance. Even if she didn't know what pressure could do to a damaged sub at that depth—let alone an undamaged one—she would have known it from the way these SEALs were acting. They didn't make *one* inquiry about provisions *Deepcore* might have for any rescued seamen. They didn't even try to find out how they might manage getting survivors from some compartment of the sub—presumably still at one atmosphere—into this pressure chamber, so they could get blown down to sixty atmospheres in order to stay alive in *Deepcore*. No, the military knew that there were no survivors on the sub.

Which meant that the whole purpose of sacrificing her test well was just to keep some damned secret for the government. What, were the Russians going to slip in some super-secret equivalent of *Deepcore* during a hurricane and snatch all the secrets out of the sub? Steal all our warheads? Nonsense—they didn't even *have* an equivalent of *Deepcore*. She knew this because if the Russians *had* one, then the U.S. government would have panicked and built their own in order to keep up in some meaningless submersible-platform race. Which they hadn't, which is why somebody like Lindsey was the only one working on the problem in any serious way. *Now* the government decided a platform like *Deepcore* was useful. *Now* she was expected to sacrifice everything for the government. Where were they when she was looking for development money?

Lindsey didn't like secrets. She especially didn't like secrets on *Deepcore*.

And there was a little metal suitcase, just the thing the SEALs would use for keeping their best secrets—it was right under the bench, within easy reach of Lindsey's left foot. Coffey and Schoenick were so busy reading, they wouldn't notice if she reached out her toes like *this* and popped the left-hand latch like *that*, almost silently, and got her toes inside and lifted the lid of the case. Just to get a peek inside. It wasn't papers. She caught a glimpse: silver-colored metal, shiny, ribbed; a cylinder maybe three inches in diameter.

Coffey didn't even look up. He stamped his foot down on the lid of the case so hard that if Lindsey's reflexes hadn't been so good, if she hadn't pulled her toes away in time, they would have been dealing with five little amputation wounds with the minimal first-aid supplies in the pressure chamber.

Only after the lid was safely shut, Coffey's heavy boot resting on it, did he look up at her with a half smile and a twinkle in his eye. "Curiosity killed the cat."

What bothered Lindsey most about it was that Coffey didn't seem annoyed the way he had before. When she'd just been insulting their male pride by reminding them of pressurization problems like HPNS, he'd been ticked off at her. Now, when she had actually been doing something wrong, he seemed to have enjoyed the momentary conflict. As if he didn't really have fun unless he was on the verge of doing something violent.

It didn't occur to her that maybe he smiled because he absolutely understood her—exactly how much of a threat she posed, and how to handle it.

The time was up. Everybody inside the pressure chamber was breathing the same mix of argon and a tiny bit of oxygen and nitrogen that the rest of *Deepcore* was using. Catfish spun a couple of valves closed and then cranked the wheel on the chamber hatch. It popped open with a faint puff of air like a virgin's sigh—the pressure is never *exactly* equal, but with Catfish running it it was damn close.

"Y'all are done to a turn and ready to serve," said Catfish. "Everybody OK?"

The SEALs shouldered past him as if he didn't exist, carrying the largest equipment cases out toward the moonpool. Wilhite and Coffey led the way. Lindsey came out in the middle of the group. She could see that Catfish was annoyed at how the SEALs didn't so much as say hello, didn't even acknowledge the guy who'd given them every breath they took for the last eight hours. She patted Catfish on the shoulder. "They're really very sweet," she said. He grinned.

Almost at once she came up against Jammer, who was so tall his chest was at Lindsey's eye level. "I don't remember putting a wall here. How're you doing, Jammer?"

"Pretty good. How're you, little lady?"

"I'm OK." Monk and Schoenick moved through, carrying a grey, trunk-size metal equipment case. With Lindsey standing there talking to Jammer, there wasn't room to get by. They got through anyway, without saying excuse me. Lindsey watched them as they slid the case along her backside. "OK," she said, echoing herself.

The SEALs set down their stuff in the sub bay, the open area around the moonpool. Lindsey could hear Coffey talking—but he was talking only to his own men. "I want a full check on that gear."

"These guys are about as much fun as a tax audit," said Lindsey. Catfish nodded. What he didn't mention was that Lindsey wasn't exactly a one-woman party herself.

Coffey pushed back through the little clump of civilians. He heard Lindsey's remark, but he didn't care. His team wasn't here to entertain take-charge stunters like her. He understood more about Lindsey than she thought. For instance, he knew from the minute she came over to Cab Three back on the *Explorer* that she wasn't authorized to be their pilot. Before she even raised her hand to call for the crane to lift the cab, he had considered what to do. He had been briefed about her long before the helicopter picked her up in Houston—if he hadn't thought she might be useful, he could have refused to take her with him even then. So he knew she was an experienced deep-sea diver, knew that she understood *Deepcore* better than anybody else. She could get them down, and if there was some damage to *Deepcore* or they had to improvise something mechanical, she'd be an asset. If he had concluded otherwise, he would have drawn a weapon and arrested her on the spot. If she had resisted him, he would have disabled her. She thought she had bluffed him, but you didn't bluff Coffey. He knew what you could do, or he found out damn quick.

What he didn't know was her motive for going down. A hot-dogger? Or perhaps an enemy agent determined to be on-site when they went into the *Montana?* Sticking her toe into the case, that was what gave her away as a pure hot-dogger. No agent would be stupid enough to try that when two wide-awake SEALs were in the room—especially when popping the latch of the case wasn't silent. She was too amateurish to be a spy. She was just a meddlesome jerk. She might get in the way, but she wouldn't try to interfere actively.

Coffey bent down, picked up the case Lindsey had been prying into, set it on the bench. It was then that he noticed his hands were shaking.

Coffey's hands never shook. He knew immediately what it meant—he was at least as aware of the danger of HPNS as Lindsey. He had the jitters. Did he have it bad? Would he become delusional? He paused a moment, thinking through the alternatives. Would he *know* if he had a lapse in judgment? He should immediately turn command over to . . . who? Wilhite would be true to the mission, but he didn't have the initiative, the drive—he wouldn't be able to push these civilians into doing what was needed. Schoenick had the strength for it, but he didn't really have the brains. He wasn't good at looking at the whole situation and making the right decision. Monk? Monk could do it, but Coffey felt uneasy about him, felt that Monk was holding something back. Not much, but there was just a tiny part of him that didn't belong to the team. A tiny part of him that resisted discipline. Not that Monk had ever done anything wrong, had ever rebelled or disobeyed. But Coffey had felt it, that even when Monk was working right alongside the rest of the team, sweating his guts out, doing his all, there was something inside him that was just watching, observing it all, but not *part* of it.

Or maybe I'm paranoid. Maybe the HPNS is making me find weaknesses in all my men. Find reasons to mistrust them. After all, I must have trusted them enough to pick them for the original assignment in the Central American mountains. I didn't have any qualms about them until I got down here, until I got pressurized.

No. Coffey knew himself, knew exactly what he was capable of, and he knew his men. His judgment was *not* impaired. He was the only man here who understood all that was at stake, who was able to deal with any contingency. If the mission was to succeed, he had to lead it.

What Coffey didn't know about himself was his absolute reluctance to surrender command. He might follow general orders, but when it came down to the split-second, moment-by-moment tactical decisions of an operation, he had never, ever yielded to anyone else's judgment. It had never been necessary—he had never been in a situation where decisions mattered and he wasn't making them. He didn't realize how difficult it would be for him to surrender command even if he was in perfect control of himself.

And he wasn't in perfect control of himself.

He clenched his trembling fingers into a fist. Couldn't let anybody see this. It would jeopardize the mission to let anybody know he had the jitters. He picked up the case and carried it on out to the sub bay. Things would be fine.

Chapter 7

Breathing Fluid

Lindsey probably should have checked in with Bud the minute she arrived. After all, he was toolpusher on *Deepcore*. It was like reporting to the captain the minute you went on board the ship—the commanding officer had a right to know who was on his craft at all times. But then, Lindsey didn't think of *Deepcore* as being anybody's craft but hers.

So she went straight to the locker room, just off the sub bay. The various test crews on *Deepcore I* and *II* had long since learned never to clean out her locker, even if they *knew* she wasn't coming along. Lindsey wasn't very good at staying away from *Deepcore,* and so it was always a good idea to have a couple of changes of clothes on board. Especially now, since she hadn't brought anything else with her.

She pulled out the clothes. They stank. But the clothes she'd been wearing all day—on the *Explorer,* in Cab Three, and in the pressure chamber—smelled considerably worse. She'd get used to stinking pretty soon, but she wasn't used to it yet. She stripped off her orange jumpsuit right there in the locker room and put on the blues from her locker. Halfway through changing her clothes, it occurred to her that it was a little late to start dressing up to please Bud.

What an absurd thought. She wasn't dressing to please anybody but herself. Bud had nothing to do with it. She wasn't even nervous about seeing him; she certainly wasn't changing clothes just to postpone talking to him. Why, *he* should be the one trying to avoid talking to *her*. Wasn't he responsible for letting them take her drill rig on this cockamamy errand to rescue *codebooks?* That's why he hadn't come looking for her the moment he knew she was out of the pressure chamber. That's why he hadn't come by to chat during the eight long hours she was in there.

Not that he should. Not that he had a duty or anything. But it would have been *nice.* It would have been common courtesy. Bud was probably trying to get even with her for being mad at him. Or maybe he was punishing her for coming down to *Deepcore* in the first place. Well, he'd find out that it didn't work. She wasn't his wife anymore. She was his project engineer, and she had a right to come down to her project whenever she wanted to, so if he didn't like it, screw *him.*

Clothes changed, she walked out into the sub bay, behind the dive platform. The SEALs were still there, playing with their toys. She ducked through the hatchway into the corridor and made her way down to the end. A left turn would take her into the infirmary trimodule. Since it also included the lounge and mess hall, it was bound to be full of lazy, bored, lousy-joke-telling crewmen. She turned right.

Bud was in the command room, of course, with Hippy off to one side in the sonar shack. Bud looked busy. Lindsey tried to think of something to say to him. Some greeting that wouldn't start a fight but also wouldn't sound like an apology. For what? What would she apologize for?

Hippy was holding his white rat up to his lips. Kissing it. Or nibbling at it.

"Hippy," said Lindsey. "You're going to give that rat a disease."

That was their first clue that she was in the room—but

they obviously weren't surprised to see her. Bud turned around slowly. "Well, well. Mrs. Brigman."

"Not for long," she said. Just like him, to try to pick a fight with his first words. He used that name like a suitcase label, to assert ownership. Well, she wasn't going to fight with him. She was going to ignore him. She walked up to the command center and scanned the monitors and readouts. She could tell at a glance what each one said, like a mother looking at her baby, knowing right away if there was some problem. Lindsey's big iron baby.

"You never did like being called that, did you?" said Bud.

As if you had forgotten. "Not even when it meant something." Back in the dark ages. She looked out the viewport. She could see Flatbed's lights floating out there in the darkness, leading *Deepcore* through the permanent nighttime at two thousand feet. Who would Bud have riding scout? "Is that One Night in Flatbed?"

"Yeah, who else?" said Bud. "Here, say hi." He handed her the headset.

She held it so the mouthpiece was in position and one earphone was at her left ear. "Hi, One Night, it's Lindsey."

Lindsey heard One Night's cheery answer. "Oh, hi, Lindsey."

Out in Flatbed, where nobody could see her, One Night pantomimed gagging herself with her finger.

Lindsey didn't need to see it to know how One Night felt. She knew One Night wasn't glad to hear her voice—the very cheeriness of her answer was a lie. Jammer and Catfish might have joked with her, One Night might fake a pleasant answer, but Lindsey knew that she was an outsider, an interloper. And worse—she was the woman who was divorcing their beloved toolpusher, Virgil Brigman. I broke their poor hero's heart, and so I'm slime. Screw you, One Night.

She handed the headset back to Bud and turned away. Might as well tour *Deepcore* and see just how screwed up everything is. Bud's precious crew wasn't exactly perfect. They let things slide. Everybody did, after a while. Nobody kept their edge underwater. Except Lindsey. She *always* kept her edge.

Behind her, Bud signaled to Hippy to come take over for him at the joystick. Hippy had the good grace to get the message silently. Bud got up and followed Lindsey out of the command module and out into the corridor.

Lindsey being here was a problem, and, just like any other problem, Bud knew he had to handle it. He'd done it before, back when their marriage was still alive, and even earlier than that. Teased her a little—just enough to let her see she was being a bit ridiculous. It always worked. Or at least it used to work. Turn a point of friction into a kind of game. Verbal karate, only never quite connecting hard enough to hurt.

This time wasn't going to be so easy, though. Things had changed. For one thing, just having her down here made Bud a little crazy. All these months without her—not so bad since he'd been down in *Deepcore,* but the months before that. Thinking about her in bed with that college-educated asshole. Trying to figure out what he'd done wrong. Trying to pretend that he didn't love her, that she absolutely wasn't lovable, wasn't *worth* it, and then remembering what it was like when they were still working well together, when it *clicked.* It was smooth, no effort at all, both of them concentrating on something outside themselves, something they both cared about—then they meshed like well-tooled gears, at work and at play, the whole rhythm of their life perfect.

Perfect, and then she started picking at him, and no matter what he did she got pissed off. It came out of nowhere, there was no *reason* for it. She just decided one day that she was going to hate everything he did, even his crew, and then after a while she tells him, Bud, it isn't working, we fight all the time. Damn right we fight all the time! So if you don't want to fight, don't divorce me, just stop the fighting! And if you *are* going to divorce me, why do you have to keep getting into my face? The divorce didn't stop the fighting, it just stopped the stuff that made it so I could *stand* your sniping at me; you still won't leave me alone, only now I don't even get to sleep with you.

So even though Bud meant to simply tease her out of her foul temper, he couldn't help pushing it too far. Saying it with a sort of half-smile, so that it would look like he meant it as a joke. Only it wasn't a joke. Not really.

"I can't believe you were dumb enough to come down here." Just kidding. Right? You can hear in my voice that I'm teasing. "Now you're stuck here for the storm. That was dumb, hot-rod, real dumb." I'm teasing, but it was dumb.

"I didn't come down here to fight with you."

Oh, really? What was that crap about Mrs. Brigman and rubbing his face in how that name didn't mean anything anymore? But take it easy. Don't let her attitude get to you. "Then why *did* you come down?"

"You need me." She kept on walking down the corridor. "Nobody knows the systems on this rig better than I do. Once you're disconnected from the *Explorer,* you guys are on your own for however long this storm lasts. I mean what if something was to happen after the surface support clears off? What would you have done?"

"Wow, you're right," said Bud. He followed her down the ladder to the drill level. "Us poor dumb ol' boys might've had to think for ourselves. Could've been a disaster." What did she think they'd been training for during the last year and a half? How did she think they managed to survive through their first one-month shift and most of their second without her?

But I'm smiling, see? Just trying to joke you out of your bad mood.

She headed for the compressor room, started checking the life-support systems.

Except the jokes weren't working. Bud wasn't a fool, he knew he was even more pissed off at her than he was showing.

Get it under control, Bud. You know how to handle her.

"Do you want to know what I think?" Bud asked.

She was paying no attention to his argument. Or rather,

she *was* paying attention, and intended to answer by proving that they *did* need her. "Do you see where this is set?" she demanded. She turned a valve. Not all that much. It wasn't far off, but it wasn't right on where it was supposed to be, either. Sloppy. Lazy.

"You want to know what I think?" He wasn't giving up.

"Not particularly." She moved away from him again. He followed.

"I think you were worried about me." Now *that's* a joke, right? She'll laugh at *that*.

"That must be it," she said. Not exactly a laugh, but kind of a joke, so his teasing was beginning to work. She was lightening up.

They turned a corner and Lindsey nearly ran into a rigger. "Hey, Perry," she greeted him.

Since she was beginning to respond, Bud kept up that line of conversation. "No, I think you were. Come on, it's OK." Bud said it to make her laugh. At the same time he didn't want her to laugh. He wanted it not to be a joke. He wanted her to turn around and say, Yes, as a matter of fact I *was* worried about you. "It's OK, you can admit it."

She heard the pleading, not the joking tone. So she explained it to him like he was a three-year-old who didn't catch on unless you talked clearly. "I was worried about the rig. I've got over four years invested in this project."

She meant it, he knew that. The rig was all, it was everything, it always had been, their marriage was a lie right from the start. Well, what the hell. At least we can laugh about it, can't we? "Yeah, you only have three years invested in me."

She paused in the doorway. She said it so he couldn't miss the meaning. "Well, you have to have priorities." Then she turned and walked out.

I did this to myself, Bud thought. I set myself up for this, I begged for it, I was *begging* her to tell me she cares about me, and she won't do it, she can't do it because she doesn't. It's that simple, only I'm too *stupid* to remember it, because I need her so much, I care about her so much, think about her all the time, I keep forgetting that it's nothing like that with her. She never thinks about me at all, just the rig. I know this about her, I know she isn't even *human* about some things. I always knew that.

Only I didn't always know it. When I married her I thought she loved me. Why didn't I know it then? Why didn't I know what was coming and run away?

He took off his cap, leaned against an overhead brace. Breathed deep a couple of times. This wasn't a time to start feeling sorry for himself. Nor was it a good idea to leave things like this with Lindsey. They were going to be in *Deepcore* together for weeks. They'd have to get along, like it or not. He had to get her to lighten up. He had to smooth things out between them well enough that they could make it through several weeks together. Teasing didn't work, so he'd play it straight.

He followed her, found her checking out the drill room, making sure everything had been stored properly so they could resume drilling without having to go back to Galveston for supplies. No joking this time. "You'll need a place to sleep. We'll get there in a few hours, you'll want to rest."

It was true. She *was* tired—the pressure chamber wasn't exactly restful, since she was too worried about everything to sleep.

"My room," he said. "I won't be in there."

She took it for what it was—a peace offering. "Sure. Thanks."

"You can check out everything else when you get up. I'll have somebody wake you when it looks like we're nearly there, OK?"

She nodded. He led the way, opened the door to the only private stateroom on the rig. Rank had its privileges. The room wasn't much, but at least he could get off by himself.

As she walked in, his hand on the door was about level with her eyes. She noticed he was wearing the massive titanium wedding band she'd bought him. That was part of why they were so good together at first. A lot of guys she knew at MIT would know that titanium was the toughest metal, that it symbolized something that would really last. Bud knew that, too—but the ring also looked right on his hand. He was as strong as the titanium. She could count on him. If that's all the ring meant, then it told the truth. He had never let her down. He'd been there every time, no matter what. But the ring also was supposed to say that *she* would be just as faithful. Well, that was before she knew that she just wasn't cut out for marriage. You had to give up too much of yourself.

Except that wasn't it at all, was it? What drove her crazy about Bud wasn't that he demanded so much from her, but rather that he demanded so much from himself, *gave* so much to her, and she could never, never deserve it.

"It's kind of messy, but I guarantee it's the only bunk that won't be occupied." Bud was gathering up his dirty clothes off the bed, cleaning up so the room would be good for her. It's what he always did—saw what she'd need, took care of her. Like knowing she was tired before she realized it herself. Giving her his bunk, cleaning it up. "You can grab a couple hours rest before we get there."

No! He wasn't really giving her anything. He was manipulating her now just like always. Even wearing that damn ring, trying to make her ashamed of her broken promise. "What are you still wearing that for?" she demanded.

He looked down at the ring as if he'd forgotten it was there. "I don't know. Divorce ain't final. Forgot to take it off." He looked kind of embarrassed to have been caught wearing it.

"I haven't worn mine in months," she said. She didn't mean to hurt him—it just occurred to her. But it was good for him to hear it, so he'd know that she *didn't* feel that way anymore.

But of course he took it wrong. "Yeah, well, what's-his-name wouldn't like it. The Suit." He pretended he was joking, but it wasn't funny.

Was he still jealous? "Do you always have to call him that? The Suit? It makes you sound like such a hick. His name is Michael."

"So how *is* Michael, then? Mr. Brooks Brothers? Mr. BMW?" When she didn't laugh or smile or answer at all, a new possibility occurred to him. "You still seeing him?"

You mean are we still humping away, as you no doubt call it? "No, I haven't *seen* him in a few weeks."

He smiled. He loved hearing it. "I'm terribly sorry. What happened?" He was snatching at this like a drowning man grabbing a lifebuoy.

"Why are you doing this, huh? Why? This is—this is none of your business, it's not a part of your life anymore."

She was arranging things a little so she could lie on the bed—pulling up the covers. He came up behind her, leaned over her, echoing her movements like a shadow, like they were dancing. He was kidding with her. He also wasn't kidding. "I'll tell you what happened. You woke up one morning in those satin sheets. You rolled over and there was this good-looking guy. Well-groomed, expensive watch on. And you realized, this guy never makes me laugh."

Finally, finally she lost it. No more pretending to be calm, no more lowered voice. "That's it, Bud, that's it. Aren't you clever, Jesus you're clever! You know you should start your own talk show or something, Ask Dr. Bud, advice to the lovelorn from three hundred fathoms!"

He raised his hands in surrender, backed away, backed out of the room. Hey, it was just a joke. Ease up. No offense.

Bullshit. "Thank you," she said, with mock politeness. "Thank you."

As soon as he closed the door, she turned the wheel to seal it shut. Then she went back to the bed, sat down, gave a quiet, contained, careful little scream. What the hell kind of idiot *was* he? Michael made her laugh all the time, what did Bud think? She didn't love Bud because he made her laugh, she loved him because he was the one man she could be *serious* with, the one man she could *work* with, not like Michael, who thought a woman should give him a good strong tickle every night and otherwise be entertaining and decorative. And when Michael *did* talk about business it was always very stupid, uninteresting business, which he thought was so *important*. She finally broke up with him because he made her laugh all the time—but mostly when he wasn't there.

She snapped off the light. She could still see from the floodlights outside *Deepcore*, letting a dim bluish light in through the porthole. It was a sad kind of almost-darkness.

Even now Bud didn't make her laugh. Even when he tried to talk her into coming back to him or to punish her because she wouldn't, all these stupid, pointless refusals to recognize that it was over. Even that didn't make her laugh. It just made her sad. Made her almost wish that she was somebody else, somebody who was just dumb enough to fall for all his manipulative little well-meant kindnesses. Any other woman in the world would think he was the perfect husband.

So of course he married me, the poor schmuck.

She idly reached for a bottle of aftershave sitting on the little bedside table. Same brand. He never changed brands of anything. She opened it. Sniffed. It was him. It made her a little dizzy, just for a moment, as if he were right there in the room with her, just out of sight behind her on the bed, reaching out—he'd touch her in just a moment, pull the shirt from her shoulders, hook a hand around her waist and slide her back, pull her close. . . .

She closed the bottle and set it back down, angry at herself. "Shit," she whispered. I'm not fifteen years old. I never *was* fifteen. I'm not going to distort my life because I still have a meaningless crush on my husband. Ex-husband. Almost-ex-husband.

Bud went straight from her room—*his* room—to the head. Why did he do that? He wasn't teasing her, no matter what he thought at the time. When it came to Lindsey he just didn't have the same kind of self control he had in other situations. He ended up baiting her, goading her until she got mad, just like at the end, just like before she moved out. What, did he have to prove to himself again that it was really over? Well fine, the point was made, now I know it's over, and I'm damned if I'm going to wear the ring another minute, not with her here for the next few weeks, looking at the ring and laughing at him for wearing it.

He could hardly get it off his finger—it hadn't been off since she first slid it on. But it came free, eventually—he gladly would've taken half the skin off with it. Then he flung it down into the blue chemical water of the toilet. Let it wind up on the bottom of the ocean where it belongs.

He got maybe two steps away from the head and stopped. He couldn't do it. It was wrong, he hated himself for it, but he couldn't just let the thing get flushed away. Even if the ring meant nothing to her, even if she mocked him for it, it still meant something to *him.* Three years with Lindsey, they were real even if they were over, and the ring was part of that, part of the best times.

So he opened the door and went back in, knelt down beside the toilet, plunged his hand into the chemicals, and fished around till he got the ring. He didn't think to rinse it off first, just pushed it back onto his left ring finger.

Then he looked at his right hand. Blue up to the wrist. And the color looked like it was sticking, it wasn't draining away with the water. Now if that wasn't brilliant. I not only have the ring on my left hand to make me look ridiculous, but my right hand has been dyed blue. *Permanently* dyed blue—they'd all been warned that the liquid waste disposal chemicals don't wash off. He'd probably die with one blue hand. "How did that happen to poor Virgil Brigman?" "Oh, you know old Virgil, couldn't keep his hands out of toilets. That's where he found his wedding band, you know."

"Oh, shit," he whispered, and he meant it.

They got there. One Night spotted the steep downslope that led to the edge of the Cayman Trench just about the moment McBride reported that the *Explorer's* sonar had located them at the exact spot.

Bud was at the controls. He sent Hippy to wake Lindsey up while he got One Night to drop the tow cables, turn around, and survey the landing site to make sure it was generally smooth and clear—no rock outcroppings that might tear into a module somewhere, no slope that might make her rest unsteady. Lindsey was there by the time he was ready to let *Deepcore* set down. Like a spacecraft landing on a barren planet, the rig settled into the bottom ooze.

One Night brought Flatbed back under *Deepcore,* then rose up into the moonpool.

Bud expected they'd take some time for sleep before they went out to start work at the sub. He was wrong. The SEALs didn't intend to make entry into the *Montana* a solo effort. They intended to use all of *Deepcore's* support facilities—the ROVs, Flatbed, both Cabs. And not just hardware. Coffey immediately had all the trained divers in the sub bay and made them study the layout of the ground around the sub and the plans of the sub inside, getting them ready for the operation.

Bud stood there, listening, fascinated at first, but more and more frustrated as time went on. What Coffey was forgetting was that the very people who were trained divers were the same crew that kept *Deepcore* running—and therefore the ones who had been up for hours, tending *Deepcore* as Flatbed led her through the darkness. The only rested people on *Deepcore* were the drillers, and they were useless on this job. Coffey would have to wait.

"I just want to go through a couple of high points one last time," said Coffey. He laid out the computer-composite scan of the area where the sub was, with the exact location marked and the contours shown in dark lines. "All right, this is us, sitting right on the edge of the Cayman Trench. This is the *Montana,* three hundred meters away, seventy meters below us. We think she slid down the wall and is now lodged on this outcropping."

In the meantime, Wilhite was going around giving everybody little plastic badges to clip on. One Night looked at hers. There wasn't a picture, so it wasn't I.D. "This tells us how much radiation we get?"

That was the first time most of the crew had thought about the fact that this was a *nuclear* sub. Nuclear weapons, nuclear engine. If it got really crashed up, bad stuff would come out. "Whoa," said Hippy. "I'm not going in no radiation, no way."

Catfish was contemptuous. "Hippy, you pussy."

"What good is the money if six months later your dick drops off?" Hippy was walking away.

Coffey thought he could solve this by explaining it rationally to them. That'd work with most of them—but then most of them weren't worried about it. Hippy was, and Bud knew that Hippy didn't connect with rationality. Still, he sat tight while Coffey did his best. "We'll take readings as we go. If the reactor's breached or the warheads have released radioactive debris, we'll back off. Simple."

"Oh, great!" said Hippy. He understood, intellectually, but what did that matter? He still had the fear, gonad-level fear, and he wasn't going to move until that was gone. Coffey didn't know how to get past that. Bud did.

"OK, Hippy's not going," Bud announced. "McWhirter, you can run Little Geek." Bud patted the top of the smaller of the two ROVs.

That did it. Bud knew how Hippy felt about Little Geek—and McWhirter. Hippy was right back in the group, bitching. "Goddammit! You know that McWhirter can't run an ROV worth shit." Only then did he remember that McWhirter might not share his opinion. "No offense," said Hippy.

McWhirter knew Hippy well enough not to take him seriously. Besides, McWhirter was only marginally qualified with ROVs. The only thing Hippy loved better than Big Geek and Little Geek was Beany. Hippy was back with the program. "I'll go," he said.

Catfish was with him. He rumpled Hippy's hair. "What a guy," he said.

It was a good moment. Coffey killed it. He turned on his military voice and shut them all down. "On the dive, you do absolutely nothing without direct orders from me, and you follow my instructions without discussion. Is that clear? All right, I want everyone finished prep and ready to get wet in fifteen minutes."

It was about the worst thing Coffey could have done for

morale and loyalty. Just the fact that he thought that speech was necessary was insulting to the crew. How did he think they had stayed alive all these years together if they didn't know that you don't screw around underwater and you obey your leader's orders instantly? Bud could see how it hit them—Catfish was pissed, Jammer was contemptuous, Hippy hung his head like he was being chewed out—the worst mood you could get any of them into.

The dumbest thing about it was that Coffey didn't seem to be dumb in general. He handled his own guys great. He should've known better. Bud couldn't figure why he'd done it—surely Coffey wasn't one of those military guys who had to strut all the time. Maybe it annoyed Coffey that Bud had got Hippy back into line. Or maybe it worried him to see that the divers could be marginally bonkers like Hippy, so they *needed* to be teased into doing stuff. Maybe it bothered him to be depending on people who weren't right-down-the-line disciplined military types. Whatever the reason, it wasn't a very good one. It told Bud that Coffey had bad judgment. He didn't like sending his crew out under the orders of a man with bad judgment.

Still, they were going to do the job. This wasn't the time for Bud to do anything openly that might undermine Coffey's authority. Perry had a few guys helping him load Little Geek and its control boxes into Cab Three. "Let's get suited up," Bud said. It was his way of saying, It's OK, let's do the job, who cares what he thinks.

But he made a point of getting Coffey alone, by the dive platform where the SEAL leader was doing the last of his own prep. Bud didn't like this whole dive right now. The timing was bad, morale was bad, and Coffey wasn't too good himself. If something went wrong, nobody was going to be sharp enough to deal with it.

"Look, it's three A.M." Bud said. He was choosing his words carefully, making sure he didn't sound threatening, making it sound like a suggestion. The kind of suggestion that a commander could take without losing face. Bud's dad had been a non-com—he'd watched him handle officers like this all the time. The smart officers listened. "These guys are running on bad coffee and about four hours of sleep. Maybe you could think about cutting them some slack."

Coffey didn't even look at him. "I can't afford slack."

Pure military bullshit. Didn't the guy have a brain? "Hey, you come on my rig, you don't talk to me, you start ordering my people around, it's not going to work." No, that didn't sound right. Sounded like Bud was ticked off because he was losing authority, and that *wasn't* the problem. He tried to explain what he really meant: "You gotta know how to handle these people. We've got a certain way of doing things here."

"Right now I'm not *interested* in your way of doing things. Just get your team ready to dive." Coffey walked off, leaving Bud to stand there burning.

He ate it. Just swallowed it down. No point in arguing now. They were going, and so the best thing for Bud to do was make sure he was sharp, everybody was sharp, no open quarrels, everything going smooth. He walked back to the locker area and sat down, started pulling on his boots.

Finler was sitting next to him. Looking at him. What're you looking at?

"Bud. You know your hand is blue?"

That was Finler. Always trying to be helpful. Probably walked up to double amputees and said, Hey, you know you got no legs? Bud looked at him. "Will you shut up and get your gear on?" He meant to say it funny, but it wasn't funny, it was mean. So he said, "Please." So Finler would know it was OK.

If I wasn't tired, if I wasn't pissed off at Coffey, I wouldn't have talked like that to Finler. Looks like handling people badly is contagious.

Monk was also a little bothered by the way Coffey had dealt with the civilians, though not for the same reasons as Bud. It was Coffey himself that Monk was worried about. Not that Monk had time to stop and think about anything— but then, part of being a SEAL was the ability to do about ten things at once, purely by habit, so your mind could be on the most important thing. So Monk busied his hands draining the Deep Suit fluid breathing system, which he had been testing, while his mind was busy thinking back over the way Coffey had just offended the entire civilian crew of *Deepcore*.

In his time in the service Monk had known officers who antagonized everybody they talked to—but Coffey wasn't one of them. Coffey was a master of MCT. They had a trainer who taught them the MCT principle, which was that when you were on a mission, all you say to civilians is the Minimum Correct Thing. For most SEALs that meant shutting up most of the time, because it was too hard to figure out what the correct thing was in time to say it. But Coffey always seemed to know. Till now. And that worried Monk. Coffey didn't *make* mistakes like that. Maybe it was the tension of being on an assignment that no SEALs had ever had before. Maybe Coffey had some reason for antagonizing the civilians. Or maybe Coffey wasn't completely healthy.

Monk also was aware of what was going on around him—SEALs who can't keep watch while carrying out a task generally end up coming home in a bag. So he knew that the ROV operator, a short nervous guy named Hippy, was walking along the edge of the moonpool toward Monk, kind of watching as people worked on the submersibles.

Catfish called to him. "Hey, Hippy, toss me a couple of cyalume sticks!"

Hippy reached down, got them out of the box, tossed them to Catfish. When Hippy turned around again he almost bumped into Monk.

"Excuse me," said Monk.

Which was more than he should have said, since Hippy immediately took it as a friendly gesture, instead of the slightly sarcastic rebuke that Monk meant it to be. As usual, Monk had varied from the MCT by talking too much.

Naturally, Hippy noticed that Monk was working with some weird equipment he didn't understand. Hippy made sure he understood every piece of equipment he ever saw. "What is all this stuff?"

Monk didn't look at him. Is it all right to tell him? The Deep Suit was top secret, but fluid breathing systems weren't. Monk thought back over his training—he knew a lot about fluid breathing because it had been his specialty since they first started working with the Deep Suit while training with the Experimental Dive Unit six months ago. They'd been testing fluid breathing with rodents all through the sixties, and it was clear back in 1973 that Johannes Kylstra first got a human breathing in liquid—a hyper-barically-oxygenated saline solution, tested in just one lung, since if a two-lung experiment had failed, the patient would have had trouble filling out his report afterward. Liquid fluorocarbon had been used by Thomas Shaffer in his demand-regulator breathing system, and Peter Bennett had done a lot of testing with it in his hyperbaric chamber in the mid-80s, so even the breathing fluid was a matter of public record. Hell, the fluid they used was nothing more than the medical grade of a 3M product used for leak testing in electronics. Anybody could buy it. It was OK to talk about it. "Fluid breathing system. We just got them. We use it if we need to go really deep."

"How deep?" asked Hippy.

"Deep."

Hippy didn't respond well to evasive answers. Maybe that was one of the reasons his father kicked him out of the house when he was fifteen. *"How deep?"*

But Monk wasn't being evasive just for the hell of it. Partly it was because it was against military policy ever to reveal the limits of any equipment. Partly it was because nobody had ever found out Deep Suit's limits. "It's classified."

So that was that. Hippy left the question alone.

Monk understood, though, that Hippy didn't mean to be a problem. To these guys in *Deepcore,* experimental hyperbaric equipment was a fact of life. Any new piece of equipment had to be understood completely—all that it could do, all its limitations. Especially a guy like Hippy, who got along a lot better with machines than he did with people. So Monk went ahead and explained what he could while he drained the liquid fluorocarbon out of the Deep Suit tank, letting it flow into a clear plastic box. He couldn't tell him details, but he could tell him the stuff that was in the library at Duke University. "Anyway, you breathe liquid, so you can't be compressed. Pressure doesn't get you as bad."

Catfish was with them by now, working at the same table, so he heard that last bit. He couldn't let it go by. "You mean you got liquid? In your lungs?"

Monk turned off the drain valve. "Oxygenated fluorocarbon emulsion."

"Bullshit," said Hippy.

It didn't bother Monk not to be believed. He wasn't a salesman. Whether they believed him or not made no difference in his mission. Still, it'd be fun to show them. They were divers, weren't they? They spent a lot of effort making sure they never had to breathe anything liquid; but they also knew that it was that very dependence on gases that put a bottom limit on how deep they could go. They'd know just how important it was. Besides, Monk kind of liked these guys. If he weren't a SEAL, this was the kind of work he might like to be doing—something that took real courage, but not the kind of thing you'd ever get famous for. Even though Monk was a SEAL and therefore completely separate from them, he still felt a bit of kinship. A bit of brotherhood under the skin.

Monk reached out and got a wire-mesh box from the table and dumped out the valves that were stored in it. "Check this out," Monk said. Then he reached out and snaked the rat off Hippy's shoulders. "Can I borrow your rat?" It was the correct way to get what you need from civilians. Ask permission after; finish the mission before the civilian finishes saying no.

"Hey, what're you doing, man! You're gonna kill her!" Hippy was grabbing at him, but Monk paid no attention. He put the rat into the wire box as if it were a cage, then turned it upside down and pushed the cage, rat and all, down into the fluid. The liquid was tinted pink, so it could be distinguished immediately from water. But it was still liquid, so Monk knew what it looked like to Hippy—the rat was going to drown.

Monk tried to reassure him. "It's OK, I've done this myself." No need to mention that it was probably the most terrifying experience of his life, even though they doped him up a little to help stifle his gag reflex and keep him from thrashing around so much from raw, naked panic as he felt the liquid burn its way into his lungs. That information would only increase Hippy's resistance. All Monk explained was the MCT.

"You're going to kill her!" Hippy was trying to grab the wire box, pull it out. But he wasn't trying extremely hard. Not *hysterically* hard. Monk stopped him just by keeping his shoulder in the way.

"I've breathed this myself," said Monk again, sounding calm, soothing him. "He's going to be fine."

"She's gonna drown! Look, she's freaking out!"

"He's just going through a normal adjustment period." The moment when you know you're going to die and you're afraid it's going to take too long.

"Normal! That looks normal to you?"

The rat *was* panicking—swimming around, struggling to get out. But there's only so long that any air-breather can hold its breath underwater. Eventually the rat had to open its mouth, had to gasp at the liquid. Except that this time when liquid flowed into its lungs, the air-breather didn't die. "He's taking in the fluid," said Monk. "See his chest moving?"

Catfish was finally turning into a believer. "He's breathing it. This rat is breathing that shit!"

Monk enjoyed this, watching their amazement. He'd brought them something they valued—an experience, a new thing. There weren't all that many new things in life. Monk liked feeling their excitement about it. "See? He's digging it."

"She's *doing* it," said Hippy. "She ain't *digging* it."

True enough. The rat opened its mouth each time it took a breath. This stuff was thicker than air, it had to be breathed through the mouth. It worked, carrying oxygen to the lungs.

But there was no chance that the rat was actually getting pleasure from it. Monk remembered his own experience with this stuff too well.

Hippy didn't know that, of course. He only knew that nobody had asked Beany if this experiment was OK. The rat was scared half to death. It was a shitty thing to do, and just because Beany wasn't belly-up dead didn't make it any nicer. "Let her out now," he said.

Monk was content to obey. They'd seen; that was enough. Besides, the liquid wasn't heated yet, and the rat was very small. Rodents weren't like larger animals. Hypothermia didn't cause a rat's body to collect blood—and therefore heat—in the brain. If Monk left the rat too long, it would come out with brain damage, and that really *would* be a lousy thing to do.

Monk lifted up the cage, pulled out the rat, and held it by the tail, upside down over the dish, draining the fluid out of its lungs. He knew from experience that this was the most painful part—it hurt down in your lungs, burned, stung, so you knew you didn't want to do this every day. But pain or not, fluid breathing was real. Lungs didn't care what they sucked in, as long as it had oxygen in it that could be picked up by the bloodstream. This stuff could actually hold sixty-five percent oxygen at one atmosphere of pressure, even more when the pressure was higher—that was more oxygen than there was in air, more than there was in blood. And because it was liquid, it cleaned out the gas pockets in the lungs, allowed a diver to get down past the depths where gas-breathing lungs started to burst and bleed. It allowed a diver to get so far down that the synapses of your brain would begin misfiring from the sheer pressure squeezing all your brain cells together. So deep that you had to be doped half out of your mind just to be able to think at all.

I don't ever, ever want to go that deep, thought Monk.

Hippy was chattering at the rat as it hung there from Monk's hand. Hippy was reassuring it like a nervous mama. He kept reaching out, his hands fluttering, hungry to take Beany, to touch it.

"Let the fluid drain out of him for a minute," said Monk.

"Easy easy easy easy easy," said Hippy, chanting it like a prayer. "Whoa whoa whoa, give me give me give me."

Catfish was praying, too, after his fashion. "That is no-bullshit hands-down the goddamnedest thing I ever saw."

Well, why not. It looked like a sure-enough miracle. Monk handed the rat to Hippy. The kid started moaning with relief as if he'd been the one breathing liquid. Monk tossed him a towel. The rat moved as Hippy dried him off. "Oh, Beany, are you all right?" He started kissing the rat, cooing to it, petting and patting it. For all the world it looked like what you'd expect from Mary and Martha after Jesus raised their brother Lazarus from the dead.

"See? He's fine," said Monk.

Hippy looked at him with withering contempt. "It's a *she,*" he said.

What was I supposed to do, thought Monk, check for a little teeny dong? But he didn't say it. Didn't say anything more. In fact, he was already regretting having done this demonstration at all. Not because he'd breached security— he hadn't, he never would. It was mostly because he realized that he had been showing off. He really wanted these guys to like him. And that was scary. This was the first time since he joined the SEALs that Monk had cared even a little bit whether somebody outside his team liked him.

It wasn't Coffey who was losing it, Monk realized. It was himself. This was not a good time to go native.

Chapter 8
Seeing Things

For all his misgivings, Bud couldn't help but catch the sense of excitement that everyone felt as they set out for the *Montana*. Civilians could talk all they like about how they'd hate to be in the military, how they couldn't stand the discipline, even how they disapprove of war and despise the military mind—but when it came down to it, the idea of being led by crack soldiers on a dangerous mission stirred up something inside a man. As the son of a Marine, Bud might see right through all the phony talk of guts and glory, but when it came right down to it, battle-hunger was built into his genes as sure as the thinning and receding of his hair.

He was never completely lost in his thoughts, however; one part of his mind was listening intently to the headset chatter. Lindsey's voice, coming over the UQC from Cab One: "Com-check, everybody. Flatbed, you on line?"

One Night was piloting Flatbed, of course—even though she'd just spent twelve hours straight doing the same job, without much more than a catnap in between. "Ten-four, Lindsey, read you loud and clear." It was kind of fun listening to her speak so calmly to Lindsey, knowing that

One Night resented Lindsey with a deep and abiding rancor that began even before Lindsey filed for divorce from Bud. One Night didn't hate Lindsey solely out of a sense of duty to Bud; One Night was a volunteer.

The communications check went on. "Cab Three?"

Hippy came on. "Cab Three, check. Right behind you." Everybody was on line.

So now it was time to check their progress. "What's your depth, Cab Three?"

Hippy didn't have to concentrate as much on finding his way, since he could follow the two sets of lights in front of him, had the best opportunity to read the gauges. "Eighteen-forty. Fifty. Sixty. Seventy." Ticking off the depths like decades through history. Going down.

Bud looked around at the other men standing on the back of Flatbed as they moved through the water, packed together like bizarre migrant workers, off to pick hyperbaric lettuce. Only these guys had the wrong attitude for tedious manual labor. They were after war, wearing the armor of the underwater uniform, helmets on, backpacks loaded with breathing mix, ready to fight it out with their old enemy, the sea. They were all pretending to be calm, almost business-like about the whole thing, but if they could act out what was going on inside them, Bud was pretty sure they'd be just like a troop of chimps when it was time for battle—waving their arms, jumping up and down, hooting and screeching.

Especially the SEALs, directly across from Bud. Coffey looked icy calm through his mask. But he had eyes of fire, Bud thought, eyes all lighted up with danger. Coffey might not have invented the business of death, but he was an ambitious young executive in America's killer corporation. He'd go far, if he didn't get everybody killed first.

Bud's father never had eyes like that. He was just a guy, just Dad. But maybe Dad changed when he got to Vietnam. Maybe when some VC looked at him through his telescopic sights he saw murder in Dad's eyes and he knew: This is the one I've got to kill so these Americans will all go home. He didn't know that Dad was just a regular guy when he was in the U.S.

Maybe when Coffey isn't on a mission, he's just a regular guy, like Dad.

No way. Not possible.

Lindsey's voice interrupted Bud's thoughts. They were at the edge of the Trench. "Going over the wall. Coming to bearing zero-six-five. Everybody stay tight and in sight."

One Night was right behind her. She was the one with passengers out in the open. "Starting our descent," she said, like a tour guide at Disney World. "Divers, how're you doing?"

Bud looked down the row, his men *and* the SEALs. Everybody in place, nobody in distress, all hanging on tight. "Okay so far," he said.

Now that one of the divers had spoken, it was like giving the others a license to chatter. "How deep's the drop-off here?" asked Jammer.

"This here's the bottomless pit, baby," said Catfish. "Two and a half miles straight down."

Thanks, Catfish, you're always helpful in building morale, thought Bud.

Coffey shut them all down by getting back to business. "Cab One, do you see it yet?" This wasn't officiousness, Bud knew—idle chatter could be dangerous. Channels had to stay open for serious communication. Somebody might die while another guy was joking around. Still, Bud knew that his crew all understood that. Jammer's question, Catfish's answer, that would have been the last of it. These men weren't fools. But then, how could Coffey know that? Bud couldn't resent him for making sure.

Lindsey answered Coffey's question. "The magnetometer is twitching. Side-scan is showing a big return, but I don't see anything yet. Are you sure you got the depth right on this?"

Lindsey was good at this, but Bud knew there were some things that only came with experience she simply hadn't had the time to get. It took a while to get deepwater eyes, to get used to how far you could see at this depth, even with bright lights. Lindsey knew it intellectually, of course, but, as Bud well knew, knowing it didn't stop you from feeling uneasy when you knew you were close and still couldn't see a thing. So he reassured her. "You should be almost to it, ace."

"Yeah, roger that." And then she had it. Like a magician's black drape suddenly dropping to show what had been hidden behind it all along. The giant propeller loomed in front of her, so massive that she felt like her own submersible was dwarfed beside it. Yet this huge thing had been bent and scraped like a child's toy. We build our monsters out of metal, but the earth and the sea are still stronger. "Found it," she said.

Coffey listened to the chatter, learning from it. Even though he had shut down Brigman back at the moonpool, he got the message, and he saw that Brigman was right. These civilians had their own way of doing things, and it worked pretty well. Coffey was used to civilians being chaotic, unorganized, unpredictable, each one acting for himself in ways that were dangerous or hurtful to other people. Only with the eleven other men in his own team of SEALs had he ever found human beings who behaved rationally, predictably, cooperatively. Until now. Maybe the training was different, maybe the rules allowed more room for individual choices, but Brigman's crew worked well together, and the more Coffey studied them, the better he was able to predict what they'd do and the more he could count on them.

I should have known that earlier, thought Coffey. Should have seen the way they take care of each other, the way me and my men do. And who's to say their way isn't just as good? We work to erase our individual differences, to become one soul with twelve bodies, so I could have taken almost any three with me on this mission. But Brigman's guys keep their quirks, their strangeness, and the others just learn to work around them, to use those quirks, count on them, make allowances for them. And when things got tight, when somebody got hot or jumpy, there was Brigman, like a drop of oil into the mechanism just before the friction gets bad enough to cause a squeak. It made a smooth machine out of a bunch of parts that otherwise couldn't fit.

The only one who wasn't part of that team was this

Lindsey bitch, and that wasn't Brigman's fault. She was crazy with selfishness, the kind of person who was incapable of subordinating her own judgment to somebody else's. She was so smart it never occurred to her that maybe somebody else had a better idea. Why Brigman ever married her was beyond comprehension—maybe Brigman thought that rolling her down was the way to control her. Well, to hell with that. She was a danger to Brigman's crew at the best of times, and if Brigman didn't know how to neutralize her, well, Coffey did.

For now, though, he had to deal with her—and she *was* the best at piloting the Cabs. That's why Coffey had her at the point position. Flatbed was too vulnerable, with the divers exposed on the back, and Hippy was piloting the other Cab; no way did he belong in front. You use your best asset for every job. Even when your best asset happens to be Lindsey Brigman.

With that exception, though, Coffey now understood that these guys worked well together, even if it wasn't the same way his team did it. Above all, he respected the way Brigman held them together; he understood that the way to work with these guys was to work with Brigman.

He understood it *now,* that is. He asked himself: Why didn't I see it sooner? Before I hurt morale by saying what I did? Before I shut down Brigman and pissed him off completely there in the moonpool? I don't miss things like that. I don't make mistakes like that. Am I slipping?

Coffey couldn't help but think of his hands. If he took his hands from the railing, right now, would they tremble again? Nobody would see it if they did. Not in this light, not through the suit. But he'd know.

Hell, he wasn't afraid to know it. So he was trembling a little—so what? This was a tense mission. This had implica- tions far beyond a little jungle work, a little bit of strategic excision of key enemy personnel. If he blew this one, it wouldn't lead to a few deniable problems in a minor country. A lot more was at stake. Peace, for instance, and no matter what civilians thought, a good soldier like Coffey loved peace; he risked his life in order to preserve it. Win the little wars so there's never a big one. Use your small M-1 in Central America so nobody puts down an artillery barrage on Dallas or Denver. Trembling hands didn't mean his judgment was impaired. And it hadn't been a mistake to do what he did back at the moonpool. No sir, that wasn't bad judgment, that was *good* judgment. He had to get control, had to make sure they knew that this was not a civilian operation. Had to make sure they weren't asking questions and prying into things they shouldn't know about. What if this operation had to go on to Phase Two? The less they knew, the better.

Now the Brigman woman had the sub in sight. There were procedures to follow. Coffey knew the procedures. His judgment was right on the button. "Cab One, radiation readings?"

"Neutron counter's not showing very much."

That was one instrument's report. Now another. "Wilhite, anything?"

"Negative. Nominal."

So reactor containment integrity had not been compromised. They could go ahead. "Just continue forward along the hull."

"Copy that, continuing forward," said the Brigman woman. "You just want me to get shots of everything, right?"

Damn right—just take pictures. I don't want you *doing* anything. "Roger that, document as much as you can, but let's keep moving. Remember we're on a tight time schedule."

"Copy that."

Now Flatbed was in position as they moved along the length of the sub. It looked bigger than the *Titanic*, they were so close. Coffey tried not to let himself feel anything about it, seeing it lying there on the ledge, lame and helpless. He refused to imagine himself in the captain's position in those last moments when he knew his men were gone, when he knew they were going to die. Coffey had never lost a man. But he knew that it could happen, knew that sometimes things went wrong that were completely out of your control. And then you'd be there, still alive, your men still alive, but knowing they would soon be dead, knowing there was nothing you could do to save them. But you could still fulfil your mission. You could still do your duty. That's what made your death mean something—that you still did your duty right to the end.

Bud watched the sub go by. After the number of times he had scanned the outside of *Deepcore,* searching for structural flaws, he knew a nightmare when he saw one. The hull had obviously been flexed and twisted—metal plates that should have been snug were enough out of line that the joints were clearly visible and uneven in width. You could drain spaghetti in this thing, it had so many tiny gaps. It didn't take a barn door to let air out and water in.

It was Coffey, though, who knew what he was looking for. His voice came over the speaker in Bud's helmet. "That's the midships hatch. You see it, Cab Three?"

Hippy was on it. "Roger, I see it."

Bud didn't wait for Coffey to issue orders. He could tell from Hippy's voice that he was scared and distracted— probably imagining himself inside a cracked can like this sub. Enough to spook even somebody who wasn't as paranoid as Hippy. So Bud had to get him back to the job. "Yeah, well just get around so you can shine your light on the hatch."

"Check," said Hippy. "Then I just hang with these guys, right?" Hippy's voice was more businesslike. The edginess was gone. It was Coffey's show again.

"Right," said Coffey.

"How do you want me!" asked One Night. She sounded a little nervous, too. She could pilot Flatbed in her sleep, but she'd never had to drop off a team of sailors at a broken-down sub before.

"Just hold above it," said Coffey. She maneuvered into position. It was time to go. But nobody moved, not the

SEALs, not Bud's divers—not until Coffey gave the word. "All right, A-team."

That was all the SEALs except Coffey. Wilhite, Schoenick, and Monk unhooked their short whip-umbilicals from the central manifold of Flatbed. They were on their own breathing mix now. They had also unhooked from the direct voice connection through the umbilicals—but this didn't mean they had to rely on the short-range, erratic UQC. They'd be too spread out through the *Montana,* with too much steel and water between them for the UQC to be of much use. Instead, they carried automatic spoolers that played out disposable fiber-optic thread. It was so thin you couldn't see it in the water—but that very thinness made it so you could carry miles of it on a spool no bigger than a coffee cup. Each diver would drag a slender strand of light behind him, like a spider spinning a web. Then when they got back to Flatbed, they'd hook up with their umbilicals and leave the network of fiber-optic thread behind them in the sub. It wasn't cheap, but it was cheaper than letting divers go off without being able to maintain contact. Their voices were clearer on F-O than any of their other underwater systems.

Almost as important, though, was the psychological effect. UQC could fade; you never felt more alone than when you heard other people's voices breaking up and finally fading out completely, while you were alone in the water, surrounded by darkness in every direction. But with the thread, you didn't have just their voices. You felt a physical connection, as if you were part of them and they were part of you.

Bud watched them go, trying to see if they did anything differently from the way he'd do it. In a minute or two he'd be going with his own men into another part of the sub. And even though Coffey had sent his men on the most dangerous and sensitive part of the job, that didn't mean Bud's divers were going to have a tea party. No matter that Coffey himself would be with them. Bud was still responsible for his crew. If there was anything to learn from watching, he had to learn it. Besides, the more eyes you had on a job, the safer it was. When you're wet and deep, you pay attention every second till the job is done.

Hippy glided Cab Three closer to the hatch area, making sure not to let his lights slide away from where they were needed. Finally he was as close as he could get without interfering with Monk's team.

Monk's voice came over the speaker. "Stand by on the ROV."

That was Hippy's job. He looked over his shoulder at Perry, who was in the lockout chamber at the back of Cab Three, babysitting Little Geek, which was hanging there over the hatch. There was water directly under it, like a miniature moonpool. The air pressure inside Cab Three held the water out.

"Perry, stand by on the ROV," said Hippy. He couldn't help thinking about all the potential radiation locked up in missiles inside the *Montana,* not to mention the hot fuel in the reactor. He was sending Little Geek into the jaws of hell. He reached back and patted the ROV's tough yellow hide. "Sorry about this, little buddy. Better you than me, know what I mean?"

Then Hippy nodded and Perry dropped Little Geek through the hatch into the water. Perry fed out a length of tether, but Hippy was already looking at the screen that gave him a Geek's-eye-view of the sub, steering Little Geek with the control box like a sluggish videogame, heading toward the *Montana*'s hatch. Little Geek would serve as a self-propelled flashlight and guardian angel all the way.

The SEALs took off the deck cover and started working on the outer hatch. It came free with little trouble, like a clam opening its jaw. No surprise in that. It was the inside hatch where, if there *were* any survivors, there'd be a radical pressure difference that would make the hatch hard to open. Monk swam down into the narrow escape trunk that connected the outer hatch with the inner one. He pressed his helmet against the inner hatch and banged on the metal with a wrench.

There was no quick hollow ringing the way there would be if there was air inside. Just the thunk, thunk that meant there was water at equal pressure on both sides of the hatch. Of course. Any hope of survivors had been foolish all along, they all knew that. Still. There were sometimes miracles, weren't there?

"It's flooded," Monk reported. He tucked the wrench into its clasp on his tool belt and took hold of the wheel on the hatch. "All right, I'm opening her up."

This time there was a little resistance—there was bound to be a tiny pressure difference on a hatch that fit this tight, if only because opening the hatch caused a slight enlargement of the interior space before the seal was broken. Like opening a refrigerator.

As soon as it was open, Monk pushed himself back out of the escape trunk and beckoned to Little Geek. Hippy saw him on his video monitor as if he was looking right out of Little Geek's eyes, and at once he maneuvered the ROV into the hatch. Hippy might be warm and dry in street clothes inside Cab Three, but he was still the first one into the sub. What did he care where his body was? When he was flying Little Geek, wherever the ROV went, that's where Hippy's soul was, living inside the machine.

Flatbed moved on, following Cab One along the hull. Lindsey had seen Coffey's charts of the sub's layout, but even without that she would have recognized the great hatches of the Trident missile tubes as they slid by under the front bubble of Cab One. They looked to her like the cages of silent wild animals, waiting in utter immobility until someone flung open the door. Then they would hurl themselves out, teeth bared, slavering, to lunge and tear at anything in their path.

Coffey, of course, was paying attention only to the job. "Looks like a couple of the hatches have sprung, but the radiation is nominal. The warheads must still be intact."

Yes, the wolves still have their teeth. "How many are there?" she asked.

"Twenty-four Trident missiles. Eight MIRVs per missile."

MIRVs—Multiple Independently-targeted Reentry Vehicles. Warheads that went up together but found their own way home. Eight times twenty-four. Sixteen times twelve. She'd done enough binary math at MIT that the number rolled right out. "That's a hundred and ninety-two warheads." This sub could fling its fires at a hundred and ninety-two cities. Probably every city over a hundred thousand in the Soviet Union, with a few left over for more creative targeting. "And how powerful are they?"

Coffey didn't answer. Coffey never did when he didn't think you had a reason to know the answer. So it was Schoenick, waiting with Monk outside the midships hatch, who said, "Your MIRV is a tactical nuke, a hundred and ten kilotons nominal yield. Say five times Hiroshima."

Pop, no Moscow. Pop, no Leningrad. Pop pop pop, no Kiev, no Volgograd, no cities left in Russia. "Jesus Christ, this is World War Three in a can."

Coffey shut it down right away. "Let's knock off the chatter, please." So Coffey didn't want anybody thinking about what these warheads *meant*. Lindsey wasn't surprised. The military male couldn't bring himself to think of the consequences of those missiles any more than the average teenage boy was capable of taking responsibility when his dick exploded on target. But if *these* went off, there wouldn't be anybody left to argue about paternity.

Hippy watched the video camera to make sure Little Geek didn't bump into anything, but he kept checking the radiation counter, too. This was like walking into Three Mile Island. He kept wincing as he passed through the heart of the *Montana*, heading for the engine room. As if through any door he might suddenly meet the monster he most feared.

Little Geek showed a screen full of pipes and machinery, for all the world like a grotto of stalactites and stalagmites. The engine room. Hippy hardly noticed. He had his eyes on the gauge.

"Getting a reading?" asked Monk.

"It's twitching but it's below the line you said was safe."

As far as Hippy was concerned, the only time radiation was *really* safe was when the gauge was still as a rock.

"Let's get in there," said Monk.

Sure. Right. It's your balls.

Wilhite and Schoenick followed Monk down into the escape trunk to the dark corridor beyond. From then on, Hippy alternated between leading and following. Inside a compartment, Monk would lead the way, directing Schoenick and Wilhite in their inscrutable tasks as Hippy held Little Geek like a narrow-beam lantern over their heads. Then, when it was time to move through a hatch into another room, Monk would beckon and Hippy would glide on ahead, flying Little Geek into the strange new territory. He was right down there with them, like a big brother who was stronger and tougher, leading the way into danger, then stepping back when he was sure it was safe, so the younger, weaker ones could pretend they were having an adventure. Just follow me and you'll be OK. Even if I might be leading you into hell.

As Cab One led them toward the bow of the sub, the real damage came into view. Above them was the trailing edge of the sail, big as a three-story building, looming overhead. Flatbed moved along the floor of the ledge where the sub rested, while the men on its back surveyed the ravaged metal where the *Montana* had hit, then scraped along the canyon wall.

There was an enormous break where the bow had nearly torn away from the rest of the sub. "Set it down right here," said Coffey. "There's a breach in the pressure hull. That's where we go in."

Not the kind of door a diver hoped to enter. Too many jagged metal edges where you could cut yourself or, even more dangerously, a hose. Too many snags to catch your pack or a hose and pull something loose. A careful diver plain wouldn't go in there. As the forty-year-old hat diver on Bud's first rig told him, there's old divers and there's bold divers, but there ain't no old, bold divers.

But Bud's people had worked salvage before. They knew

how to be careful in an unpredictable area. It was still a risk, and Bud didn't like it, but that's what the triple pay was for. "Let's go, guys," said Bud.

Coffey led the way into the narrow wound in the side of the sub; in the shadow of the lights from Flatbed and Cab One, it looked like a mouth, grinning malevolently. Bud, Catfish, Jammer, and Finler followed him.

Inside, it wasn't as scary—their lights dispelled the shadows. There were rows of bunks, twisted and disheveled. "This is the forward berthing compartment," said Coffey. He sounded impersonal—he was just noting their position on the charts, nothing more. But to Bud, this was a place where men had slept. The bedding hung from the bunks like the lolling tongues of dead dogs. Papers floated in the gentle eddying currents caused by the divers' movements. Letters that would never be answered. Paperback novels that would never be finished. Photos of girlfriends who would shed a few tears and then marry somebody else.

If they were tempted to linger, Coffey wouldn't let them. "This way," he insisted.

Bud knew that if *he* had been distracted by what they were seeing, so would Catfish and Jammer. "Take it slow and stay in sight," he told them. "Watch for hatches that could close on you, or any loose equipment that could fall." The last thing he needed was for them to get spooked. "We ain't pros at this. We got nothing to lose. Let's just take it easy."

"OK," said Catfish, "but it looks bad, chief."

They all knew the plan—get to the attack center, where Coffey had to find some top-secret stuff and get it out. They'd memorized the plans, but it was different when the lines on paper became corridors and companionways, hatches and bulkheads. Coffey swung up a companionway toward the attack center; the others followed behind him, pulling themselves up the railing of the stairs. Once sailors had slid down these steps with their feet hardly touching, most of their weight on their hands as they skidded down the rails. Now it was hand-over-hand up the railing, against the resistance of the water. The sub wasn't designed to be traversed this way. It was awkward, and the steps weren't much help.

The watertight door had buckled. It wouldn't open. "It's jammed," said Coffey. "Give me a hand."

Bud moved in to help. Even working together they couldn't budge it. They didn't have the leverage. "Jammer," said Bud. "Bring that pry bar over here."

Jammer and Bud squeezed in around Coffey. They could never have fit in that space if they'd all had to stand on the steps. But they were floating free, and so there was room. They felt rather than heard the vibration of the squealing hinges as they wrenched at the door; then it gave way, suddenly, flying open. The suction of the door's movement pulled something large through the door, right at them, like a huge animal that had been poised on the other side, waiting to pounce. Only it wasn't an animal. It slammed Jammer's shoulder, and when he turned to look at what had hit him, he found himself staring into the face of a young officer.

The ensign seemed unmarked, uninjured, but his eyes and mouth were open wide, as if he was surprised by his own mortality. Jammer froze there, staring. Bud and Catfish and Finler weren't much better off. It was Coffey who reached past Jammer and pushed the ensign's body out of the way.

"All right, we knew we were going to see this," said Coffey.

His words brought them back to their senses. His tone of voice shamed them a little, made them determined not to let this throw them. They followed him into the control room, but they were all a little dazed. Dad saw this all the time, thought Bud. He saw guys he knew get blown to bits. I can take this.

But it wasn't their being dead that was getting to him. Bud kept thinking of them drowning. He felt it like a pain in his chest. He knew what it felt like. His lungs had sucked water that time when he was a kid. Only when it happened to him, there'd been somebody there to pull him out, to press the water out of his chest and let him live again. These guys weren't so lucky. The ocean got them and they'd never breathe air again. Like Junior. Carried down to the bottom, pressed down by the heavy merciless hand of the sea.

There were a lot of bodies, and between the currents caused by the divers' movements and the way their lights kept moving, changing the patterns of shadows on the walls, it kept looking like the corpses were alive, waving, pleading for help or else gesturing mildly, a faint movement of an arm, as if they were conversing, inviting you to sit down for a minute, got something to tell you, don't go off like that, can't you see I want to talk to you?

Bud got control of himself. They had work to do, and they'd be no good if they kept looking at how dead people could get when they lost air this far down. Bud looked at the others. Right away he saw that Jammer's helmet was fogging up—he was breathing too fast. It'd be lousy if Jammer hyperventilated right now. You can't exactly give smelling salts to a guy who faints in a helmet. Somebody'd have to drag him out, watching all the time to make sure Jammer's breathing mix stayed connected and balanced. No good— Jammer had to snap out of it. "Hey, Jammer, you doing all right?"

Jammer made a show of nodding his head. Bud could hear over his F-O that his on-demand breathing apparatus was slowing down. The hyperventilation episode was over. Bud turned to the others—they weren't much better off. "How are you guys doing?"

"I'm all right," said Finler. "I'm dealing."

Catfish sounded kind of sheepish. "Triple time sounded like a lot of money, Bud. It ain't. I'm sorry."

This was no time for laying blame, even when it was well deserved. "Yeah, well, we're here," said Bud. "Let's get it done."

Bud moved from man to man, touching, making contact, reassuring them. He was sweating rivers inside his helmet, partly because he wasn't fully recovered himself from the shock of what they saw, partly because he knew how dangerous it would get if they didn't keep control.

* * *

Coffey didn't just stand there while Brigman got the civilians to stop wetting their pants over a few bodies. While men were alive you did all you could to keep them that way. But that was over. Dead was dead and there was work to do. The most important thing was to find the captain.

And there he was. Coffey turned him over, looked him in the face. I don't know what happened, he said silently, but if it was your fault, you died knowing that you killed your men, and that's punishment enough. At least you did your duty and got your position marker off. At least you made it possible for me to get here. That's something. You pulled something out.

So did Coffey. He reached into neck of the man's shirt and pulled out the chain that held the missile arming key. It was the power of nuclear war, right there in a little piece of metal; that's how much America trusted its boomer captains. The key was useless now—the safeguard systems aboard the sub would never be used. Coffey had to take the key so that there was no chance of it ever falling into enemy hands. He'd never use the key himself.

Yet still he knew the trust had passed to him. He held onto the key and gave it a hard yank. The captain would feel no pain now from the key coming off. But Coffey felt it like a pain himself, to have it. It was so light he could hardly tell he was holding it; it was so heavy that he could barely hang on. I've got the power to make one of these babies blow, thought Coffey. And if we get to Phase Three, I'll have to do it. That's something no boomer captain in history had ever had to do—actually *use* the key and set a warhead off.

Coffey stowed the key in the pouch at his belt. He'd trained almost as much in gloves as bare-handed—he had no problem manipulating even something as small as the key. He looked around—none of the civilians had seen him take it. Good. Fewer questions, fewer lies to tell. Yet he was vaguely disappointed, too. There should be some ceremony for the passing of this key. Like a scepter or a magic wand—it gives more power than any king or wizard ever had.

He saw that Brigman had his crew under control. The

man was good at what he did, and Coffey was able to rely on that. "Brigman, take your men and continue aft. Split into two teams. Let's get moving. We head back in fourteen minutes."

Brigman did it, just like that. The man knew when and how to take an order. Just like me, thought Coffey.

As soon as the civilians were out of the control center, Coffey went to the wall safe and, consulting the plastic card they'd given him back in Houston, he spun the dial until the safe door sprang open. Inside were several plastic binders. The code books. Except for a map of the location of all the nuclear subs, which was impossible to get since the Navy didn't even know, these binders were the things the Russians would most love to get their hands on. But now Coffey's hands were on it, which mean the Russians would never get it. America's security was safe in Coffey's hands.

He checked through the binders, making sure all the material was there. It was. He put the codebooks back into the safe. Then he took an underwater thermite grenade out of his pouch, pulled the pin, put it in the safe, and closed the door. He backed away. A moment later there was a flash. One danger eliminated. There were a lot more of them—electronic circuitry that Soviet hardware experts could translate or imitate. But then, Coffey had a lot of thermite grenades.

Bud led his men along the corridor until they came to a companionway leading down. Toward the missiles. It wasn't necessary for them all to go down there in order to check them out, and for safety it was better to leave men at the halfway point, in case something went wrong. Besides, they could make themselves useful, check out these compartments. "OK, Cat, Lew," said Bud. "I want you guys to stay on this level. Check it out. Me and Jammer are going down below."

"OK, you got it," said Catfish. There was no question that Catfish would be in charge when Bud was gone.

"I want you to be back here in ten minutes sharp." Bud

watched as Catfish and Finler checked their watches. Underwater, ten minutes meant ten minutes. This wasn't a bunch of kids promising to meet their mom somewhere at the mall.

"Ten minutes," said Catfish. "Okie-dokie."

And a last word of warning. "Be careful." As if the warning was necessary. What it really meant was, I care about you. Maybe it wasn't so different from a mom turning her kids loose at the mall, after all. Bud dropped down into the hole in the deck, using his hands to push himself feetfirst down the ladderway. Jammer came right after.

Bud had originally chosen Jammer to come with him because if something was wrong, some physical obstruction, Jammer was the biggest and strongest. But now he was glad to have him along because he wanted Jammer where he could keep an eye on him. Bud was still worried about how he'd responded to the bodies in the control room. Everybody was thrown a little, but Jammer had it the worst. Jammer was on the edge right now.

Bud led the way through a long, claustrophobically narrow corridor. There were more bodies, but now Bud was getting used to them. They didn't seem so *personal*. Just crumpled shapes in khaki or blue. They reached a hatch, undogged it, opened it up. Beyond it the space was so big their lights couldn't find any wall at all.

They went through into the darkness. Now, instead of walls, their lights struck forty-foot vertical tubes, extending up through three levels, divided by floors made of open steel grillwork. An ant's-eye-view of crayons inside a Crayola box.

"Where are we?" asked Jammer.

"Missile compartment," said Bud. "Those are the launch tubes." It worried Bud that Jammer had to ask. He'd been there when they were briefed. If Jammer was thinking straight, he would've known right off.

They swept their lights around the chamber. It was huge—a hundred and twenty feet long. But it was something small that caught their eye. Jammer's light fell across something moving, and so it drew his gaze. A seaman in coveralls was turning slowly in the eddying current. In Jammer's light, they watched as small albino crabs crawled slowly over the man's face. One crab scuttled out of his gaping mouth.

Jammer went bugfuck. "Lord God Almighty. Shit, aw shit, aw shit!" He turned away, as if he was trying to escape. Bud reached out, caught his arm, turned him back around, held him there helmet to helmet. Jammer couldn't hold still, couldn't stop clenching and unclenching his hands.

Bud asked him, "Hey, you OK?" but he sure as hell wasn't. Jammer was hyperventilating now, and from his face Bud guessed that he was close to puking. Vomit inside a helmet was worse than a mess. It could screw up the breathing system. It could kill.

"Deep and slow, big guy," Bud said. "Deep and slow. Just breathe easy."

"I—they're all dead, Bud. Everybody's dead."

Right, Jammer, but let's not add to the total. "I'm taking you back out," Bud said. It was the only sensible decision. If anything else happened, Jammer would surely panic. Better to get out now while Jammer could still do his own swimming.

But Jammer knew what that meant—part of the job aborted, Bud having to get him back to one of the Cabs, the Cab heading back to *Deepcore* prematurely. Somebody else having to come in here and do his share. A lot of extra work, all because Jammer lost control. "No no no! I'm OK." He didn't mean that he was *OK.* He only meant that he didn't have to go back right away. Jammer was no fool—he knew the danger. "I can't go any further in."

If Jammer had pretended he could go on, Bud would have known his judgment was shot, would have insisted on taking him back immediately. But because Jammer knew his limitations, Bud was pretty sure he could trust him to stay in place, not do anything that might lead him to panic again. "OK, Jammer, no problem. You stay right here, all right. I have to go down there to the end of this thing. We'll stay in voice contact. You'll be able to see my lights, right?" Like a father telling his kid not to be afraid of the dark because there was a nightlight plugged into the wall. But that was all right, that was what Jammer needed right now. When things started going wrong underwater, anybody could turn into a frightened child. There was a five-year-old inside everybody, just waiting to get scared out of hiding. "Just hold onto the rope," Bud said. "If you have any problems, tug on it twice, right? Five more minutes. Relax, OK?"

"Yeah, OK. OK."

Bud made his way farther in, checking the integrity of the launch tubes, paying out lifeline as he went.

Jammer felt like a shit-eating fool. Of course everybody'd been listening in. Everybody knew that it was Jammer who lost it, Jammer who couldn't take it. He knew that it might've happened to anybody, that they were always on edge down there, that you never know who's going to blow. But the fact was that it was him this time, calm cool Jammer, and even now he was still so jittery that it took real effort to breathe slow and steady. The worst thing was that Bud's lights weren't always visible. Sometimes he'd go behind something. And now he was just plain getting too far. This room was too big. It was possible to lose the lights at the far end of the room, if they were pointed the wrong way. Jammer clenched and unclenched his hands. It's OK. Bud's still there, I've got his tether. He'll be back, I've just lost him for a minute, at least I still have *my* lights, I can still see what's going on right here except I just don't want to look, that's all, I don't want to see—what I saw before. Just keep looking for Bud, for his lights, and—

Suddenly Jammer's own light faded. It didn't just blink off, it *faded* down to nothing, as if it was powered by a rat in a treadmill and the rat was slowing down for a rest. Trouble was, Jammer knew there was no way that could happen. A power *fade*, from batteries? And now he was alone in the darkness. This was not a good thing to happen. He knew he might panic. He knew he was on the edge. In fact, worrying about panicking might make him panic. This was just a bad thing to happen, really bad, a very bad thing to happen. "Bud? Bud! I just lost my lights! Bud, *Bud!* You reading me? *Bud?*" It was completely black all around him. He couldn't see anything. He was going to lose it, he knew that. He pictured an albino crab crawling on him; he could feel it, even though he knew it was just imagination. He imagined a crab inside his helmet, finding a way in somewhere and crawling across his faceplate.

No, he shouted silently, don't think about that. Don't think of the crab scuttling to the side of the faceplate and moving over onto your cheek. Don't think of it crawling across your face, trying to find your mouth, trying to crawl inside.

Bud's own lights were flickering, dimming—but not completely to black. It wasn't supposed to happen, he didn't understand it, didn't know if it was dangerous. But his first concern was Jammer—if this was happening to him, he could lose it all, right then, and if Bud's lights went out while Jammer was panicking, there'd be no help for it. "How you doing, Jammer? Are your lights dimming on you?" Keep it calm, make it sound like it's no problem.

But Jammer didn't hear Bud, and Bud didn't hear Jammer, because the power was down on their speaking systems, too, UQC and F-O alike. The explanation was simple enough. The builders pulled their energy from any ambient source, setting up highly conductive molecular chains to draw it in. They didn't think about it any more than we humans think about making our hearts beat or our stomachs digest. We know it's happening but since it's keeping us alive it doesn't occur to us that we might want to stop the process.

So as a builder came near to Jammer, by reflexively drawing from the ambient energy source it shut down most of the electrical functions of his suit. It didn't drain his batteries—that was potential energy, not actual electrical flow. But it did siphon off whatever current the batteries were putting out. She knew, of course, that humans were fragile at this depth, and that the current they were using was probably important to their survival, so as quickly as possible she slackened her own energy demands, trying to leave the human as much as she could. Enough that his lights still glowed dimly. Enough that his air regulator continued to function, though sluggishly. Not enough for their F-Os to send signals strong and clear enough to be made into words on the other end of the thread.

The builder hadn't gone to the *Montana* in order to meet with humans. As far as the builders knew, all the humans there were dead, their memories and bodies long since recorded. The city was working steadily, trying to decode human memory and comprehend the functions of the strange, fragile human body. Whatever they learned was immediately disseminated by direct memory transfer among all the builders in this city, and by messenger would soon be known in every city under the sea.

So this builder, like any other, knew that as the danger from human beings became steadily more serious, it became more and more urgent to make some kind of contact with the living creatures, not just with their abandoned dead. She was working on the nuclear warheads in the *Montana*, studying how they might be destroyed without being detonated, when she felt the warmth and movement and smells from human beings and their machines coming nearer, coming right into the sub. This might be important. She waited until two of them came directly into the same large chamber where she was working, waited until they separated, one remaining stationary, the other exploring further. Then she approached the stationary one, hoping to make contact, using what had been learned so far about the human body and mind.

Because she was not riding in a porter or performing a particular, specialized function, she appeared in her natural state; and because she was absorbing energy not only from Jammer's and Bud's batteries, but also from the nearby vehicles, she glowed brightly with the channels of energy flowing through her.

Jammer couldn't hear anything—he realized that along with the loss of his lights, his speaker was out. He wasn't hearing anything from the others, not even the chig-chig-chig of their regulators controlling the flow of oxygen. He was alone. The only thing he had left was the tether linking him with Bud. As his lights began to return, he tugged on the line. Urgently. Sharply. With all his strength. The line resisted so stubbornly that surely Bud had felt him—with all Jammer's pulling he might well be dragging Bud back toward him.

The taut line abruptly relaxed. Jammer rocked backward with the sudden release of tension. Then, as he recovered and pulled in the line, he saw that it had been severed only ten feet away. The tether must have caught on a snag, and his pulling had cut it. Probably cut Bud's F-O thread, too. Bud was completely alone down there. And Jammer was completely alone up here.

He looked all around in the darkness, trying to see Bud's helmet lamp, trying to see *something.* Hysteria was only a few quick breaths away. Then he became aware of a soft radiance flickering over the walls, over the launch tubes. He turned gratefully toward the source of the light. It was coming from under the steel grating of the deck. Bud must have gone down to the level below, and now that the tether was broken he was coming back. "Bud, is that you?" he asked.

Jammer shielded his eyes, staring into the source of the light. Something was wrong. It wasn't a pinpoint source, like Bud's headlamp. It was much larger, more general. And it was too big to be Bud, whatever it was. Oh, God, it wasn't Bud at all. It wasn't a person at all. It was glowing with light, it had huge, towering shoulders—or were they wings?—and the eyes were staring into him, right into his soul. It was coming for him. How did he know that? It was coming for him, it wanted him; the nearer it came, the more powerful the feeling of dread and loss that swept over him. Everybody was dead, everybody was going to die, this was the angel of death, it was coming to take him, to take everything out from inside of him, to crawl inside his head and eat his mind out like one of those crabs. Jammer screamed and turned away, gulping air, clawing hand over hand through the wreckage, trying to get away, trying to get up where Catfish and Finler were, up where this thing couldn't see him, couldn't crawl inside his head. Only he couldn't get away, he was caught on something, he was snagged—no, *it* had him; and now he banged his backpack against a wall, trying to get away. Then something went wrong with his breathing mix. He really was going to die. That thing, that angel of death, it had cut off his air, it was killing him, he was going to die, just like the sailors, just like the dead men floating all through this sub.

The builder tried to communicate. It sent invisible tendrils out into the water, reaching until they found the man. Then they swarmed over his suit, probing until they found an opening large enough to get through. Surface tension kept the water from breaking through, but these intelligently guided tendrils weren't blocked. In moments they were inside the man's helmet, into his ears and nostrils. The builder sent molecular codes along the tendrils, which duplicated them inside the man's brain, reordering the electrical patterns enough to give him back some of the memories they had taken out of the dead men on the *Montana.* This seemed to get the man's attention—he was standing, frozen, staring at the builder as she came nearer and nearer. She had no way of knowing that she was sending into Jammer's brain the point-of-death panic and despair that had filled a sailor's mind in the final moments of his life.

In the meantime, she tried sending the messages that the decoders in the city had thought might work in speaking to humans. A message of good intentions, explaining how the builders would try to speak to them, by introducing chemical messages into his brain. But all he seemed to do was breath more shallowly and rapidly, and then he opened his mouth and caused powerful high-pitched vibrations inside the vessel that enclosed his head. She did not understand. Apparently it was impossible to communicate with these creatures—or perhaps she had done it badly.

At least she could salvage something from the botched attempt at contact. She made a rapid scan of Jammer's brain-state, then quickly analyzed his body functions. This could be important, since Jammer was the first living human they had examined. At that moment he turned and ran, when he struggled to get free of a snag that caught at his pack harness, and finally when he broke loose and rammed his breathing regulator against the ceiling. She could tell at once that he was in a life-threatening condition, with bad air coming into the lungs, and it was all the worse because of his rapid, panicked breathing. Immediately she did what the city had suggested might have prolonged the lives of the men in the submarine—she introduced chemical changes in some of the molecules in his brain, causing him to drop immediately into a deep, relaxed sleep. It would last for several hours, causing much less stress on his body.

Despite her best efforts, the human had obviously misinterpreted her actions and had tried to flee. No doubt others would do the same until a new contact strategy—and, perhaps, a better contact vocabulary—was developed. So the best thing she could do at the moment was leave the sub until the humans were gone. This one human would be all right until the others came to restore his equipment to proper functioning. She could already feel the new currents and taste the stronger flavor in the water, clear signals that one of them was approaching. She sank back down into the depths of the sub, then linked with her porter and found her way out of the missile chamber.

Just as Bud got near to where he had left Jammer, his lights brightened again, and from Jammer's panicked gasping he could tell that his speaker was alive again—UQC instead of F-O, but it was good enough at this range. He spotted Jammer almost immediately, thrashing violently where he lay on the floor. A seizure. Something was wrong with his breathing mix. "Jammer!" he cried. "Jammer! Hang on!"

Bud knew he had to get to the regulator, find out what was wrong, but with Jammer casting his huge arms violently around him it was impossible to get in close enough. Then Catfish and Finler arrived, brought by Bud's cries on the UQC.

"He's convulsing!" cried Bud. Immediately they started grappling with the big man, trying to get him under control.

Catfish was the first to see a gauge clearly. "It's his mixture!" he shouted. "Too much oxygen."

It was Bud who got his hands on the controls. Finler and Catfish held onto Jammer while Bud tried to adjust the valve.

Finler shouted at him. *"Crank it down, man!"*

"Shit, it's stuck," said Bud. *"Goddammit!"*

"You're losing him! Have you got it? Have you got it?"

The control gave way, sluggishly. It still worked. "OK," said Bud as he cranked it down. "OK."

The moment the mix reached its proper level of oxygen, the seizure stopped. Jammer's body went slack. But he was definitely *not* OK. A seizure like that could cause permanent brain damage. Some guys ended up as vegetables, kept alive by machines, their brains turned off forever. And even if it hadn't done that much damage, Jammer wasn't going to be doing anything on his own for quite a while.

"Let's get him out of here," said Bud. "Come on! Move it! Move it! Move it!"

Coffey heard all this on the speaker in his helmet—or hat, as the civilian divers called it. He could tell that Brigman had it under control, that he was doing what had to be done. Coffey wouldn't have done it any differently—you get your man out alive, if you can. Protect your men first.

What worried Coffey was the way the speakers had gone dead for a while. The slight dimming of the lights. That was no failure of equipment—not when it happened to several men at once, not when all the equipment came back to full function at the same time. It scared him, right to the bone. If somebody had a weapon that could do *that,* could dampen their power supply from a distance, they were in deep shit. They'd be helpless against something like that. He imagined the same thing in the air—some American fighter pilot getting set to lock onto a MiG, and suddenly his power damps down, his computers blink, and when he fires his missile it goes anywhere, nowhere. All our advantage over the Russians was in high-tech stuff that absolutely depended on electrical current. If they could screw that up, then we had nothing to offset their huge advantage in raw force, brute quantity.

The question was, Were they down here? Had they noticed the increased activity at GITMO, guessed what was happening, and found some way to crawl in under the storm? Who knew what kind of secret weapons they might have? They could do anything, anything. How could Coffey deal with them if they were everywhere, if they could do anything they wanted?

Lindsey had spent the whole time cruising the length of the *Montana,* taking close-up videos so that the full extent of the damage could be assessed. Her pictures would be essential, she knew, in order to plan an eventual raising of the hulk. Probably the *Montana* would have to be raised in two sections, the nearly-broken-off bow and the main part of the boat.

Lindsey was nearing the bow when she heard some confusion over the speakers. Because she couldn't see what was happening, the voices made no sense. Somebody was in convulsions. Bad stuff, but she didn't know what was going on and so she couldn't take any useful action. She could hear Bud's voice among the others. "Bud, do you read? Bud?"

But the only answer she got was from One Night in Flatbed. "Do you see the divers? Are they out yet?" Which meant that One Night didn't know any more than she did.

Lindsey would have answered, but at that moment her lights went dim and her thrusters lost power. Cab One drifted in the water, no longer responding to her controls.

She tried to check the fuses and throw switches, but nothing helped. Then she saw something through the dome window that made her forget everything else for a moment. A bright light was making a corona around the *Montana*'s sail, and then from the light there emerged . . . something. Something laced with light and moving unbelievably fast through the water, right toward her.

And then it was past her, before she could comprehend its structure or even its size. Now it was only a dazzling light with something hard and glassy at its core. Magenta and purple, colors so dim they usually couldn't be seen more than a few feet underwater. She was seeing light of that color, dozens, hundreds of yards away from its source. Whatever it was, it was *bright*. Lindsey crammed her head into an awkward angle in the front bubble of Cab One, trying to follow it with her eyes. But in a moment it was too far off. There was nothing to see.

She knew—*knew*—that it wasn't made by any human hand. Wasn't designed by any human mind. She had caught only a glimpse of it, but she knew there was no material, no structure, no engine, no light-source ever conceived by the human mind that could do what this had done. Move so fast, drain Cab One's power, give off so much high-frequency light. This was something *new,* strange, impossible. Yet she had seen it with her own eyes.

As she strained to see it, Cab One bumped into the leading edge of the sail; her momentum was enough to slam her around inside. Silt rose up from the seafloor, obscuring her view. She should immediately check on hull integrity, buoyancy, make sure there was no damage—she knew that, but she couldn't take her eyes off the thing as it dropped away, down into the chasm.

Bud's voice came loud over the speaker. "Cab One! Cab One! Meet me at Flatbed. *This is a diver emergency!* Do you copy? Lindsey?"

Whatever it was, it had to wait. Diver emergencies came before everything. Even before visions and miracles. "Copy you, Bud. On my way." *If I can.*

She could. Now that the thing was gone, she had power again. Cab One responded normally, none the worse for a little bumping. She headed off through the water as fast as the submersible could take her. It had always seemed quite fast to her. But after the thing she had seen rush past her, it felt unbearably slow.

Chapter 9

International Incident

It took time to get Jammer out to Cab One, and more time to bring everyone back to *Deepcore*. Fortunately, they didn't have to waste much time on decompression—when you're already at sixty atmospheres, the few meters down from *Deepcore* to the *Montana* and the brief time the divers were there made little difference. A much harder problem was Jammer's size. He was big. He was heavy. Getting him out of his suit and into the infirmary took a lot of effort, especially considering how tired everyone was.

The infirmary was in the same trimodule as the mess and the lounge. Everybody hovered around outside as Monk and Bud examined Jammer, partly because they were worried, partly because this was where they normally went when they were off duty.

"What do you think?" Bud asked.

Monk refused to overpromise. "I'm a medic, which is mostly about patching holes." That wasn't strictly true, of course. He had trained exceptionally well in hyperbaric medicine because it intrigued him. He wasn't licensed to hang out a shingle as a doctor, but he had prepared himself well enough that the rest of the SEALs on his team could trust him to do the right thing.

So Monk knew that whatever caused the accident, the result was a coma from oxygen poisoning. He knew—and mentally reviewed—all the possible consequences. Jammer might stay unconscious for a few hours or days, and then come back to consciousness little the worse for wear—with no more brain damage than from a drunken weekend or a few hours at very high altitude. Or he might stay in a coma forever, or emerge from it hopelessly brain damaged. Or he might die.

However, since they had no way of knowing how long or how badly Jammer's regulator was improperly adjusted, Monk couldn't predict which of the possible outcomes might actually happen. He didn't want to promise anything. But it would be just as bad to put too bad a face on it and hurt morale among the other civilians. "This type of thing —there's not much I can do. The coma could last hours or days."

Monk looked at Brigman. How was he taking it? Hard to tell. Just stood there, looking down at Jammer. Monk tried to put himself in the same situation. Jammer had been teamed with Brigman; Brigman decided to separate. If Jammer suffered permanent consequences, Brigman would blame himself. I would, in his situation, thought Monk. But I'm not in his situation, so from the outside I can see the truth: Jammer was the one who panicked. Jammer was the one whose personal weakness had brought him to this. There was no blame in it. Jammer's systems malfunctioned and now his body would do its best to restore itself. They could keep him on I.V. so he didn't die of shock or thirst or hunger while he slept. It's out of my hands, out of your hands, out of everybody's hands.

But that doesn't change how you feel when it's your man Monk looked at Brigman and felt a little of his pain. He also felt: Thank God it isn't me.

Coffey debriefed everybody and made his report to DeMarco. The toughest part was what the Brigman woman told him. A vehicle of some kind, moving incredibly fast, giving off a lot of light, heading toward deeper water. How seriously was he supposed to take this? She seemed edgy as she told him. Reluctant to tell what she saw. Why? Because she didn't trust her own observations? Or because she did, but didn't think she'd be believed? Or was she holding something back?

One thing was certain—she was emotionally upset, and he was pretty sure it had nothing to do with Jammer. She didn't hover around him like the others. Instead she seemed distracted, off in her own thoughts. That was hardly a surprise. She wasn't exactly a loyal or compassionate person, as far as Coffey could tell—she was a loose cannon, always off in her own thoughts, working on her own projects, and to hell with anybody else's problems. But something about this *had* engaged her emotions. Because of that, he didn't know what to make of her report. Was she concealing something? Was she unreliable by her own estimation?

Certain or not, Coffey had to say *something* about it to DeMarco. The on-site commander, even if he was a couple of thousand feet up on the *Explorer,* had to know all the available information in order to make the best decisions. So Coffey had to sit there in front of the video and explain that some unidentified vehicle had been sighted near the sub at precisely the time a civilian diver panicked and nearly killed himself.

DeMarco was as confused about what to do with the information as Coffey. "Did any of *you* see it?" By which he meant, and Coffey understood, Did any of you SEALs, any of you trained observers, see it?

"No sir," said Coffey. "The Brigman woman saw it." DeMarco had met her topside. Let him reach his own conclusions about the reliability of the observer. But if she actually saw something—and the power *had* dimmed—then there could only be one nation with the technical capability to make such a vehicle and the political will to deploy it here without informing the U.S. "It could have been a Russian bogey," said Coffey. That was the primary danger right now—that the Russians might be competing for access to the sub.

"CINCLANTFLT's going to go apeshit," said DeMarco. "Two Russian attack subs, a *Tango* and a *Victor,* they've been tracked within fifty miles of here. And now we don't know where the hell they are."

Russian attack subs were known to piggyback submersibles in order to carry them unobserved into an area where they were needed for underwater operations. So they both knew the situation: There were Soviet attack subs in the area, a strange unidentified vehicle had possibly been sighted near the sub, and the Commander-in-Chief of the Atlantic Fleet—CINCLANTFLT—was very tense about the whole situation. No time for the *Glomar Explorer* to come and raise the sub at leisure.

"OK," said DeMarco. "I don't have any choice, I'm confirming you to go to Phase Two."

There it was. Coffey heard it. He had just been assigned to retrieve a nuclear warhead and arm it, so he'd be prepared at a moment's notice to set off the first nuclear weapon the U.S. had exploded outside of tests since Nagasaki. It was a bad assignment. Too many things could go wrong. And the worst possibility was that they'd have to go to Phase Three—set the detonator, then evacuate to a safe distance before the warhead went off.

In the middle of a hurricane a nuclear explosion probably wouldn't cause much damage to commercial shipping, since everybody was already in port if they could help it. But who was to say the Russians wouldn't regard it as a provocation, especially if they had a vehicle in the area that might be damaged? This was the kind of dangerous situation where things could fall in any direction. Yet there was no time or opportunity to ask for Washington to decide. The storm was coming too fast, the potential danger was too immediate. DeMarco had fulfilled the responsibility he was given to make the decision on-site if it seemed necessary to go to Phase Two. It wasn't Coffey's choice. But it was still Coffey's act to perform. His job to carry out flawlessly, with perfect judgment at every moment. And once he had accomplished

Phase Two, he'd have a live nuclear warhead in his possession, under his sole control. Not even the President had that.

DeMarco responded to Coffey's silence. "Is there a problem?"

"Yes." But that wasn't what Coffey meant to say, was it? What had he been thinking at that moment? Did he have some problem in mind? No, he was answering yes to the original order, that's all. "I mean, no sir. Negative, sir."

DeMarco stayed on the screen for a moment, perhaps to see if Coffey meant to modify his answer. Then he switched off. Coffey took a deep breath. As if he had just averted a serious problem. But he hadn't, he knew it. He now had about the biggest problem in the whole world on his shoulders.

One thing was certain. Phase Two could not be explained to the civilians. Hippy probably wasn't the only one who'd panic at the idea of being under the same ocean with a nuke. And none of these people had security clearance. Who could trust them if they knew there was a live warhead on board *Deepcore?* Who could guess where their loyalties lay?

There wasn't a space on *Deepcore* that couldn't be used for about five different things. So Lindsey was in the photo workstation—which also doubled as a maintenance room. The adjoining head was the only darkroom. It was pretty good, even if it was cramped. Light-tight, had a sink, and you didn't have to go very far to take a leak.

But Lindsey was pretty glum as she reassembled Cab One's camera housings. She had seen the way Coffey looked as he listened to her. It was obvious he didn't really trust her. For that matter, did she trust herself? She saw it, but she couldn't make much sense of it. She only knew that whatever she saw was *strange*. So strange that she, an engineer who had memorized every deep-sea structure ever made, didn't have the vocabulary to describe it.

She was as helpless as a layman trying to talk about a structure—"Why do you use those roundy things instead of triangles?" "What's that thingummy for?" Her descriptions were at the same level. "It was kind of round like an arched turbine, and it might have flexed in the water a little." Yeah, that'll get you an A in structural engineering. Hear that level of precision and you know they'll offer you a job designing airplanes, you can bet on it.

She could only describe what it wasn't. "It didn't seem to be propelled by backward thrust, like a rocket or a jet. But it didn't undulate enough to be swimming, and it was going so fast it could have been flying through air." Coffey had nodded wisely when she said that. She wondered if that was his private way of saying, Bullshit, ma'am. And then he starts talking about how maybe it's a new Russian submersible. Did he think she was so dumb she couldn't have seen for herself if it looked like a submersible craft?

And now here was Bud, giving her a second debriefing as he scanned through the rolls of developed film. It was obvious he thought the whole thing was kind of funny. "So you didn't get anything on the cameras," he said. There was a hundred thousand dollars worth of camera gear in Cab One, and her job at the *Montana* was to take pictures, nothing else—and yet she hadn't thought to take a single picture of the thing she saw.

"No," she explained again. "I didn't get a picture of it." Didn't Bud describe losing power himself? She couldn't have taken pictures if she'd tried.

But that's what bothered her most of all—that she hadn't tried. This thing she saw had so surprised her, unnerved her, that she hadn't remembered she *had* cameras until it was gone. She felt like an idiot.

Still, if Bud knew her at all, he'd know she wasn't hallucinating or exaggerating, he'd know she really saw what she said she saw.

"What about the video?" he asked.

"No." Of course, he didn't know her at all. That's why she was divorcing him, wasn't it? So it shouldn't bother her a bit that he wanted objective proof. She shouldn't take it so *personally.* "Look," she said to him. "I'd just really rather not talk about it."

"Well fine. Be that way." He stepped back by the dome

window where the stuffed Garfield hung on for dear life with his suction cups.

She could tell from his voice that he was a little bit disgusted with her. He was acting as if she was refusing to talk about it out of personal pique, because she didn't *feel* like talking. And because that was in fact part of her reason, she had to answer.

"Look, I don't *know* what I saw. OK?" How can I explain it to you when I don't understand it myself? Do you think I can turn a glimpse of something strange into a clear vision of something familiar, just by having you ask me more questions? If you want to turn it into something more familiar, do it yourself. "Coffey wants to call it a Russian submersible, that's fine. It's a Russian submersible. No problem."

She was trying to end the conversation without a conclusion. Bud wouldn't let her get away with it. He never did, if he could help it. "But you think it's something else. What? One of ours?"

"No." If it was American, I would have known it. Hell, I would have known who designed it, even if it was so top-secret nobody had seen it outside the military. I *know* this field.

"Well whose, then?" That was Bud. Always pushing too damn hard. Always insisting on knowing what *she* thought. Always wanting to get inside her head even when she didn't know what she was thinking herself. "Come on, Lins. Talk to me." How many times had she heard those words?

And yet this time she really did want to tell him. If only she knew anything to tell. All she could do was explain her own confusion. "Look, Jammer saw something down there, something that scared the hell out of him."

"His mixture got screwed up. Jammer panicked and he pranged his regulator."

That's right, Bud. You've got your explanation for what happened to Jammer and that's it, that's enough, even if your explanation is no better than saying, This guy's dead because his heart stopped beating, without bothering to find out *why* his heart stopped beating.

He had to see it her way this time. He had to realize how very strange this whole situation was. It was very important for Bud to understand that this was *not* a Russian submersible or anything else that made sense.

So she put the real question to him. "But what did he *see* that made him panic?"

Once again he threw it back at her. "What do *you* think he saw?"

And there it was. Should she tell him what she *really* thought? That whatever it was she saw, there was no trace of human thought or experience in its design? She didn't dare tell him that. He'd start muttering about HPNS getting to her, about pressure-induced hallucinations. So she had to fall back on what she had told Coffey.

Yet Bud was *not* Coffey, and so when she spoke, she couldn't help but put a little pleading in her voice. "I don't know. *I don't know! I* should, and I don't." Believe me, Bud, she was saying. Take me very seriously on this one.

Maybe he understood her. Maybe not. The hatch opened at that moment, and Hippy stuck his head into the room. "Hey, you guys. Hurry up, check this out. They're announcing it!"

The *Explorer* was piping the satellite TV signal down to them. It wasn't a rerun of "The Waltons." They were on the news.

To Bud it came as a relief. The secrecy lid was off. They might be alone at the bottom of the sea, but at least now the whole world knew they were down here. Of course, that meant that if they screwed up, the world would see that. But it also meant that nobody could do anything to them without it being noticed. That was what scared him most when Coffey started talking about Russian submersibles. If the Russians really could build something like what Lindsey described, what could stop them from destroying *Deepcore?* Now, though, under the glare of publicity, even the Russians would try to behave.

Everybody crammed around the topside-fed television in

the rec room, making noise and telling each other to be quiet.

"Quiet, quiet!"

"Turn it up, bozo."

It took Lindsey to shut them down and get them to listen.

". . . and the Kremlin continues to deny Russian involvement in the sinking of the Trident sub USS *Montana*. The Navy has not released the names of the hundred and fifty-six crew members, all of whom are presumed dead at this time."

Catfish reached out and started fiddling with the controls, trying to adjust the signal. He was taking his life in his hands, doing that. Everybody hates it when somebody starts fiddling with the TV in the middle of a story they want to see. Better to have a good-enough signal than to screw it up completely. So they practically jumped down his throat. "Leave it alone, 'Fish!"

"Civilian employees of an offshore drilling rig owned by Benthic Petroleum . . ."

"Hey, that's us!"

"Shhh!" They were like little kids, thought Bud, excited about seeing their hometown mentioned on the news.

". . . are apparently participating in the recovery operation but we have little information about their involvement. Bill Tyler is at the scene of the sinking now. Bill, there seems to be a massive naval presence out there already—"

"Bullshit! We want names!"

Right, boys. A hundred and fifty-six dead on the *Montana,* and you want your names mentioned on TV. Not that Bud was angry about it. You don't get angry at people for being human. It's just that he kept hoping that people would be just a little better than that, just a little less concerned about always being the center of the universe.

Well, if their names couldn't be mentioned, they got the next best thing. A helicopter shot of a lot of ships being tossed by dangerously high and irregular waves—and among them, wallowing in the water with far more stability than any of the others, a ship they recognized. "There's the *Explorer!*"

What caught Bud's attention was how many *other* ships there were. Down on the bottom of the Caribbean, Bud hadn't imagined anything more up top than the *Explorer*, tethered to *Deepcore*'s umbilical, and a lot of wind and water. Now he realized that on the ceiling of the sea the Navy was scooting around like bathtub toys. Doing what? There was a *hurricane* coming, didn't they know that? Ships didn't belong out there in such waters.

And if Bud knew that, the Navy surely knew it. So they must be really scared of the Russians, if they felt a need to keep an escort for the *Explorer* in seas like this.

The reporter made it clear that the situation was even worse than it appeared. "With Cuba only eighty miles away, the massive buildup of U.S. ships and aircraft in the area has drawn official protest from Havana and Moscow and has led to a redirection of Soviet warships into the Caribbean theater."

Bud could feel the mood in the control room change. No more we're-on-TV excitement. Soviet warships in the Caribbean. What bothered Bud was the way it seemed to be cycling upward. The Navy gets scared that the Russians might move in on the *Montana,* so they bring a large escort to protect the site. Then the Russians see our big military force building up, and so they move in on the *Montana.* As if the fear itself caused the thing they feared to come true.

The anchor asked the standard asinine follow-up question, so it would sound like he was doing something more important than just reading the news off a prompter. "Bill, how would you describe the mood there?"

"The mood is one of suspicion, even confrontation. A number of Russian and Cuban trawlers, undoubtedly surveillance vessels, have been circling within a few miles throughout the day, and Soviet aircraft have repeatedly been warned away from the area."

It was like an anthill up there. The red ants and the black ants. It made Bud feel a little bit better on the bottom of the sea. For all he knew, this might be the safest place on Earth right now.

When the broadcast ended, Bud and Lindsey headed

toward the moonpool. If the news broadcast had shown Bud anything, it was the fact that the *Explorer* couldn't stay above them much longer. There was no hope of the storm passing far enough away that they could stay connected. It was time to see if One Night had got Flatbed prepped to go out and disconnect the umbilical so the *Explorer* could leave.

He didn't even have to tell Lindsey where he was headed. She knew what had to be done as surely as he did. For a moment it felt like the old days when they could work together almost without talking, because they understood each other and *Deepcore* so perfectly.

Only this time Hippy tagged along. He was agitated, almost frantic in his tone of voice, his gestures. Bud had seen Hippy in this mood before. Things are going wrong, Do something! Do something! The solution was usually for Bud to give Hippy an assignment. When Hippy actually had something to do, something that required his concentration, then he calmed down, he did the job. But what was there for Hippy to do right now?

Still, Bud had to get him calmed down somehow.

"This *really* sucks!" said Hippy.

There was only one thing to do: Let him have his say. Bud stopped, turned back in the corridor, faced Hippy. "Hippy, what's the matter with you?"

"What's the matter with me? Now we're right in the middle of this big-time international incident. Like the Cuban Missile Crisis or something."

Bud was listening patiently, but Lindsey didn't catch on to what he was trying to do. She so rarely did. So instead of encouraging Hippy to talk it out, she tried to shut him down with ridicule. "Figured that out for yourself, did you?" she said.

Smooth, Lindsey. You should give a Dale Carnegie course.

All Lindsey accomplished was to make Hippy even more agitated. "We got Russian subs creeping around. Shit! Something goes wrong, they could say anything happened down here, man. Give our folks medals."

Yes, I know exactly what you mean. I thought of it myself. "Hippy, just relax." Bud tried to make a joke out of it. Pointing at Lindsey, he said, "You're making the women nervous."

"Cute, Virgil," said Lindsey.

The distraction calmed him a little. Hippy was winding down. From a whine to a mumble. "Those SEALs aren't telling us squat. Something's going on."

"Hippy, you think everything's a conspiracy." Bud walked away, taking Lindsey with him.

Behind them, Hippy tried to figure out why Bud would bother to say something so obviously true. "Everything *is,*" he said.

Maybe so, thought Bud. Can you call it paranoia if everybody really is out to get you?

No sooner had they left Hippy behind than One Night came pounding down the corridor from the sub bay. It was a bad sign.

"Hurry up!" One Night shouted. "Coffey's splitting with Flatbed! He got me to show him the controls and he's out of here!"

This was a little more serious than a kid taking off with the family car. Before she finished talking Bud was already past her, running toward the moonpool. "Goddammit!" he said as he ran. "Didn't you tell him we need it *right now?*"

"Yeah, but he wouldn't listen to me. I told him we had to get the umbilical unhooked ASAP."

It was the most nonsensical thing he'd ever heard of. Coffey was supposed to be a smart guy. The umbilical couldn't be uncoupled at the top end; it had to be done here, at *Deepcore.* Did Coffey think he could accomplish the rest of his mission if the *Explorer* sank or got damaged? Or worse—what if the umbilical got damaged while they waited for him to come back? Did he think they were going to find a spare in one of the neighboring countries? You don't go shopping for specialized equipment like that in Haiti or Honduras. "Where the hell is he going?"

"I have no idea," said One Night. "You told us to cooperate with him."

Yeah, that's right. And it should have been OK. How could I know he had his head up his ass?

When Bud got to the moonpool, Wilhite, Monk, and Schoenick were standing on Flatbed in full gear as Coffey piloted it down. They were facing Bud as he ran into the room. He screamed at the top of his voice, knowing they could probably hear him. "We need the big arm to unhook the umbilical. There's a goddamn hurricane coming."

In the meantime, Lindsey had grabbed a headset. "Coffey, Coffey, do you copy?"

The SEALs' heads disappeared under the water. No answer came over the speakers. No explanation. Nothing. Just the dumbest, most dangerous, most irresponsible kind of behavior Bud had ever seen in all his years of work on oil rigs—landside, over the water, or under it. He turned away from the moonpool. "Son of a bitch," he said. Softly. Like a benediction. "Unbelievable." I knew I should never have let them come onto *Deepcore*.

He looked at Lindsey, waiting for her to say the same thing. Waiting for her to say, Didn't I tell you not to let the military take over? Didn't I tell you they didn't give a shit about the safety of the rig or the crew?

But she didn't say it. Maybe because she knew she didn't have to. Maybe because she knew that when Bud was *really* wrong, nobody had to stick it to him because he already stuck it to himself so bad.

McBride gripped the handrail as he looked out over the deck of the *Explorer*. There were still men scurrying around in lifejackets, trying to keep things secure in the storm. But it was clear that this storm was far too big to deal with. The *Explorer* was designed to cut and run when it got this bad. Even now he wasn't sure they could get out of the way of Hurricane Frederick without sustaining major damage. The wind was eighty knots. The Hurricane Center was telling them about the possibility of two-hundred-knot winds near the eye. Which was heading for them as directly as if they had hooked it on a fishing line and were reeling it in.

McBride staggered across the heaving deck and pulled

himself back into the *Explorer*'s command center. There was DeMarco, standing around as if he had all the time in the world. Surely he couldn't be so stupid as not to know the danger they were in. Most of the Navy escort was standing much farther off now, for fear of ships getting tossed into each other by waves and wind. "We need to get unhooked and get out of here now!"

DeMarco looked at him with no expression. "All right, then, do it." Somebody handed DeMarco a foil-wrapped sandwich. He was going to have lunch. Perfect. Next thing he'd say would be, Let them eat cake.

But McBride had to make damn sure DeMarco knew where the responsibility lay. "No problem except your boys go sightseeing in Flatbed when my people need Flatbed to get unhooked on their end."

DeMarco unwrapped his lunch. "They'll be back in two hours." Then he brought the sandwich up to his mouth and took a bite.

"Two hours? We're gonna get the shit kicked out of us by our pal Fred in two hours!"

It was no use trying to get DeMarco interested in their problems. He just stood there, calmly chewing, looking out over the Caribbean as if there were anything to see out there besides hell.

The SEALs opened one of the missile hatches. It took a few minutes, but Coffey got the hang of controlling Flatbed's arm well enough to help them hoist the plastic diaphragm out of the way. And then there it was, the blunt nose of the Trident C-4 missile. Like looking down the barrel of a gun at the bullet aimed right at you.

Only the bullet would never get fired. The missile would never launch. The only useful things inside were the MIRV warheads, short metal cones with the power of a small star locked inside. If any of them went off right now, Coffey thought, all the water for miles around would be vaporized, instantly. It would rise up at once and make a bubble on the surface, which would instantly pop, releasing poison into the atmosphere. Not that much water, really, compared to the amount there was in the whole ocean. Just a little belch in the sea. Along with a shock wave like an underwater earthquake.

Trouble was, this was no longer speculative information in a training session on land. This was real. He, Coffey, was going to arm a warhead so it *could* happen.

They lifted away the nose cone, exposing the warheads. Monk read off the instructions from the plasticized card he had been given in Houston by a man who acted as reluctant as if the card were his only child. Schoenick and Wilhite followed each command as he read it; Monk watched to make sure they were doing it correctly.

"Separation sequencer disconnected," said Wilhite. "Next?"

"Remove explosive bolts one through six in counterclockwise sequence."

"Check," said Schoenick. "Removing bolt one."

Coffey looked down through Flatbed's window at his men working on the missile. He felt the same flat sense of inevitability that he had felt long before, standing halfway up a flight of stairs in an apartment building in Los Angeles, holding a cinder block, waiting for Darrel Woodward to come home. It's going to happen. Wait. Wait. Maybe he'll come, maybe he won't. Wait.

Not far off, a builder hovered in the water. She was watching, but not with her eyes; light was not that helpful here. Instead she used other senses. Tendrils she had spun out of her embraced Flatbed, the *Montana,* the SEALs, and the missile in an invisible web, each strand only molecules thick; next to these, the threads of the fiber-optic communications system seemed thick and clumsy. With these she tasted and touched to discover what was happening.

The humans were opening the missile and removing the death inside. It might be a good sign. But then, it might not. Who could understand these creatures who allowed each others' precious memories to perish when their bodies died, who fought against death with terrible fury, but made weapons that could shatter all their works and lay waste an entire planet?

Still, the city had been studying. The fleeting contact with Jammer's living brain had given them a great deal of information on how to interpret the memories of the dead they had taken from the *Montana*. They had figured out how to translate radio broadcasts into sound and television signals into pictures. They had even decoded human languages, after a fashion. Now, though, they were finally able to make sense out of our actions and our words. By seeing how our brains worked, what we remembered, how it felt to be human, words that had been empty code-patterns to them suddenly took on meaning. Decades-old broadcasts that had lain dormant in the city's spires of memory were now being examined in a frenzy of activity. The builders had shut down almost all activity except the effort to comprehend what these strange creatures meant by the incomprehensible things they did.

Long before they understood our languages, they had developed a label for us, a way to think of us, in their own wordless communications. They thought of all nonbuilders, whatever their species, as *forgetters*—the equivalent of our concept of *animal,* creatures that move as if with purpose but are not capable of real thought. Until the *Montana,* we had belonged in that category in their minds. Now, though, they knew we were rememberers like them, though our memories were cut tragically short by one of the morbid accidents of biology. So to distinguish us from themselves and from the forgetters, they thought of us as *those-who-kill-each-other-on-purpose.*

In the meantime, the city gathered more and more heat out of the waters of the Caribbean till it warmed the sea directly under Hurricane Frederick, as well as the water in front of the storm. The radiating warmth heated the air above it, steadily lowering the air pressure inside the hurricane. Eventually it would surpass all previous records. Frederick was a controlled storm; with the builders herding it toward *Deepcore,* it was going to be the worst hurricane in history.

There was no malice in this. The builders were going to probe *Deepcore* in an effort to gather information about these air-breathers. Though *Deepcore* was at the lower limits of survival for human beings, it was near the upper limits for builders who were not safely locked within a porter's body. They were genetically reshaping several porters into a probe that could survive in the breathing mixture that filled *Deepcore.* But in order to take it up to the dangerously thin seawater at two thousand feet, the builders themselves would be exposed. Vulnerable. Therefore they had to be sure that *Deepcore* was alone. Hurricane Frederick would sweep the sea above them and keep it clear until they had learned from *Deepcore*'s crew all that could be learned.

On the outer edges of the storm, Russian warships and gunboats probed the U.S. Navy's formations. They played with each other like children. Tag. Chicken. Frighten the other guy. See how resolute he is. See what he's capable of doing.

What the U.S. missile cruiser *Appleton* was not capable of doing was avoiding a collision with a much smaller Soviet destroyer. They never saw each other until the last moment, but each certainly knew, from radar and intercepted radio communications, that the other was nearby. Even when the destroyer came in view, the captain of the *Appleton* tried to steer away, and thought he had succeeded. But the *Appleton* heeled over in a monstrous wave; another wave, coming at a different angle in the chaotic sea, tossed the destroyer in its path.

The *Appleton* was crippled, but the Soviet ship was mortally hurt. She was taking on water rapidly, and burning savagely above the waterline, in spite of the heavy rain. It took only a few minutes for the destroyer to founder and sink.

Even before the crew of the *Appleton* had finished assessing its own damage, they were radioing for help in rescuing survivors of the Soviet ship. But there were only a few men plucked out of the violent sea, and all of them were rescued in the first few minutes by American sailors in rafts, or by climbing up swaying rope ladders dropped down the sides of American ships.

In calmer times this would have been an enormously dangerous incident, more so than the shooting down of the Korean Airlines jet, since this involved military forces on both sides. But this collision happened while both sides were already viewing each other with fear and suspicion.

The Russians were trying to figure out why their new sub-tracking satellite had blown up less than an hour after it became operational; if the Americans did it, how did they know what it was, and how did they kill it without the Russians detecting a launch? Now the Americans, claiming a submarine had been sunk, were gathering a fleet off the southwest coast of Cuba. The link between a "lost" submarine and a lost sub-tracking satellite could not be pure coincidence, could it? Were the Americans searching for an excuse to invade Cuba and test the Russians' will *now,* before they could launch another sub-tracker and neutralize the American strategic force?

There were just as many questions on the American side. Why did the new Soviet satellite explode? Was it linked with the loss, only a few minutes later, of the *Montana?* Why were the Russians moving such a large fleet into the area of the lost sub? What was the strange, incredibly fast submersible craft that had been reported by the SEALs working to secure the wreck of the *Montana?* Were the Russians trying to provoke the U.S. into actions that would give them an excuse to launch a first strike?

In this climate the collision did not look like an accident to anyone but the captains of the *Appleton* and the Soviet destroyer. The destroyer's captain was dead. Captain Sweeney of the *Appleton* reported accurately to the Navy, but the Navy doubted his assessment of Soviet intentions, and the Russians flat out called him a liar. The official Soviet statement denounced the collision as an unprovoked attack. Soviet negotiators walked out of the START talks.

The Soviet Army raised the level of readiness of their troops in Europe.

U.S. satellites took photos showing that every Russian warship that could move was steaming out of port; there seemed to be unusual activity at ICBM launch sites as well. The President had no choice but to reciprocate, sending all American bombers into the air and all American ships out to sea. In short, U.S. readiness was now raised to DefCon 3.

Neither side could understand the actions of the other. It did not occur to them that a third party might be involved. Instead they were forced to interpret all events as if the ones they did not cause themselves were caused by the other side. In the mind of every man and woman in either government who was involved at all, there came a question that had not been asked since 1963:

Is this it? Is this finally it?

While they waited for the SEALs to get back with Flatbed, there was nothing for the crew of *Deepcore* to do but wait and watch with increasing horror the television news reports being piped down the umbilical from the *Explorer*.

"Bud, this is big time," said Lindsey.

It was on every channel. The TV newspeople were doing man-on-the-street interviews. Nobody seemed to know how to take the news. Hadn't things seemed like they were getting *better* these past few years? Everybody expected this back in the bomb-shelter fifties—even in the sixties and seventies. But ever since Gorbachev came to power and presented a new Soviet face to the world, everybody had felt safer, had given a sigh of relief and started counting on things going on the same way forever. How could they snatch it away now?

Some people sounded outraged, betrayed; others laughed —it's a joke, right? Still others nodded wisely—we knew it all along. Others were angry—if they sank our sub, then they deserved to lose a ship of their own. And some almost wept with fear. What can we do? What can anyone do?

Out in space, builders were intercepting and recording the same broadcasts—and the military transmissions as well.

One after another they rode their gliders down to the sea, reporting to every city of builders that those-who-kill-each-other-on-purpose seemed to be getting ready to act out their name on a massive scale.

Finally, Flatbed came back. Immediately Bud gathered the crew into the moonpool. The broadcasts had sobered them—their rage at Coffey was long since swallowed up in their fear for the world above them. Besides, there was no time for recriminations—they could chew Coffey's ass later, topside, back home, if there was any home to go back to by then. In the meantime, even if everything went perfectly from now on, they'd still have three weeks with these guys decompressing. Bud knew he had to keep things cool.

So when Flatbed rose up out of the water, three SEALs standing on its back like statues from a dark undersea pantheon, Bud and the crew meant to be nothing but efficient and helpful. Lindsey stood there looking on like the face of a vengeful god, but even she recognized that there was nothing to be gained by recrimination.

As soon as Flatbed was on the surface, they sprang to life. Bud gave the command. "Let's get their gear off and clear the sub. We've got to get out of here." The sooner they got the SEALs off Flatbed, the sooner they could get out to the umbilical connector at the top of *Deepcore* and cast off from the *Explorer.*

The SEALs, for their part, offered neither apology nor explanation. Their mission had been accomplished; they had every reason, now, to cooperate with the crew in *theirs.*

Except in one area. Hippy started to untie a conical object wrapped in one of the SEALs gear bags. Coffey saw him as he emerged from *Deepcore*'s hatch. "Don't touch that," he said sharply. "Back away."

"Excuse—moi, said Hippy. He raised his hands as if to say, I'm not touching anything. But he didn't take his eyes off the bag. Coffey couldn't have done a better job of telling him there was something *very important* in that bag if he had put up a sign. And right now, with the world upstairs in chaos, Hippy knew that whatever was in that bag, it was not going to be good for anybody, least of all for him. Hippy wasn't a believer in the maxim that curiosity kills the cat. What I don't know will almost certainly kill me, thought Hippy. Nothing in his life had given him the slightest reason to believe otherwise.

Coffey and the other SEALs unlashed the gear bag and hefted it carefully, gingerly; even though it was obviously quite heavy, it must also be fragile. One Night was already at Flatbed's controls, ready to go, waiting for them to get off. Bud urged them on. "Coffey, we're a little pressed for time." It was the closest he would let himself come to reaming Coffey out for risking all their lives and the lives of all the people on the *Explorer*.

Finally the SEALs were clear. Bud leaned down over Flatbed's hatch, where One Night was checking out the controls, making sure everything was working right. "This ain't no drill, slick," he said. "Make me proud."

He meant it—and she took it—as encouragement. Nobody had ever had a faster time than One Night at attaching and unhooking the umbilical during training. "Piece o' cake, baby."

Bud dropped and sealed the hatch, then stepped away as Flatbed slowly sank into the moonpool. Intellectually, Bud was aware that One Night was descending at the fastest possible rate. That didn't stop him from muttering under his breath to hurry up, goddammit, hurry up.

One Night hurried. But moving through water was always slow, and at this depth there was a limit to how fast anything could go. Except whatever it was that Lindsey said she saw. No, *saw*. Lindsey might be the queen bitch of the universe, but she didn't go making stuff up. Nor had One Night ever known her to exaggerate. So maybe there *was* something that could go fast through two thousand feet of water. One Night only wished it was her.

She went all the way under *Deepcore* and around the outside, and finally reached the umbilical connection at the top of the A-frame. It was a big structure, sturdy-looking as a railroad bridge; the umbilical looked kind of little and weak by comparison—but One Night knew that the umbili-

cal was as tough as they could make it. The umbilical still
had some slack, but it was moving, swaying. There were no
currents at this depth—the movement was carried down
from the surface, where the waves must be real bad by now.
Hold on just a minute longer, boys of the *Benthic Explorer*.
One Night is here to ease your pain.

She got into position and hovered, then deployed the big
hydraulic arm. It unfolded from Flatbed like a huge steel
spider leg; One Night opened its gripper like a claw. She felt
the strength of the thing like her own fingers, her own arm. *I
am God when I've got this thing, I am the finger of the Lord.*

Only the umbilical wouldn't hold still long enough to get a
firm grip on it. "Goddammit." She tried again. "Son of a
bitch." The arm wasn't designed to catch a moving target.

The swaying that was giving One Night such a hard time
was a symptom of much more serious problems topside.
The crane that suspended the umbilical over the launch well
was so massive that it looked too big for the ship; if the
Explorer's center of gravity had not been so deep in the
water, the crane would have made the ship top-heavy and
unmanageable. It had to be that large to deal with the weight
and drag of the umbilical, which weighed about sixty
pounds per linear foot. Even so, it was not designed to
withstand infinite stress—nothing is—and it certainly
wasn't supposed to have to deal with more than slight
sideways and vertical movement. Much of the stress was
supposed to be borne elsewhere.

For instance, the dynamic positioning system was supposed to keep the *Explorer* in place horizontally. Like
positioning rockets on spacecraft, the side-mounted thrusters gouted jets of water to keep the ship from drifting in any
direction. Because there are no landmarks at sea, the
computers controlling the positioning system marked the
ship's position by constantly checking with satellites. The
Explorer could normally hold its position within a few feet
over a given spot on the ocean bottom.

As for vertical movement, caused by the up-and-down of
waves, that was taken care of by the heave compensator, a

huge rack of pulleys, cables, hydraulic pistons, and sliding counterweights hanging from the crane directly over the launch well. It served to keep just the right amount of slack in the umbilical, despite the vertical motion of the sea.

So the crane was not supposed to have to handle much in the way of horizontal and vertical movement. It was simply supposed to bear weight. Unfortunately, as Hurricane Frederick approached, the waves got too big. The vertical movement was too large, too rapid for the motion compensators, and the *Explorer*'s violent shifts across the surface were more than the thrusters could handle. It wasn't any flaw in the system's design. The system was designed for the *Explorer* to cut loose and get the hell out hours before the seas got this bad.

The only reason the umbilical connection had held out this long was because Lindsey had designed everything to withstand far more pressure than the project specifications. But now the stress was so far out of line that something had to give.

The first thing to fail was a pair of tunnel thrusters. Its motors overloaded from the strain of trying to fight sixty-foot waves and eighty-knot winds with gusts of double that force.

Up on the bridge, Bendix watched with fatalistic calm as the worst storm he'd ever seen tortured the sweetest ship he'd ever sailed. A sudden violent lurch threw him against the control panel; others all over the control room stumbled and, if they didn't have a tight enough hold, fell.

Bendix knew at once what was happening. The motion compensators weren't coping. "We've got a problem." The only question was which thruster was going to fail first. "We're losing number two thruster. Bearing's going."

It was already showing up in the ship's position. Everyone could feel the sideways movement. A warning klaxon went off—part of the alert system. Everybody was already alert. There was simply nothing they could do. "It's not holding," Bendix shouted over the noise of the horn. "We're sliding out of position!"

As the ship slewed, the umbilical was pulled taut and

drawn off its vertical position. It was pulled against the side of the launch well, tight as a bowstring against the nock of the arrow. As it screeched along the edge, tearing loose ladders and floats, Bendix expected at any moment to see it tear through right at that contact point. It was tougher than he expected. Too bad—if something had to go, that was the least dangerous spot to have it happen.

Down below, One Night finally had a firm grip on the umbilical's decoupling mechanism. It was going to happen, just another couple of minutes at the most and she'd get it free.

Then the umbilical went taut with such force that it jerked the whole mechanism, the whole A-frame. It dislodged Flatbed's arm and threw One Night forward, then back. For a moment she lost control. Then she grabbed the controls and jinked Flatbed out of the way as the umbilical moved toward her, dragging the A-frame with it. One Night pivoted. There was no way to get in and disconnect the umbilical now. The whole rig was moving.

Inside *Deepcore,* Lindsey was standing in the corridor, sipping at a cup of hot tea, when the whole rig boomed like a gong and lurched sideways. The tea splashed all over her. Bud was already tearing through a doorway, pounding past her, heading for the control room. Hippy's voice came over the intercom, telling them all what they already knew. "Bud to control! Emergency! Bud to control!"

As Bud clawed his way up the ladder to level two, the rig boomed again, as if the whole thing were a musical instrument—which it was, with one long, tight string and *Deepcore* at the bottom of it serving as a resonance chamber. A great big washtub bass. Only the rig wasn't going to sit still and play music. The rig didn't stop lurching, bouncing.

It was almost impossible to keep his footing as Bud struggled through the corridors. He kept getting tossed against the walls, the floor. Worst damn earthquake he'd ever been in. He had a dozen new bruises that hurt like stab wounds when he finally got to the control room. His pain didn't matter—dying would feel a hell of a lot worse. He ran in, past Hippy, and grabbed the mike.

"Topside, topside! Pay out some slack, we're getting dragged!" Bud knew that things must be terrible up top, for the motion compensators to give way like this. They could have disconnected any time in the last two hours and this wouldn't be happening. Any damn time, but now it was too late.

Lindsey joined him in the control room. Together they looked out the front viewport. *Deepcore* wasn't bumping into the seafloor now, because the bottom was sloping lower. And lower. They both saw it; Lindsey said it. "We're heading right for the drop-off."

McBride tried to give Bud what he was asking for. He ran to the window and looked down at the crane shack, where Byron was squinting up through the cab window, trying to see what was going on through the driving rain. "Byron, down on number one winch! *Down on one!* Pay out some umbilical. Now! *Now!*"

Byron tapped on his headset to signal McBride that he couldn't hear. It wouldn't have mattered if he had. It was already too late.

At that moment, down on the bottom, *Deepcore* was dragged into a collision with an outcropping of rock. For an instant *Deepcore* stopped moving and the *Explorer* didn't. It was more strain than the connection could bear—something had to go. It wasn't the umbilical. It wasn't the connection with *Deepcore*. Lindsey had designed them to be too strong. It was the crane supporting the umbilical that gave way. The heave compensator bottomed out, its stabilizing cables snapping like guitar strings.

Byron saw the broken end of a cable coming at him, just in time to duck as it smashed the window of the cab. Crumbs of safety glass showered over him. He could feel the cab, the whole crane assembly tipping. He clawed for the door, but there was no time to get out.

McBride watched in horror from the bridge as the next

heave from the waves tore at the crane. It tilted, bent, twisted, as all forty tons of it toppled into the launch well with a roar of tortured steel that was louder than the storm. Water exploded upward as the crane fell in. It broke away clean—no part of it was still attached, dangling from the ship. Byron had been carried down in the cab; he was on his way to the bottom, beyond all hope of rescue. The pressure would probably kill him before he had time to drown.

How long would it take for the crane to strike bottom? It would get there far too soon for *Deepcore* to get out of the way. But at least with warning they might be able to prepare for the crash. McBride could warn them on his headset—with the umbilical severed, the direct line was gone. He turned away from the window. "Get them on the UQC!" he ordered. He held the underwater telephone to his ear. "Bud! We've lost the crane!"

Down below, Bud wasn't getting it. "What? Say again."

McBride struggled to make himself heard over the backup system. "The crane! We've lost the crane! It's on its way down to you!"

And that was it. There was nothing more the *Explorer* could do. Either the crane would hit *Deepcore*, completely destroying it and killing everybody aboard, or it wouldn't. And if it didn't, there was still nothing the *Explorer* could do until the storm cleared out. They were on their own down there.

Even though there was no more umbilical, McBride gave orders to stay in place over *Deepcore,* as far as that was possible. If they strayed too much, the UQC would go out of range, and they wouldn't know what happened. But with one set of thrusters out, the heavy seas were too much. The *Explorer* was drifting away from the site. The *Explorer* tried to reestablish UQC contact with *Deepcore,* but there was no answer from below. Again and again, answered only by silence, until it became obvious that either they were out of range or there was no one down there to answer them.

McBride stopped trying to make contact, then waited a few moments for the truth to dawn on everyone else. In his helplessness he had to lash out, had to do *something.* And for once the person who was actually responsible for all of this was standing right there. DeMarco. The on-site commander. The military expert. McBride could actually vent his rage on the man who deserved it. And everybody else was right there to hear it, so it would be a public satisfaction.

"We missed our chance to do this safely," McBride said. "Byron's already dead. God knows how many died down there when the crane hit. All because your boys took a ride on Flatbed without checking with the people who actually *knew* what the hell they were doing."

DeMarco looked at him wordlessly, but McBride saw the look in his eyes. No longer so sure of himself. No longer so maddeningly in command.

McBride had no pity. "You better hope your team completed their assignment, because they sure as hell aren't going to do it now. You fucked up, DeMarco, you *failed*. And *you* did it, nobody else, *you* did it!"

Still DeMarco said nothing.

Probably he thinks he can talk his way out of it, thought McBride. Tell his higher-ups about civilian non-cooperation. Equipment failure. Well, that will not happen. I will make my own report, and it *will* be read. "I swear to God I'll have your balls in a jar."

DeMarco stood there. Taking it. It felt to McBride like a confession of guilt. It was enough for now.

McBride turned to his own crew. "We'll come back and try to find them when the storm blows out. Right now let's get out of the rain."

Chapter 10

Cut Off

Deepcore had already bumped—hard—into a sea-bottom crag. The miracle was that there seemed to be no serious damage—nothing that showed up on the instruments, anyway. Now, though, something much worse was on its way.

"All right, everybody! Everybody rig for impact!" Bud shouted into the P.A. "Close all the exterior hatches!" He slammed his hand into the alarm button. Everybody knew the drill. They'd done it a hundred times in training.

The worst thing Bud had feared till now was that the *Explorer* would drag *Deepcore* out into the Cayman Trench. He'd been hoping the umbilical might rupture—he figured they could live through having the heavy cable impact with *Deepcore*. It had never occurred to him that the umbilical might have been stronger than the crane's mooring to the deck of the *Explorer*. Now he had forty tons of steel headed straight down. *Deepcore* wasn't designed to withstand impact from above. If the crane hit them it would crumple the rig like an aluminum can.

"Let's *move it!*" he barked. "Let's go go go go go *go!*"

Lindsey was already in the sonar shack. She put the

signals over the speakers so everybody could hear them. Ping, ping, ping. Like in a World War II submarine movie. Listening for the enemy. It was like a counterpoint to the alarm siren. Whoop whoop. Ping ping ping. The music of fear.

Coffey knew immediately that this was his fault. But he had to take Flatbed, didn't he? Had to get the warhead. He had orders—Phase Two.

But taking Flatbed had delayed the disconnection from the *Explorer,* and now the result of that was the possible destruction of *Deepcore.* Very smart, Lieutenant. Got the warhead, lost the rig, the mission's over, you're dead, you failed. Should have realized the priorities here. Should have realized it was more important to secure *Deepcore* and *then* go after the warhead. Why didn't I realize that? I always take the safety of my men into account first. I *always* make sure I don't jeopardize success by being in too much of a hurry.

Worst of all is that here I am wasting time thinking about what a bad job I did when there are things to do *right now.* Assess the situation, do what is necessary *now.*

Where is my team best utilized? I can make that decision. Fast, no time wasted. He spoke to Monk and Wilhite. "You two help secure the rig." And then to Schoenick. "Let's go."

They moved. Monk and Wilhite toward the control room, securing hatches behind them. Coffey and Schoenick toward the warhead. Had to be there with the warhead. If the warhead made it through a collision, it still wouldn't do any good if Coffey wasn't with it.

Bud knew what was happening all over *Deepcore.* All the hatches getting sealed, separating all compartments from each other. His crew dispersed. If the crane hit them, some would certainly die. A few might live, if one of the trimodules wasn't hit, if some of the tanks survived. Even if they had enough submersibles to get everybody out, there wasn't time.

Then he remembered Flatbed, which *was* out. He grabbed his headset, yelled into it. "One Night, One Night, can you hear me? Get the hell out of there! The crane's coming down!" He tried to see out the window, cursed himself for delaying, even for an instant.

Outside, One Night struggled for control, writhed and twisted Flatbed, struggling to find a course through the erratically falling umbilical. It had already struck a glancing blow against Flatbed's port pontoon, which bounced her brutally inside the cabin; if some of the umbilical hung up on Flatbed, it would smash her right down to the bottom, and there'd be no escape for her then.

Catfish came into the control room, slammed the hatch shut, sealed it. He'd been passing people in the corridors, none of them sure what was happening, all of them scared shitless. Finler had asked him what the hell was going on. Catfish hadn't known, not then. But now he could see the whole story. The umbilical coming down fast. That was bad enough—but Bud looking so flat-out scared and the siren whooping away told him that there must be something big and ugly attached to the other end of it.

Bud was barely aware of Catfish. He just kept checking the video monitors, gauges. Still no bad damage. The rig rang and shuddered as loops of umbilical struck it, but he could see some of the umbilical cable now when he looked out the viewport. Part of it, at least, wasn't banging onto the roof of *Deepcore* anymore; it was coiling and curling over itself, forming a pile on the seafloor a few yards away from the viewport. Like a heap of pasta on a plate. Was that a good sign, that so much of the umbilical was coming down beside *Deepcore* instead of on top? After all, before the crane broke away, the *Explorer* had been off at an angle, stretching the umbilical, dragging them along. So the crane might be coming down just a little off center. A little. Enough?

"I've got it!" said Lindsey. "I've got it, it's heading straight for us!"

You don't know that, Lindsey. *Maybe* it's off. Just a little bit. Please, God. Just a few meters.

A stretch of the umbilical hit *Deepcore* again. It rang like the inside of a bell. So maybe *Deepcore* was ground zero after all.

Lindsey came over to join Bud in looking out the view-port. Catfish just stood there, holding onto the steel bracing. Hippy grabbed a plastic bag, stuffed Beany into it, and zipped it shut.

And they stood there, waiting, watching. Bud leaned into the viewport, so he could look up, see it coming. Fat lot of good it's going to do me, knowing three-tenths of a second before it hits that it's going to hit. But I've got to know.

So did Lindsey. She left the sonar, leaned into the viewport beside him. Both of them looking up. Say a little prayer, Lins, that's what I'm doing.

And if we die, we die together, and you're still my wife on this day at this hour, so I guess I win. It's about the only way I could.

The pinging of the sonar got faster and faster and—

The jumbled, broken crane landed not twenty yards off, with a crunching noise so loud they could hear it easily inside the control room. Mud roiled up from the seafloor in a sluggish cloud. They were alive.

They laughed. Lindsey's laugh was a little bit hysterical. Bud's was more like a gasp than a laugh. It occurred to him that he'd never been gladder to see anything than to see the crane land outside the viewport window.

The crane was poised right at the brink of the chasm. Part of it had landed vertically, and some of the rock underneath it, right at the cliff edge, was too weak for the strain. It crumbled. The vertical hunk of steel began to tilt. It groaned under the strain as it tipped slowly, gracefully over the edge.

It slid down, down, the slope ever steeper, nothing there to stop its fall. Behind it, the umbilical began to uncoil and follow it down into the chasm like a snake slithering away from *Deepcore.*

Then Lindsey remembered that this particular snake could never get away from *Deepcore,* because it was attached, first at the A-frame, and then at every point where the falling umbilical had tangled in the structure of the rig. "Oh shit," she said.

The crane was over the edge now, tumbling down the slope, tangled together like puppies playing. It reached a ridge and hung for a moment, but the forward momentum rolled it over, carried it over the lip to an even steeper slope. There was no stopping it now.

From the viewport Bud could see the umbilical unwinding itself, racing ever faster over the edge. Forty tons of steel, falling fast, and all of it attached by an unbreakable line to the top of *Deepcore*. There was no anchor, no mooring. *Deepcore* was already on a gentle slope, resting on skids up against an outcropping of rock. If the rock held the skids, then the A-frame might break—that was the best hope. What Bud feared was that *Deepcore* would roll or slide, get dragged to the edge, and then get sucked down into the canyon. Once they got down there, they'd never live to get back out. No one would ever find them. Like his brother, Junior. Lost forever. "Oh no no no no no no no no no *no,*" he said.

"Oh my God," said Lindsey. "Bud?"

As if she expected him to do something. Like what? For once Lindsey actually looks to me to do something, actually treats me like there's something she needs me for, and there's not *one* thing I can do.

The umbilical snapped taut as a sail in the wind. *Deepcore* lurched, twisted as the umbilical tugged at it. Alarms went off all over the rig. But *Deepcore* didn't roll or break. The structure was too sturdy for that, too low-centered. Instead it began to slide. Right toward the edge.

When the *Explorer* had dragged them, it hadn't been so bad—the umbilical was actually lifting them slightly then. Now, though, the umbilical was pulling them downward, so that they felt every irregularity of the seafloor. But what did they care about getting jolted and bounced? They were at the edge of the downward slope. And then they were over.

Gliding down the slope, following a path already cleared of obstacles by the crane. *Deepcore* was meant to stand level on the ocean bottom; it wasn't meant to flex over the edge of a cliff. That was a strain that Lindsey couldn't have planned for, not if she meant to make it affordable to build. She could hear, could *feel* things giving way, seams splitting, joints torquing out of alignment; it was as if she had nerves running from every part of *Deepcore,* straight to her brain, so she felt it like the agony of her own body being torn apart.

Light flashed, seared; there were shorts in the wiring, a fire in the control room. "Battery room exploding!" Bud shouted—at least some of the gauges were still reporting.

Lindsey followed Bud out of the control room. On the way, she pointed Catfish toward the fire. "Take care of that!" She could feel Hippy's hand on her back, following her as she ducked through the hatch. Catfish had the fire extinguisher hissing away before she was out of earshot.

They raced out into the corridor. Finler was coming up from the drill room. "Bud!" A cry like a little boy, calling for help.

Bud stopped, looked down where Finler was standing. "Yeah!" he shouted.

"Bud, the drill room's flooding!"

Then what the hell are you doing here talking to me? "Get back down there!" Bud shouted. "I'll be right with you! Move it!"

Finler was gone. Another jolt from the skids hitting some obstacle, bouncing. Lindsey wasn't holding on at the moment—she got slammed against a wall. She immediately turned around, back to the wall, out of breath for a moment.

Bud saw Hippy was there. Another tag-along. "Hippy, get to the sub bay. Lock it up!"

There was no reason for Lindsey to stay with Bud—they both knew what to do, they could accomplish twice as much if they split up. So why was she sticking so close to him? Why didn't she want to let him out of her sight? Did she think she could save him if something went wrong? Or did she expect him to save *her?* Bullshit. "I'll deal with this!" she shouted. Bud heard her, and agreed by not arguing. He ducked into a doorway. Lindsey turned away, raced on down the corridor, heading for the ladder to the machine rooms.

In the compressor room, Monk was working in a spray of seawater, turning valves to stop the flow from ruptured pipes. Then a sheet of sparks licked out of the battery room. Seawater had hit the batteries; they were arcing violently. He knew what would happen—the sheets of electricity would ignite the hydrogen from the batteries. But there was no time to react, to get away. The battery room exploded, blowing the hatch off its hinges. The slab of metal rocketed straight for Monk, hit him, knocked him down, pinned him on the deck.

In the ladderway down to the machine room, Lindsey caught the edge of the same explosion—searing light, then fire. The heat was immediate and intense, but it was breathing that worried her. Fire used up oxygen so fast and put so much smoke into the air that she was already coughing as she grabbed a Drager pack hanging on the wall. She got the mask on first, so she could stay alive long enough to swing the whole pack onto her shoulders. Only then did she get a seawater hose and started spraying it on the flames. That's one thing they had plenty of—seawater.

Hippy lurched down the corridor, almost stumbled past the door into the sub bay. He ducked through the hatch. Because of the slope of the rig, water was flooding from the moonpool down into the lower part of the rig. Across the pool, Hippy could see one of the SEALs—Wilhite—fighting a fire. It was insane. Didn't he realize that the moonpool had to be sealed off? It was a gaping hole in the center of Deepcore, and now that the rig wasn't level, it was the surest route for water to get into everything. It had to be sealed off—fire was the last problem here.

But then, not everybody was acting sensible. Hippy knew that. Hell, here he was with his hand gripping a baggy with a rat inside.

"Get out of there!" Hippy screamed.

Wilhite heard him. He knew. "Hippy, close the watertight door!"

Hippy hit the switch. It was still working—the door shut, sealing that entrance. He started running toward Wilhite.

Deepcore took a sharp bounce. Cab Three picked that

moment to break loose from its cradle and slide straight toward Wilhite. With Cab Three coming, there wasn't any room left on the deck for Wilhite to stand. He took a dive into the moonpool.

Cab Three slammed into the end wall, then spun with the movement of *Deepcore* and began skidding straight toward Hippy. Hippy splashed through the water, scrambling to get out of the way. He plunged through a hatch. Safe.

Except he had dropped something. He looked back. Beany's plastic bag was floating on the water, caught in the current from the moonpool, bobbing directly in front of Cab Three as it slid toward the hatch. Hippy scrambled through the hatch back into the sub bay, caught up Beany's bag, then dove back through and out of the way a split second before Cab Three slammed against the hatch.

Wilhite barely noticed Hippy getting out. He was scrabbling at the rim of the pool, trying to get out. The water was so cold, his fingers were so numb, that he couldn't get a firm purchase on the deck, couldn't climb up.

Then *Deepcore* lurched again. Cab Three rolled over, straight toward Wilhite. He put his hands up, as if he could save himself by holding the twelve-ton submersible out of the water. It fell into the pool, shoving him down, plunging him deep into the water. He was under the rig. He tried to hang on, to climb back up into the pool, but he couldn't. His fingers were too cold to hold onto anything. The water held him as the rig swept on. He stayed behind. But he never realized he'd been left. Hypothermia had him unconscious before *Deepcore* had finished passing over him. Before he even had time to drown.

Deepcore hurtled down the slope to the lip where the crane had hesitated, then rolled over, off the cliff. This time, though, the structure was up to the strain. *Deepcore* was so massive and its center of gravity was so low that when it reached the lip, it held. Teetered there, yes—but it held.

Somewhere down below, the crane was arrested in its downward plunge. Pieces of it fell away, but much of it still hung on the end of the umbilical. When *Deepcore* refused to give way, to follow it down, the crane's momentum was transferred from vertical to horizontal. It swung like a pendulum.

Far above, *Deepcore* groaned with the strain of the swinging umbilical. Again, though, it held. *Deepcore* wasn't going to fall over into the abyss. It was in a shitload of trouble, but the rig wasn't going to die yet. Not completely.

In the living quarters, Perry had sealed the hatch to his module. So far so good—but he knew he wouldn't be safe there. Too much seawater was spraying in from above him. He had to get the roof hatch open, climb up to level three. Lindsey Brigman may be a bitch to work with, but she designed a good rig—there was always a way out.

The overhead hatch was too high to reach. He'd have to stand on a bunk. Only at the moment he started to climb, *Deepcore* reached the edge of the cliff and jerked to a stop. The strain opened a vertical seam in the wall. Water gouted into the module, tipping over the bunk, knocking Perry down. The water was so cold it nearly stopped his breath, but he struggled to his feet, clambered up onto the bunk frame.

Now he could reach the hatch. He tried to turn it, but it wouldn't go. All these hatches had checked out at turnover, when they came on duty. It must have been the twisting of the frame when *Deepcore* stopped that jammed it. If he could just twist hard enough.

But he couldn't get the leverage. The water kept rising, higher, higher. The hatch wouldn't budge. And finally, with the water pressing him against the roof, he stopped trying to turn it. He was hanging on, that's all, as the cold slowed down his blood, made his fingers so thick and clumsy that he couldn't hold on anymore.

He hovered in the water as the compartment filled to the top, his arms and legs drifting lazily with the last remnants of turbulence, like gentle breezes in the water.

Lindsey fought her way down to the compressor room, spraying seawater, making some headway against the fire.

Through the smoke she saw the door that had blown off the battery room. There was somebody under it.

Catfish came down the ladder. Lindsey handed him the hose. "Hold it on me!" she told him.

With the stream of water keeping the worst of the flame off her, she made it to the hatch. It was Monk lying there, not completely unconscious, feebly trying to move, to wriggle out from under the slab of metal. Lindsey grabbed him, dragged him out of the way of the flames.

When she was far enough back from the flames that she didn't need the spray on her, Catfish ran in, picked up Monk, tossed him over his shoulder, and headed up the ladder. The infirmary was in the same trimodule, one level up, and so far there wasn't any flooding here.

Lindsey picked up the hose, kept putting out the fire. She looked through the flames into the battery room. On the other side of that compartment was the toolpusher's office —Bud's room. Beyond that, another ladderway and then the long corridor down to the drill room. Bud had promised Finler that he'd go down there. Was he there now? Had the fire blown off a hatch on the other side, too? Could Bud have been in his stateroom, trying to save something? *I save one of these goddamn SEALs, and maybe Bud's on the other side of the fire, lying under a hatch the same way, only I'm not there, I won't pull him out.*

Grimly she stayed in place, directing water on the flames. *If I go off chasing everything I imagine might be happening, I'll be worse than useless. Do my job, Bud'll do his, everything will work out OK. Please God.*

Down in the drill room, Finler and Dietz and McWhirter had the fires under control, the flooding stopped—until the last brutal jolt and the twisting as the crane swung on the end of the umbilical. Then they found out what flooding was. The water rushed in like it was coming over the top of a dam. It jammed them into the machinery; they tumbled head over heels. But finally they got to their feet, scrambled away through the water; nothing to do but get out, try to find some part of *Deepcore* that was intact.

But the big automated door was already closing, its motors sliding it shut like a bank vault door. Slogging through water, they didn't reach it until it had closed.

They pounded on the door. They looked through the window into the corridor beyond, desperate for help. There was no one there to hear them, no one to activate the door from the other side. They pressed their hands, their faces against the tiny round window as if they could push their way through.

That was when Bud finally came running down the long corridor to the drill room. He saw the closed door. Saw hands, someone's head.

There was no way he could open the door from this side. The motor would keep forcing the door closed until it was shut off. The only way to do that was to cut the pneumatic hose, which was on the other side of the door.

"Cut the line to the motor!" Bud shouted. "Cut the hose! I can't open the door from this side!"

They didn't hear him. Or they didn't understand. Or panic had taken over, and they weren't rational enough to do anything but pound uselessly at the window. And so Bud stood there, outside in the corridor, knowing how to save them, only inches away from them, and yet powerless to act. It was the worst thing in the world, to watch somebody die like that. How many times had he seen Junior drowning in his dreams? Always just out of reach. Always where Bud couldn't do a thing to help him. Just like now.

Suddenly the bulkhead next to him gave way. A freezing torrent thundered in. It blew him off his feet. He knew what would happen next. The automatic door at the end of the corridor would immediately start to close. If he didn't get there first, it would be *his* face and hands pressed hopelessly against a tiny window.

He got up, splashed through the water. He was luckier than the others—the break wasn't as large, so the corridor wasn't filling up as fast as the drill room had. Still, the water slowed him so much that he didn't reach the door soon enough. Desperately he reached out, stuck his hand into the gap, tried to hold it open. There was no chance. He didn't have the strength.

The door closed on the fingers of his left hand. He braced himself for the agony of having them crushed. But it didn't come.

The door was still open. Something was holding it just wide enough for his fingers. It was his ring. The harder-than-steel wedding band Lindsey had given him. The door could bend it a little—he could feel the pressure on his finger—but it couldn't break it or crush it. Nor could he slide out his finger—the ring had bent just enough that it locked over the bone of his knuckle. He couldn't pull free.

The water was filling up behind him—but some was leaking through the gap in the doorframe. The notch at the top was large enough for him to see through. This was no damn good for anybody. He was going to die here, and he knew that was right, that's the way it worked underwater, sometimes you ended up on the wrong side of a hatch and to save the lives of the people on the other side, that door had to stay closed and you had to die. But this door wasn't doing its job of holding back the water, either. He was going to die and the rest of the rig wasn't going to be one whit safer because of it.

He yelled. "Hey! *Hey!*" Again and again, refusing to give up. Somebody had to hear him.

It was Catfish. He and Sonny pounded down the ladderway, down the corridor to the other side of the automatic door. Catfish mashed at the Open button. Nothing happened. Sonny, always more direct, wedged a crowbar into the narrow opening and tried to pry the door.

None of this was going to work, and Bud knew it. "Cut the hose! Cut the pneumatic hose!" Finally they heard him over the noise of the water spurting through the crack in the door. Catfish whipped open his jackknife and slashed the hose on the door actuator.

Bud immediately felt the pressure ease up on his ring. Now Cat and Sonny could force the door open fairly easily. Too quickly, in fact—Bud was blown through in a torrent of water, knocking Sonny back against the pipes in the corridor. One of Sonny's arm bones snapped from the force of the blow.

The corridor was filling up fast. "All right," yelled Bud, "let's go go go go go go!"

Catfish saw that Sonny was holding his arm, dazed with pain. "Sonny, you all right?"

"Come on, move it! Go go go go go!" They plunged through the next hatch into the ladderway. "Get the hatch!" shouted Bud. Catfish shoved it shut, turned the crank. There was no leak here. Bud slumped against the wall. They'd sealed off the water. As commander that's all he was supposed to care about. But shit, he wasn't Coffey, he didn't pretend not to feel anything but officially sanctioned feelings. He was damn glad to be alive.

He looked down at the ring on his finger. A tiny band of metal. It would never come off now, but that was fine. He kissed it emphatically.

"You all right? Everybody OK?"

Yeah. They were OK.

First thing they did was send out Big Geek and Little Geek to survey the damage, see if any of the other modules had held, if there were any other survivors, what their remaining assets might be. They had this asset: They were alive, perched on the very edge of the chasm of hell.

From the inside, Bud could figure out this much: They had dim emergency lights. They had the command module and the side of the rig with the mess hall, the food, the infirmary. The other side was gone, flooded out. They'd lost Wilhite of the SEALs, Perry, Finler, Dietz, and McWhirter of the crew. Jammer had slept through the whole thing, still in his coma in the infirmary. Sonny had his arm in a splint and a sling, but he was still useful; he could get around, so Bud had him on the UQC, trying to contact the *Explorer*. Monk's leg was broken—it had to be the medical specialist who was pinned down in the infirmary. Everybody else was more or less healthy. All of them were shaky, some were scared shitless, some were grieving over the dead, others were glad to be alive and ashamed of being so glad.

And Beany. The rat was alive and crawling around on Hippy's shoulders.

Bud came into the control room. He felt the deaths more than anybody, because he not only grieved for his friends, he also felt responsible for them. He had let them down. He had watched some of them die, and hadn't done a damn thing for them. Never mind that there was nothing he could have done. No, there *was* something he could have done. He could have told McBride and Kirkhill and that military guy—Martini, DeMarco—told them to go stuff themselves. Told them that this was a goddam *drilling rig*, not a military craft. If he'd done that, if he'd done what Lindsey told him he should have done, then all these people would be alive. In fact, they'd be coming off shift tomorrow. Waiting for the new crew to pressurize, then climbing into the chamber and depressurizing for three weeks. Bored silly. Bored out of their minds but *alive*.

Sonny was still chanting into the UQC to topside. "Mayday, mayday, mayday. This is *Deepcore Two*. Do you read me, over?"

He'd been at it for a long time already. If they were going to answer, if they could hear at all, they'd have answered by now. Probably the hurricane was right overhead. Probably they were so far out of range that calling for them was a joke. What could they do, anyway, till the storm passed?

"*Benthic Explorer, Benthic Explorer,* this is *Deepcore.* Do you read me, over?"

Bud went over to him. The flashlight he was carrying made shadows dance on the walls. "Forget it, Sonny. They're gone."

Sonny stopped, slumped in his chair. But after a pause he went right back to it. "Mayday, mayday, mayday—"

Bud put a hand on his shoulder. "Hey, they're gone."

Now Sonny got the message.

"Are you OK?" Bud asked.

Sonny held onto the mike in his hand like it was a magic

charm—if he fondled it enough, it'd give him what he wanted. "I just want to get out of this. I want to see my wife one more time."

Bud understood then. Sonny wasn't calling because it was practical. He was calling because if he stopped then that would mean he was giving up hope. Give the guy a chance to get himself back together. In the meantime, let him do what he has to do. "All right then, you better keep trying."

Sonny began to chant again. "Mayday mayday mayday, do you read me, over."

Bud went on down the corridor to the infirmary, finding his way with his flashlight. Here and there an emergency light marked a path—but it was dark.

He went to the bed where Jammer lay, still in his coma. Touched Jammer's head. "Hey, Jammer," he whispered. "What did you see down there?" He pulled the blanket up over him. It was getting colder in here.

Bud heard a soft cry from the other room. For a moment it was as if Jammer had answered him. But it was the SEALs. He pushed the door open and looked in. Coffey and Schoenick were setting Monk's leg, putting a splint on. Coffey looked up when Bud stuck his head into the room.

"Did you find your buddy?" Bud asked him.

"No," said Coffey.

They locked eyes for a moment. Bud bit back the words that came to mind. Either Coffey already knew why all this happened, in which case Bud didn't need to say anything, or he was too damn stubborn to believe it, so why should Bud bother? Still, he couldn't keep his judgment out of his eyes. You did this, Coffey. I said yes back at the beginning, but the deal was that I had the say-so about safety, and you knew it. If you'd kept the bargain, your boy here wouldn't be groaning in pain, and that other kid wouldn't be dead in the water somewhere, so deep even the fishes wouldn't find him.

Bud turned wordlessly away. Behind him, Coffey took a few steps toward the door. "Brigman," he said.

Bud stopped, turned partway around. "What?"

"I was under orders. I had no choice."

Bud heard the words, but he knew better. My father was a

Marine noncom, Coffey. I know all about orders. I also know that a commander has discretion. If you had waited half an hour for One Night to unhook the umbilical back when it was possible, you could have spent all the time since then doing whatever your mysterious mission was. If you'd said so, DeMarco would have gone along. You *always* have a choice.

Still, he knew that it was tough for Coffey to admit he'd been wrong. And that's what his words meant—an admission that it was his actions that had caused all this. Caused the death of his own man, too—Coffey must feel that as keenly as Bud felt the deaths of his own crew. They had that much in common, at least. So he didn't reject what Coffey said. He lingered long enough for Coffey to know he'd been heard, heard and not refuted. Then he left the infirmary.

He headed down the ladder toward the machinery room. He saw Catfish, welding a weak point. But it was Lindsey that Bud was looking for. She was the one who knew every wire, every damn electron *on* those wires.

She was dragging a length of cable through the knee-deep water, getting set to hook it up with some wires on the wall. The water on the floor was cold and unpleasant, but it wasn't dangerous anymore—it was the stuff that had splashed from the moonpool, having settled at the lowest point in *Deepcore*.

He looked at her for a few moments. This was Lindsey at her best, working on something that took up her whole attention, *building* something. God, she was beautiful. And she was alive. Covered with grease, cold and filthy, but alive. If he'd lost her, if she'd been in one of the flooded compartments, if he had to think of her floating somewhere in the cold black ocean, he couldn't take it, he'd lose it all right then. Hell, I thought I'd lost her before, when she left me. I grieved like it was the end of the world. What did I know then? Even if she isn't with me, she's still in this world, and that makes it worth living in myself.

But he couldn't stand there looking at her forever. "What's the scoop, ace?" he said. He did a damn good job of keeping the emotion out of his voice.

She didn't stop working to answer him. "I can get power to this module and sub bay if I reroute these busses. I've got to get past the mains, which are a total meltdown."

"Need some help?"

"Thanks. I'll handle this." She thought of something else he needed to know. "There won't be enough to run the heaters. In a couple of hours this place is going to be cold as a meat locker."

"What about O_2?"

"Brace yourself. We've got enough for about twelve hours—if we close off sections we're not using."

That wasn't good enough. "Well, this storm's going to last longer than twelve hours."

She thought for a second. "I can maybe extend that. There are some storage tanks outboard on the wrecked module. I'll have to go out and tie onto them."

Maybe that would be enough, maybe not. They didn't have to discuss it. They'd do all they could to last as long as they could, and if that wasn't enough, then it wasn't enough. There were so many absolutely sure ways to die that hadn't come true, Bud wasn't about to complain about the possibility of dying twelve hours from now. Twelve hours was like a whole second lifetime.

He watched her crimping wires together, her fingers deft and sure, her arms stronger than they looked—everything about her stronger than she looked. He thought of how she came down here yesterday—was it even that long ago?—talking like they couldn't make it without her. Well, it was true. They couldn't have made it through *this* without her. And if Coffey could admit he was wrong, so could Bud. He put his hand on her shoulders.

"Hey, Lins," he said. "I'm glad you're here."

She laughed a little. "Well *I'm* not."

But he knew she'd understood the apology and accepted it. That was enough. He left her to her work and headed back upstairs to the sub bay.

Hippy and One Night were both there, concentrating on piloting their ROVs. They'd jury-rigged a decent setup.

Monitors on top of a stack of other equipment, the control cables running down into the moonpool. Not as nice as doing it from the control room, but a lot better than not doing it at all.

One Night heard him come in. Probably caught sight of his flashlight from the corner of her eye. "Found Cab Three," she said. "Deader than dogshit, boss." She showed him on the monitor. A girder from the base of the drilling derrick was jammed right through its front dome. "Right through the brainpan."

Bad news, but it could have been worse. One Night had got Flatbed back inside, still in one piece, and Cab One's damage was minor, certainly repairable. Two out of three was almost a victory.

He went on to Hippy, looked over his shoulder at his monitor. "Where are you?" he asked.

Hippy answered. "Quarters. Level one."

Bud didn't have to ask what he was looking for. He watched as Little Geek rose up through the open central hatch in the living quarters, then pivoted in a circle to scan the flooded interior. It was a shambles.

They came to a pair of shoes. Followed up the body. Lying there like he was asleep. Peaceful. Dead. "Aw, jeez," breathed Hippy. "That's Perry."

Bud already knew it, but seeing it with his own eyes somehow made it final. "That's it, then," he said. "Finler, McWhirter, Dietz, and Perry." They deserved something from him. Something better than him standing there, naming them. They needed a memorial, a service, some kind of prayer. But all Bud could come up with was a single word. "Jesus."

"Do we just leave him there?" asked Hippy.

"Yeah, for now," said Bud. "Our first priority's to get something to breathe."

As he stood there, looking at Perry's face in gentle repose, he felt a kind of relief. He couldn't understand why he felt that way. Until he realized that he'd been imagining this scene all his life, for years and years. Ever since he was a kid and Junior was lost. He'd seen his brother's body a hundred times, a thousand times in his mind—in dreams, but sometimes awake, too. Sometimes Junior looked like this. Relaxed. Almost as if death had tasted sweet. There were other dreams, not as nice. Dreams that made him wake up shouting, screaming, moaning when he was young. He had learned to control that response. Now he just woke up sweating, gasping for breath, remembering how it felt to have water in his lungs, still seeing Junior's face from the nightmare, twisted in the agonized rictus of death.

It was such a relief to know it could look like this. That not everything had to be as ugly and terrible as possible. Not always, anyway.

Out of the range of the lights, the builders watched; they reached in with their slender filaments, touched, tasted. They found the bodies of the dead long before the ROVs did, scanned and recorded their memories. The city had learned much since their contact with Jammer. They understood the memories they found, and now, with hundreds of dead— the men from the *Montana,* the Russians whose bodies sank far enough down before their brains were cold, and these men from *Deepcore,* they were building up a thorough picture of mankind.

And they were horrified. How well they had named these creatures—most of them were filled with memories of planning and training to kill, memories of the fear of death, anger and terror and loneliness. At times the city almost despaired of finding any common ground with these creatures.

There was Barnes, the sonarman from the *Montana.* In his last moments, he had *not* been lonely. He had gone back in his own memory to a place where he was happy, a place where he belonged. To people who were part of him. People in whose memory he would live on, so that death held more of grief than terror for him.

Most of the men had memories of family, of course—but their memories were ambiguous, muddy, and filled with conflict and rebellion. Their lives were focused around war; their most important associations were with their fellow soldiers. The builders had no way of knowing that most of these men were really still adolescents, only recently on their own, still celebrating their independence from their families, still in search of their identity. And the older men were career soldiers—good ones, but by necessity—and choice—they had opted to leave their families behind for months on end. It was not a balanced sample of humanity. But it was the only sample the builders had ever found.

So the preponderance of evidence was that human beings loved war, lived for killing, a swarm of vicious worms swallowing each other, but reproducing faster than they could devour. The city could not imagine communicating with them.

And yet they *had* to find a way, didn't they? Now that the builders could make sense of the humans' broadcasts and transmissions, they knew what both sides of the current troubles did not, *could* not know—that neither side would back down, that each was so terrified that the other meant to strike that both were planning to strike first, before their weapons could be destroyed. The world was days, hours away from the order for missiles to fly.

The builders were in no immediate danger. On the bottom of the sea, there would be little direct damage. But the planet would die at the surface, and within a few years that death would lead to stagnation, then starvation at the bottom of the world. The builders would have to leave this world with their work unfinished. The plan was for each city to become an ark, rising out of the ocean to soar upward into space, flying off in search of other worlds where they could start the cycle again. But that was still a long time away. The only city that was ready for flight was this one, here in the Cayman Trench; and it was only ready because it had arrived here ready. It was the first, from which all the other cities had been founded. So if they had to leave, all they could do was gather together the memories of the other cities and then embark on its voyage as a single ark.

A failure, because this world had given rise to no more arks than had arrived here. The only profit from their sojourn on Earth would be the memory of this mad species, which had somehow become intelligent without ever learning how to understand themselves.

The worst of it, though, was this: The crisis that these humans faced was not entirely of their own making. Their weapons, their enmities had all existed before. But from their broadcasts and messages, the builders knew now how much of their fear and anger was caused by things the builders themselves had inadvertently done.

We are not responsible for their nature, said the city. We didn't make their weapons.

But they had those most terrible weapons for a long time, as they measure time—through many wars, and yet they never used them once they saw how terrible they were. Until we destroyed their satellite.

To save them from war, answered the city.

Yes, but they didn't know it, they didn't understand us. And so they were terrified. And then we destroyed their submarine, killed their crew.

It was an accident, an unattended glider; they didn't move out of the way.

They didn't know us. They weren't prepared for us. *We* were the ones who caused the things that made them so afraid. And if they now use these weapons that they so long refrained from using, will it be their fault or our own?

Partly ours.

More than that. They were learning to control themselves. Out of fear of each other, true—but it was serving them well enough. We did what each of them was too terrified to do. We provoked them. The fault is ours.

And the city tasted the strange and bitter flavor of shame. How can we leave now, with this memory? Yet how can we undo what we've done? How can we explain to them the truth about what has been happening, when seeing one of us so terrifies them that they almost die?

There's one who saw us and wasn't afraid.

Then she's the one we'll try to speak to. Go to her and see if you can put your thoughts into her mind. See if she can understand.

One Night found undamaged tanks on the far side of the rig. Lindsey suited up and took Catfish with her out into the water to make the connection. Little Geek came along with them, with Hippy in the sub bay at the controls.

There was enough oxygen in those tanks to triple their life expectancy. That might be enough, if the *Explorer* got back in time.

They walked along the bottom. "Cat, I want you to tie onto this manifold. Do you see it?"

He looked up, saw it overhead.

"I'm going to go around the other side and check out some tanks," said Lindsey.

So he'd be on his own with this job. It meant she trusted him to do it right. Was this Lindsey Brigman? "Be careful, darlin'," Catfish warned her.

The tank was too high for him to reach it by jumping—he was wearing too much gear to have much buoyancy. So Lindsey hooked her hands under his foot. He balanced, got ready. "One," she said. "Two, three." He pushed off with his other foot, and when he was high enough, she shoved him upward. A slow-motion boost.

He caught onto the railing. "Geronimo," he said. "Thank you, Lindsey."

She left him behind to do his job. Little Geek followed her.

Bud was in the sub bay, inspecting electric cables and splicing the broken parts. He could hear through his headset what was going on, since he was hooked into her F-O line. Hearing the conversation between Lindsey and Cat, knowing she was on her own now, Bud reached down to the control box at his hip and switched his mike on so Lindsey could hear him. "How's it look?" he asked.

What could Lindsey say? Building *Deepcore* had been her life for years, and it was trashed. On the other hand, it pleased her to see how well it had held up under some pretty extraordinary stress. And a lot of it was repairable. So she was almost jaunty in her answer. "Well, you guys really screwed up my rig. There's a lot of wreckage out here."

Bud heard the tone of her voice, knew she was OK. He also worried that when she was in an eager mood like this, she sometimes moved too fast, didn't watch what was going on around her. On land all that led to was people with hurt feelings. Out there in the water, especially with unpredictable wreckage around, moving too fast could be deadly. Your hoses could hook on a snag; something could slip suddenly and you could get pinned. "Well, don't get fouled," he said. I sound like her mom. Be careful, don't get hurt, and make sure to be home by nine-thirty.

She was busy—so was he. He switched off his mike, so he could hear but was no longer transmitting to her.

A few feet away, One Night was repairing some of the damage to Cab One. She reached toward him, indicating a wrench. "Give me that nine-sixteenths, will you?"

He did.

Seeing that his mike was off, she reminded him to go on with what they'd been talking about before. How he and Lindsey happened to get married. To One Night that was one of the supreme mysteries of the universe. It was obvious to her that they were the two most unlikely, impossible, *absurd* people ever to tie the connubial knot. "So there you were," she said.

Bud went on with his story. "There we were, side by side, on the same ship, for two months. I'm toolpusher and we're testing this automated derrick of hers. We get back on the beach and we're living together."

"Doesn't mean you had to marry her."

How could he explain it to One Night? I was with her and it felt like I was more myself than I ever was when I was alone. I was proud to be with her, I was proud of what we *were* together. I liked *us* better than I liked myself. If he tried saying that to One Night, she wouldn't even believe it, she'd wonder why he was shitting her like that. So he smiled and told her the other reason—the practical reason, what you might even call the true reason, since it was the only one that Bud and Lindsey admitted to each other at the time. "We were due to go back out on the same ship. Six months of tests. If you were married you got a stateroom. Otherwise, it was bunks."

She bought it. "OK, good reason. Will you come over here and tie this for me?"

He looped the cable over a stanchion so it wouldn't slide back down into the water. Then he went over and lent her a hand.

"Then what?" she asked.

"It was all right for a while, you know. But then she got promoted to chief engineer on this thing, couple of years ago." It was the only time he'd ever seen Lindsey flat-out cry, the time she thought they'd decided to put somebody else on it. Her design, her rig, and they were going to let somebody else supervise the construction and testing. She needed to be project engineer like some women need to have babies. Exactly like that. And I wanted her to have it too, because she wanted it so bad—and because we could be together. Instead it drove us apart.

"She went front-office on you, man."

That was how it looked to One Night, but Bud didn't believe it. Not like the suits, Lindsey was never like that. She didn't get too *important* for him, just too . . . distracted. Or no, she just found *him* too distracting. "Well," Bud said. "You know Lindsey, just too damn aggressive. She didn't leave me. She just left me *behind.*"

One Night stopped what she was doing and looked him in the eye. "Bud, let me tell you something. She ain't half as smart as she thinks she is." And she held his gaze till she was sure Bud got the message.

He got it. One Night was telling him, She's dumb to lose you. One Night was saying, I know who you are, Bud Brigman, and you didn't blow it with Lindsey, she blew it with you.

You just don't know, One Night. If I'd been smarter or

tried harder or not so hard or done better somehow, I'd still have her with me. But I know what you're telling me, and I thank you for it.

One Night had another idea in mind, though. She took Lindsey's air hose in both hands and made as if to kink it, which would cut off Lindsey's mix. Just a little favor she was willing to do for Bud.

He reached out to stop her.

A joke. That's all it was. One Night whooped and cackled. Boy, you're so screwed up in love with her your brain's in backward.

A few yards away, Hippy started fiddling with the knobs on his monitor. He was getting some interference. Static. A weakening signal. That was ridiculous—Little Geek was on a tether, he should be getting absolutely clear signals.

"Hey, Lindsey," Hippy said, "do you read me? Over."

Outside *Deepcore,* Lindsey heard him, but his voice was breaking up as if he were getting farther away. Only distance shouldn't make any difference, and she wasn't moving anyway. "Yeah, Hippy, I read you." She was standing at the edge of the canyon, checking the valves on a rack of oxygen bottles, trying to find which ones should be hooked up and which were spent. Behind her there was a sheer drop to nothingness. But it didn't bother her till now, with Hippy's voice fading. She needed that connection. "What's the matter?" she said.

Inside the rig, Hippy had lost visual contact completely. If Lindsey answered him, he didn't hear. "Lindsey, come back." Answer me.

The lights inside the rig dimmed sharply. Bud's first thought was that the power supply had been damaged. But that couldn't be it—that wouldn't cause a sharp fade like this, and then hold steady. He remembered the power loss back on the *Montana.*

When the outside lights dimmed, Lindsey began to get spooked. She wasn't getting anything from Hippy now, and the last thing she needed was to be stuck out here alone in the dark. If the lights went out, her chances of getting back in without getting snagged or trapped or just plain lost were pretty slim. "Catfish, do you read me?"

Hippy and Bud weren't hearing anything, either, as they both called for Lindsey. Communications were dead.

A hundred meters below the lip of the abyss, the builders hovered in the water. So far everything was working well. They had waited until Lindsey was separated from all the others. Then they had moved closer, which damped the power in *Deepcore;* but they sent forth tendrils to draw away *all* the power from the communications systems. They would be alone with Lindsey, without distraction or interference.

Now they sent new tendrils out to her, only a few molecules wide. They found the cracks in her suit—at the neck, at every fastening—and, gathering and polymerizing the ambient water vapor in her suit, the tendrils grew until they had found their way through her ears, her nostrils, her mouth, her eyes, back into her brain. There they followed the pathways of her mind—touching every neuron and bridging every synapse. This was no project now for a single builder. A dozen of them were scanning her brain, and then, together, interpreting what they read there.

She's afraid.

They didn't want her to be afraid, to panic and hurt herself the way Jammer had. So now, in order to calm her, they made their first effort at direct communication.

If they had been human, using human speech, they would have whispered to her, gently assuring her, a sort of lullaby: Don't be afraid, be at peace, be at peace. But they were not human. So their meaning came, not as words, but as molecules. Chemicals that they believed would communicate the feeling of peace to Lindsey.

Lindsey was still hearing nothing. She tried to reach everybody, using her F-O, then her UQC. "Catfish, do you copy? Over." She felt herself starting to panic, heard the desperation in her own voice. "Bud, do you copy? Over."

Then the power dimmed even further. It should have

frightened her more. But instead, she felt somewhat calmer. "Catfish, I seem to be having a problem here. Over." And then she felt no need to call out anymore. What was she so worried about? Everything would be all right. She had no idea why she should feel that way, yet she did—she had complete confidence. She had nothing to fear. She was at peace.

It's working, they said. She heard us.

It was time for the next step. Something small. The porter that she had caught a glimpse of before. It would be somewhat familiar to her. It would also seem like a machine to her, with a firm, unfluctuating structure—from what they knew of humans now, and what they knew of Lindsey, they were quite sure she'd feel less threatened if she thought it was a machine. So the porter darted upward from the chasm. It saw her, and like a puppy recognizing its master, it quickly moved into place behind her.

Lindsey saw only the patterns of light on the equipment in front of her. She turned slowly, still completely unafraid—and saw before her a machine. Was it what she had seen before? The body of it was smooth, slightly arched, like a leaping fish—but it was no fish. At the front there was an opening like the front of a jet engine—but it was no engine. Inside was a circle with bright points radiating outward, like a child's drawing of the sun; it was spinning. Light danced inside it.

Then it turned sideways. Its shell—or skin, or body—was transparent, like perfect crystal glass. Colors shone in patterns on the skin as it moved, as if it were reflecting some outward source of light. But there was no light except what came from inside the thing. Structures of different colors, glowing, connecting inside like in a machine—or was it a biological system? She couldn't tell, nor could she guess what its purpose was.

But it was beautiful. She marveled at its perfect grace.

She admires it. She wants to know and understand it. When she sees without fear, then she can love.

The builders remembered this thought, because they knew it was important. Fear was the great controller of

216

human beings. Fear was bringing them to the brink of war. Fear drove them away from each other, kept most of them from risking anything in their lives. There was good evolutionary reason for fear to be so strong in them—they could die, not just in the body, but in the memory as well. Of course they feared death. If we died so completely, we would fear it, too.

But with the fear removed, the true self remained behind. Lindsey was filled with eagerness to see more, to understand all. She was ready.

Still, the builders were careful. The sight of a builder in her natural shape had frightened Jammer. And Lindsey had a particular affinity for machines. So the builder Lindsey would meet would be inside a glider, not in her natural shape. Again, it would be like a machine, but this time a machine filled with intelligence.

The porter was reluctant to leave, sensing that Lindsey desired him to stay—though it received this information more from the builders than from Lindsey herself. It drifted backward, then rose up out of sight.

Lindsey's gaze followed the porter as it disappeared. Then she saw a sight that took her breath away—a large, smooth shape rising upward slowly from below. It was bright with inner light, its surface smooth and perfect, its shape gracefully undulant. Interior lights moved and danced within it. It was the light of life, of thought, of memory. It was transparent, its walls so perfectly clear that they were almost invisible. There was no building material known that could be so transparent and yet so strong that it could hold such a structure without twisting or shattering.

No architect or engineer could have designed this thing. It had no place in the natural order of the Earth. She knew at once that this was the work of a stranger, a newcomer—but not an interloper. Not an intruder. It would not interfere with her or any other human, if it could help it. It lived in the deepest part of the sea, where human beings could never go. There was no enmity between humanity and these things. These people.

How did she know this? She had no idea—but she was

certain of it. It was beyond question. Like the way she knew that she could reach out her hand and touch it. It was a dangerous, unreasonable thing to do—yet she had no doubt that she could do it. And she wanted to, with all her heart. It would be unbearable to see such beauty and leave it untouched.

So she laid her hand against its winglike arch as it slowly rotated over her. The surface was smooth and hard—it did not yield under her fingers. And yet it glided by under her hand utterly without friction—she saw it moving, yet could not feel its motion.

What are you? Who built you? Who is inside you? And then a desire she remembered from childhood, the desire that had kept her with her father, forsaking all the other attractions of youth: Teach me how to make such things.

Plenty of time for that, she thought. There's no hurry. Now that we've met, there's plenty of time. You can tell me all your memories. Voyages across the endless abyss of space, the hot flaring light of suns, the exquisite relief of sinking down again into the cool deeps of a new sea, there to begin again. You are builders, I know that—builders like me, only far older and more experienced. Our bodies are so utterly different that we can only meet here, in this difficult place; but our minds are not so unlike that we can't communicate.

I wish that you would speak to me.

Then she remembered her camera. The ROV's video wasn't working, of course, with the power down, but she had an underwater camera that was purely mechanical. She could take a picture, she could show the others; then they'd know that these creatures were nothing to fear. She fumbled with the settings—hurry, hurry, it's leaving.

As the glider sank down into the canyon, she finally got set for a picture. But just as she was ready to click the shutter, the small porter darted past her from behind, startling her. She completely missed the shot of the glider. Well, at least she could take a picture of this one, though it refused to hold still, zigzagging down the canyon. She got one shot, only a second before it disappeared.

My God, we're not alone down here, she thought. We've come down so far that almost nothing lives here, only to find out that even farther down, at the bottom of this trench, there live the most beautiful creatures with the most perfect machines on this earth.

The lights came back up. The communications systems sputtered back to life. Little Geek woke up and arose from the seafloor, stirring up silt. And there was Catfish, coming around the flank of the rig, looking for her.

"You better not say you missed that," Lindsey said.

Catfish was baffled. "Missed what?"

Never mind. She *knew* now. She had a picture. They would see.

It was only partly a success. They had spoken to Lindsey, and she had understood. The problem was that she didn't *know* they had spoken. Because they communicated by directly manipulating memory and emotion at a chemical and electrical level, the builders' messages entered Lindsey's brain exactly the way her own thoughts and feelings did. So she thought their messages were her own ideas. She trusted them, believed them, but thought it was intuition, deduction, something inside herself.

Humans aren't used to receiving others' thoughts directly, the builders told each other. They can't taste the flavor that tells us when a thought comes from someone else. So how can they possibly recognize someone else's mental voice inside their heads? Worse, how can they distinguish between their own thoughts and those we give them? We told her to be at peace. We told her where we come from, who we are, what we do. But she decided for herself that our works were beautiful, that she wanted us to teach her. Yet if she knew that some of her thoughts came from us, she'd be unable to tell where our messages left off and her own desires began.

And they discovered other things about her, too. They could take away her fear, but that wasn't the only barrier between one human being and another. From her memories they could see the countless times in her life when she had separated herself from other people, not from fear, but because of her intense concentration on the things she cared about. Human beings were capable of deliberately not knowing each other, shutting others out and cutting them off; and she didn't see this as a tragic loss, a bitter loneliness. She saw it as a necessity, the only way to concentrate on her work, to accomplish anything.

So it won't be enough for us to remove fear, even if we could do that in the open air, where these humans live.

Then there's no hope of changing them. We might as well begin our preparations to leave, and let them destroy each other. It isn't our fault—they would have done it eventually, since they refuse to belong to each other.

No. We can't dismiss them all so easily. We've still seen only a few of them. Unlike us, their utterly separate memories mean that each person is different from others; knowing one or even a hundred doesn't mean we know them all.

We have time. We can watch. We can see what they do, see if there's some hope for them. But we'll surely be disappointed.

Chapter 11

Crazy People

Lindsey told them what happened, all that she saw. Then, when the film was developed, it was there in the picture, just like she said. She had caught it.

Unfortunately, it looked like a little squiggle of light surrounded by pitch black.

Bud teased her about it, of course. "Great shot, Lins."

"What did you do?" asked Sonny. "You drop your dive light?"

It was too far away to see clearly—what did they expect, a studio-quality portrait, with a pretty painted background? Go ahead, tease me. I still got the picture. "Come on, you guys, come on. Now that's the small one, the smaller one, right here. You can see how it's kind of zigging around."

"Yeah," said Bud. "Whatever it is."

Maybe he *wasn't* teasing. Maybe he really didn't believe she saw anything. "I'm *telling* you what it is. You're just not hearing. There's something *down there*. Something—not us."

She looked around at them. Nobody was buying it. Not that they were calling her a liar. Or crazy. Not yet.

"You could be more . . . specific?" said Catfish.

Bud tried to answer—with a joke, of course. "Something that zigs."

But Lindsey wasn't going to stand for that. Bud was *not* going to *handle* this by making it a joke. It was real, and he was going to have to deal with the reality. She barely let him finish what he was saying. "Not *us*," she insisted. "Not *human*. Get it? Something nonhuman, but intelligent."

They looked around at each other. Hippy was smiling. Because he liked the idea? Or because he thought she was crazy?

"A non-*terrestrial* intelligence," Lindsey said.

Oh, Hippy was *loving* it. "A Non-Terrestrial Intelligence," he said. "NTIs. Oh, man, that's better than UFOs. Oh, but that works too. Underwater Flying Objects."

Catfish finally got it. "Are we talkin' little space friends here?"

"Hell yeah!" said Hippy. "Hot rods of the gods! Right, Lins? No, no, really! It could *be* NTIs. The CIA's known about them forever. They abduct people all the time, man. There was once—"

The more Hippy said, the stupider he made it all sound. "Hippy, do me a favor," said Lindsey. "Stay off my side."

Bud wasn't laughing anymore. He touched her arm, drew her aside. "Will you step into my office, please."

She followed him. Hoping that this meant he was about to take this seriously.

He was. He was downright grim. "Jesus, Lins—"

She didn't want him to humor her, or lecture her, or *handle* her. She wanted him to *hear* her. "Bud, come on, something really important is happening here."

But he wasn't accepting it. "I'm trying to keep this situation under control, and I can't allow you to cause this kind of hysteria—"

"Who's hysterical? Nobody's hysterical!"

"Shh," he whispered.

He was right. She *was* getting agitated. He wouldn't listen if she didn't stay calm. So she forced herself to take a deep breath, relax a little.

When he saw she was listening, he said, "All I'm saying is when you're hanging on by your fingernails, you don't go waving your arms around."

She knew that. She knew that Bud was the best at keeping people calm, getting them to work smoothly together. But this time, just this once, he needed to stop being responsible for creating everybody else's reality and let somebody else change reality for *him*. "Look, *I saw something!*" she said. "I'm not going to go back in there and say I didn't see it when I did. I'm sorry. Please."

He turned his head, then faced her again, squinting at her the way he did when he was trying not to be angry. "You are the most stubborn woman I ever knew."

It was true, and at this moment she regretted it. All their time together she'd been stubborn over everything. Even the things that didn't matter. So that now, when it was important, he didn't think she was insisting on this because it was absolutely true. He thought she was insisting on it because she was Lindsey, because she insisted on having her way in everything. For the first time she realized the price she paid for so rarely being willing to bend. She didn't know how to make him see the difference. Except to admit the truth. "Yes, I am," she said. "But I need you to believe me right now."

She could see it in his face—he'd never heard her talk like that before. He'd never heard her say she needed *anything*. He wanted to believe her. And she knew that it wasn't easy, either. A smudge of light on a photograph—what proof was that? None at all—unless he believed what she told him about where the camera was pointed when she took the picture. Unless he believed that she actually saw what she said she saw, touched the thing, the creature, the *person*. It all came down to whether he had faith in her.

"Now come on," she said, "look at me, come on. Am I stressed out? Do I have any symptoms of pressure sickness, any tremors, slurred speech?"

He thought about it. He sounded almost defeated when he answered. "No."

"No," she echoed. "Bud, this is me, Lindsey. OK? You know me better than anybody in the world." She didn't know how to make it any plainer. She was *begging*. And he knew it. He was looking at her with his eyes soft and caring, like so many times back when things were still good between them. He wanted to give her what she asked for. He'd have to believe her now. "Now watch my lips. *I saw these things*. I touched one of them."

But that wasn't all, that wasn't enough to explain what it meant, what it was like. "And it wasn't some clunky steel can like we would build. It glided. It was the most beautiful thing I've ever seen. Oh, God, I wish you'd been there."

It was the first time it dawned on her that this was true. She really *did* wish he'd been there, and not just because then he would believe her. It was because she knew that he would have felt the same things she did. He would have loved it, the way she did. "It was a machine. It was a machine, but it was alive. Like a . . . dance of light." He would have understood all this if he'd been there. Because there really were moments when they saw as if from the same eyes.

"Please, you have to trust me," she said. And maybe he would have. Except that she suddenly realized that it wasn't just what she saw that she wanted him to trust. It was what she *knew* about it. How *did* she know that the creature was good, that she was safe, that there was no danger? How could she be so certain of that? "I don't think they mean us any harm, I don't know how I know that."

He squinted, looked away, twisted his head. She'd gone too far, expecting him to trust her conclusions as well as what she actually saw. But it was just as true. Just as true and much more important. "It's just a feeling," she said.

She'd lost him. "Jesus," he said. He pinched the bridge of his nose. She knew what it meant—he was going to say no. He was going to refuse. It hurt like he was stabbing her. "Am I supposed to go on a feeling?" he said. "How can I go on a feeling? You think Coffey's going to go on a feeling?"

She didn't understand her own reaction. Why does it hurt

so bad, that he doubts me? If I wasn't the one who saw it, I wouldn't believe me either. I'm asking him to do for me something that I don't think I'd do for him or anybody else. But that doesn't change anything. Just because I wouldn't be trusting enough to do this doesn't mean that he can't. Bud is a better person. I've always known that. Bud's better than anybody. That's why if he doesn't trust me, nobody will.

"We all see what we want to see," she said. "Coffey looks and he sees Russians, he sees hate and fear. You have to look with better eyes than that." She smiled at him. She tried to put all her need, all her feelings right there on her face, in her voice, so he'd see, so he'd *know*. She tried to show him everything. And he understood her. She could see it in his face. He knew how much she needed him to accept this. "Please," she said.

Bud could hardly bear it, having her talk like that, *look* like that. She had never been so open, so vulnerable; he had never loved her more than he did right then, never wanted more to give her what she wanted. But even if he could change his own beliefs, what could he do about it? He had a crew that was depending on him. He had to deal with Coffey. If he suddenly started believing stories about space creatures in the Cayman Trench, he'd lose his credibility with everybody. He'd lose his ability to lead. And that meant that there'd be nobody to hold all this together, keep them all alive and stable till, somehow, they got out of this.

"I can't, Lins," he said.

It was the worst thing he'd ever done to her. She put everything on the table, and he was shoving it away. She held her smile, but he knew she was wounded. She would never come to him like this again, if he refused now. But he couldn't jeopardize everybody else out of love for Lindsey.

"I'm sorry," he said. "I can't right now."

He turned away, left the room, hating himself, but knowing he'd done the right thing.

She stood there after he was gone. She'd never felt so lonely in her life. It wouldn't matter if anyone else believed her—Hippy, Catfish, Sonny, what did they matter? It was

Bud's faith she needed. And when she didn't have that, she had nothing.

Coffey wasn't surprised by what Lindsey saw. If an intruder had come once, it was to be expected that it would come again.

Of course, the conclusions she had reached were absurd. He was glad to see that no one else took them seriously, either. The woman was a good engineer—her jury-rigged life support for *Deepcore* had been quick and thorough. But that didn't mean she was automatically a reliable witness. She was under stress. She saw something strange. She got a picture, and the more Coffey looked at it, the more he realized that it had to be *something* from outside *Deepcore*. If she'd taken a picture of any of the light sources on the rig, then part of the rig would be showing in the picture. So when she said she took the picture when the intruder was heading down into the canyon, he believed her.

Something was out there. It had made no attempt to communicate with them. Therefore until he knew otherwise, he assumed it was Russian and he assumed it was hostile. That meant they had to function under military discipline from now on. No more of this lackadaisical attitude that Brigman liked so much. That was fine while they were recovering from the crash, when they needed to restore morale. Now they had to be watchful.

Instead, they were busy setting up tables, laying out blankets and pillows, trying to turn the mess hall into a reasonable bunk area. As if sleep were the most important thing on their minds. He was trying to explain this to Brigman, trying to work out with him what was needed. All Coffey wanted was cooperation. So he was asking Brigman, "We've got to set up twenty-four hour surveillance on the exterior cameras." One Night brushed past him, carrying blankets. "How many men have you got? You've got six people, I've got—"

Catfish hustled a table into the room, calling out, "Watch out, coming through."

It was impossible to concentrate with all this going on. Coffey turned to the group and spoke loudly, his command voice. "Everybody just *stop!*"

They stopped. They looked at him.

He waited. Waited until they changed position, set things down, got ready to listen and stay listening until he was done. Waited, in other words, until they had reached the civilian equivalent of standing at attention. They didn't like it, but they did it.

"All right," he said. "I want round-the-clock manning of the sonar shack and the exterior cameras. If that Russian bogey comes back, I don't think we should be taking a nap."

It was the Brigman woman who resisted, of course. "Give me a break, Coffey. Those things live three and a half miles down on the bottom of an abyssal trench! Trust me, they're not speaking Russian."

Coffey knew that nobody took her ideas seriously— except the kid with the rat, maybe. But the contempt in her voice, that was damaging. It let the others think that they didn't have to treat him with the respect that was essential for a commanding officer. She was dangerous, even when she was crazy.

Still, this wasn't the time to shut her down. The best way to deal with her disdain was to answer with even more disdain. He ignored her completely, went on with making assignments as if she hadn't spoken. He turned to One Night. "Have you finished the repairs on the acoustic transmitter yet?"

"Nope." She sounded sullen.

Coffey knew how to deal with this sort of thing. You hold people accountable, that's what you do. "Why not?" he said.

She turned around slowly, her face filled with hostility. "I was having my nails done."

This was open insubordination, not like the Brigman woman's whining about UFOs. He had to meet one challenge with another. "Well, get it done," said Coffey. Nobody ever talked back to him when he spoke like that.

"Kiss my ass," said One Night.

Coffey looked around at the others. Nobody was acting embarrassed or apologetic. They were all looking right at Coffey, which meant they were joining One Night in her challenge. Especially Catfish. He thought of himself as a fighter. If he got out of hand, this could be very bad. Not that Coffey was afraid he couldn't take the man. But if it actually came to blows, then it wouldn't be a challenge anymore. It would be mutiny.

This had gone far enough. Coffey looked them all in the eye, one by one. "All right. Get something straight. You people are under my authority, and when I—"

Catfish interrupted him, stuck out his hand—but it wasn't a threatening gesture, not yet. His hand was open, as if to ward away danger; not a fist, not an attack. Catfish was as much scared as belligerent—like a cornered animal. This wasn't some barroom brawl shaping up here—Catfish knew that Coffey was trained as a killer, not a fighter. But Coffey was pushing them farther than any of them meant to go. Scared or not, it was stopping here. They had been willing to help the Navy out of a bind—for triple pay—but they sure as hell hadn't enlisted. "Look, partner," said Catfish. "We don't work for you, we don't take orders from you, and we don't much like you. Besides which, your mama dresses you funny."

Nobody laughed at the old ritual insult. Fighting words. Catfish was drawing the line. Daring Coffey to push any further.

Until now, Bud had been content to let Coffey run his own show. Now, though, it was plain that Coffey wasn't functioning very well. He was sweating, tense. Didn't he realize that his very nervousness was a confession of fear? An open invitation to rebellion? You don't lead independent-minded people by letting them see how much you fear their disobedience. "Hey Cat," said Bud. "Cat.

Catfish turned to him. Reluctantly. "Yeah?"

"Why don't you take the first watch in sonar. OK?" He looked at him steadily, not in challenge, the way Coffey had, but in a way that told him, I need you to do this, for all of us.

Catfish got it. He looked back at Coffey, as if to say, For

228

Bud I'll do it. "Right on," he whispered. Then he walked out, past Coffey, heading for the sonar shack.

"Sonny," said Bud, "you get a couple hours' sleep, then you spell Cat, all right? Hippy, you handle exterior surveillance." They went, avoiding Coffey's gaze. That got easier when he turned his back, leaned on an overhead beam.

Bud came up behind One Night. Because Coffey had as much as accused her of not doing her job, she was the angriest, the one least likely to go along. So he sat down behind her, close, like he was flirting. It was an old joke between them, to flirt a little bit. He was reminding her of all their years of friendship. That she was somebody he could trust. "One Night, will you do me a favor and see if you can get that transmitter fixed? All right?"

For Bud. She'd swallow her pride for Bud. "Give me a couple of hours." It was a good thing Coffey didn't see her glare as she walked on past him out of the mess hall. It might have turned him to stone.

Coffey took it. It was humiliating, it burned deep, but he took it because he was a soldier who would do his duty for his country even if his country was represented on this rig by a bunch of disloyal, selfish, mutinous shitheads.

Even with all the oxygen Lindsey had found, he couldn't count on more than twelve hours in which to complete his assignment. And with the civilians acting like this, he might have even less time. It was certain that he couldn't count on any of them to help him at all, not now. Wilhite was dead. Monk was laid up with a broken leg, so he was only marginally useful. That meant it was up to Schoenick and him to get the warhead into place and blow the *Montana* off the ledge and down into the abyss before the Russian bogey could get any more information from it.

So little time. He felt it like somebody's breath on his neck. He had to *hurry*.

Hippy was in the control room, driving Big Geek around outside *Deepcore*. Officially he was supposed to be watching out for the NTI Lindsey had seen. But hell, she said it was friendly, didn't she? If he saw it, he'd be glad, but in the meantime he wanted to look for what really scared him: Coffey. He found him through the viewport of maintenance room B. There was a light inside, and he carefully jockeyed Big Geek until the ROV's video camera was pointing straight in the window. "Come on, A.J. Squared Away," murmured Hippy. "Move to the left. That's it."

He had a pretty clear view. He couldn't see details, but he didn't have to. You didn't need a Ph.D. in nuclear physics to figure out what the silver cone on the table was. It sure as hell wasn't part of *Deepcore's* equipment, which meant it was the thing they'd brought back from the *Montana.* It had to be a nuclear warhead. And there it was, opened at the base, with Coffey sticking his hands right up the warhead's ass.

"Oh, man. This isn't happening," Hippy murmured. "Oh, come on. I am not here."

He had to get a picture of this. Nobody'd believe these guys would be stupid enough to arm a nuclear weapon right here in *Deepcore,* not unless Hippy got the evidence. He stepped over to the VCR that was always hooked to Big Geek, pushed in the tape, pressed Record.

"Oh, man. Are you for real?"

Bud knew Hippy was a little paranoid, but he'd never seen him this flat-out scared before. Either Hippy was over the edge or something pretty bad was going down. Either way, Bud had to take it seriously. So he sat in front of the monitor, watching Hippy's videotape. One of the SEALs had his back to the window, blocking out whatever was on the table. Bud looked around the edges of the screen, trying to figure out what room he was looking at. "This is the maintenance room, right?"

"Yeah, this is the maintenance room. Look at me, I'm shaking, man."

Right, Hippy, I already noticed that.

Hippy put his hand down on the VCR, as if he could squeeze the right information out of it if he pressed hard enough. "All right, wait wait wait wait. And now, heeeeere's MIRV."

Bud saw the cone. He heard what Hippy said. He just didn't want to jump to a conclusion.

Hippy knew what Bud's silence meant. "Come on, man. What else could it be?"

"Why bring it here?" It's got to make sense before I believe it.

Hippy had it all figured out, of course. "It's got to be some kind of emergency plan to keep it away from the Russians, right? Look look look, they hotwire one of the nukes, they use some kind of detonator that they brought, then they stick it back in the sub, fry the whole thing up, bam, slicker'n snot."

Bud just sat there, watching the screen, thinking.

Hippy answered him, though, as if Bud were arguing with him. "I'm telling you, and I'm not being paranoid—" He saw some kind of motion out of the corner of his eye and looked toward the door. "Hi, Lins," he said.

Bud turned around, saw her standing there. How long had she been there? She must have seen and heard enough to know what was happening—or what Hippy *thought* was happening. Otherwise she'd be in here asking questions, demanding to know.

She stood there for a long moment, waiting for Bud to say something. But he couldn't think of anything to say. So she turned and left, moving like she meant to go somewhere and do something major.

If Hippy was right, Coffey was up to some real crazy shit down in the maintenance room. This must be the Phase Two DeMarco had ordered back when they reported the first time Lindsey saw something. But that also meant that the craziest thing anybody could do was try to confront Coffey about it.

Bud got up and followed her down the corridor. "Lins! Will you just wait a second!"

"Look, goddammit, if you won't do something about it, I will."

"Lindsey, we'll do something about it, just wait a second!"

She was at the door. She looked in the window, trying to

turn the wheel. It was dogged down from the inside. "Hello!" she cried, a challenge, not a greeting. She slapped on the door.

"Lindsey!" said Bud.

She didn't stop. She took a fire extinguisher from the wall and started banging on the door with the bottom of it. "What?"

"Will you just stop and think about this for a second!"

"For what?" She kept banging.

The door opened.

Schoenick stepped back as Lindsey came in. Coffey stood there in front of the table, a blanket over the warhead. Lindsey went straight for the table. Coffey sidestepped a little, but he could tell by the way she was acting that she already knew what was there. So when she reached around to pull the blanket off, he didn't break her arm. He let her do it. What did it matter now if she saw what a MIRV looked like? Besides, Brigman was with her. Coffey had to find out whether he was with this woman or if maybe he was still reasonable. If not, if things went too far, he was ready.

The Brigman woman was all full of moral outrage. "You've got some huevos bringing that thing into my rig. With all that's going on up in the world, you bring a nuclear weapon in *here?*"

What, thought Coffey, your little rig is some holy temple of peace? What do you think has kept you free and safe to build your little underwater toys, Mrs. Brigman? It's been weapons like the one behind me, it's been men like me. So go ahead, be righteous about what is too filthy and vile to bring into your rig. All your life you've been spending the freedom that this filthy weapon earned for you.

But he said nothing. Let her wear herself out with talking.

She turned to the others—Brigman, the kid with the rat, even Schoenick. Didn't she know that Schoenick was loyal to the core? She'd get no support there.

"Does this strike anyone as particularly psychotic, or is it just me?" Lindsey demanded.

Coffey was still in control of himself. Just like always. He spoke to her calmly, reasonably. "Mrs. Brigman, you don't

232

need to know the details of our operation. It's better if you don't."

In reply, she got even more unreasonable, her voice rising in pitch and volume. "You're right. I don't. What I need to know is *that thing is off this rig!* You hear me, Roger Ramjet?" By the end of her speech she was yelling.

As if she really believed that this would impress Coffey, would cause him to recognize that she had authority over him, would cause him to deviate from his mission. "You're becoming a serious impediment to our mission," Coffey said. He spoke in careful, measured tones. "Now you either do an about-face and walk out of here, or I'll have you escorted out."

She shook her head, laughing in fury. "I will not do an about-face and get out of here." She began yelling again. "Who the hell do you think you're talking to?"

Coffey nodded at Schoenick, who was standing behind her. Schoenick moved quickly, seized her around the body, pinning her arms to her sides. She went apeshit, yelling, struggling to get free. Coffey wasn't worried about her. It was Brigman who worried him. If he suddenly got macho about protecting his woman, somebody was going to die right here.

Bud reached behind him and punched the fire alarm on the wall by the door. It rang loudly as he held down the button on the P.A. and said, *"Emergency!* Maintenance room B. *Emergency!"*

Hippy dodged out into the corridor, yelling for the rest of the crew. "Now! Come on! We got trouble! Now! Come on!"

Coffey was taking all this in, trying to decide what to do. The rest of the crew were pounding down the ladders, along the corridors. But so far Brigman hadn't made a move. Brigman was clearly angry. He was watching Coffey, never took his eyes off him. Didn't even bother watching Lindsey as she struggled to get out of Schoenick's grasp. The man was smart. He knew that until Coffey said the word, no way was anyone getting that woman out of Schoenick's hold. And as long as Brigman didn't lose his head, Coffey wouldn't have to do anything final.

Catfish, Hippy, One Night, Sonny—they were all crowded around the door. They would have charged in, would have mixed it up right away, but Brigman stopped them. "All right, all right, all right, all *right.*" They stopped. They waited.

So did Coffey.

For the first time, Bud turned and spoke to Schoenick. "All right, man, you let her go. Do it." Schoenick didn't respond in any way. Bud raised his voice. "Do it, now!"

Coffey had to decide. Brigman was beginning to lose it. Whether it was real or just for show didn't matter. What mattered was this: Coffey's mission. Phase Two. The warhead behind him. Not holding this Brigman bitch. So Coffey softly gave the order to Schoenick. "Let her go."

Instantly Schoenick released her. She moved quickly away, backed up to where Bud stood at the front of the crowd. Solidarity.

Bud glanced at her to make sure she was OK. Then he looked back at Coffey. "That's the smartest thing you ever did."

Maybe, Coffey said silently. Let's see what *you* do next. Let's see if *you're* smart.

The Brigman woman thought that she was still part of the battle. She picked up right where she left off. Yelling. "Coffey, you son of a bitch!"

But this time Brigman didn't stand by and let her do it. *"Lindsey!"* he shouted. Then, softer: "Cool it." It seemed to startle her, make her realize that this wasn't a problem she could solve by yelling louder or cussing harder. She had no authority here. She fell silent.

Catfish spoke up. "What's the problem?"

That's right, fighter, tough guy. You butt in, prove you're hot stuff. Coffey watched Brigman, to see what he'd do.

"Nothing," said Brigman. "We were just leaving." He turned to Lindsey. "Weren't we."

That was what Coffey was looking for. Brigman knew what was at stake here. He knew Coffey was never going to back down. He knew that if things went one inch further, somebody was going to die. The Brigman woman had been way out of line coming down here, poking her nose into top-secret activities.

The crew backed out through the hatch. Bud lingered in the doorway, never taking his eyes off Coffey, never turning his back until all of his people except Catfish were safely out. Then he stepped back through, letting Catfish have the last glare, the final gesture of defiance. Then the hatch swung shut. Coffey and Schoenick were alone again.

Coffey pulled the pistol he had been holding from behind his back, rested the muzzle on the table. The confrontation hadn't turned into a showdown, but if it had, Coffey would have been ready. He would have had to kill Brigman first, then Catfish. That would slow down the others, make them think again. And the Brigman woman. He would have had to kill her, because nothing else would ever stop her.

"We don't need them," Coffey said to Schoenick. "We can't trust *them*. We have to take steps. We're going to have to take steps."

Walking down the corridor, Bud knew he had to have it out with Lindsey, right now. It was one thing, her going off half-cocked back during the days when they were building the rig, training for it. Then all she did was offend guys in suits, crewmen, civilized people. Bud always had time to go back, smooth things out. Not so much was at stake.

But Lindsey didn't have sense enough to know that Coffey was a different kind of person. And it wasn't just that he was in the military. Bud had been watching him there in the maintenance room. The way Coffey was sweating. The way his glance kept sliding off sideways, like he couldn't keep looking straight at anything.

"Lins, I want you to stay away from that guy. I mean it."

Hippy had seen it, too. "Yeah. That guy is gone. You see his hands?"

Lindsey finally got the picture. "What, he's got the shakes?" It was unbelievable to her that she hadn't noticed it. If Coffey had been a machine, she would have noticed in a fraction of a second that it was malfunctioning, that it was dangerous. But because he was a person, he could wear the signs of HPNS as bright as neon and she'd never see it. So Bud would have to explain it to her, clearly, so she couldn't mistake it. Maybe this time, after Schoenick roughed her up a little, maybe this time she'd get the message. "Look, the guy's operating on his own. He's cut off from his chain of command. He's showing signs of pressure-induced psychosis. And he's got a nuclear weapon. So, as a personal favor to me, will you put your tongue in neutral for a while?"

Hippy chimed in. "I can tell you, I give this whole thing a sphincter-factor of about nine-point-five." He'd never sounded more excited in the whole time Bud had known him. It finally dawned on him. Hippy wasn't paranoid because he was paranoid. He actually *loved* being scared. That's why he was always looking for reasons to frighten himself.

Only now that it was over did Lindsey realize what had happened. She found out about the warhead, it was like finding out there was some malfunction in the electrical system. The second you know about it, you go fix it. But this wasn't that simple. She didn't have a wiring diagram for people. But Virgil did. He had warned her, he practically begged her not to get into it. But she didn't listen. She didn't *trust* him to know better than she did.

Why should she feel bad about it? It was just what he did to her, not believing her about the NTIs.

Except that he'd taken her off in private, he'd listened to her, he really wanted to believe her. While *she* flouted *him* right in front of everybody. Not just this time, but over and over again. He'd tell her, Do it this way, it'll work out better. And then she'd do the opposite because what business did *he* have telling her what to do?

I'll tell you what business he had, Lindsey said to herself. He was *right*. Things really would have worked out better if I'd just stopped when he said to. Thought about it for a few seconds. Figured out something intelligent to do. If somebody acted around my rig the impetuous, arrogant way I act around Bud's *people,* I'd throw them off the rig, I'd want to kill them.

One time he lets me down, one time he doesn't believe

me, and I feel so betrayed I want to die. I've done it to him a dozen times, a hundred times in the years we've been together. How does he feel? Why the hell did he ever love me?

Right then, right at the moment when she was about to reach for a real understanding of what Bud was about, the emotions were so strong inside her that she couldn't handle it. She didn't know what to *do* with feelings like that.

So she stopped. Right on the verge of losing her self-control she just—stopped. Didn't feel anything. Like all the times her schoolmates froze her out, all the times her sisters or her mother sniped at her. I don't have to deal with this. This is nothing to me. It's stupid to get emotional about this. Bud wasn't going to do anything about the warhead, so I had to, it's that simple. He's always weak, always conciliatory. Well, I'm not. I *act*. That's why it never worked between us, why it could never have worked. Bud and I are completely different people, that's all. At least I was trying to do something. All *he* did when he took over in there was give in to Coffey, give in *completely*. Virgil Brigman is a weak man.

How many times had she said that to herself? Especially after she filed for divorce. Every time she noticed he wasn't there, every time she looked for him or thought about him, she went through the litany of reasons why he just didn't measure up.

This time, though, it didn't make her feel better. Just made her feel bitter. Toward Bud? No. Just bitter. What are you, Lindsey?

You're bullshit, that's what you are.

Only she didn't want to believe that. She refused to believe it. *Bud* knew she wasn't bullshit. After all that had happened, after all the times she'd stung him with a word, all the times she'd humiliated him in front of his friends, his crew—he still loved her. He still wore the ring she gave him. What about that? If she was bullshit, why would somebody like Bud Brigman feel like that about her?

Coffey leaned into the conical well leading to the round window of the maintenance room. His reflection was in the window at first, but the farther he leaned in, the more his shadow blocked out the light, and then he could see past the glass, out into the void.

There was something out there, an enemy. And now he was surrounded by enemies inside, too. He had originally planned to plant the warhead with the timer set for several days. It'd give them time for the *Explorer* to come back, hook up a new umbilical, rig a towline and drag them away from here. They could keep watch here until the *Explorer* returned, drive off the intruder whenever it came back. Then, when ships got through the storm, the Navy could clear the area, keep it safe until the warhead went off.

But there was no time for that now. He couldn't use any of the civilians now—they'd never cooperate. They'd probably sabotage the operation if they had a chance. The Brigman woman certainly would, probably One Night, too. And Catfish was bound to get belligerent, start a fight. Hippy was certifiable. Sonny was on the edge of hysteria. Bud was his enemy now. They were all dangerous. All of them.

Even me.

Stuck to the acrylic bubble beside him was one of those suction-cup Garfields. Somebody's idea of a joke. Pressed up against the window, spread-eagled, naked, hanging on. Any second he could lose his grip and fall screaming into the abyss. Any second.

Chapter 12

Friends and Enemies

Sonny and Catfish were in the galley. Catfish was having a bite to eat before he crashed; Sonny was having a cup of coffee before he went on duty in the sonar shack. Since the eating area was now the sleeping quarters as well, Monk lay on one of the tables in the galley, so wrapped up in blankets it was hard to see a man-shape under them.

"Damn cold," said Catfish.

Sonny nodded and sucked down a deep draught of coffee. "This stuff don't stay hot long enough." His arm also hurt like hell and he wanted so bad to be home that he could taste it. Sonny'd got control of himself in the last few hours, so he didn't feel like crying all the time, but he was still scared, he still figured he was probably going to die and never see his family again. It was safer, though, to complain about the coffee.

Catfish hummed something, staring off into space. Sonny knew the song but couldn't remember what it was. Then Catfish broke into words right at the end. "Jesus, Savior, pilot me."

It was a hymn. Sonny never figured Catfish for the religious type.

Which he wasn't, as Catfish proved with the next thing he said. "The way I figure it, partner, if God loved me I'd be home in Houston right now."

"How do you know something worse wouldn't've happened to you in Houston if you was there?" asked Sonny.

"You tell me one thing that could happen to me in Houston that's worse than this. I'm twenty-one hundred feet under the ocean with a hurricane over my head, cut off from the world, we got maybe ten more hours of oxygen, our rig is crippled and can't move under its own power anymore, we got one member of our crew seeing UFOs whenever she's alone, and there's a crazy man with an atom bomb giving orders and seeing Commies everywhere." Catfish took another bite of his peanut-butter-and-cracker sandwich. "Only thing worse'd be if you cut my dick off and put me in a room full of whores."

Sonny laughed. Best thing about Catfish, even when he was pissed off and scared shitless, he could find a way to make it funny.

"Lieutenant Coffey is a good man."

Sonny looked around, surprised. Who said *that?* Monk. Forgot he was here. "Thought you were asleep," said Sonny.

"We've been through hell with Lieutenant Coffey a lot of times." Monk didn't sound angry. Just telling them stuff they didn't know. "He always brought us back. Every one of us."

"Well, not this time," said Catfish.

"He's never lost a man before," said Monk.

Sonny hadn't thought of that. It explained part of why Coffey was so jittery, so upset-looking.

"Well, isn't that what soldiers get paid for?" asked Catfish. He was joking again, but this time, thought Sonny, it wasn't time for a joke.

"No sir," said Monk. "That's what soldiers get *honored* for."

Sonny got to thinking then, about what soldiers do, and about how he hadn't thought of *why* Coffey might be so upset right now, and so he told them a story. "When my daddy was in the Navy, back in forty-nine, his ship put in at

240

Havana and he got shore leave. This was before Castro. Well, they acted like sailors on leave, getting drunk and having enough fun to kill a normal man, and they're walking through Central Park in Havana and my dad has to take a leak. There's this statue right in the middle of the park, on top of a big stone whatever, like a wall, and so my dad whips it out and hoses down the stone. And while he's doing that, one of the other guys thinks he's a mountain climber and he goes right up to the top of the statue and sits on its head."

"Is this going somewhere, Sonny?" asked Catfish.

"Well, see, it doesn't sound like a big deal to you guys, does it? Just a bunch of drunk sailors, right?"

Right.

"Only it was a statue of a guy named Marti, and to the Cubans it's like he's George Washington and Abraham Lincoln and Nathan Hale all rolled up in one, and this is the most sacred shrine to his memory. I mean, what if a bunch of Cubans came into the Lincoln Memorial and climbed up and took a dump in Lincoln's lap and then wiped their asses with the flag?"

"They'd be licking it off with their tongues in about ten seconds," said Catfish.

"If the police hadn't been right there," said Sonny, "the crowd in the park would've torn my daddy and the other sailors into pieces. Little teeny pieces so small the ants would've carried them off before they could collect enough to fill one coffin. That's how my daddy always said it. It was the most scared he ever was in his life."

"What happened to him?"

"Back in those days the Cuban government was just a bunch of suck-ups to the U.S., so they turned my daddy and his buddies over to the fleet. The Cuban people *hated* that. They were screaming for blood. Their honor was besmirched, my daddy said. That's the worst thing that can happen to a Cuban. They still fight duels, you know. Anyway they had demonstrations in the streets, and when the U.S. Ambassador went out and tried to make a speech to the demonstrators, the police show up and start beating people up. So the only ones that got punished was Cubans."

"I bet your daddy caught hell," said Catfish.

"They didn't say a damn thing to him about it. If the Navy'd punished the sailors, then maybe the Cubans could have forgiven what happened, because that would be saying, Our boys did wrong and we're sorry. But when *nothing* happened, it was like the United States was saying, Fuck you and the horse you rode in on. My daddy always told that story. Every time one of us kids got in a fight with somebody, my daddy'd say, What did you do? And we'd say, I didn't do *anything*. And he'd say, What did you do? And we'd say, All I did was this one little harmless thing. And then he'd say, What do you think that looked like to the other guy? And most of the time we'd end up saying, It looked like I was as low as a rat's asshole. And Daddy'd tell us that story again and then he'd beat the shit out of us."

Catfish laughed.

Monk didn't.

"You're a philosopher, partner, and I never knowed it," said Catfish.

"I'm just saying that we don't know what Coffey means by what he's doing, and he sure as hell don't know what we mean by what *we're* doing. Nobody ever understands anybody in this world."

Catfish's smile faded and he leaned in close, looking as serious as Sonny ever saw. "You're probably right, partner, but I'll tell you something else. Right now Coffey's crazy with HPNS. He's shaking, he's paranoid, and he's sweating so much he probably doesn't have to piss anymore. So we're not talking here about simple little misunderstandings or guys who got drunk and peed in the wrong place. We're talking about a guy who knows how to kill people with his bare hands who thinks the ocean's full of Russians and we're dangerous Commie sympathizers, and on top of all that, he's got him a bomb that could make a tidal wave that'd wash up pieces of *Deepcore* on the beaches of Nebraska."

"It's not that powerful a device," said Monk softly.

"Now don't tell me that," said Catfish. "If I'm gonna get my ass blowed off by your lieutenant, I want to think it's a first-rate bomb that did it, OK?" He turned to Sonny. "And you know what else? I'm not even gonna brush my teeth after eating." With that he swung himself around on the table, dragged a couple of blankets up around his neck, and curled up to sleep. Sonny reached over to a pile on another table and came back with a pillow, which he tucked under Catfish's head.

"Thanks, Mom," said Catfish.

"Just don't have any dirty dreams while you're sleeping," said Sonny. He remembered tucking his kids into bed and felt the forbidden emotions swell up inside him again. Keep control of yourself, Sonny. What happens, happens. He rinsed off his cup and headed off for the sonar shack, so he could keep watch for possible intruders.

Lindsey couldn't do anything about Coffey, but that didn't mean she had to do nothing at all. Nobody else believed her about the NTI. Except Coffey, and he only believed her enough to be convinced that it was a Russian submersible. And Hippy—*he* believed her. It really annoyed her that he of all people was the only one, but he was somebody, wasn't he? He could help.

She found Hippy doing maintenance on Big Geek. The camera in Big Geek's nose was on; from time to time Hippy made it go through a series of test movements. She watched him work for a minute or so. She tried to think of some easy way of starting up this conversation. How would Bud start up? Hey, Hippy, I been thinking, why don't we—

Why the hell am I trying to be Bud? I'm me, and if they can't deal with that, too bad.

"Hippy," she said, "I can't just sit up here in *Deepcore* hoping for one of them to come back."

He stopped working and looked at her for a moment. Then he realized what she was talking about. "The NTIs?"

"I want to go down and see if we can find *them.*"

Hippy looked at her like she was crazy. "You can't go down there," he said. "It's very deep."

"Not *me,*" she said. She patted the nose of the ROV. "Big Geek."

He laid a protective hand on his ROV. "Big Geek is on a

tether." That was a bad sign, him touching Big Geek. Hippy had a way of thinking that the machines he worked with were people. Friends. He didn't like them taking risks.

"Does he have to be?" asked Lindsey. "Look, you can just punch into his primary guidance chip where you want him to go, and he goes, right?"

Hippy waved his hands in the air like he was trying to wash the idea right out of the air. "No, no. Bad idea, Lindsey. Bad."

"Why, Hip? Come on." Hippy always had reasons why things wouldn't work. That was one of the things that made him valuable. It was also one of the things that drove Lindsey crazy.

"Because even *if* he can take the pressure at that depth—which I don't think he can. Without the tether, you know what happens down there? It would just sit like a—please?"

She had been fiddling with the joystick controls lying there on the workbench. She didn't realize it until he told her to stop. She drew her hand back.

Hippy went on. "It would just sit like a dumbshit. Something would have to pass in front of the camera for you to see anything."

He was right. It was a farfetched chance. But it was something, wasn't it? "I know, but we *could* get lucky, right? We should go for it."

"I really ought to talk to Bud about this."

"No, this is between you and me. We get proof, then we tell the others. Hippy, look. If we can prove to Coffey that there aren't Russians down there, maybe he'll ease off the button a little bit."

That set him off in a different direction. "I gotta tell you, that guy *scares me*. More than anything we're gonna find down there. He's a goddam A.J. Squared Away jarhead robot." Just talking about Coffey had moved Hippy squarely to being on Lindsey's side. Nothing like having a common enemy to make Hippy into your loyal friend. "OK, give me a couple hours," he said. "I'll see what I can do."

* * *

Coffey looked into the control room to see if the civilians were still keeping watch. They were, sort of. Sonny was there in the sonar shack, headphones on, the sonar equipment working fine. Only thing wrong was that Sonny was asleep, holding onto his broken arm like he was afraid even in his sleep that the thing was going to fall off.

Coffey wandered around the control room a little. He snapped on the monitors. About half of them were dead— the ones on the flooded side of *Deepcore*. The others showed empty rooms, or guys sleeping. Except the observation camera in the sub bay. Hippy was down there, working on the ROV with a big toothy shark's grin painted on its face. Big Geek. And in comes the Brigman woman, and so Coffey sat down and listened to every word they said.

Jarhead robot.

Coffey refused to take any of the things they said personally. Little weasely rat boy thinks I'm crazy? Fine. But the crazy one is you, boy. Letting her talk you into acting out her plan for you. You start letting a woman give you your instructions in life, you never know where it's going to lead. It'll turn you into something you never meant to be. Because women don't think of men as people. I finally caught on to that. They think of us as particularly useful machines. You and that ROV, rat boy, you're both the same to her, she can't tell where one leaves off and the other begins. You watch a woman with a machine, boy. They'll act the same way they do with you. They'll try to make the machine do what they want, and when it doesn't, they'll yell at it, they'll turn their backs and pout, they'll cry, they'll do all the same shit they do with you. Only the machines are smarter than us. They just sit there and let it all roll off their backs. Machines don't have to pay attention to women because machines don't want to fuck 'em. And machines don't have no mamas. So Big Geek doesn't give a shit if that bitch walks off and leaves him and starts using Little Geek instead. A machine can't be *betrayed*.

Coffey suddenly broke off his train of thought. What am I doing, sitting here thinking about stupid shit like this? I have a mission to think about. Enemy vehicle in the area. Hostile civilian crew in this rig. Only Schoenick and Monk left on my team, a man and a half. God, I lost Wilhite. I never lost anybody before. Things were out of control, completely out of control down here. But it was my fault. I went off on Flatbed and the rig didn't get unhooked and so Wilhite died. *Bad judgment, Coffey*. No shit. No shit. Very bad judgment. But it's the only judgment I got down here. Act in the best interest of your country, Coffey. Maybe you should've backed off right at first, when you saw your hand shaking. Only what would've happened different? Who would've taken over? When DeMarco said Phase Two they would've done the same thing I did because that was the order, proceed *at once* to missile, remove warhead, carry it to a safe place and arm it. Same result. Not my fault. Did what I was told.

Why am I still sitting here whining to myself? Think about what's going on. Just think about it. Review the current situation. Assets and liabilities. How have things changed with what they're doing to the ROV? They're programming it to go down. Straight down into the Cayman Trench. Think about that.

The lights were down. The pseudo-night that landside creatures with a built-in twenty-four-hour clock had to have. Catfish, One Night, and Bud were crashed out on the tables in the mess hall, wrapped in blankets. Monk was lying in the galley, nursing his broken leg, sometimes sleeping, sometimes not. The cold was intense. Water dripped everywhere, not from leaks, but from water vapor inside *Deepcore* condensing on the walls. But with enough of them in the mess hall and the infirmary next door, their body heat kept it from getting impossibly cold.

Lindsey was making coffee. She had seen when she came in that Monk wasn't asleep. So when the coffee was ready, she poured two cups. She carried a cup over to where he lay, nothing but a face in a pile of blankets. His hand came out, took the coffee.

As she turned away, she felt his hand touch her sleeve. She turned back to him. "Thanks," he said. With her eyes she acknowledged him, then moved away.

He wasn't like Lieutenant Coffey. Maybe he used to be, but he wasn't anymore. That tough, businesslike edge wasn't there. That air of unapproachability. Monk had turned back into a real person. Maybe the pain had done it to him, but he remembered how to be human, how to be a kid in his early twenties, still not sure how to be a grown-up, still not sure he even wanted to be. It was a good sign—maybe there was a human being hidden away inside Coffey and Schoenick, too. Maybe that meant there was a limit to their arrogance. A line they wouldn't cross. She remembered Schoenick gripping her, how helpless she had been. No matter how she struggled, it was like he barely even noticed. He had so much unused strength left over, she knew he could have killed her like *that*. Just slap her on the side of the head and snap her neck like a pretzel. She hated that. Somebody having that much power over her.

She walked from the galley into the mess hall. Bud was in there, snoring softly. She went over and sat down beside the table where he was sleeping. The breeze of her movement must have disturbed him a little, or maybe it was her soft footfalls, but anyway his snoring downshifted to a loud rasp. That used to happen whenever she came to bed late. A wordless rebuke, as if he were saying, I was alone here, where were you?

She spoke to him as she used to do at home. "Virgil, turn on your side."

Bud grunted, turned on his side. An automatic response. The well-trained husband. She'd almost forgotten that. So much between them that came like reflex now. They might not understand each other, but they knew how to live together, how to *be* together. They had a lot of mileage on the marriage, more than most people got in so few years, because they'd been together waking and sleeping, on the job and at home. But if the old car won't run anymore, you have to get a new car, don't you? Can't hang on to the old one till it rusts on the front lawn. We were good together for a while, Virgil and me, and then we weren't. That's all. Too bad, yes, but not the end of the world.

Alone now in the sonar shack, Sonny slept on. If he really believed there was something out there, he might have stayed awake, might have kept watch. But he was a skeptic, and so he slept. He didn't hear the interference that came up on the passive sonar. He didn't see the almost imperceptible trace that appeared on the active sonar screen.

It arose out of the chasm, a single tube of water within water. Usually sonar completely missed the builders and the porters, because they made no sound, and when sonar transmitted high-frequency sound waves, their bodies absorbed the energy of the sound vibrations within the water, reflecting nothing back for sonar to pick up. Now, though, they were trying something new. Instead of trying to reach the humans in the water, they would reach inside *Deepcore* itself and observe them, communicate with them if that was possible. It meant developing a new structure that could thrive in a gas environment instead of liquid. It meant reshaping and merging several porters into a flexible tube like a single thick tendril. Within this tube, builders could pass freely. They had to collapse their own bodies in order to fit, just as they did when traveling inside a glider. This was dangerous—they had none of their natural protection against the relatively low pressure this close to the surface. That's why the builders sent out the tube from a glider far down the cliff, so they never had to venture out into the open water. The tube would protect them, allow them to carry the ocean with them inside the gaseous interior of *Deepcore*. They could see the humans as the humans saw each other.

Because the new tube had a much thicker outer layer, the builders couldn't draw energy of any kind through it. Sound waves were no longer absorbed; the tube's movement could now be picked up, faintly, by *Deepcore's* active sonar.

It also meant that as the tube rose up out of the canyon, there was no dimming of the lights inside *Deepcore*. The builders knew from Lindsey's mind that there was no energy to spare, and little oxygen—the risk of more human death was a serious matter to them now that they knew how permanent and complete human death was. They would do nothing to increase the risk. Besides, the dimming of power made the humans more fearful. By coming this way, into the gaseous human environment, without any harmful act like the draining of power, surely the humans would not be afraid of them. Then they could begin to converse.

In the sub bay, Hippy had just finished the modifications to Big Geek. He looked at the front of the ROV, its front bubble window like a single eye, the shark's smile painted under it. "All set, big guy," he said. Then, sternly: "I told you to wipe that grin off your face." Hippy yawned, turned off the lights, left the sub bay.

Behind him, the builders' probe reached up out of the water into the air—the tetramix—that the humans breathed. The structure solidified, flexed, held. The brightness of the life inside the tube reflected from the water, making shadows dance on the ceiling and the walls. Swiftly, steadily, it followed Hippy out of the sub bay, the tube growing at the tip, water and energy flowing along its length to provide the materials for its growth, drawing them ultimately from the sea far below in the abyss. It was the first time the builders had ever had to make a structure that could move flexibly over solid surfaces while being fully self-contained in fluids and energy. The gliders had to fly through open atmosphere and the wide emptiness of space; they didn't have to move through narrow corridors. So their rigid, skeletized structure wouldn't do at all. Fortunately, the atmosphere inside *Deepcore* was pressurized to balance with the ambient ocean, so the probe didn't have to withstand a serious pressure differential. All the strength of the structure was spent on holding it balanced in the air, not touching anything unnecessarily, since each friction point would require much greater energy and attention to support the walls of the tube.

It worked splendidly. It rose out of the water, balancing precisely as it turned and extended over the sub bay deck, then thrust its swiftly-growing tip through the hatch and into the corridors of *Deepcore*. They had built something new and it worked; even if nothing else came of it, this would be worth sharing with other builder colonies on other worlds.

But something else *must* come of this. They were so close to being able to make themselves understood. If the humans could hold off just a little longer, the builders could explain it all to them, so they wouldn't kill each other over offenses that no one meant to commit.

Hippy trudged along the dark corridor. He reached the men's head and went inside. Behind him, light shimmered on the walls and door. The lead builder took the tip of the probe past the door and went on toward the chambers where the builders outside *Deepcore* told her the most humans were gathered. Another builder stayed behind in the tube and sent tendrils through the door into the john and began scanning Hippy's brain as he sat there.

The probe reached into the room where Monk lay sleeping. The builder nearest the tip of the probe sent out tendrils to examine him. He was in pain, but the damage to his leg was structural only, and the body was healing itself. The builder didn't understand human body structure well enough to meddle. She went on.

The probe found Jammer next. Here the builder's tendrils brought her more disturbing information. Jammer's oxygen poisoning had caused serious brain damage. Many of the connections within it had broken down, drastically changed from the condition it had been in when one of the builders scanned his brain back in the *Montana*. She passed the information back to the builder that was next behind her in the tube. Immediately the second builder set to work reconstructing the brain to the state it had been in when it was scanned before. She wasn't carrying all those memories with her, but it took only a few moments for the question to be passed down the tube to the glider waiting under the edge of the cliff. The questions was relayed by messenger to the city. Moments later a builder returned with the full and perfect memory of exactly how Jammer's brain had been before the accident. The second builder sent out her own tendrils and began the work of reconstruction. Because it was delicate work, requiring much intelligence on the spot, she passed a significant portion of herself along the tendrils, so that for a brief time she dwelt inside Jammer's head, overseeing the work where she could make instant decisions on a dozen subjects at once.

In the meantime, the leader pressed on, trusting that the work of undoing the harm they caused would be carried on behind her. The tip of the probe reached into the mess hall, where Bud, One Night, and Catfish were asleep on tables, and Lindsey dozed lightly on a chair. The builder recognized her from her smell—the tiny flecks of skin that every human sheds, floating in the air, each fleck containing countless molecules that tagged her identity perfectly. Immediately the builder thrust out tendrils to Lindsey and to all the others sleeping in the room. Because they had to stretch across such a long area of gas, without the support of water, the tendrils were thicker than before—dozens of molecules across. But to human eyes they remained completely invisible. They entered all the sleepers through the nostrils, the ears, the eyes, and quickly scanned their brains. It was a habit now, though only a short time before they were exploring the human brain for the first time. Within moments, memories were being transferred back down the tube to the builders waiting high in the canyon, and they in turn carried them to the city deep in the abyss. At once the city began to analyze. Soon they would learn what had been happening in *Deepcore* from several different perspectives. But not soon enough.

Lindsey stirred. The others felt nothing and remained asleep, but Lindsey had been touched before, and felt the surge of new thought within her mind, not as a dream, but as an event. She opened her eyes and saw it at once, a glassy tube of water suspended in the air, reaching through the door into the room.

"Bud," she whispered, afraid to alarm it, but determined that this time she would not be the only witness. "Bud. Bud, get up."

He began to awaken. She felt a terrible dread that he would look and see nothing, that she really was going mad. Then his eyes widened, his body stiffened, he rose up from the bed like a wakening lizard. Yes, he saw it, too.

One Night heard the whispering, felt the movement, woke up. When she saw the tube, she reflexively tried to back away. There was nowhere to go.

Bud also heard movement from the galley, where Monk must also be awake. That left only Catfish asleep. "Cat!" he said. He threw a pillow at him. "Cat!"

Catfish woke up surly, wanting to go back to sleep. He tossed away the pillow, drew his cap down over his eyes. Then he realized what he had glimpsed through squinting, sleepy eyes. He jumped up, grabbed the first heavy object that came to hand. A potted plant sitting in the window well. He held it up like a weapon. He was ready to do battle.

The builder that led the probe felt the fear in them, but this time did not remove it. The city had decided that a little fear was so natural to humans that to deprive them of it completely would deform them. The only message that she sent directly to their brains was a feeling of hesitancy, a desire to wait and watch. Since this desire was already present in them, it was a matter of reinforcing what was already there. Only Lindsey watched with no fear at all.

So the builder decided to begin her attempt at open communication with her. Since humans did not understand that they were being spoken to when thoughts were put directly into their minds, they had to try another way. Language was still too strange and difficult for them to attempt it with confidence. But since they could sense light themselves, they thought a visual message might work. So the probe twisted and darted forward until it hovered in the air in front of Lindsey's face.

This startled her, and now she *was* afraid, for a moment. "Bud—" she said. But then the probe hesitated in the air, its tip a foot or two from her. "No, it's OK, it's OK," she said. She touched him with a restraining hand.

He obeyed her because he trusted her completely now.

She was the one who had been proved right. If she said it was OK, then it was. "I think it likes you," he said.

The builder felt Bud's anxiety ease along with Lindsey's. They were surprised at this. All she had done was touch him and say a few words, and yet his brain filled with calm as if she had put the thought directly in his head. This was a surprise. They hadn't thought humans capable of such a thing. How was it done, with no physical connection, brain to brain?

No time to explore that—let the city do it as the memories reached them. The builder began the task assigned. Carefully it formed the growing tip of the probe into a mirror image of Lindsey's face. Not perfect—the folds and creases were softened because of the material the probe was made of, and the hairs were not even attempted. But it was her face, unmistakably. The builder scanned her thoughts to see what she made of it.

My face, she thought. Which means they know me, or want to know me. They want me to see myself as they see me. Or maybe they want to see as if through my eyes, to understand how things look to me.

She smiled.

It smiled back at her.

They want to wear my face, to *be* me. "It's trying to communicate," she said. And as she did, the builder filled her mind with certainty. Yes. That's right.

But it was easier with her, because she had already received so much communication from the builders. Now for the man beside her, the one who figured so powerfully in her recent memories.

Bud saw his own face take shape on the tip of the NTI probe. Lindsey laughed. "It's wonderful!" she said.

He couldn't help being delighted. Catfish and One Night were even laughing—nervously, but laughing. "It's me," Bud said.

Fearless again, Lindsey remembered touching the large one that came so near to her before. So she reached out a hand to touch the probe.

"No, no, no," Bud warned her.

"It's OK," she said. Trust me. "It's OK."

He trusted her. She reached out, pressed a finger against the probe. It was cool but not cold, and it yielded as easily as if she had put her fingers into a basin of water. Not at all like the hard but frictionless surface of the big one outside. She brought her finger back to her mouth, tasted it. "Seawater," she said.

But the builder was disappointed. These humans had no visual language beyond a few vague concepts. It was all speech—even their writing was a visualization of speech. They would have to find another way.

Nevertheless, there still should be *some* communication. So the builder quickly surveyed the immediate questions in their minds and reordered their minds to hold the answers they wanted. Then she backed away, withdrawing from the room. On the way out, she passed near Monk, reached out tendrils into his mind. She sensed at once that he was different, that he knew things the rest of them didn't know. He knew how to kill, for one thing, and he had done it. But he was complicated, surprising—he took no pride from this, no pleasure.

Monk also knew about the warhead that had been brought aboard *Deepcore;* and even though she detected in him no will to use it, she learned from him that the warhead had been armed. Far from trying to dismantle their weapons, the humans were preparing them for use.

She ordered the probe to rush down the corridor to the place where Monk's mind had told her the warhead was hidden. The city had to know what was being done with the warhead, what they meant to use it for, how it worked. With Bud and Lindsey, Catfish and One Night running after her, she pushed the probe down the ladderway to the maintenance room where the warhead was kept.

Her tendrils examined the weapon. It was still alive; the machinery was set up so it could explode. Why were the humans preparing to do this? If the builders could understand this one thing, then perhaps they could unlock the key to all the madness they had seen, perhaps they could comprehend humanity and find a way to survive on the same planet with them. She probed again into the minds of the people watching her, but none of them knew. In fact, they were afraid of the weapon themselves; they loathed it almost as much as the builders did—even Monk had felt that way.

Then why did they tolerate it? Fear of Coffey. A sense of duty and responsibility to their nation. Awe of the power of the thing. Reluctance to take the responsibility of acting against it themselves. In Lindsey's mind, a memory of being held by Schoenick, pinned, unable to move, as terrible to her as being suffocated. Many reasons in many combinations.

And as the builder held the tube near the warhead, she could also feel their fear. They were terrified that she might set off the weapon, or that she'd be angry at them for having it, that she'd retaliate. There was also hope in some of their minds—hope that she'd disarm it, that she'd take it away from them. These humans—they don't even trust themselves.

Coffey and Schoenick had been back in the locker area, talking where they knew they couldn't be overheard. Then they heard a commotion as the others ran down a distant corridor. Something was going on, something unknown and therefore dangerous. Coffey suspected rebellion, mutiny; he and Schoenick came into the sub bay with pistols drawn, prepared to act. Then they saw the probe rising out of the moonpool like a giant tentacle, reaching through the door. It was unbelievable. Coffey dropped his gun, recoiled from the thing. He couldn't deal with it. I'm gone, he thought. My brain is completely gone and I'm seeing things that can't be there.

Except that Schoenick was seeing it, too. So it had to be real. And that meant that whatever it was, it was reaching into the rig. And that was too dangerous to tolerate. Yet he had never been so frightened. This was an enemy he was completely unprepared for. There was no protocol for dealing with impossible underwater monsters that could reach a two-foot-thick arm into your craft. There was no special weapons training.

But Coffey had dealt with new situations before. He could improvise. The tentacle was reaching into a door? See what happens if the door closes.

He stepped quickly to the button that worked the automatic watertight door. He pressed it. The door began to close.

It took only three seconds for the door to close. In that moment, the probe recognized the danger and informed the builders. They instantly stopped what they were doing and raced back down the tube. It took less than a second before they were gone. Then even the porters that sustained the probe withdrew, leaving behind water-structures that, without constant replenishment and direction, were already collapsing. By the time the door closed, there was nothing alive in the probe. They had gone, all their memories intact, and what splashed on the decks of *Deepcore* was nothing but seawater.

In the maintenance room, the rig crew had no warning. The tentacle was there, its tip hovering near the warhead, and then, suddenly, it was gone, and water splashed onto the floor, spattering them. What happened? What killed it?

Back in the sub bay, the stump of the probe recoiled from the door. For a moment it looked like it meant to attack Coffey and Schoenick. Coffey cried out, put up his hands to ward off the thing. In fact, the builder inside the probe was reaching out with her tendrils, doing a quick scan of both their brains. It found unspeakable terror inside Coffey—even worse than what Jammer had felt. This is the one that tried to kill us, thought the builder, and now it fears retaliation. Fear of us is driving him to madness; if we stay we'll cause him harm. She withdrew her contact with Coffey and pulled the probe back into the moonpool.

The stump of the tentacle fell back into the water with a

splash. Coffey, gasping, watched it go. It didn't touch me, thought Coffey. It knew who I was, it *saw* me, but it didn't touch me. I cut it off and it didn't hurt me. We beat it. He felt the way he did after the cinder block hit Darrel Woodward's head. As Darrel lay there and Coffey stood over him for just a moment, realizing what he'd done. Not a speck of remorse, because he was only doing his duty. But he was filled with a sense of his own strength.

As he sat there, panting in relief, he realized that the Brigman woman had been right. This wasn't the Russians— there was no way in hell they had something like this. What was incredible to him was that she thought it was *better* this way. She was out of her mind. This thing was so much more dangerous than the Russians that he could hardly conceive of all the possibilities. At least the Russians were human, bound by the same constraints as he was. They had to breathe, they had to carry fuel with them, they had *limits*. But these things, whatever they were, they *belonged* down here.

And whatever they are, they've got a technology beyond belief. They've also got access to dozens of warheads on the missiles in the sub. And nobody knows about it but us. They could come out of the water and do whatever they want, anytime they want. We're the only ones who know about them, and *we can't warn anybody*. There's a military doctrine about this. Something—can't remember. Always the rule is, Get back and give warning. Don't engage an unexpected superior force without orders, just get back and report. Only what do you do if you can't report, if there's no way to give warning?

You do what you can to neutralize the enemy. You expend yourself in the effort, if need be, but you neutralize the foe and shield your main forces from the surprise attack.

Only what if you can't do anything to harm it? What if the enemy is so superior that all you can do is stand up in front of it and die? I don't want to die for no purpose. It's too much to ask.

Maybe, though, maybe there's something we can do. It

was easier to hurt the thing than it looked at first. It'll think twice before it comes back here. And even though we still don't know much about it, we know that it can be damaged. Maimed. Broken. And that means that we *can* win. Maybe only a tiny chance of it, but if I can figure out exactly the right thing to do, then I can beat them. The most dangerous, terrible enemy that any soldier ever had to face, but I can beat them.

In the sonar shack, Sonny woke up, startled. It was the sound of the splash of water in the corridors that woke him, but all he could hear now was the hum of the sonar. He struggled to get a fix on the thing as it rushed away from *Deepcore,* but it was gone before he could accomplish anything.

Hippy came out of the can, feeling much better, but still ready for some sleep. If there was any bed space left. When he stepped on the deck, it splashed. He looked down, saw water an inch deep running the length of the corridor. What the hell could have caused it? There weren't any alarms. It couldn't be a leak. He followed the water until he found the others coming up from the maintenance room.

A few minutes later, they were all gathered in the mess hall. Lindsey was feeling so exuberant she could hardly contain it. They had doubted her, but now they knew. Coffey had been so *damn* sure it was Russians, and now he was absolutely proven wrong. Or maybe Coffey didn't get it. "So raise your hand if you think that was a *Russian* water-tentacle. Lieutenant? No? A breakthrough. Takes a while, but . . ."

Bud listened to her. She had a right to gloat a little, but Coffey was looking thoroughly crazed right now, and it wasn't a good time to goad him. He smiled and said, "Hey, Ace."

"Yeah," she said. She gave a little laugh of embarrassment. She knew what he was going to say before he said it. She'd been pushing too far.

"You done impressing yourself?" he said. He said it

teasingly, even affectionately. But for a moment Lindsey felt the rush of anger that always came when he started doing this, when he started *handling* her. But this time she caught herself. Bud knows how to make this work. He's the mechanic in charge. She pinched the bridge of her nose, held her tongue, *took* it. It was damn hard. But it didn't feel as bad as she had thought it would. In fact, it felt kind of good to cooperate with him for a change, even when it cost her a little embarrassment.

It was One Night who spoke up at once, taking the pressure off Lindsey. "No way that thing could be just seawater."

It was a question, a problem, and Lindsey began searching for possible explanations. The ideas came easily to her. "They must have learned how to control water. I mean at a molecular level. You know. They can plasticize it, they can polymerize it, do whatever they want to do with it. They can put it under intelligent control." As she said it, it sounded so right to her, so certain, that she could not possibly doubt that it was true. Why? Why was she so *sure?*

Bud was doing the same thing. "Maybe . . . their whole technology is based on that. Controlling water." She heard him, and recognized that what he said was the truth. How did they know this stuff?

Hippy was full of questions, since he hadn't seen anything but water on the floor. "Was it the same thing you saw last time?"

"No," said Lindsey.

An idea came to him—an idea he was sure of the moment he thought of it. "You know, I don't think that thing was them."

Catfish didn't get it. "Hippy, what are you talking about?"

"I mean I don't think *it* was an NTI. I think *it* was like their version of an ROV. Like Big Geek."

"Hippy, you mean they were just checking us out?" asked Catfish.

"Yeah."

"How come?" asked Catfish.

Lindsey was willing to guess. "Curious, I suppose. We're probably the first people they've seen, right? Who's been down this far?"

Sonny thought back to what had been going on here the past couple of days. What was going on topside, with war looming. "Hope they don't judge the whole race off of us."

Catfish thought that was pretty funny. "Maybe I ought to shave."

"Naw," said Lindsey.

Coffey listened to all this, kept still, heard them out. The Brigman woman was so cocky, they all thought they were so smart. All excited about this stuff, like it was a game, like they were playing scientist and these NTIs were all going to be as sweet-tempered as dolphins. Well, Coffey knew something about the world, and one thing was sure: Nothing had the kind of terrible power these NTIs had without *using* it. He heard them talking and laughing, and the whole time he was shivering inside with fear. He could feel it as an inward trembling, and he knew that if he once let that shaking show on the outside he'd fall apart completely, and then who would stop these things, who would defend the world from an invasion that would make the Huns and the Vandals look like Brownies? He had to keep control, had to, and so he did the only thing he could think of. Pain worked. Pain kept him in focus, it always had before. So he took his K-bar knife in his right hand and held it under the table and carefully, slowly, methodically, cut crosswise into the flesh of his left arm. One cut, then another, then another, working down his arm.

The pain came into his brain like a drug, clearing out his head. The shaking eased up, and a kind of strength took its place. The strength he'd felt before, every time he was right at the cusp of a mission. Those last terrible, glorious moments when he heard the downstairs door open, heard Darrel Woodward walking up the stairs, those moments just before it was time to *act*.

He was in control again. And now they were laughing, making jokes about dressing up pretty for the NTI visitors.

He stood up abruptly and left the room. Schoenick followed him. They walked through the group as if they were smoke.

Outside in the corridor, Coffey reached up and leaned on the ductwork in the low ceiling. Schoenick was right there, waiting to be told what to do. A perfect man. Loyal to the core. Not like those fools inside. "It went straight for the warhead," Coffey said gruffly. "And they think it's cute."

Coffey turned and led the way down to the maintenance room. He reached for his gear bag, pulled it out from under the worktable. Inside it was a short-barreled CAR-15 assault rifle. It was time to take action.

Coffey was right about Schoenick. He was absolutely loyal. But not to Coffey. He was loyal to his orders, to the rules. One rule was that you obey your commanding officer at all times. Fine. But another rule was that you evaluate your team to see what's in their best interest. There was blood on Coffey's arm. A row of slices. Nobody could have done that but Coffey himself. He was actually cutting himself. This was not good. And now he was pulling out a CAR-15 and loading it up. For what? Where was the enemy? He reached out and gripped Coffey by the left arm—up high, above the bleeding. "You need to get some sleep," Schoenick said.

Coffey slapped his hand away and finished with the rifle. Then he set it down and held his hands out in front of him the way he always did when he was about to begin an explanation. As if he held a box of truth between his hands and he was about to open it and show what was inside.

"We have no way of warning the surface," Coffey said. His voice was measured, but Schoenick could hear the chaos behind the words. "Do you know what that means?"

Schoenick didn't know.

Coffey reached out and grabbed him by the front of the shirt, pulled him close. He spoke directly into Schoenick's face. "It means whatever happens is up to *us*. Us."

It registered. Schoenick understood. Of course Coffey was tense. Schoenick knew as well as Coffey did that the civilians weren't with them, had no respect for their mission. Now the mission was changed, now it was ten times, a thousand times as important. They couldn't have *any* interference.

Coffey pressed the assault rifle into Schoenick's hands. Schoenick took it. Snapped the bolt. Safety off. Ready to go.

A few minutes after the SEALs left the mess hall, Bud caught Hippy's eye, then nodded toward the door where the SEALs had gone. Hippy got the message. Go after them. See what they're doing. Hippy got up and left.

He went down the ladder to the bottom level. The maintenance-room door was slightly ajar. He looked in the window. Couldn't see anybody inside. He pushed the door open. It creaked a little, but it didn't matter. The room was empty.

Completely empty. Including the table where the warhead had been lying all this time. They were taking the warhead somewhere. This was bad shit, them taking it God knows where to do God knows what. Hippy headed back upstairs. Before he got back to the mess hall, though, he heard a loud hissing sound coming from the sub bay. He turned and followed along the corridor. The noise got louder, and now there was pounding. No, he knew that sound. The winch. Somebody was moving one of the vehicles into the water.

He got to the door and looked in. He was right. It was Big Geek, being moved over the deck, out toward the water. Only Big Geek wasn't alone. The warhead was tightly strapped under it. Big Geek was now a guided missile with a single nuclear warhead. And Hippy himself had set the target only a few minutes ago.

He backed away from the door, leaned up against the wall, thought about what that could possibly mean. Only one thing. These guys were setting up to blow the NTIs. Smart. So smart. They don't know how many there are, they don't know for sure what kind of weapons they have, don't even know if the NTIs are hostile, and here they are starting a goddam nuclear *war* with them. Bud is not going to like this.

Hippy turned to head back for the mess hall. But he didn't get to take a single step, because there was Coffey, looking at him real calm. His lips were almost brushing the barrel of his pistol, which he held diagonally, his finger on the trigger. Not pointing at Hippy, but the threat was very clear.

"Did you sniff something? Did you, rat boy?"

Then with his left hand Coffey grabbed the front of Hippy's shirt and jerked him out into the corridor.

In the mess hall, Bud leaned into the dome of the window, his back to the others. He was looking out and down. Not that he expected to actually see one of the NTIs. He just had to look into the dark of the ocean while he was thinking about them. Things—no, not things, a kind of *people* that lived down here where the ocean was most terrible. People that could tame the water and make it do whatever they wanted. People who were smarter and stronger and tougher than the ocean. People who looked at this place and thought of it, not as the enemy, but as *home*.

Behind him, the others were still working on the curiosity the builders had encouraged in them. "You think they're from down there originally?" asked One Night. "Or from— you know." She pointed up toward the sky. Hesitantly. It was embarrassing to suggest the idea, even though she knew that it had to be true.

Lindsey was beyond embarrassment. She always had been. It was plain that these creatures came from a completely different evolutionary track. It didn't make sense to think of them as having been there all along. "I don't know." She laughed. "I think—I think they're from you-know. Some place that has similar conditions. Cold, intense pressure."

"Oh, man," said One Night.

"Happy as hogs in a waller down there, probably," said Catfish. He speared a breakfast sausage with his buck knife and brought it to his mouth.

The door swung open and Hippy plunged into the room, Coffey pushing him. They all looked up in time to see Coffey give a shove that sent Hippy down on the ground among them. Before they could react, Coffey was pointing his pistol at them, and there was Schoenick beside him with a wicked-looking rifle. "Freeze!" shouted Coffey. He raised the pistol to aim squarely at Bud, then back down again at the others. "Don't move," Coffey said. The message was clear: I can move this quickly. I can kill any of you before you take a full step toward me. Mother may I? No you may not.

Once Coffey saw that they were all holding still, he backed out into the galley, where Monk was sitting up on his makeshift bed, watching. Schoenick immediately moved into the center of the archway, where he could see everybody, shoot anybody.

Always with an eye on the gun, the crew helped Hippy get up. Now he could deliver his message. "They're using Big Geek to take the bomb to the NTIs." Hippy spotted Lindsey, spoke right to her. "We set it up to go right to them."

"What are you talking about?" asked Bud.

"Oh my God," said Lindsey. How did Coffey know they had set the ROV to go down into the abyss? He was going to nuke the NTIs, even though Lindsey knew, *everybody* knew that they were harmless. And without meaning to, Lindsey and Hippy had helped him do it.

In the galley, Coffey handed his pistol to Monk. "Here, hold this a second." He helped Monk get up and half-carried him into the mess hall with the others. "We're going to Phase Three." He leaned Monk up against the wall in a place where he could keep watch. It was all that Monk could do right now to help the operation—keep the others under control.

Monk, though, was shocked. Phase Three—set the detonator and evacuate. But how could they possibly evacuate? Explode the warhead at the Montana or down in the chasm, and the effect would be the same—*Deepcore* was so close to the edge it would be blown off by the shockwave either way. Even if they could all suit up and ride Flatbed and Cab One out of harm's way, they couldn't carry enough tetramix with them to stay alive more than a few hours. Certainly not enough time to decompress and get to the surface. One way or another, Phase Three would be fatal. Unless Coffey had made contact with the surface and knew that rescue was imminent. Maybe they were setting up a towline to pull *Deepcore* to safety behind some underwater ridge. That would make sense—but how could Coffey have communicated with the surface without the rig crew knowing about it? Impossible. Coffey was sentencing them all to death.

The most terrible thing about it was that Coffey was going to do this in order to kill the NTIs. Monk understood why Coffey feared them—Coffey hadn't seen how the tentacle tried to communicate with them, how it played at making faces with Bud and Lindsey. Coffey couldn't possibly feel Monk's absolute certainty that there was no danger in these creatures. To Coffey, there was nothing but danger. Somehow, Monk had to get him off alone, had to explain it to him, keep him from making this terrible mistake.

But Coffey had already turned back to face the civilians. Of course it was the Brigman woman in front of the group, coming toward him. Her hands were reaching out toward him, open, in supplication. She was trying to be meek and persuasive. He almost laughed out loud—as if she expected him to buy an act like that at this late date. "Coffey? Coffey, just think about what you're doing, OK? Just one minute, just think about what you're—"

But Coffey wasn't going to listen to this anymore. The need to listen politely to pure bullshit from meddling civilians was over. She was no longer an ally or even a neutral. She was the enemy. He reached out and grabbed her, threw her up against the wall. She gasped in fear.

Brigman and the others started to surge forward, but Schoenick was on them, the gun pointed right at them. "Get back!" he shouted.

Lindsey looked into Coffey's eyes and saw only rage and madness. He was pressed close to her, crushing her body against the wall. His voice was measured, dangerous: "This is something I've wanted to do since I first met you." His hands were out of sight, below his waist; she heard a tearing sound, and for a terrible moment thought that he was so insane he intended to humiliate and dominate her with rape.

Then he lifted his hand into view. He was holding

something silvery-gray. A strip of duct tape. He laid the tape firmly across her mouth, pressed it tight all the way back to her ears. He was shutting her up. It would have come as a relief, except that she could breathe only through her nose. She had to calm herself deliberately to keep from panicking about her inability to breathe. She wanted to reach up and tear off the tape, but knew that was the most dangerous thing she could do.

Coffey pushed her into the galley, then went back and started ushering the others in. They pissed and moaned, but they obeyed. Coffey couldn't help thinking that if they'd done that before, there wouldn't have been a problem. They just didn't understand that Coffey was going to fulfill his mission. Period.

Hippy was the last one in. He stopped in front of Schoenick, rifle or no rifle, and tried to talk to him. "Your boss is going to pull the pin on fifty kilotons and we're all ringside." Coffey grabbed him and dragged him into the galley. Hippy kept talking. "He's having a full-on meltdown."

Schoenick didn't respond, but Monk was listening. "What's the timer set for?" asked Monk.

Schoenick answered. "Three hours."

Coffey snapped at them. "Shut up. Don't talk!"

"Three hours," said Monk. There was only one explanation for Coffey's irrational behavior. From the moment Coffey came into the room, Monk could see that he had most of the symptoms of HPNS. Coffey was out of control. It was frightening—the one thing Monk had thought he could count on in this world was Coffey. When everything else was falling apart, Coffey was always cool, Coffey was always thinking. But now Coffey was unreliable, even dangerous.

Still, Monk tried to reason with him. "We can't get to minimum-safe-distance in three hours." Monk was in terrible pain—he shouldn't be standing up yet. But screw the pain—Coffey was out of his mind, and Monk had to *do* something. "We can't go to Phase Three. What about these people?" The orders for Phase Three didn't include blowing the civilians to hell. Coffey took orders very seriously. It was unthinkable that he would exceed them now.

Coffey faced him, close. "Shut up. *Shut up!*" He was scared—Monk could almost taste the fear, Coffey was sweating it, rivers of it pouring down his face. "What's the matter with you?"

What's the matter with *me,* thought Monk, is that you aren't going to snap out of this. You aren't going to act like the real Coffey. So somebody else is going to have to do it.

How much of this could Coffey see in Monk's face? Whatever he saw, Coffey reached a decision. He reached out and took the pistol from Monk's hand. Monk knew what that meant. Coffey had determined that he was unreliable. He was no longer with the SEALs. He may not be inside the galley with the civilians, but he was no longer part of the mission. Even though he knew Coffey was not himself, this hurt him worse than the pain in his leg, it knifed through him. Coffey's cutting me off, Coffey doesn't trust me.

The worst of it was, Monk knew Coffey was right not to trust him. Any commander who was taking actions like these could not expect Monk to obey his orders. Monk might be a SEAL, but he was a human being first, an American, a citizen, a *person.* A person who didn't collaborate with soldiers who meant to set off nuclear devices on their own authority, in order to destroy strangers who meant no one any harm.

Coffey went to the door of the galley, moved Schoenick aside, and addressed the civilians. "Everybody just stay calm. The situation is under control." Then he backed out of the room, closed the watertight door, and dogged it down. He looked at Schoenick. "If anybody touches this door, kill them." Since the only person who could touch the door was Monk, the meaning was pretty clear. Coffey had lost confidence in Monk's loyalty.

Coffey left the room, heading back to the sub bay, closing and sealing hatches behind him.

Inside the galley, they did the only thing they *could* do.

They talked to Schoenick through the door. "Schoenick," said Lindsey. "Your lieutenant is about to make a real bad career move."

Hippy was more direct. "The guy's crazier than a shithouse rat!"

Then the voices became a cacophony of pleading, demanding, explaining.

Schoenick paid no attention to the voices inside the galley. The only voice he heard was Monk's, there outside with him, as Monk leaned against the wall. "We're going to lose it, man," Monk said.

"Shut up!" said Schoenick.

Monk could see how torn up Schoenick was. Of all the men on the team, Monk knew that Schoenick was least able to make independent decisions. But this time he had to. "The shockwave will kill us. It'll crush this rig like a beer can."

"Shut up, man!" Schoenick demanded. "What're you talking about?"

"We got to stop him!"

"Shut up!"

Monk shut up. But now Bud's voice came clearly from inside the galley. "Schoenick, you don't have to follow orders when your commanding officer's out of his mind."

Inside the galley they had stopped yelling all at once. Now they were taking turns. Lindsey gave it another try. "Schoenick, listen, he's about to make war on an alien species, Schoenick, just when they're trying to make contact with us. Please!" No answer. Surely the silence on the other side was a good sign. She spoke softly to Bud. "I think I'm reaching him."

Bud shook his head. He didn't think so. He'd seen a lot of soldiers in his life, and he didn't think Schoenick was going to be persuaded very easily.

Then the wheel on the door began to turn. He was letting them out. "See?" said Lindsey.

The door opened. Only it wasn't Schoenick who came in. It was the tallest human on *Deepcore*. Jammer. And he was holding Schoenick's assault rifle.

"Is everybody OK?" he asked.

They acted like he had returned from the dead. They froze there, all of them, just looking at him. It was Hippy who finally acted. Grabbed the assault rifle out of his hands and charged through the door into the other room. Schoenick was lying on the deck, unconscious—Jammer must have taken him by surprise and put him out of commission—at least for the moment. Hippy pointed the gun at Monk, who was sitting on the deck, weak with pain.

Monk waved him away. "I'm the least of your problems," he said.

Bud had come through the door right behind Hippy. He put a hand on Hippy's shoulder to calm him down—Monk wasn't against them, Bud knew that.

"I'm all right," said Hippy.

Now he turned back to the door where Jammer was standing, pretty much filling all the available space. He was the sweetest sight Bud had ever seen. Not just out of the coma, but standing up, looking like himself, looking fine. Our secret weapon—so damn secret we didn't even know we had it. The one guy Coffey didn't bother to lock up in the galley. "How you feeling, big guy?"

"OK, Bud. I just figured I was dead back there, when I saw that angel coming for me."

"Uh." Angel. Still another shape for the NTIs? "Yeah, OK." No time to explain to Jammer all that had happened since then. The guy already knew the only thing that mattered right now: which side he was on. "Yeah, why don't you tell us about it later."

Bud led the way out of the mess hall into the corridor. He ran down to the door leading into the sub bay. It was sealed. It wouldn't budge. "He's got it tied off with something," Bud said. So Coffey didn't trust even Schoenick to be able to keep them in. He must have been a hell of a soldier when his brain was in gear. He and Lindsey tried to open it, putting their whole strength into trying to turn the wheel. Didn't move. "We're not going to be able to budge it."

"Now what?" Lindsey asked. "This is the only door to sub bay."

Right. Right. They were trapped inside trimodule-C and the control module. Since the wreck, all the other hatches led to water.

So, if water's the only route to sub bay, somebody's going to have to swim. And since the water's so cold the only reason it doesn't freeze is the pressure, it better be somebody who can swim fast and knows right where to go. He ran back to the mess hall and dropped down the ladder to level one, into about two feet of water. Right under him was the emergency lockout hatch. It was designed for exactly this problem—a way out of the trimodule if they couldn't get to the moonpool. He opened it.

Just like the moonpool, the water was held down by the pressure of the air above it. Real good design, putting this here, Lindsey. Good thinking.

She was still with him. So were One Night and Catfish. "What are you doing?" Lindsey demanded. She knew exactly what he was doing, of course. He wasn't pulling off his boots to go wading.

"I'm going to free-swim to hatch six. I'm gonna get inside. Then I'm gonna open the door from the other side."

"Bud, this water's freezing," said Lindsey.

Not much he could do about that. All the heated suits were in the sub bay. "Then I guess you better wish me luck, huh?" It's got to be done, so why argue about how hard it's going to be?

"Wish *us* luck," corrected Catfish.

"You coming along?"

"Looks that way." It wasn't something Catfish wanted to do, but he was going to do it anyway.

Bud didn't know whether he wanted Catfish to come. Nice to have another man with him when he got there—if he got there. Pretty bad to have them both die if it didn't work. But it was Cat's decision, not his.

Catfish handed One Night his wallet and the chain he always wore around his neck. "Here, in case I don't die." He turned to Bud, who was stripping his coat and belt off. "Come on, Bud. Let's go, partner, I ain't got all day."

Bud heard the fear in his voice. I know the feeling, Cat.

270

Bud dropped down into the hatch, caught the rim, and hung there on his hands for a second. The water was so damn cold it knocked the breath out of him. But that meant they had no time to waste. Every second of this meant his body was going to get all the more convinced that it was dying and it'd start shutting down on him. He took one last look up at Lindsey, then took a deep breath and dropped down through.

There was enough light in the water to see—if he had been wearing a mask or helmet. When you get used to wearing something over your eyes all the time, you forget that human eyes were meant to work in air, not liquid. All Bud could see was bright blurs here and there; he was pretty sure which blur was his destination, but what if he was wrong?

No time to worry about that. He had to avoid tangles of cable and twisted steel, had to *move* through the water. He swam with all his strength. The harder he worked at it, the warmer his body would be. Big, powerful strokes. It took maybe forty seconds to reach the hatch, but it felt like he'd used up all the breath he ever took in his life. Cat was right with him. For a split second it felt like the hatch wasn't going to move—was this one of the ones that buckled and jammed in the crash? Then, with Catfish helping him, it came open. Dropped down.

Catfish backed away. That was right—Bud was the first one into the water, so he should be the first one to go up for air. Bud pulled himself through the opening.

They weren't home free yet. There was a lot of water inside. Was there any air at the top? Or just another hatch? Six feet straight up, and Bud found the air—a two-foot bubble of tetramix. Catfish splashed to the surface right after him, gasping and sputtering. "That was worse than I thought," said Catfish, "and I thought it was gonna be bad." Bud could hear it in the way he was breathing—that swim took everything Catfish had. And still he had waited his turn through the hatch. Good man.

They reached up, tried the wheel on the hatch above them.

"Come on, yank on it," said Catfish.

This one *was* jammed. No way. And no time to keep trying it, either. The cold was going to get to them.

"Have to—have to go to the moonpool," Bud said. "It's the only way."

That meant an even longer swim, all the way under and back up into the pool. Catfish had just found out his limitations. "Can't make it, partner. Sorry."

"OK, Cat. You head on back."

Bud took a few quick breaths to hyperventilate, then dropped back down under the water. Catfish watched him go, disgusted with himself for not being in better shape, for letting Bud *down*. He slammed the heel of his fist into the wall of the module. If anything happens to Bud cause I'm not there. . . .

Down under hatch six, Bud oriented himself and swam deeper, toward the moonpool entrance. The lights marked it clearly—it was the garage door for the submersibles and the ROVs. Easy to see it, not so easy to get to it. Only trouble was, it was about nine miles ahead of him. No. No, just five strokes, six, seven. Getting colder, weaker. Push harder, get more heat into the muscles. I'm losing a pound a second under here. Got to recommend this as a weight-loss technique. A real incentive to exercise.

Wherever he could, he grabbed onto pipes and pulled himself along. Under the pool. Took only half his life. He swam upward. It'd be nice if he could get to the top silently, but there was no way in hell his body would let him do that. He splashed up, gasped for breath. But he was lucky. Coffey was making some noise of his own, sitting there on the deck, playing with the chain from the winch, passing it through his hands. It clicked in the gears overhead. Once the first air came into his lungs, Bud got control of himself, breathed silently. A couple more breaths. Then he swam over to where Cab One hung over the water. Out of Coffey's line of sight.

He reached up to one of the metal bars of the cradle, tried to pull himself up. His fingers were so cold they didn't want to respond. He gripped anyway, pulled himself up. It felt like he was ripping away sheets of muscle inside his arms. But he got up out of the water, pulled himself onto the deck beside the moonpool. He had never been so cold, so exhausted in his life. He wanted to rest, *needed* to. But he couldn't.

He looked around for the door. It was pretty clear. Given where Coffey was and where he was, he didn't have a chance of getting to the door without Coffey seeing him. And once Coffey saw him, he wouldn't have a chance at all. The man had a gun. Even if he hadn't, Coffey wasn't worn out and frozen from swimming in a T-shirt in sub-freezing water at twenty-one hundred feet. All this way, all this work, and he was no closer to opening the door than he had been when he was on the other side of it.

Coffey sat there, pulling on the winch chain, trying to keep from crying, not making it. Why was he crying? That wasn't rational, that suggested he wasn't in control. But he *was* in control, he'd done everything right, every single thing. He'd followed orders perfectly. But he didn't have any orders about what you do when you suddenly got a tentacle thicker than your body coming up out of the deep and you realize these guys have power that makes our stuff look silly *except* you got a nuclear warhead and a delivery system and you can take them out *right now* only you don't have any orders. There's nobody to tell you that this is the right thing, nobody to say, All right, Coffey. This is what's right for your country, this is what's right for *us,* so *do it.* Instead he had these other guys, these other *civilians* telling him not to, telling him he's crazy, well he wasn't crazy, he was maybe stressed, maybe a little bit of HPNS, but he was still functioning just fine because if he wasn't how did he get control of these people so easy? Only now he was down here and he was *alone.* Why did you go off and leave me when I needed you? I *never* would have left you, never, I was with you forever, just you and me, and you married that asshole and when it came right down to it you preferred *him* and I wasn't worth shit to you and I made Darrel Woodward into a brain-damaged moron for you, Mom, I did everything you wanted and you left me down here all alone in the water with this goddam warhead and I'm supposed to know whether to send it down into hell or not.

In the control module, One Night and Jammer were busy taping Schoenick to a chair. They knew enough about SEALs to know that if they didn't tie him down pretty tight, he could wipe his way through them with his bare hands in ten seconds flat. The only one there who would know how to stop him was Monk, and even if they could trust him to help, he was crippled up with his broken leg.

Lindsey was at the video monitor, watching the sub bay. The same view Coffey had a while ago when he heard Lindsey and Hippy talking about modifying Big Geek. She'd been staring at Coffey, trying to figure out what was going on in his mind. Everything was ready to go—but still he wasn't going. Maybe he'd change his mind. Maybe he'd come back to his senses, realize that he just couldn't nuke a bunch of peaceful NTIs with no provocation whatsoever.

Lindsey was shocked when Bud came up through the water of the moonpool. He was supposed to get up through hatch six and come into the sub bay on his feet. "Bud's in the pool," she said. "And Catfish isn't with him."

"Jesus," whispered One Night.

Jammer gave an extra jerk as he wrapped more tape around Schoenick. Hippy joined Lindsey at the monitor.

"What's he doing?" Lindsey asked. Bud wasn't heading for the door, he was moving up behind Coffey, walking slow, quiet. Then he reached down and picked up a length of steel pipe—a drive shaft.

"He can't get to the door," said Hippy. "I think he's going to try and take him himself."

"He couldn't be that dumb!" Lindsey cried. "The guy's a trained killer."

"He's got three feet of pipe," said Hippy. "Of course he's going to try to take him out." Didn't Lindsey know Bud at all?

Yeah, she knew him. That's why she was so scared for him. He didn't have any sense of what was *possible*, just what was necessary. It was necessary to take out Coffey, so Bud was going to try it, even though he didn't have a chance in hell of doing it. Lindsey reprimanded him, spoke to his image in the monitor. "Bud!"

Bud raised the pipe, ready to slam it down on the back of Coffey's head. But he hesitated. Made as if to swing, then hesitated again.

He can't do it, thought Lindsey. He has this one chance to take Coffey from behind, and his goddam sense of fair play won't let him do it. Fair play is great for touch football, but it's a luxury we can't afford right now.

But it wasn't some chivalric ideal that stayed Bud's hand, it wasn't some "you draw first" ethos drawn from the bad TV westerns he'd grown up with. It was a much deeper sense of justice. Bud knew that if he hit Coffey anywhere but in the head, it wouldn't stop him—and if he *did* hit him in the head with this pipe, it would probably kill him. Before I execute this guy, where's the judge and jury? Coffey's probably a decent guy. It isn't the real Coffey doing this stuff, it's HPNS-induced paranoia. Get him topside, get him out of this pressure, and Coffey'd be horrified at what he was planning to do down here. He'd thank Bud for stopping him. But he wouldn't thank anybody if he was dead.

Still, Bud would've hit him if he hadn't found any other course of action. It had to be better for one man to die unjustly than to launch an unprovoked nuclear attack, to unleash war between species. So Coffey would've died right then, except that Bud realized that Coffey's pistol was right there in easy reach. Pull that out, point it at him, and Coffey would do what he was told. Or else Bud could shoot him in the leg or something, take him out of commission without killing him.

In the control room, they watched as Bud lowered the pipe and reached out with his other hand for the pistol at Coffey's belt. It was a bad move. Whether Coffey felt the wind of the pipe moving down or heard something or had some sixth sense, he knew Bud was there. He turned, pulling his gun, leveling it at Bud's head.

"No!" Lindsey cried.

Bud stood there looking into the barrel of the gun. "Coffey," he said. Sounding reasonable. "Coffey." He knew that talking wouldn't make any difference. There are men who are content to wave their guns around and make threats. Then there are the men who shoot. Bud's dad used to talk about that, and one time Bud said, "Yeah, I heard that in wartime maybe only twenty percent of the guys ever fire their weapons."

"Bull*shit*," Daddy said. "Whoever said that was a plain liar. You get out there in battle, under fire, it's you and the guy next to you, if he isn't firing you *know* it, only he always is. The hard part is to get your boys to *stop* firing. I'm not talking about battle, anyway. I'm talking about one on one, when a guy's holding a weapon on you and nobody's looking and he has a choice, he can either capture you or blow your brains out, either one's a fair choice, it's his *option*. There are guys who'll shoot, and guys who won't."

"How do you know which one is which?" Bud asked him then.

"If you're still breathing, he wasn't the kind that shoots."

Which kind are you, Coffey? You don't have to kill me. You can disarm me, you can get me out of the way just fine. But you're crazy with HPNS and scared shitless about what you think you've got to do and besides, I saw you crying.

Coffey pulled the trigger.

Bud flinched, but nothing happend. No bullet through the head, no hot red impact above the eyes.

Misfire, of course. The next bullet would do it.

Coffey pulled the trigger again. Click. Again.

Back in the control module, they couldn't believe it when the pistol didn't fire. How could something that lucky possibly happen?

Monk knew. He reached into his coat and pulled out the answer. Sonny caught the motion out of the corner of his eye, grabbed Monk by the wrist—but then they realized what he was holding. The ammo clip from Coffey's pistol. How did he get it? Back when Coffey gave it to him in the mess hall, when Coffey still trusted him. Monk must have realized he was crazy even then, must have taken it while he still had the chance.

Schoenick looked at him with eyes full of venom. "You son of a *bitch!*"

In the sub bay, though, there was no explanation. They only knew that now it was just the two of them, no gun. Bud, worn out from swimming, armed with a drive shaft, and having no serious training in combat, against Coffey, with his knife and years of training as a killer, and the craziness of HPNS. And both of them convinced that the fate of the human race depended on what he did here. God help me, thought Bud. I've got to kill a man here, and I don't want to. I also don't have the faintest idea how I'm going to do it.

Chapter 13

Drowning

In the city at the bottom of the Cayman Trench, the builders were at the border of despair. They had put themselves at risk to meet the humans in their atmosphere. They had tried to show their desire to communicate. What was the result? A doorway closed across the probe with no warning. They had come to help the humans save themselves from their own murderous instincts, and in response the humans had tried to murder the messengers. They knew that the human who tried to kill them was not the same as Lindsey and Bud and the others. The builders also knew that most of the crew was afraid of the SEALs, especially Coffey. But who decided to put the weapons into the hands of these men? Just because they delegated their killing to specialists didn't mean that the gentler humans weren't responsible. The humans, as a species, weren't even trying to curb their desire to kill.

No, they *are* trying. They're afraid that if one side gives up their weapons, then the side that doesn't will rule them all.

A vicious quandary. One that can't be resolved, for the very good reason that if one side disarmed, the other certainly *would* take advantage of it—or some third party would. We've seen their television—they're no different up in the atmosphere than these that have come down nearer to us. Therefore we should leave and let them destroy each other. That will sweep away the problem well enough.

We can't give up. Part of this is our fault. Even inside *Deepcore* it's partly the fear of what he thinks we are that has made this Coffey so afraid.

What more can we do? We can't safely go inside again. When we speak to them, they don't know we're speaking. We could force them to think the thoughts we want them to have, but what would that accomplish? That isn't communication, it's slavery. Let them be.

We can still watch them, can't we?

Watch, then. See them act out the murder and destruction that has filled their history.

In the bubble of air inside hatch six, Catfish knew that he should head back for the hatch he had come from. The longer he waited, the colder he'd get, here in this water. Yet he couldn't stand the thought of giving up, leaving it all up to Bud. If Bud made it, he'd have to come out of the water and face Coffey, and dammit, Bud wasn't up to it. He didn't have the fighting skills. Catfish did. They made fun of him for talking about it, but he really *was* a fighter, and he still had the arm.

I'm a damn fool, but I'm going for the moonpool or I'm gonna die trying.

Catfish hyperventilated, then dropped down into the water. It took only a moment to spot the moonpool. Not that far away. Not impossible. I can make it.

He surged forward through the water, big sweeping strokes. Caught the pipes, pulled himself along. But he wasn't making it. He was too tired, the cold was getting to him The air was burning in his lungs like icy fire. Dumb macho schmuck, you ain't worth shit alive *or* dead but if you're gonna die, do it under the moonpool so you'll float up and they'll know what happened to you.

He did not see the builder that floated in the water out beyond the reach of the lights, far enough away that she didn't damp the power in the rig. She was aware of the debate that had raged in the city after the humans tried to kill the probe. She knew that their role now was only to watch. But here was one of the humans, struggling to survive out in the water, almost naked, as fragile as the probe they had sent inside *Deepcore*. He was only following his friend, who seemed to be younger and stronger than he was. Wouldn't it be as great a crime to let this one die out here as it was for the one inside to try to kill our probe? Isn't letting them die a kind of murder, too?

So she thickened the tendrils and reached out part of her own intelligence toward him. She slipped between the crease of his lips, down his throat, into his lungs. It wasn't hard for her to make the catalysts that broke the carbon dioxide in his lungs back into carbon and oxygen. She absorbed the excess carbon herself and carried it back along the tendrils. It wasn't much, really, not too much interference. Just enough oxygen that he could rise up to the surface of the pool and breathe for himself. When he broke out into the gaseous space, she drew back her tendrils and retreated. She would be rebuked for this, probably. Her memories would probably be shameful ones when she brought them to the city. But she was alone, and she had made the decision she would certainly have made if Catfish had been a builder and not a man.

Catfish breathed deep, astonished that he had made it after all. Right at the end it had seemed like he found new reserves. A spare lung.

He looked around and spotted Coffey and Bud. It was ugly as sin, watching them fighting. Bud was about as ready to fight Coffey as a baby squirrel is ready for a hunting cat. They were dodging around in some cables and chains and a light fixture dangling from the ceiling, but it was a matter of time, that was for sure.

Catfish heaved himself out of the water. He could barely stand up, he was so cold. He flexed his muscles, swung his arms, twisted around as he staggered across the deck to where they were fighting. Coffey was tossing a cable around Bud's neck, strangling him. Damn, thought Catfish, can't I move any faster? "Hey!" he shouted. Anything to distract Coffey from his killing fever.

Coffey whirled around to face him. Completely unprepared. Easiest punch Catfish ever had the pleasure of taking. Caught the lieutenant in the jaw with a right and laid him on his ass. Down for the count, yes sir. Didn't call it the Hammer for nothing.

He went to help Bud, who was unwinding the cable from around his neck. But Buddy-boy wasn't interested in no howdys or how-the-hell-did-you-get-heres. "Get Coffey!" he shouted.

Coffey was up. Catfish could hardly believe it. Nobody got up after a punch like that. But it wasn't more fight that Coffey was after. He could count—there was two of them and one of him, and he had a mission to perform. So he ran for the edge, jumped over onto Flatbed floating there in the moonpool, clambered up the side and down into the driver's seat. Catfish was right behind him, but by the time he got to the hatch it was already closed. And locked down tight. "He's dogged it off!" he shouted.

Now Bud was on Flatbed, staggering but upright. Seeing how bad off Bud was after the fight made Catfish feel more useful than he'd ever felt before. He took a chance, trying to be a hero, and by damn if he didn't make it.

Bud didn't seem impressed, though. He was already busy, grappling with Big Geek, trying to get it free from Flatbed's huge steel claw. "Help me get this off," he said.

Catfish helped as best he could, but it was no good. They could hear Flatbed's motors starting to go. Bud switched from trying to unhook Big Geek from Flatbed—now he was reaching underneath, trying to unstrap the warhead from the ROV. No good. Coffey was submerging Flatbed right under them, taking them right back down into the water. Too cold, they couldn't do any more than that. He was down.

They clambered out of the water. Bud was about worn out. "You go get the door," he said. Catfish hit the button and went through the automatic door the second it was wide enough for his body to fit. He pounded down the corridor like he'd never run before, his beer gut doing a rhumba. He hit the door and pulled out the piece of pipe Coffey had wedged in the wheel.

Of course they'd been watching all this in the control room, so they were ready by the time Catfish got there. Too ready. The second the wheel could turn, Hippy shoved the door open so fast it rammed Catfish right up against the wall. Then Hippy was down the corridor to the sub bay, carrying the assault rifle like he thought he was in a Chuck Norris movie. Catfish managed to pry the hatch wheel out of his belly and took off after him; he could hear Lindsey right behind him.

By the time they got to the sub bay, Bud was out there on the deck pulling on a dry suit. Hippy was standing there like an idiot looking down into the pool. No sweat—Coffey was still down there. With all the damage to *Deepcore*, it wasn't easy finding a way to get something as big as Flatbed out through the wreckage without getting fouled on something. So there he was in the bubble, big as life, looking right up at the assault rifle and not even looking worried.

"Shoot!" Catfish shouted. "Shoot!"

Hippy was squeezing the trigger and nothing was happening.

Hadn't the fool kid ever handled a gun before? "The safety's on!" Catfish screamed at him. "The safety's on!"

Hippy didn't seem to know what a safety was. Catfish grabbed the gun, flipped the safety, and let fly. Recoil damn near tore his arms off. The bullets went just about everywhere except into Flatbed's dome.

"Forget that!" Lindsey shouted. She was over with Bud. It had nearly killed her, watching the fight, helpless to do anything. When Catfish showed up on the monitor she thought he was God. Now she wanted to know Bud was OK, just wanted to touch him for a second.

Bud didn't have time for that right now. He still thought it was possible to stop Coffey. "Come on, let's go! Help me on!" He pulled the neck-dam over his head. "Give me a hand, let's move it."

Lindsey could see that Jammer and Sonny would be

enough to get Bud's helmet and pack on him. So she thought about what *she* could do. "What about Cab One?" she asked One Night.

"Ready to launch." One Night was already headed around the pool to the winch that held Cab One halfway over the water. "I'll unhook."

Lindsey started to climb up the side of the submersible, then hesitated. One Night would expect to drive this.

"Go!" One Night shouted. "You're better in these than I am."

Lindsey recognized this for what it was: a sign of respect. Reconciliation. Something that she never thought she'd get from One Night. She nodded, clambered up onto the top. One Night already had the winch going. Lindsey rode the submersible out over the water. How many hours ago was it that Byron lowered her out over the *Explorer's* launch pool in Cab One's twin? If only I'd crashed Cab Three right then, with Coffey inside. I wouldn't have been down here in *Deepcore,* but then I wouldn't have been *needed* down here, either.

Over on the deck they had Bud's pack on him. "All right, give me the hat." Sonny lifted the helmet with his good arm; Bud took it, lowered it down over his head.

They were babbling, checking everything, checking again. "Got air?"

"Got air."

"That's it, you got air, you got air, you got air."

It was all chanting, meaningless by now, but they had to do it. They were praying. They were giving him a benediction before he went down into the labyrinth to fight the minotaur. He felt them locking down the ring, getting a firm fit between the helmet and the neck-dam. The tetramix was coming in strong. Go. Go.

He jumped straight forward into the pool, pulled himself down. Flatbed was out from under the moonpool now, but not free of the wreckage. Coffey still had to pick his way—Bud, being a lot smaller, didn't have the same problems. His problem was just getting to Flatbed in time to hitch a ride. He pulled along the steel pipe of the frame, making good time, good time. But he was still fifteen feet, maybe twenty behind Flatbed when Coffey saw his clear path, started to accelerate.

But Flatbed wasn't exactly a sprinter. Bud managed to swim his way forward and gain on Flatbed, despite the resistance of the water, the drag of his pack, the sheer mass of his body and his clothing and his gear. He just missed the last handhold on Flatbed, but he managed to catch onto a tie-down strap trailing along behind.

He held on with both hands as the submersible jerked him along, tossing him around in the turbulence behind the thrusters. They got out into the open and headed straight for the edge of the canyon. The faster Flatbed went, the harder it was to hold on. But he still managed to inch his way forward, hand over hand, until he had a hold on the stern rail of Flatbed's platform.

It was easier to hang on now, but the current was still dragging at him; he couldn't make any headway. Then they got to the rim of the canyon and Flatbed stopped. It was the break Bud needed. He made his way forward to where Big Geek was strangling in the mechanical arm. Tried to get the ROV loose, but he couldn't do it. Tried to get the warhead free, but it was impossible, not in gloves, not in time.

Bud cast about, looking for something, some kind of tool he could use, anything at all. The only thing he saw was one of the yellow nylon safety lines. That was something. Yes, sir, he could tether it onto something, keep it from going down there. Never mind that it meant a warhead with a three-hour timer was ticking away not fifty yards from *Deepcore*. If they could keep Big Geek up close, then they had a chance of getting the warhead off and disarming it. And even if they couldn't, better to have it blow up here than down there, an act of war against the NTIs.

Inside Flatbed, Coffey could hear the shuffling of somebody's feet against the deck. So you caught up. Too bad. Nothing you can do. Soft-hearted, weepy-eyed, you'd love to sit back and wait till these sea monsters come out of the water and start blasting their way through America's cities. Well it isn't going to happen. I know my duty, even when there's nobody to tell it to me. Only why wasn't he doing it? Why was he still sitting here? I'm sitting here, I'm telling myself to do it, go, now. Only nothing's happening. The connection's broken. Body's not doing what the brain says.

Coffey shook his head, shook it violently, spraying sweat and saltwater around the inside of the cabin. I'm inside Flatbed and there's a button here that turns on Big Geek's engine. There it is. That's the one. Push it.

He found it. He gripped the lever. His thumb found the button. He pushed. All done very slowly, but he did it.

Bud finished tying the line onto Big Geek just as the ROV's thrusters came on. Big Geek was straining against the grip of the arm. No time to lose—how long was this line, anyway? How fast could Big Geek go? Bud kicked away, paying out line behind him.

Coffey opened up the grippers on the end of the arm, and Big Geek shot away. Bud had the answer to his question. Pretty damn fast. And no hesitation, either. Hippy did a good job of reprogramming the little sucker. It went out and then turned downward. Coffey watched it, satisfied. Until he saw the nylon rope zipping by, tied onto Big Geek. Immediately he knew what that meant. There *was* a way they could ruin it all.

He slewed Flatbed around, looking for the source of the line. Bud had the end of it already wrapped around the nearest of *Deepcore's* heavy steel-pipe skids. Coffey swung out Flatbed's arm, straight forward, and drove directly at the spot where Bud was trying to tie a knot. A moment later the line went taut—down in the canyon, Big Geek was straining against his leash, trying to get away. Fine, thought Coffey. Make it hard for Brigman. Keep him busy, hold him there, hold him still, I've got him.

Bud had the knot partly done, enough to hold for a while, when Flatbed got there, arm extended like the lance of a charging knight. Not very sporting. Bud ducked down, pushed away from the skid just before Flatbed smashed into it, destroying the arm and breaking off both manipulators. Debris and silt sprayed out, but Bud was out and alive.

Unfortunately, despite the damage, so was Flatbed. Bud watched Coffey pull away from the skid. He could even see him inside the bubble, sweating in his shirtsleeves. He was crazy—he looked like a wild animal, crouching over the controls, waiting to pounce.

Inside Flatbed, the collision had smashed Coffey around more than a little. Dazed him for a moment. In the impact, the back of his head had struck the boom box One Night kept in there. The cassette started playing. A woman's voice, singing. "I been kicked by the wind. . . ." Coffey didn't want to hear it, didn't want anybody shouting in his ear. Shut up! Stop yelling at me! He jammed his elbow into it, smashed the plastic case. It shut up.

Bud swam clear of the collision, moving diagonally down the wall of the canyon, trying to stay on Flatbed's blind side. Down below him he could see Big Geek, writhing around on the end of the rope, remembering only that it was commanded to go downward, trying desperately to please. Bud knew his knot wouldn't hold unless he could get back up there. Already he could see that Big Geek was making progress, jerking the line inches at a time. How many inches till the end of the rope passed out of the knot?

At the moment, though, Bud's biggest concern was Coffey. He had pulled Flatbed clear of the debris, and now he was drifting downward, facing the wall, Flatbed's lights playing across the surface. Bud was in a pretty bad position here. Completely exposed on the face of the cliff, nowhere to go. He tried to scramble across the rock wall, tried to dodge, but he was too slow compared to Flatbed's thrusters. Coffey had already proved he didn't mind smashing himself into things in order to kill Bud. I'm a bug on the wall and here comes the swatter.

Coffey had him. Right there in the lights, he could take him out, get rid of this liability once and for all. Had his head in sight, coming right up the stairs, and all I have to do is take this big old cinder block and—

Right at that moment a blinding light stabbed at him through the window. He winced—what was it? One of those

NTIs? Too late he realized it was Cab One, and it was coming right at him. Full throttle. No time to dodge.

At the controls of Cab One, Lindsey slammed the thrusters full lock and her submersible slewed sideways, slamming its starboard side into Flatbed's cab. She knew the collision was coming and braced herself. Coffey wasn't ready, wasn't braced. He got bounced around pretty bad; he fought to control his vehicle, but he was so disoriented himself that he didn't know what he was doing. Nothing responded right. Then he realized that the two submersibles were locked together in a tangle of crashbars, spinning around each other. Lindsey knew that, she was controlling it. Just as he realized what was wrong, Lindsey forced Flatbed to smash stern-first into the cliff.

An electrical fire broke out in Flatbed's cabin. Coffey grabbed the fire extinguisher and sprayed across the flames. Fire went out, but so did Flatbed's lights. He was hanging in the water, untangled from Cab One now, but without controls, drifting slowly along the wall under *Deepcore*.

Lindsey looked up and saw that Coffey was disabled. Time to go for Bud, bring him inside. She cruised over, hovered above him. "Get in," she said over the UQC. There was nothing more he could do outside alone, a fragile diver.

She heard the lockout hatch open and then the splashing as Bud came up into Cab One. She opened the hatch leading into the back compartment. "Are you OK?"

He gave her the OK sign, answered, "Yeah."

She backed Cab One away from the cliff, maneuvering carefully, searching for Big Geek. She spotted the ROV, started toward it. Then, course set, she looked back through the hatch. Bud had his helmet and pack off. "You owe me, Virgil," she said.

"We'll negotiate later." He came forward, leaned through the hatch. "You see Big Geek?"

"Yeah, right out in front. Straight ahead."

The ROV looked helpless, dangling on the end of the line. Then, suddenly, he didn't look so helpless. He was moving. The knot must have given way back at the skid.

The line was sliding by. "Oh my God!" she cried.

"Get after him! Get after him!"

No point in chasing Big Geek. Instead she moved Cab One's arm out in front. It was nothing compared to the arm on Flatbed, but it would do the job, if she could just get the gripper in place.

There. She had the nylon rope sliding through the grippers.

"Hold it really steady," said Bud.

She clamped down. The grippers held. The line stopped moving. Big Geek was once more dancing around on the end of a string.

Then Cab One got smashed from behind like some giant dropkicked them. Lindsey was thrown against a wall; Bud ended up on his butt in the back of the Cab. They got bounced around some more as Flatbed brushed past them, rolling them over their port pontoon. That was bad, that was dangerous, but the worst was the last thing Lindsey saw before she got thrown away from the window: Cab One's arm opening. Big Geek breaking free, heading for the bottom.

It was over. Coffey had won.

Trouble was, Coffey was crazy with HPNS and more than one blow to the head. They had no way of knowing whether he'd consider victory grounds enough for quitting. "Where is he? Bud, do you see him?"

Bud struggled to get to the dome on top. "I'll take a look."

Flatbed was really moving, coming right at them. Trust Coffey to know how to get everything running again inside a submersible. He probably trained with similar craft in the Navy till he knew how to build one out of grass and coconut shells, just in case he needed one on a desert island. "He's coming up fast. Step on it."

"Shhhhh-*it*," said Lindsey. The thrusters had stopped during the collision. Were they damaged? No, she must have kicked the throttle full back. She got them going. They moved.

Bud stayed in the back, watching Flatbed through the dome. "Go to the right," he said. "Swing to the right."

Coffey was on them, tight. Lindsey was the best pilot Bud had ever seen in a submersible, and here was Coffey, sticking with her. Partly that was because Flatbed had more powerful thrusters. But he was also matching her, move for move, as she dodged around *Deepcore*, swinging under and around the twisted steel. Partly, though, it was because of the HPNS. The pressure was making the synapses in his brain fire too fast. Made him crazy but it gave him great reflexes.

"Now he's swinging around on your right. Hard left, baby."

She could barely hear what he was saying, she was concentrating so tightly on picking her way through the obstacle course. "What side?"

"Left, left, left."

"Hold on."

They skirted *Deepcore*. If the guys inside were watching, they were getting a hell of a show. Ben-Hur's chariot race, Luke Skywalker at the Death Star, watch us go.

"He's coming up behind you. Go to the right!"

Great idea, Bud. I go to the right and we end up inside trimodule-B.

She got past *Deepcore* and swung right. Now they were out, away from *Deepcore*, moving along the slope. It wasn't the best place to be. In the open, Flatbed's superior power was bound to tell—and sure enough, it only took about ten seconds for Coffey to get in position to ram them from behind. They rattled around inside Cab One.

Somehow Lindsey managed to keep Cab One trim and moving. "You all right?" she asked.

"Yeah," said Bud. "The son of a bitch."

Coffey wasn't through. He got them again. And again. Lindsey was skimming along the bottom as low as possible. The one advantage she had was experience. She could dodge around better than he could. If they didn't have *Deepcore* to provide obstacles, she'd use the rocks on the ocean bottom.

Lindsey at least had something to hold on to. Bud was rattling around in back like dice in a cup. "People pay for shit like this at carnivals," he said.

As if in answer, Lindsey bashed into a sloping rock on the seafloor. It knocked them upward; she had them under control instantly, but it was the worst jolt of all for Bud, because he could see that Coffey was too far back at the moment to hit them, so he wasn't expecting it. Could've bit his tongue off, his jaw got slammed shut so fast. "Jesus Christ, lady," he said.

She didn't appreciate the criticism. "Bud, if you think you can do any better, you're welcome up here."

It was definitely not a tempting offer. Besides, now Coffey *was* close enough. From the back. Bang! Then from the side. Bang! Then from the top, smashing them down onto the seafloor. Bang!

Lindsey was really getting pissed off. She was past fear now, running on pure adrenaline. The killer instinct. The cornered bear. "Is he right on us?"

"Yeah," said Bud, "he is right on your ass."

She rose up, fast, then smashed deliberately into a rock outcropping. It rained down a small avalanche of silt and rock, right into Coffey's path. It blinded him; he ran into the rock, hung there, couldn't see, didn't know which way was out.

Lindsey rose up, cut to the right, and smashed down on top of Flatbed as it finally emerged from the silt cloud. She forced him down, slamming him into another rock, tearing off Flatbed's port pontoon. Coffey was good at the chase, but he wasn't good at recovering when his vehicle was out of control. Lindsey kept after him, ramming him from behind. The collisions were nowhere near as hard on Flatbed as they had been on Cab One, but Coffey couldn't handle it when they took him by surprise. He was disoriented. He flailed around with his hands, but for whole seconds he couldn't remember what the controls did. His thrusters weren't working right even when he had the controls.

Flatbed hit the bottom, hooked on a rock, spun around just as Lindsey came in with Cab One for another collision. They tangled, slid together down the slope. And now Lindsey could see that they were on the edge of the cliff again. Sliding, sliding—they stopped. Flatbed mostly over the edge, Cab One completely on. Nose to nose. They could see right into Flatbed's cabin. Coffey was lying up against the side of the cabin, his face streaked with blood from a cut on his head. His eyes were open, but he wasn't there.

No, he was. He raised himself up, just a little, enough to turn his head, to look at them.

Bud leaned forward through the hatch, looked out the window with Lindsey. Flatbed's weight was too much. It began to pull away from Cab One. Slide backward. Did Coffey even realize what was happening? There was nothing they could do. Just watch as Flatbed broke free and began to drop, faster and faster, down into the abyss.

Coffey knew something was wrong. He shouldn't be falling like this. The controls should be responding, things should happen when he moved the joystick, when he flipped the switches. He was depending on something and it just *let him go*. Shouldn't have done that. Should never depend on anything or anybody. Always let you take the fall. Never count on anybody. Monk, you bastard. They got past you, Schoenick. You, Mom, you married him and I was never shit to you again after that, well it doesn't matter because I saved you anyway. I sent the warhead down there and they'll never get it back, it's down there and it'll blow those monsters to hell and so even though you dumped on me, every motherfucking one of you, I saved your lives, every breath you take from now on is a gift from me because you would have been dead if I hadn't done it and I did it all for you.

A tiny silver fracture shot partway across the front bubble. It grew. The pressure outside Flatbed was now much greater than the pressure inside. That crack in the bubble, Coffey knew what it was. It was the gate into hell.

Water sprayed into his face from a tiny gap in the metal—a gap now opened by the driving pressure outside the cabin. Coffey knew what was coming, knew now that he would never come out of this place. What hurt him most, in his madness, was that he wouldn't be alive to see the fruition of his work. He wouldn't see the blossom of light in the abyss, wouldn't feel the shockwave roll over him. Instead of dying at the moment of victory, he would die unsure of whether he had fulfilled his assignment.

A moment of lucidity. A moment of outrage at the fact that they had ordered *him* to do this. Why should I die for this? Why shouldn't I, just once, do what *I* want? No orders, no assignment, just what Hiram Coffey wants to do. And what Hiram Coffey wants right now is to live, is to hold this bubble in place, keep the water outside. What I want is to rise up out of the water, to breathe clean air under the open sky, to see other people and not have to decide whether they're my enemies, decide whether to kill them or use them. What I want is to take Mother by the shoulders and scream one last time into her face that she had *no right* to send me down here and then abandon me as if I never mattered at all, after everything I did for her.

He pressed his hands against the plexiglas, though he knew it was useless, because he had to act. He would not surrender. Instead he screamed his defiance and—at last— his rebellion.

Suddenly, driven by tons of pressure, a scythelike curtain of seawater burst through the slender crack in the window and slashed into him. A moment later the whole bubble imploded, and Coffey died in a bloody froth of churning water, air, and clear plastic shards, his cry unheard in the roar of the ocean's victory.

The builders watched it all in sorrow. Even the peaceful ones engaged in war. Even Lindsey, who hated the warhead more than anyone, even she could fill with the same bestial, mindless rage as any of the soldiers. Even she could charge again and again until her enemy was shattered. Even she could watch him die. And Bud, the one who seemed to be a healer, a builder of connections among people, he approved of all she did. Why? Because Coffey made them so afraid, because the fear was so unbearable, that they would do anything to destroy whatever made them feel that way.

Bud and Lindsey tried to help him, to persuade him.

But they gave up, didn't they? In the end, these people are

all alike. When they're afraid, they kill. And they will always be afraid.

So the builders held back. No more interference. The one who gave breath to Catfish was sent away, sent deep, kept busy with important tasks—but work that had nothing to do with the humans.

They watched Coffey fall into the chasm, but they did nothing to help him. Only after he was dead did they move swiftly in and scan his memory, to preserve him.

We can do that much, for these humans who came so far to meet us. When we leave this world, we can take the memory of these wretched fearful creatures with us. In only a very short time, our memory will be the only place where any of them remain alive.

Coffey was gone. Flatbed was gone. Big Geek was gone. But they were alive inside Cab One. Bruised, beaten up, but *alive.*

Bud could hear water trickling into Cab One. He pulled out of the hatch, moved back to check it out. It was coming from behind the control box for the outside umbilicals. A pretty steady flow. Not under pressure—they were equalized at this depth. But a leak in meant a leak out—they were losing breathing mix as gravity brought the water flowing in.

Lindsey looked back through the hatch. "Flooding like a son of a bitch."

"You noticed," said Bud.

"You know, you did OK back there, Virgil. I was fairly impressed."

It took him a moment to realize she was referring to his exploits with Big Geek and the rope and playing dodgeball with Flatbed's manipulator arm. "Yeah, well, not good enough. We still got to catch Big Geek." He was trying to get behind the panel. The leak had to be coming through a connector that had been knocked loose by the last impact. There wasn't any leak at all till the last crash.

Lindsey was still checking things out. Flipping switches. Nothing was happening. "Not in this thing," she said.

Bud laughed. "You totaled it, huh?"

She got the joke, laughed. "Yes, dear, I totaled the car." They might be immobile, but it shouldn't be hard for them to come out from the rig and get them. Bring her a drysuit and a pack. She tried to wake up the UQC. *"Deepcore. Deepcore,* this is Cab One, over." She hit the box. Nothing. *"Deepcore,* this is Cab One, we need assistance, over."

She flipped another switch. It was the wrong one. Something shorted out in a shower of sparks. She ducked, covered her hair—this wouldn't be a good time to have a spark ignite it and have her head go up like a torch.

The sparking stopped. The cabin was dark now, no power at all.

"You all right?" asked Bud.

"Yeah."

Bud turned on the underwater flashlight that was always kept in the back of Cab One. He played it across her face to make sure she really was OK.

"Well, that's that," she said. Phone's disconnected. No more calls. Should've paid the long-distance bill.

"Wonderful," said Bud. He realized that even when he turned the light away from her, he could see her OK. A bluish light coming through the window. "There's some light from somewhere. Somewhere back to the right."

"Yeah, it's the rig."

He looked out the window, found it. "It's a good sixty or seventy yards, I'd say." It could've been worse. They must have been angling back toward *Deepcore* at the end, without noticing it.

"They're gonna come out after us," said Lindsey.

Bud kept hearing the water coming in. Seemed to get louder. The flow seemed to be getting stronger all the time. "Yeah, but it's going to take them a while to get here. We gotta get this flooding stopped."

She came through the hatch, back into the compartment with him. "You see where it's coming in?"

"Yeah, can you hold this?" He handed her the light. She trained it on the leaking panel. "There's a busted fitting here in this panel. Problem is, I don't think I can get to it." He

294

tried to pull the panel away from the wall so he could see behind it. "You got any tools?"

"I don't know. Look around."

He did, but without hope. "Yeah, well, I looked already." He turned back to the panel. "Goddammit, all I need's a goddam crescent wrench." Wishing gets you nothing but wishes, as his mom used to say. He hooked his fingers behind the panel on the top and the right side. Lindsey got the idea and hooked her fingers on the top and the left. Bud braced his feet against the wall and pulled. So did she. He strained, groaning, until his fingers couldn't hold on anymore and they came free, scraping the skin.

"Shit!" Bud shouted. "Son of a *bitch!*"

It made her nervous to see him so upset. "Calm down, Bud." She needed him to be calm, because as long as he was calm that suggested there was something they could do about this. But the water was up to their waists now as they knelt on the floor in back, and that suggested that they didn't have much time to figure out what to do. "Calm down." She wiggled her fingers, tried to get some feeling back into them.

"OK," said Bud. The confidence was coming back to his voice. "OK, uh. We've got to get you out of here."

The water was really cold. He was in a dry suit. She wasn't. "Yeah. How?"

"I don't *know* how!"

"All right, all right." It was hard to think of something when there was nothing to think of except a single terrible fact. "We've only got one suit."

"I know! I know! But we gotta think of something."

She wasn't listening to him. Even though she was standing up now, bent over, to keep more of her body out of the water, it wasn't helping. "Oh, God, I'm freezing," she said. It made her realize what it meant, him swimming under the rig to get into the moonpool. That was a dozen yards, though. Not sixty.

"Here, give me your hands," he said. She did. He held them—his hands really were warmer. He wasn't losing so much heat through his suit. "Listen," he said. She thought he was going to tell her the answer. What he said was something a good deal less helpful. "You're smart," he said, "think of something. Can't you think of something? Think of something."

It was absurd. But the way Bud asked her, calm, expectant, that made her feel more confident. And she thought of something. "OK, why don't you swim back to the rig and bring back another suit."

"That'd take me about seven, eight minutes to swim, get the gear, come back. I wouldn't make it." He held up her hands. They were stiffening, turning blue with cold. "Look at this. By the time I got back you'd be——"

"Yeah. OK. Look around, just look around." There had to be something they could use, something to give them an idea. She found a breathing mask.

"See if that works," Bud said.

She already had it up to her mouth. Nothing. She let it drop. Looked around some more, trying to move her arms, keep them moving, keep warm. She kept making involuntary sounds. She made herself stop. It sounded too much like whimpering. She wasn't going to go out whimpering.

Suddenly Bud started moving with real purpose. "All right," he said. He was handing her his breathing pack. "Put this on." He got his hands under his neck-dam, started pulling it off over his head.

It took her a second to realize. He didn't have a plan. He had just decided to give her the suit and make her go while he stayed back here and died. "No, no! What are you doing, growing gills or something? You got it on——"

"Don't argue with me, goddammit, just——"

"Look, this is not an option, so just forget about it." She thought of him drowning. Thought of him sucking water into his lungs like Hippy's rat did, only this wasn't going to end with somebody hanging him upside down and squeezing the juice out like Hippy said Monk did with Beany.

"Lindsey, shut up!"

"No!" Let me think, there *is* a way.

All he knew was that if she didn't have the suit she was going to drown. This wasn't a time when he was going to put up with her stubbornness. This was the worst thing in the world. He knew. He remembered. He'd felt the water come into his lungs, and it wasn't going to happen to her. He wasn't going to live and have to spend the rest of his life imagining how she felt as she died the way he had to do with Junior. "Shut up and put this thing on!"

"Would you just be logical for one—"

"Fuck logic!"

"Listen, *listen!* Just *listen* to me for one second. You've got the suit on and you're a much better swimmer than I am, right?"

"Yeah, maybe."

"Right? Yes. So I got a plan."

"What's the plan?"

"I drown, you tow me back to the rig."

He couldn't believe she was saying this. He rocked his head back and yelled at her. "What the hell kind of plan is that!"

"I drown—"

"No!"

"Yes."

"No!"

"This water's only a couple of degrees above freezing. I go into deep hypothermia. My blood goes like icewater. My body systems slow down, they *won't stop.* You tow me back and I can—I can be revived after maybe ten, fifteen minutes."

"Lins, you put this on! Put it on!" He was begging now, pleading with her. But he was also hearing her, processing the information at some level in his mind. He knew it was true that if you got to coldwater drowning victims soon enough, they could sometimes be revived. Often. But not *always.*

"It's the only way," she said. "You just put this on. Put this on, you know I'm right. *Please,* it's the only way. You've got all the stuff on the rig to do this. Put this on. Bud, please."

She was right. There was no other plan except the one he'd been working on—both of them staying in Cab One, arguing, until they both drowned. Her way offered some hope. "This is insane."

"Oh my God, I know, but it's the only way."

He pulled the neck-dam back over his head. She held the breathing pack, helped him shoulder it, even though her fingers were so numb from the cold that she could hardly grasp anything. They both kept chattering, murmuring, concentrating on the task.

"You can do this, you know," she said. She looked at him with eyes that said, I trust you. For the first time in all their years together he looked into her eyes and saw that she absolutely, absolutely believed in him. She was going to go right down to the edge of death and it was up to him to bring her back, him alone, and she trusted him. She touched his cheek. Her hand was ice, but it burned him. He would feel that hand on his cheek forever. "You can do this."

"Oh God, Lins, I—"

He was going to say he loved her. "No. You can tell me later." Then she told *him,* not in words, but by reaching to him, leaning toward him in the eight inches of air left at the top of the compartment and kissing him, long and deep, not a kiss of passion, not meant to arouse, but a kiss of belonging. It said, I'm part of you, I love you, I trust you with everything. He never thought she'd say a thing like that to him, and yet he understood it all as if she'd said it to him a thousand times. He believed it. It was true.

He put the helmet in the water, ducked down, put it on. Then he came up, the helmet not yet fastened to the dam, and held his breath while the regulator built up breathing mix inside the helmet, driving the water down and away. It was the ugly way of doing it, with water inside the helmet, but there wasn't enough room left between the water and the roof to put it on dry. All the time he was doing it, he heard Lindsey coughing, sputtering—the water was so high now that she was angling her head sideways or tipping it back to keep her mouth out.

He was clear. He fastened down the helmet clamps. Then he hung there in the water, watching her gasp for the last bit of air at the top of the compartment. It was one thing to decide this. It was something else to do it. She couldn't help panicking, couldn't help crying out, "Bud!" And then: "Help me." And then there was no more room. She knew it, she sank down, facing him, holding her last breath, looking into his face.

And he looked out of his face mask, saw her watching him with terror in her eyes, her mouth partly open. Then she leaned forward and pressed her lips against his mask. Supplication. As if she were trying to breathe the air he had inside there. And all he could do was look at her, all he could think was It's happening again, oh, God, it's happening again.

She reached behind him, clamped her hands behind his helmet, put her head on his shoulder and held onto him, embraced him so tightly, and he also held her. He was holding her when he felt her chest heave as she finally, deliberately filled her lungs with water. She shuddered, spasmed, her chest heaving again as her body tried to expel it.

All the times he had wished, If only I could have been with Junior at the end, if only I could have held onto him as he died. And now it was happening, he was holding on to her, she was drowning, and it was worse to be there, to be helpless, to have her cling to him and feel her body losing control, knowing I can't do *anything* to help her, it's the worst thing in the world.

Then her hands went slack. She was unconscious.

No, she was dead. Everything had stopped. The only hope they had was that she was also being killed by the cold, which was slowing down all her systems so they couldn't die as *fast* as they normally would. Her life was being strung out by the conflict between the two deaths. Virgil Brigman was holding the string.

He opened the lockout hatch, put his feet through, then reached up and took hold of her. He worked quickly, but not so fast that he fumbled, not so fast that he couldn't watch carefully to make sure he didn't hurt her as he drew her through the hatch. When she was out, he reached in and took the light. Maybe they'd be watching from inside *Deepcore*. Maybe they'd see him coming, see his light and come down to the moonpool. Maybe they'd be ready, and that would save a few seconds, and those would be the seconds that would make the difference, that would allow him to pull her back out of the abyss.

Chapter 14

Candles

When Lindsey died, the builders noticed a most curious thing. As they sent out tendrils to scan her brain, they themselves were filled with grief. They never grieved for their own who died, as long as their memories had been gathered in to the city. Yet Lindsey's memories were being gathered—they were doing it themselves—and still they were filled with sorrow. Why?

The question circulated quickly through the city, and in a far corner it was heard by the builder who had dared to help Catfish make it to the moonpool. She knew the answer, but for a brief time she hesitated to supply it—to venture into this debate again would surely expose her to further censure. But then she remembered Catfish's decision at hatch six, to attempt the swim that he knew he could not make. Was she, whose memories could never die, less courageous than he, whose life could be snuffed out, his memories lost? So she offered her answer to the city:

We grieve for her as we never grieve for each other, not because her memories will be lost, for they won't; we grieve for her because her independent actions in the world, which were so strange, which no one else would ever have done, for good or ill, those actions will stop. We grieve, not for her past, which we will have forever, but for her future, which we will never have. We knew her best of all of them, and so the loss of her future hurts us worst of all. More than the self-destruction of the entire species of humankind, the loss of this one will grieve us.

The city listened, and the idea astonished them. And they also thought of something else: This very builder who gave the answer to them had been transformed by knowing these humans, and had acted in a way that was different from what any other builder might have done. What other builder has spoken despite the city's ban? What other builder has ever dared?

For which this builder should be taken into the city, remembered, and then dispersed.

Isn't that precisely what these humans do? Destroy individuals that make them afraid?

She's one of us. She won't be destroyed, she'll be remembered.

But we'll also remove the possibility of her acting strangely ever again. And why? Because we fear the change that she has brought to us. We would remove her future influence because we're afraid of it. We have done that again and again in our history. We never thought of it as killing, because no part of their past is lost. But hasn't she shown us that it's just as grievous to cut off an individual's future?

It was a strange and terrible idea, that they themselves practiced something that resembled killing, and that their motive was also fear. They never acted in the manic rage these humans showed in battle, but they still did what every other living creature did: They acted against individuals to protect themselves. Until they met these humans, they had never valued individuals, had never really conceived of what true individuality could mean, since they shared memories so freely among themselves that each builder remembered having done what all other builders did; thus the boundaries between them meant little. Now, though, as Bud Brigman dragged Lindsey's body through the water toward the lights of *Deepcore,* they finally understood what those boundaries were, and how it was possible to prize one person and mourn her loss.

Then her memories began to circulate among the builders of the city. Above all, they were astonished at the moment of her death. She was afraid of death, and yet she had chosen to die herself rather than take breath away from Bud. An angry fear had driven her to kill Coffey, but an even stronger fear remained untinged with anger. Instead she acted on a stronger feeling—a certainty that Bud would keep her alive. They recognized this feeling. It was the same confidence the builders themselves had when one of them was at the point of destruction of her body, and another builder came and took her memories. I will live, the feeling said; I will live in you. And Lindsey meant more by this than the hope that Bud could bring her back to life. She knew that hope was slim compared to the probability of her permanent death. She also knew that even if she died, finally and forever, she would continue to live on in him.

Impossible. How could she, when they don't share memories the way we do?

Again, a quiet voice proposed an answer to the question, and this time she was joined by most of the other builders who had been close to *Deepcore,* who had experienced the humans most directly:

She knows that she has changed him, and so his future will be colored by her influence as long as he lives. She's part of who he is, and so her influence on the future won't die with her.

The city listened, astonished; they examined this answer, and then believed it. Though the process wasn't as clear and direct as the sharing of memory, it was true. The humans had found a way of living on in someone else's life.

Watch them, the city said. There still may be some hope for them. By watching them we still may find some way to undo the harm we've caused them, some way to help these humans save themselves.

One Night was watching out the window on the side that Bud was coming from. They had all seen the lights of the chase; they had seen where the submersibles struck each other and then dropped and went dark. Beyond that they had no idea what had happened. But when One Night saw a single light from a lone diver swimming toward them, she knew it had to be Bud—he was the only one who had a drysuit and helmet. "I got him!" she shouted. "I got him!" Now he was closer, and she could see that he was towing something. Some*one*. "Oh my God, that's Lindsey!"

His voice crackled to life on the UQC, faint and broken up, but they heard him. *"Deepcore, Deepcore, do you read?"*

Hippy was on the line. "Yeah, we got you, Bud. We're here."

It was hard for Bud to talk, since he was working his body so hard, swimming as swiftly as he could, trying to make headway against the drag of the water on their two bodies. It slowed him a bit, talking to them as they watched him through the window. But it was worth the delay of a few seconds if it meant they were ready for Lindsey when he got her there. "Go to the infirmary. Get the cart. Oxygen. The de-fib kit. Adrenaline in a ten-cc syringe. And some heating blankets. You got all that?"

"Got it. Over."

"Meet me at the moonpool. Make it fast."

"Now, come on, let's go," said Hippy. They were already moving, splitting up the jobs, getting it done. She was clearly dead—no one could live out there without a suit, without breathing mix. Yet if Bud said to do it, then they'd do it. And they all knew the stories of people drowning under frozen rivers and being brought back ten minutes later, sometimes even an hour later. It *might* work.

Nobody bothered with neatness. They took what they needed and let anything and everything else fall where it wanted. By the time Bud came under the moonpool they were there on the deck at the edge of the pool. Sonny saw the orange helmet rising up through the water. "Here he comes!"

Catfish splashed down onto the shallow dive platform and reached to take Lindsey from Bud's arms. He carried her to the edge of the pool, handed her up to the others. They laid her out—her eyes were open, but they were dead eyes. Hippy forced a tube into her mouth, suctioned out the liquid that was in there. Bud ripped at his helmet, shed his breathing pack, knelt over her, dripping water onto her. "Is the de-fib ready? Hurry, Cat! Get those on her." He started pressing at the base of her breastbone, pushing down in short bursts, discharging water from her mouth. Hippy was chanting—"Oh my God, Oh my God, Oh my God."

Why was Catfish taking so long with the de-fib? Smearing conductive jelly on the pads, rubbing the paddles together —all by the book. All by the slow, leisurely book. Bud grabbed for it. Catfish wouldn't give it to him. "No, you got to have bare skin, or it won't—"

Bud tore at the neck of her blouse, tore it open, laid her chest bare. Bud took the defibrillator pads and placed them, one at the center of the chest, one down along her side. "Is that right? Is this it?"

"It looks right!" Hippy answered. "It looks right! *I don't know!*"

One Night was saying something, Bud wasn't sure what she was saying. "What? *What?*"

"I got it," she was saying.

Jesus, then what are you waiting for? *"Do it!"* he shouted.

"Come on, zap her," said Catfish.

"Clear!" said One Night—the defibrillator was charged and ready. She hit the switch. Lindsey's body convulsed.

It was a pure muscle reflex. When it was over, she was as dead as ever.

"No pulse," said Sonny.

Bud kept pressing on her chest, trying to get her heart moving inside. "Do it again, One Night. Zap her again!"

"It's charging. It's charging. It's charging." Then: "Clear!"

Bud pulled his hands away. Again Lindsey convulsed. Nothing.

"Come on, baby," said Bud. "Aw, Christ." One Night was still at the machine, just sitting there, doing *nothing.* "Come on! Come *on!*"

"Clear!" shouted One Night. They lifted their hands off Lindsey's body. One Night hit the switch again. Lindsey's back arched. She fell back, still.

It was taking forever between jolts of electricity. If the de-fib would just do it faster, sooner, then maybe it would start her heart going again, every second between jolts was another second in which brain cells could die as her body warmed up. "Come on, One Night. What are you waiting for?"

"No pulse!" said Sonny. In despair, thinking of his own wife, his own children, how he could not bear it if he were in Bud's place.

One Night was reading her vital signs off the defibrillator—the pads acted as a makeshift EKG as long as they were pressed against her chest. "Goddam, it's flat, goddam, it's flat."

Bud shoved One Night out of the way, put his hands at the base of her breastbone and pushed, breathing out the count as he did. He was trying for a heartbeat, trying to make it pump the blood if he had to hold it in his hands and squeeze it himself. Her ribs flexed under the pressure. If they broke that was going to be too damn bad. Better than being dead with ribs intact. One two three four five six. One two three four five six.

"Breathe," somebody said.

Hippy was holding the mask over her mouth and nose.

One, two, three, four. "Breathe," said Bud.

"No pulse."

"Come on, baby. Come on." Over and over he said it, whispered to her, encouraged her. She didn't hear him. He kept on pushing at her chest, pushing, on and on.

Catfish gently reached his hands out, laid them on Bud's wrists. "Bud," he said gently. "Bud, it's over, man. It's all over."

Bud stopped pushing. Hippy's face was contorted with grief as he lifted the mask. The rest watched silently, in awe—at irresistible death, at Bud's agonized determination, at the pain they knew he was feeling, the pain they shared because they loved him, he was part of them, and they could know how much he loved Lindsey. They knew that this was tearing out a part of his soul and they couldn't do anything to soften it.

"I'm sorry," said Catfish. Bud knelt there, looking dully at him. Catfish reached down and drew the sides of Lindsey's overshirt across her chest to cover her.

"No pulse," said Jammer. With finality.

Bud leaned over her, looking down into her face. He felt Catfish lay a hand on the back of his head, a comforting hand. But he didn't want comfort. He didn't want affection from his friends, consolation. He wanted Lindsey back.

He brushed Catfish's hand away. *"No!"* He howled it. He wasn't saying it to Catfish or to any of them. He was saying it to Death, to God, to Fate, to the whole universe, and they better listen. "No, she has a strong heart, she wants to live!" He started pushing again. "Come on, Lins! Come on, baby." He pushed, pushed, then stopped and laid his mouth over hers, pinched her nose shut, forced his own breath down her throat. One, two, three times. Four. Then he got up and started pushing again. He paused a moment to rip his neck-dam off so it wouldn't hit her in the throat the next time he gave her air. Again he bent over her, put his lips over hers, breathed down her throat. Long, deep breaths. Take this air, Lins. Take it, use it. It's for you, dammit, *use* this, live with it, *live*.

"Zap her again," he said. "Do it. *Do it.*"

One Night got the defibrillator pads into place. She was whimpering a little; it was unbearable, to keep doing this when Lindsey was obviously dead. Like some mad preacher praying over a steak, trying to bring the animal back to life. She did it for Bud, that's all, because he wanted it so bad. Kept her eye on the box, on the dials. The charge reached full. "Clear. Clear."

Lindsey spasmed with the electricity. It didn't work. Bud went back to pumping, breathing into her. Then he stopped, leaned down close to her face. "Come on, breathe. Goddammit, breathe." It was her idea to do this, it was her idea and now she wasn't doing it, she wasn't doing what she said. He screamed at her, angry. "Goddammit, you bitch, you never backed away from anything in your life. Now fight!" He slapped her face, not hard, a stinging blow, a blow to wake her up, to call her back. "Fight!" Slapped her again. "Fight!" Again.

He took her by the shoulders, shook her. "Fight, goddammit!" He was crying now, with rage. She was letting him down. She was giving up for the first time in her life and he wasn't going to stand for that.

"Fight, fight, fight!" His voice was wearing out from shouting at her. He howled it, hoarsely, a long, painful cry. "Fight!"

They'd sent thousands of volts through her body, they'd given her oxygen, they'd pumped and pushed at her, shoved air down her throat. None of it worked. But now, Bud screaming and crying at her, swearing at her, calling her names, *quarreling* with her—that was when they saw her eyes move on their own, her throat swallow, her chest give a little heave, a spastic little cough. Her hands clenched for a moment. It might have been an involuntary spasm of a dead body. But it wasn't. Bud knew that. "Lins. That's it, Lindsey. Come on back, baby." She turned her head like she was shaking it no. Then she coughed, sputtered. *Breathed.* Bud started laughing, couldn't help it, she was making it. He heard somebody else laughing, too. Delight. Did they laugh when Jesus raised the dead? Did Lazarus hear them laughing for joy when he came out into daylight?

Hands touched him, his head, his shoulders. He lifted his face and laughed. She coughed again, gasped deeply for air.

"Get her some air," said Hippy. He put the mask over her face. Now she sucked on it, pulled down oxygen. "Breathe into it."

Her eyes opened. She was hearing them, she was doing it. Bud shouted at her again. This time for joy. "You did it, Ace!" She did what she said. She told him what to do back in Cab One, and he trusted her, he did what she told him, and then she came through on the other side, she held up her end of the bargain. She lived. He knelt over her, laughing and weeping. All of them laughing, crying. She'd gone down into death and come back out. Bud had pulled her out. Or she

308

had held on to Bud's voice, his *will,* and pulled herself out. Or both.

She was alive. She was in the infirmary, not fully conscious yet. But there was still a warhead down wherever Big Geek got to, and the clock was ticking.

"What can we do?" Bud asked the others. "Is there any way we can go down after it?"

"Cab One?"

"Wrecked," said Bud. "Ain't going nowhere."

"Send Little Geek?"

"To do what, say hi?"

"Put some explosives on it. Blow up the warhead before it can do its nuclear thing."

"We don't have anything on *Deepcore* that'll blow up at that depth."

"What depth?"

Hippy looked pretty sheepish. "I kind of set Big Geek to go down to twenty thousand. It's the maximum estimated rating. Plus a toughness factor."

"Twenty thousand?"

It was Monk who knew how it could be done. Or at least how it *might* be done. "Deep Suit," he said.

"Can it go that deep?" asked Bud.

"Maybe," said Monk. "It's the fluid breathing system more than anything. It makes it possible to take a lot more pressure. And it recharges the oxygen for a while. Gives you some more time to get down there."

Twenty thousand feet. That meant going straight down for more than three miles. That was a long way even on land. In the water, pressurizing all the way, it'd take time. They didn't *have* much time.

"The real problem isn't breathing anymore when you get that deep," said Monk. "It's the pressure on the cells in your brain. Pushes the synapses closer together. Your brain starts to short-circuit. You get hallucinations, memories, confusion. Spasms in your muscles. So I give you two anesthetics. The first one, it's mild but it's quick. It cuts down on the gag reflex and the panic when you start breathing the fluid up here. The other one's slower and a lot stronger. It starts taking effect, more and more, as you get down where you need it. Up here it would make you stupid and put you to sleep. Down there it might—just *might*—make you able to keep your mind together long enough to disarm the warhead."

It was Monk's show. Bad as his leg was, he was the only one who knew about Deep Suit, the only one who knew about fluid breathing, and the only one who could tell Bud how to disarm the thing. Schoenick knew this stuff, more or less, but they couldn't trust him. He was still taped to a chair.

So Bud listened, tried to memorize everything Monk told him. The others worked fast but carefully, following Monk's instructions, getting Deep Suit ready. Almost time to go. But he had time, just a couple of minutes, to go into the infirmary, see Lindsey one last time, talk to her if she was awake.

He sat on the edge of her bed, holding her hand. That's all he meant to do. But she woke up as he sat there, opened her eyes, looked into Bud's face.

When her eyes opened, he couldn't help himself, the tears started again. She took a couple of deep breaths. He knew how that hurt, to breathe after you'd had saltwater in your lungs. Not to mention how he'd bruised her ribs, pressing on them like that.

She spoke. A painful whisper. "Big boys don't cry, remember?"

He touched her hair, her cheek. "Hi, lady."

"Hi, tough guy." She took a few more breaths. "I guess it worked, huh?"

"Yeah. Yeah, of course it worked." He was whispering. "You're never wrong, are you?" She smiled at him. The last time he said that to her was in an argument, at the top of his voice. She liked it better, quiet like this, tender. "How you feeling, hmm? How you doing?"

She tried to make a joke of it, but her little laugh didn't sound like a laugh. "I've been better." It was the worst thing

310

she'd ever been through, holding on to him in the water, knowing she was going to die, breathing in the water, the worst terror she ever felt. If he hadn't been there with her. . . . But he *was* there, he held on to her, he brought her home. "Next time it's your turn, OK?" she said.

He paused a long time. He wasn't taking it like a joke. "Yeah, well, you got that right."

She told him how it felt to die. How she could see them as she lay there, how it seemed like they were rising up, getting smaller and smaller, farther away, as she sank down into death. And then she was looking down on them, as if she were outside, above, seeing the scene as if it were happening to someone else. And then Bud was screaming at her, and she didn't want to do anything at all, but he was *making* her do it, he was telling her what to do and even though it was so much easier to drift, to fall away, it made her so mad to hear him say she wasn't even trying that she tried, she came back. Came back and found herself inside her body, wracked with pain, but now unable to withdraw again, irrevocably bound up in a body that wanted to die. "But not as much as I wanted to live," she whispered. "Not as much as you wanted me to live."

Then he told her about Deep Suit and where he was going in it.

Hadn't it all ended when he kept her alive? Of course not. Coffey was gone, but the warhead was still at the bottom of the chasm. It might already have been destroyed or at least disarmed by the pressure—but then, it might not. Someone still had to go down and undo Coffey's last act. Yet she couldn't help feeling bitterly disappointed. She had been feeling oddly complete and content since she awoke, as if something that had long been unwired inside her had now been connected, the last circuit completed, so that emotional currents were flowing that she had never felt before. And now Bud was going down into waters so deep that even if he lived, it was likely he would suffer devastating and permanent brain damage.

She was angry and afraid. If she could have put those

feelings into words, they would have said something like this: No sooner had she found something good, something worth holding onto, than it was taken away from her. The first time she had ever trusted fate to be kind to her, she was being betrayed.

Lindsey shouldn't have been out of bed yet, let alone standing there on the deck of the moonpool. But there was no way she was going to let him go without being there. Without hanging on the end of the F-O, talking to him all the way down.

She winced as Monk put the scleral contact lenses in his eyes, covering the whole exposed surface. Monk explained that the lenses weren't to protect his eyes from the breathing fluid—it was so chemically inert that it might be less harmful than air. The value of the lenses was that they would act as tiny goggles, maintaining a thin bubble of glass at the pupils of his eyes. The incompressible glass bubbles would act as lenses, so his vision would remain clear all the way down and back. It was a very optimistic thought.

Lindsey watched Bud put on the suit, muttering to himself the instructions on how to disarm the warhead. He got the shots, which calmed him down, made him a little logy. He sat there holding Beany on his hand, almost as a good luck charm—Beany had done this, after all, and lived through it. The rat stretched up and nuzzled Bud's nose. Then Monk gave him the oxygen mask to help him hyper-ventilate. He lifted Beany up; Hippy took the rat. Bud breathed deeply into the mask.

Lindsey knelt in front of him. "Bud, you don't have to do this."

He spoke through the mask, "Somebody's got to do it."

"Well, it doesn't have to be you."

"Who, then?"

She knew the answer. Monk's leg was broken. Schoenick was so unreliable they didn't dare unbind him. She herself was too weak from the ordeal she'd just been through. Who else in the crew could be counted on to keep his head all the way down and do the job at the bottom? Maybe they could do it. Maybe not. But they all knew that if anybody could, it was Bud. So she looked at him, saying nothing except with her eyes. I don't want you to go. You could die down there, and this time nobody could bring you back. You could get down there and do the job and still not have enough oxygen in the system to get back up. I could lose you down there. I want somebody else to go. Anybody but you.

He glanced down at the keyboard built into Deep Suit on the left sleeve. It was crazy, to have an F-O connection and still have to type. He turned to Monk. "So I'll hear you, but I can't talk?"

"The fluid prevents your larynx from making sound. Excuse me." Monk reached down between Bud and Lindsey, picked up the helmet. "It'll feel a little strange." That was the most dishonest understatement Monk had ever made, but he knew that Bud knew the truth. It was for Mrs. Brigman's sake that he was softening the truth. Fluid breathing felt like hell. You would only want to do it on special occasions. Like saving the world.

"Yeah, no shit. I got to warn you all, I'm a pretty lousy typist." He was punching the keys, trying them out. Then there was nothing else to wait for. He looked up at Monk, at Lindsey, at Monk again. "The moment of truth," he said. "Come on, let's go."

They lifted the helmet over his head. "Easy," said Lindsey. Like she owned him. Like she didn't want him damaged. She gave them instructions as they put it on. Hell, she'd never put this helmet on, she had no experience, but she knew from looking at it exactly how it was supposed to go. It felt perfectly right for her to be in charge. That's who she was. The person in charge.

The helmet was secure. She knelt there in front of him, looking up into the mask, into his face. She parted her lips to say something, then didn't say it. He heard it anyway. Once the fluid went into the mask she wouldn't hear his voice again until he came back up. Maybe never. She caught herself starting to cry, stopped, then realized she couldn't stop. He brushed the tear on her cheek with the back of his massive glove. He could be gentle even with those big white cartoon hands.

He looked away from her, toward Monk, and spoke—loudly, so they could hear him through the mask. "OK, let's rock and roll."

Monk reached around the front of the suit, opened the line.

"Crack it," said Monk. Someone opened another valve on the back of the suit. The fluid started pouring into the helmet. Bud leaned forward, looking down at it collecting in the front of the mask. Monk was chanting to him, like a dentist trying to keep a kid calm while he's looking at the novocaine needle. "Relax now, Bud. Relax. Relax."

But that was background. It was Lindsey, in front of him, who raised two fingers, pointed at her own eyes. "Bud." He looked at her. "Just watch me. Watch me. Watch me."

The fluid covered his face. Monk changed his patter. "Now don't hold your breath, just take it in. Just let yourself take it in. Take it in."

He still wasn't breathing it. He heard Monk, but they didn't understand. He'd been here before, in the belly of the wave, going down, miles from anybody, worn out, scared, he didn't have any strength left, he couldn't hold his breath anymore but he *had to hold it* or he'd die. I can't do this, I can't do this. I can't breathe it in, I can't. But his eyes were on Lindsey. She was there. He wasn't out in the ocean. It wasn't going to kill him. He *could* take this breath. He knew he could, and then he did.

Immediately his body jerked, spasmed. He rocked back. They grabbed him, held him up.

"That's perfectly normal," Monk said. He spoke with the voice of command, to keep them calm.

Lindsey wasn't buying it. "That's *normal?*" She'd never seen Bud out of control like this, jerking around, panicking. It frightened her to see Bud out of control.

"Just hold him, it's perfectly normal, it'll pass in a second.

314

It's perfectly normal. We all breathe liquid for nine months, your body *will* remember."

It was true. Bud was calming down. Exhaling, he was fine. His arm still jerked upward when he inhaled. He felt like gagging as he breathed in. Again, Lindsey was in front of him. "Watch me. Watch me. Watch me." He did. He kept breathing. With each breath it got easier to take. It was thick, strange, going into his lungs. But not like the seawater had been. Not so cold. Not so harsh. Breathing in and out, it went slower than air, but it was working. He was getting the oxygen.

Lindsey picked up the F-O headset lying nearby. "Can you hear me?" she asked.

He gave her a thumbs-up.

"Bud, try your keypad."

He held up his left wrist, started punching keys. With one finger, of course—but since that was the way he always typed, he was pretty fast. Lindsey looked over her shoulder at the monitor where his message was appearing.

FEELS WEIRD
YOU SHOULD TRY THIS

She looked back at him, laughed slightly. "I already have."

He smiled back at her through the tinted fluid. The lights inside the helmet gave it a sick yellowish hue.

"OK, you ready?" she asked.

He nodded.

"Let's go," said Monk.

They helped him up. The suit was heavy. Jammer and Catfish helped him step backward into the moonpool. Hippy got down into the water with him, got his face close to the mask, and shouted so Bud could hear him through the fluid. "I redid Little Geek's chip the same as Big Geek! It should take you straight there. All you have to do is hang on!"

Bud nodded. He got it. He knew it.

Hippy gripped his hand. Bud looked at Jammer, who smiled at him. Encouragement. Good-bye.

And Lindsey's hand, held out to him. He held her hand for a moment, and even though his thick glove made it impossible to feel more than the gentle pressure of her grip, he felt a kind of warmth rise into him from that touch. More than ever before in his life, he didn't want to leave, didn't want to say good-bye.

But it had to be done. Bud looked at the others gathered around the edge of the pool and raised his hand. Farewell to all of them. Then he got a grip on the back of Little Geek, started him up, let the ROV pull him down into the pool.

As it pulled him down and the water closed over his head, he saw his friends blur, grow smaller as he sank away from them. He remembered Lindsey describing what it felt like when she was dying—how she had seen them above her, but they kept getting smaller as she fell backward into death. Is that where I'm falling now? No. I have a job to do before I can die.

He reached the seafloor, absorbed the impact by flexing his legs, and then walked along toward the edge of the cliff, letting Little Geek help pull him. It was slow going. He got to the edge, stopped, looked back. He could see them coming into the control room. Lindsey sitting down in the window. He lifted his hand. Waved. Then he turned and stepped over the edge of the abyss.

Little Geek wasn't all that powerful, but it was pulling him straight down now, so gravity was helping. He was passing along the edge of the cliff faster than he had ever moved underwater, at least in a suit, outside. He stayed close to the cliff face so he didn't lose his way, but not so close there'd be a chance of collision. Little Geek knew the way. Just hang on to Little Geek. The lights of Deepcore were gone. No light but what came from Little Geek, the light on the keyboard, the light inside his mask, the dive light he was carrying. None of them reached very far. None of them showed very much. He'd never felt so alone in his life.

He typed.

* * *

Lindsey's voice came right back to him. "We're right here with you, Bud." Her voice went softer. She had turned away from the mike. "What's his depth?" Then she came back strong—somebody'd answered her. It would be Hippy, monitoring the information coming up the F-O from Little Geek. "Your depth is thirty-two hundred feet," said Lindsey. "You're doing fine."

The light suddenly shone on something bright, metal. The wreckage of the *Explorer*'s crane. Of course—it was still hanging here, like a forty-ton yo-yo at the end of the umbilical.

GOOD DEEL ON
SLIGHTLY USED
CRANE

Up in *Deepcore,* they laughed. It felt good to know Bud felt like joking. The depth meter kept on counting down.

"Forty-eight hundred feet," said Hippy. He'd been watching for it.

"Forty-eight hundred feet," echoed Monk. "It's official."

Lindsey spoke into the mike. "Bud, according to Monk here, you just set a record for the deepest suit dive. Bet you didn't think you'd be doing this when you got up this morning, huh?"

CALL GUINESS

Hippy read off the meter. "One mile down, still grinnin'."

The cliff rushed by. Bud hardly felt like he was falling anymore. It was the cliff wall that moved, not him. He was absolutely still, right at the center of the world, and it was all coming by on a conveyer belt.

The next threshold was eighty-five hundred feet. Monk knew it was time. "Ask him about pressure effects. Tremors, vision problems, euphoria."

Lindsey spoke into the mike. "Ensign Monk wants to know how you feel."

COLD

She answered with teasing derision. "Baby."

HN HANDDS SHAKING

Monk covered the mike. "It's starting. It hits the nervous system first."

"Keep talking, Lindsey," said One Night. "Just let him hear your voice."

"What's his depth?" Lindsey asked.

"Eighty-nine hundred feet."

"OK, Bud, your depth is eighty-nine hundred feet," Lindsey said into the mike.

One Night looked at her with impatience, covered the mike. "No, *talk* to him." Didn't this woman know anything? Wasn't she married to him? Doesn't she know how to *talk?*

Lindsey got the idea. But she was suddenly shy. She had an audience around her. This wasn't a private conversation. Hell, she didn't talk to him that easily when they were alone. So she did what she *could* do. She joked. "OK, Bud, uh, you're being graded on spelling as well as sentence structure, so concentrate there, OK?"

Only it wasn't a joke. Nobody was laughing, least of all her. Lindsey had to keep Bud's attention, keep his mind engaged. She was the only one who could do it, but she could only do it if she talked about something that he cared about. Even if that meant exposing something in front of the others. Even if it meant laying herself out for a complete examination of her soul.

"Bud, there's some . . . there's some things I need to say. It's hard for me, *you* know. It's not easy being a cast-iron bitch. It takes discipline and years of training. A lot of people don't appreciate that." It was still a joke, yes, but it was also true. And saying the truth about herself, admitting

318

weakness, even when she was making it sound like a joke—that broke something inside her, it twisted something that had been blocking a passageway. Emotion welled up. She didn't have any practice dealing with this. She didn't even know the name of what she was feeling. It just came out of her as crying, so that her voice was distorted with it.

But she went on, because she wasn't thinking about the people around her in the control room anymore. She was thinking of the man on the other end of the F-O line, the man breathing fluid down there deeper than anybody'd ever gone before, the man who needed more than anything else to hear the words she was saying.

"But it wasn't all bad, I know *that*. Do you remember that bike trip? We rode the Honda up through Oregon?" She laughed a little. "It took me a week to get my hair untangled, but I've never been happier. It was the most . . . *free* I've ever felt." God, he'd begged her for this so many times. Why did she have to wait to do it till he was on the other end of an invisible thread? "Jesus, I'm sorry I can't tell you these things to your face. It's pitiful. I have to wait till you're alone in the dark, freezing, and there's ten thousand feet of water between us. I'm sorry. I'm sorry, I'm rambling."

YU LWAYS DID
TALKK TOO MUCH

She nodded. It was true. But it was also a joke. She could hear his voice saying it. Tenderly, softly. His way of saying, It's OK. I know all this. But I'm glad to hear you say it.

"Comin' up on the big ten thou," said Hippy.

"Bottom's still a mile and a half down," said One Night.

His dive light imploded. It startled him, but it was OK. He still had Little Geek's floodlight.

"Twelve thousand feet," said Hippy. "Jesus, I don't believe he's doing this." He sounded excited. Like he was watching Evel Knievel. Like it was a stunt.

It was more than Lindsey could deal with. She covered the mike. "Please," she said. "Shut up, what's wrong with you?" Then she turned back. "Bud, how're you doing?"

No answer.

"Bud?"

SLF; JAQ SFDJS I CAN'T

"He's losing it," said Monk. "Talk to him. Keep him with us."

"Bud, it's the pressure. All right, you have to listen to my voice. You have to *try*—concentrate, all right? Just listen to my voice."

YR GOINGG A WAY

"Signal's fading," said One Night.

"No. No, Bud, I'm not going away. I'm right here."

"Kill everything we don't need," said Hippy. "Catfish, knock out those exterior lights. Come on, now! Go, go!" He sounded like Bud. That's the way Bud gave orders. Everybody understood—somebody had to do the job. Somebody had to be Bud up here, if they were going to stay in contact with Bud down there. The lights went out, inside *Deepcore* and out. They saw each other only by the light from the digital monitors.

"Run it through the digital processor," said One Night, "cook it as much as you can."

"I'm right here with you, Bud. Bud, this is Lindsey, please, I'm right here with you." It was more of a test pattern than a message. But he had to hear her. Had to hear her voice.

"Seventeen thousand feet," said Hippy.

"Good Christ Almighty," said Catfish, "This is insane." Three miles down. Bud was going down there where he was probably going to get squished to death, just to save some NTIs that you couldn't talk to anyway. For all anybody knew the NTIs lived fifty miles away. Bud was gonna die for what?

Lindsey was losing it—they could see that. "I'm not getting anything," she said, but her voice was small and weak, like a child about to cry. Nobody'd ever seen her like that. Lindsey never acted like that. It was getting to them, having her be so damn human.

Bud was shaking violently, like palsy. His eyes kept rolling back in his head, he was having a hard time staying conscious. He tried to type a message but he couldn't. He kept seeing sparks, flashes of visions. Mini-hallucinations. He knew why, knew it was the synapses in his brain misfiring as the cells of his body got distorted, distended by the pressure. But knowing why didn't mean he could *stop* it.

He felt a massive jolt in his arm, a deafening pop as a shockwave hit him; the lights went out; the canyon wall disappeared. It took him a moment to figure it out. Little Geek's pressure hull had imploded.

Up in *Deepcore*, they understood it immediately. All the information coming to Hippy's monitor went dead. "Whoa whoa whoa!" he said, slapping the machine, twisting dials. "Come on, oh no!"

"Little Geek just folded," said One Night.

It was dark. Pitch black. Bud couldn't see the cliff, all he could see was the dim glow of the keyboard on his wrist. The cliff face was irregular. He could hit something. He was going so fast now. He had to see.

Magnesium flare. Have one somewhere. Here. How do I—got it.

It blinded him, coming out of the dark like that. There was the wall, but he couldn't see it very well. Too bright. He let go of Little Geek—the ROV was useless now. He was free-falling like a skydiver without a chute, half-blind, out of control.

His foot hit a ledge. He rebounded from the wall, tumbled on down, hit again and rolled along the cliff. Little Geek was rolling with him, dead but now dangerous. But he couldn't get control of himself, couldn't reach out and grab it, couldn't tell which way was up or down, he must be falling down but as he rolled over and over, flashes of rock alternating with false visions, lights, voices in his head, he couldn't even tell which way he was falling. He held on to the flare and tried to get hold of himself, tried to remember where he was and what he was doing there.

"He can still make it," Monk said. Little Geek was only taking him straight down, anyway. If he stayed alert, Brigman could still find Big Geek and the warhead. But only if he stayed alert. And that was up to Lindsey, if they had any hope of it at all. He looked at her, motioned toward the mike.

She understood. She also understood that she shouldn't need to have Monk prompting her, that she should *know* when to speak, *know* how to fill his ears with her voice. But she didn't know how or when to do it. She'd never tried; the whole labor of her life had been to avoid such public intimacy. So she *did* need Monk's prompting, and she was grateful for it, and glad that he was kind enough not to show that he despised her for not knowing how to do it all herself. She always tried to know how to do it all herself. "I know how alone you feel. Alone in all that cold blackness. But I'm there in the dark with you, Bud. You're not alone."

Bud heard one voice come clearly out of all the others. A voice that didn't sound like a memory of a time when he was twelve or twenty or nine years old. Lindsey's voice.

"You remember that time, you were pretty drunk, you probably don't remember. But the power went out at that little apartment we had on Orange Street, and we were staring at that one little candle, and I said something really dumb like that candle is me, like every one of us is out there alone in the dark in this life."

Bud saw a candle dancing in the wind of her breath. Saw her eyes angry behind it, daring him to deny it, daring him not to.

Her voice went on. "And you just lit up another candle and put it beside mine and you said, No. See, that's me, that's me, and we stared at the two candles, and then we—well if you remember any of it, I'm sure you remember the next part." But what she was thinking of wasn't the lovemaking. She was thinking of the divorce papers. She was thinking of how she made a careful, intellectual calculation about their relationship, how it wasn't good for either of them. What did it matter whether it was always comfortable or easy or pleasant or fun? Just the fact that they had each other at all, *that* was good, that was so precious and rare and yet she had decided to end it, break it off. She tried to remember why. Because she didn't need him, that's why. She was self-contained, she was complete in herself. Only that was a lie, from the very start it was a lie and she knew it, she filed those papers because she was so afraid of needing him because she didn't believe, she really didn't believe that he would always be there. She was afraid that someday she'd look for him and he'd be gone. Only she knew *now* and should have known before that with Virgil Brigman there wasn't any taking back, there wasn't any changing his mind. When he said, That candle's me, he meant it forever. He wasn't her father; she wasn't her mother. It didn't have to be like that, two empty people living together in an empty house. She could let herself belong to him because he had already, completely, forever given himself to her. She was not going to leave him. There would be no divorce. If he came back from this, it would be forever. She'd grown up that much, at least, during these hours on the edge of death. "Bud," she said, "there are *two* candles in the dark. I'm with you. I'll always be with you, Bud, I promise that."

The flare began to fade. The light dimmed. A single pinpoint moving down the cliff. But he saw that single light, he stared at it. It spoke to him with Lindsey's voice. He was sure of that—Lindsey's voice, and she was telling him that she would always be with him. It was a dream. He had dreamed of this before. Only the voice seemed to be coming out of a tinny speaker right by his ear. He saw the light again, and he remembered what it was. A magnesium flare. He was going down the wall of a cliff, looking for Big Geek and a nuclear warhead. And Lindsey was going to be with him forever. That's what was real. That's what he could count on.

Lindsey was emotionally spent, yet still quivering with fear. Bud wasn't answering. She knew she wanted to be with him forever, and he might not even have heard her, he might already be dead never having heard that from her.

Catfish reached out and gently took the microphone from her hands and draped a friendly, comforting arm across her shoulders. "How you doin', partner? Still with us?" Had to get him to answer. "Come-back, you talk to us, Buddy-boy."

Catfish was a good man, Lindsey knew it, but it was her job to talk to Bud, it was her voice he was listening for. So she took back the microphone, tried to keep the fear out of her voice. It was easier with Catfish's arm around her. She wasn't among strangers here. They'd heard her saying things that she'd never even dared to say in bed alone with Bud—things she'd never even dared to say to herself. Yet, laid bare as she was before them, they didn't think any less of her. Catfish's friendly embrace told her that maybe they even liked her for it. So she was able to speak again. "Bud? Talk to me, Bud. Now come on, you hanging in there? You have to talk to me, Bud. I need to know if you're OK!"

> FEL BETTER
> SOM LITE BELOW

"What kind of light?" Lindsey turned to Monk. "What is he talking about? There's no light down there."

> LIGHT EVYWHER
> BEAWTIFULLL

"He's hallucinating badly," said Monk.

But he wasn't hallucinating. He was moving into the nimbus of light around and above the city of the builders. It was still too far below for him to see shapes or details. But it was vast, and after so much darkness it was a relief to see light again, colors, moving in a dance that he didn't understand, yet it made sense to him. He knew it had to be them, the NTIs. He knew he was seeing their home.

The light from his flare was dully reflected by the cliff wall, except now in one spot below him, where it reflected much more brightly. Big Geek. Like Little Geek, it had also imploded, its lights were also out, but the metal was still shiny enough to give him a faint beacon.

Bud began to deliberately brush against the wall, trying to slow his descent. He grabbed with his hand, each contact, each friction taking just a little more from his velocity. He brought himself to a stop at the shelf where Big Geek rested. He was there. Below him the wall of the canyon wasn't sheer now. It sloped outward, toward the city of light. He was near the bottom of the Cayman Trench.

And his mind was just a little clearer now, clearer than it had been for some time. The hallucinations were gone. He was still groggy, sluggish, but he saw only things that he knew were real. They kept moving closer and farther away, jiggling, but they were actually there. Maybe it was because he wasn't descending, wasn't having to adjust constantly to new increases in pressure. Maybe his body was adapting.

He reached for the keyboard on his wrist.

AT GEEK

Monk took the microphone. "OK, Bud, we'll go step by step. Remove the detonator housing by unscrewing it counterclockwise."

Bud's flare went out. It was the last one. He discarded it and pulled out a cyalume stick, broke it. It gave off a dull yellowish-green light, nowhere near as much as the flare, but it was enough. He found the housing in the base of the cone, where he had seen the SEALs working on the videotape Hippy took through the maintenance-room window. Bud's hands were clumsy and stiff, but they obeyed him. He let the housing drop; it dangled from two wires. These two wires were very important, Bud remembered that.

UNSCREWD

"Great," said Monk. "All right, Bud, you have to cut the ground wire, not the lead wire. It's the blue wire with the white stripe, not—I repeat, *not*—the black wire with the yellow stripe."

CUTING NNOW

The two wires looked big as sewer pipes, but miles away, very far, down there near his hands, which were very very small. The trouble with these wires was that in the yellow-green cyalume light, they looked exactly identical. The white was as yellow as the yellow, the blue as black as the black. Identical twin wires, and cutting one would save the NTI city while cutting the other would destroy it. How could he possibly do this? How was he going to choose?

One of the wires looked right to him. Not blue and white, particularly; there was no visual difference. He just knew which one it was. The question was, could he trust his own intuition?

No, that wasn't the question. The question was, did he have anything else to rely on?

Up in *Deepcore,* everyone froze. Waiting. "Would we see the flash?" Lindsey asked.

"Through three miles of water?" said Monk. "I don't know."

He cut.

STIL HERE

They laughed, cheered.

Catfish brought them back to reality. "Quiet, quiet! Save your air, goddammit."

Monk was talking to Bud again. "Bud, give me a reading off your liquid oxygen gauge."

10 MINUTS WORTH

Hippy knew what it meant. "It took him thirty minutes just to get down there—"

Lindsey went just a little crazy. "What? Ten minutes'

worth?" How could he possibly get back? Gravity working against him, no ROV pulling him. It didn't matter. He was going to come—she *willed* him to come. "You drop your weights and you start back now, do you hear me? Bud? Bud, your gauge could be wrong. Drop your weights and start back now."

NO

"No! No, don't tell me no."

THINK ILL STAY
A WHILE

"You come back here, do you hear me? Drop your weights, you can breathe shallow, god*dam*mit Bud!" He had to try to come back. For *her*—the way she had come back for him.

He heard her. He understood. He understood that her voice was the sweetest sound in the world, and he knew that he wouldn't cause her any more sorrow if he could help it, but there was no way he could go up. He was spent. It was over. Why should he run out of air struggling to rise up through the sea? Why should he die in frustration and fear, when he could stay here and look out over a sight no human being had ever seen before—or would again, probably.

BEAUTIFUL HERE

Lindsey wasn't taking it, though. She shouted at him, railed at him. "You dragged me out of that bottomless pit, now you come back here."

But you don't understand, Lins. I can't do it. You can't tell me to do that, because I just can't.

She knew that. Knew also that it wasn't fair, it wasn't right. Her voice lost its sternness, broke. "Don't leave me here." And, at least, a prayer. "God, Virgil, *please.*"

He couldn't leave her like that. Not without a word.

DONT CRY BABY
KNEW THIS WAS
ONE WAY TICKET
BUT YOU KNOW
I HAD TO COME

She did cry, though.

LOVE YOU WIFE

She knew it was his last word to her. Knew that it meant he understood. That she was his wife, truly now, as she had never been before. There was only one thing left for her to say, and it wasn't until the words passed her lips that she realized she had never known what they meant before, had never felt them flow through her like blood the way they did right now.

"Love you."

There was no reply.

Chapter 15

Alive

$\mathbf{A}$ll the time that Bud came down the canyon, they were watching him. Their tendrils were inside his brain, scanning his memories, interpreting his thoughts, hearing all he heard, feeling all he felt.

Why is he coming down to us?

He comes because he's afraid. He fears that the warhead will explode. He fears that it will destroy our city. He fears that we'll be angry and punish his people.

Then is he a fool? We can destroy this warhead for ourselves.

He doesn't know that.

We would never harm his people.

Not intentionally—but we *have* harmed them. They're on the verge of war out on the surface of this world, in part because of us. He thinks we're also on the verge of destruction here, because of him. He's risking all he is and all he has in order to come undo the terrible thing that Coffey meant to do to us. Who is the nobler creature, then? Him or us? What do *we* put at risk, if we save them?

We can't save them. Killing is in their hearts, even the best of them.

So is fear—and yet they overcome it. You say that fear has brought him down to us. There were also fears that made him hate to come. Fear of personal death, which is more terrible to them than it is to us. His fear of breathing liquid, which is worse in him than any other human that we've seen. His fear of losing *her*—a fear that we ourselves have tasted. You asked why he's coming down to us. I think I understand. He saw two possible worlds. One, a world in which he remained alive, but in which a terrible crime would be committed against us, a crime that he might have prevented. The other, a world in which there remained the possibility of peace between us and his people, but in which he himself was dead.

This is too simple an explanation.

Is it? Then let me show you another, even simpler. I also see two worlds ahead of *us*. One in which we refuse to change our own behavior, and so we stand by and let these humans destroy each other, forcing us to leave this world behind, dead, when we could have prevented it, when its death is partly our fault. The other is a world in which we change to become a little more like them, in order to have the power to change them to become a little more like us; that's the world that remains alive, with us and these humans sharing it, at peace with each other, at peace within ourselves. I choose the second one. I choose to change ourselves a little in order to save us all.

What sort of change do you propose?

We've seen how fear controls them. How fear of each other, which we inadvertently helped to cause, is leading them to devastating war. Why not, then, let them see how irresistibly powerful *we* are, compared to them? Why not let them fear our power so much that when we tell them to destroy their nuclear weapons, they'll do it?

Fear *us*? But we would never harm them!

Wouldn't we? Haven't you nearly decided to stand back and let them destroy this world?

They would be the ones destroying each other, not us causing harm.

Bud Brigman believes this warhead will destroy us. But by

330

your reasoning, it would be *Coffey* destroying us, not him. Yet he has chosen to act as if Coffey were part of himself, to take responsibility for Coffey's actions, to die in order to undo the harm that Coffey caused. We can't pretend to be innocent if we stand by and let them destroy each other—especially since we're partly to blame for their crisis.

No! Your madness is confusing you, and you are confusing *us!* You're speaking as if these humans were as important to us as we are to each other, as if they were our equals, when plainly they aren't! They're killers!

Didn't you mean to kill *me?*

They're strangers! Monstrous, terrible strangers that we can't speak to because they don't even know they're being spoken to. They can never understand us and we can never understand them. They don't *matter* to us! Why should we change ourselves, betray our nature for them?

This is the most important thing the humans have taught me. The thing they're teaching us right now. You see, they are *all* strangers to each other. They live out their entire lives, never truly understanding one another, only making guesses, making mistakes, distorting, deceiving, misunderstanding each other. And yet, though they're permanently strangers, they choose sometimes to trust each other, care for each other so completely that they gladly die to let the other live—that they gladly change themselves to make the other person happy. They're so used to this great leap of trust and love that Bud Brigman has extended that same trust to us—even though he doesn't know us, doesn't understand us, even though we're strangers to him. All I ask is that we treat them as Bud Brigman is treating us. He barely comprehends us, yet values our lives enough to die trying to save us. We understand far more about them, and we don't even have to die to save them. We only have to change a little bit, and then when their nuclear weapons are gone, we benefit as much as they do, because we can remain in peace on this planet.

You make it sound as if you think they're better than we are.

In some ways they are. In some ways they're much worse.

Humans and builders, we're *different* from each other. But we must still value each other, in spite of the differences. Because of them.

This is hard. This is very hard. We've never thought like this before—we can't find this in any of our memories, even the oldest ones from the first of all worlds.

Then watch Bud Brigman and Lindsey Brigman. They're as separate from each other, as strange to each other, as we are from humans, as humans are from us. See how they do what I think that we should do.

Somewhere during Bud's journey down the cliff, as the city watched and listened, a mind that was made up of ten thousand other minds made a decision. The builders began to act.

By the time Bud reached the ledge near the bottom of the cliff, instead of his being helpless, his brain destroyed, their tendrils had reached into his brain, into his body, and changed him, restored him, made it possible for him to live in a place where a human could not live.

They showed him which wire to cut and made him sure of his choice. They filled him with peace at the thought of staying to see the city of strangers. And finally, as the last of the oxygen began to bleed out of his breathing fluid, a builder was sent to him.

He sat on the ledge, leaning against the wall of the cliff. He had seen the city of light, and he had saved it. There was more that he would have wished to do with his life, but if it had to end now, this was enough. It was worth living. Lindsey loved him. He had accomplished everything that really mattered to him. Now he was tired, and the breathing fluid was no longer replenishing; the liquid oxygen was gone. He closed his eyes.

Closed his eyes and saw his brother, standing on the shore. Rushing into the water to save him. Don't come. Don't save me. I'd rather have *you* live than me.

But Junior answered him and said, I couldn't live and be the one who stood on the shore and watched you die.

Yeah, that's right, Junior. Me neither. I couldn't live and be that guy. So it looks like we both bought it in the ocean, liquid in our lungs, splashing around trying to be heroes. Not a bad way to go.

But speaking of being dead, Junior, isn't this taking kind of a long time? I'm out of oxygen. Shouldn't I be gone by now? Or is this life after death, sitting around forever wondering what happens next, only nothing ever does?

He saw light. Moving, getting brighter. He opened his eyes. Turned his head to face it.

It was an angel, coming toward him in the water, just like Jammer said. Bright, glowing, light shifting inside it; two wings arching from its back, sweeping down behind it.

As it came closer, though, he saw that they weren't wings and it wasn't an angel. Where the body of it should have been, it wasn't human, not even close. What seemed to be wings was a veil, a delicate mantle that billowed as it moved through the water. No, it was the rhythmic undulation of the mantle that was propelling it. Its body and limbs were transparent, like a figure of blown glass. Its face was inhuman, but not repellent. He looked into its eyes and realized that it was beautiful.

Bud wasn't afraid. He knew he was seeing an NTI—not something it made, not an artifact or vehicle, but one of the people of the abyss. He knew that he was safe now that it was here.

Bud reached out his hand in greeting.

The NTI reached out an arm to him. The slender blown-glass fingers grasped his bulky glove. The fingers were solid and strong, belying the delicacy of their appearance. But instead of being afraid, instead of feeling imprisoned by the creature's hold on him, Bud felt protected, cared for. He wanted very much to go with this creature, to see everything that it might show him. He didn't wonder anymore why he wasn't dead yet; he knew that the coming of this creature—this *person*—meant that his life wasn't over yet, and he was glad of the delay.

The NTI pulled him up from the ledge, and then, like Peter Pan taking Wendy on her maiden flight, the NTI drew him through the water, carrying him swiftly over the last sweeping downslopes of the canyon wall. They cruised over rocks and cliffs, toward the glow he had seen at the bottom.

Suddenly the darkness exploded with light as they cleared the last cliff and saw the whole city open up beneath and before them. It was one vast, symmetrical structure, radiating outward from the center, as if it were one living body, one huge machine. Light swept along slender threads that must have been twenty yards thick, yet still looked graceful and delicate. They seemed like highways, but the only travelers were pulses of color. He saw huge spires rising upward in graceful spirals, with arches and webbing and tissue stretched across ribs, like microscopic photographs of delicate internal organs. None of the structures made sense —where were the highways, the shopping districts, the suburbs, the parks? This city wasn't built for any purpose Bud could understand. But he knew, without comprehension, that it was perfect for its purpose, that not a spire, not a channel, not a ridge or arch or bend was out of place.

They swept toward the center, descending as they went, and now Bud could see thousands of creatures moving through the city. They didn't follow the channels or ridges —when they all could fly through the dense water at the bottom of the sea, why would they need roads? There were many like the one who was leading Bud; there were also other shapes, dozens of them, all going about their business with purpose and intelligence. Many of them stopped and touched each other as they passed—not like ants, with their chaotic dance of indecision, constantly touching antennae to discover where they were and what they ought to do, but rather like a city of people who all knew each other so well that they must greet with brief but real affection everyone they pass.

The NTI led him toward one of the spires. As they sank down toward its base, he realized how tall it was, hundreds of feet high. The closer they got to it, the more detail he could see. Each feature—a rib, an arch, a sweep of wall— was really composed of hundreds of smaller structures that echoed the shapes and patterns of the spire as a whole, and each of those smaller structures was composed of others, smaller still, so that he believed that the entire thing was grown, not built, taking its shape naturally from the myriad forms within it. Even the buildings are alive, he thought. The whole city is alive.

They approached one of the large openings. It was not an archway; it opened in so smooth and gradual a curve that it was impossible to tell the moment when you stopped being outside and started being inside its yawning mouth. Instead of slowing as they came near, the NTI accelerated, as if they had been caught in a current, like blood cells being swept through the veins toward the heart. Inside, they rushed through a curving, three-dimensional maze of tunnels, not dark and forbidding, but full of light and life, a safe place, a place of memory.

There was so much of it that Bud gave up trying to make sense of the route they were taking, of the things he saw. Lindsey would understand this. Lindsey would figure out what all these structures are for, what each of these creatures or machines we pass are doing. All I can do is witness it, see it without understanding. That's enough for me right now. When they want me to understand, when I *need* to understand, they'll speak to me.

Tunnels divided. They followed narrowed tubes, turning at startling speed, then abruptly moved out into main thoroughfares hundreds of feet across, crowded with NTIs of every description. Finally, though, they came to a smaller chamber where they settled on the floor. The NTI let go of his hand then, and floated back a few feet.

Bud found that he missed having the NTI's hand in his. The flight had been exhilarating, but now his feet were on the ground again, and he was alone, touching no one. He wasn't afraid. But he felt solitary, weak, insufficient for whatever they meant to do with him. He was also physically weak, still exhausted; he didn't stand, but half lay, half sat on the floor of the room, straddling a recessed oval on the floor, whose purpose he couldn't begin to guess.

A shimmering division appeared in the water, bisecting the chamber they were in, like an almost-invisible curtain. Then the one curtain became two, drawing apart, wider, wider—and between them there was no water. It was the parting of the Red Sea, only smoothly, as if the sea had been sliced by a laser beam. It passed over his head, his body, and beyond him; at the end, Bud found himself sitting in a short, shimmering hallway between two walls of water. Twenty thousand feet under the Caribbean Sea, he was dripping wet in a pocket of air.

For a moment he didn't understand why they should do this. Then he did. If they wanted him to talk with them, then he needed to be breathing air. For a moment he worried that they might not know how to create a breathing mix that wouldn't kill him at this depth, at this pressure, but almost at once the fear subsided. Of course they knew. They would not be careless with his life.

He reached up, uncoupled his helmet, and pulled it free. The breathing fluid splashed out. It hadn't occurred to him that it would be no easier to quit breathing fluid than it had been to start. He bent over, his body wracked by spasms as fluid exploded from his lungs. He thought, No wonder babies cry, when they have to give up the water of the womb and start breathing fire. Finally he lay gasping and coughing on the floor, dragging in deep, painful breaths of air. I've done this before, he thought, but I never want to do it again.

In a short time, though, he recovered enough to sit up, to look around. Behind the shimmering curtain of water he could see the NTI who brought him being joined by others, all of the same general appearance. He couldn't tell them apart, except to count that there were seven of them; their inhumanness was so powerful that he couldn't have noticed any individual differences. If they had any.

What were they waiting for? Perhaps for him to show that he could speak now. So he spoke. "Howdy." Then he realized that was too informal, these guys might be ambassadors or government people or something. So he tried again: "Uh, how're you guys doin'?"

His voice echoed metallically in the room; he could hear a soft lapping of water from the walls. Then in the water wall before him there appeared a pattern of glowing horizontal lines, with colored dots appearing at random along each line. Then the patterns resolved themselves. They were the horizontal lines of a raster screen. He was watching a twenty-foot TV.

"You watch our TV? Is that what you're trying to say? That you know what's been going on up there?"

It was the solution they had finally come up with to the problem of how to talk to a human so he'd know that the builders were talking to him and he'd understand what they were saying. Humans used television to talk to each other; the builders could use the same television programs to communicate with Bud Brigman. When they could see in his mind that he understood them, they'd release the chemicals in his brain that gave him a feeling of certainty. It was the best combination of human and builder speech that they could think of.

Recorded in the vast memory of the city were every frame of every television broadcast that their gliders had received as they passed back and forth between space and the sea. But it was current broadcasts they wanted Bud to see. They had to show him the action they had finally decided to take, so that he could go back and explain it to the rest of humanity. It was not enough to act—they had tried that before, when a builder destroyed a potentially deadly satellite, and it led to exactly the sort of trouble the builder had been hoping to prevent. Their actions had to be clearly identified as coming from the builders, not any group of humans. And their purpose had to be explained and understood. Since Bud and Lindsey had been at the heart of their decision, it seemed only right that he be the messenger to explain them to the humans at the surface of the world.

What they were doing had a simple goal: to show humanity that the builders existed, that they had irresistible power, that if they wanted to, they could devastate and slaughter at will. It was important that the demonstration be worldwide, so the builders had carried the memory of all their decision-making to every other city of builders. Having received a complete memory of this city's experiences with the humans of *Deepcore*, they reacted as if they had all gone through the same process and reached the same decision. They couldn't bring all of humanity out to the ocean, to see their power in the place where they lived. So, together, they set out to take the ocean to the humans.

A wave. A tsunami. Rising out of the ocean for no discernible cause, a huge, continuous wave surrounding every inhabited continent. The technology to produce and control the wave was simple enough for the builders, but the energy cost was enormous. They tapped the vast reserves of geothermal energy, drew enough heat from the ocean and the atmosphere to offset the greenhouse effect. They used far more energy to create this demonstration than all the energy released by human beings throughout human history—all the woodfires, all the coal furnaces, all the oil and gas, all the nuclear reactors had not produced enough energy to duplicate what the builders could do with only a few minutes notice, acting together in perfect unity.

They showed Bud the news reports. Baffled scientists being interviewed about the approaching wave. No, we don't know what caused it. We don't know how to stop it. But we do know what it will do. A half-mile-high wall of water striking every coastline in the world? It will utterly destroy everything in its path for miles and miles inland. No, there's no point in evacuating coastal areas—if you're close enough to be threatened, you have no hope of getting away in time. Most people in the world live within the threatened area. It will be a far worse disaster than any plague or war; the whole fabric of human civilization will be unwoven in the aftermath.

And interviews with common people, terrified as much by the impossibility of what was happening as by the physical danger of it. What could you count on in the world if the sea could suddenly rise up and attack the land for no reason? No pictures of the wave itself, not yet—it was moving too fast for that, the news of it had come from radio reports from airplanes, or from ships that radioed in panic and then fell silent. But it was coming. It would be visible from the shore in a minute or two.

Bud listened to the news. He realized at once what was causing the wave. "You're doing it! Right? That's what you're telling me. Yeah, you can control water. That's your technology. But *why?*"

Yes, he knew the question. That's why they had brought him here, to tell him why.

The huge television screen went blank, then came to life again. Not with current news, now, but with old broadcasts: a brilliant flash of light, and then the mushroom cloud rising. The same film, repeated again and again, faster and faster, until the whole thing merged into an unbroken white glare.

Bud thought of the news reports they had been getting while the *Explorer* was still with them. The nuclear powers on the verge of war. "Hey, you don't know they're really going to do it. Where do you get off passing judgment on us, when you can't be sure? How do you know?"

The screen exploded with searing images of cruelty and killing. U.S. soldiers in Vietnam, Afghan children with limbs blown off by Russian toy-bombs, a car bomb in Belfast, street fighting in Beirut, corpses being bulldozed into mass graves at Auschwitz; a picture of humanity that sickened Bud; an indictment; a condemnation.

Bud understood what they were saying. Not that humanity was pure evil and deserved to die—quite the opposite. They were answering his specific question: How do you know that the superpowers are really going to launch a nuclear war? The answer: When has an act of war ever been so terrible, so monstrous, so self-defeating that *no* nation on earth was willing to do it? The NTIs knew that this time the threat of annihilation was real. The wave was designed to prevent it.

Still, Bud refused to believe that it was right to destroy half of humanity like this, with only a few minutes warning, with no chance to realize their mistake, to change. On a cosmic scale perhaps it might be right to kill so many in order to keep humanity from killing everyone. But to carry out such an act would be monstrous in itself. Have you no compassion for the people you're about to kill?

Their answer was to fill the screen again with the present broadcast. The wave was visible now from shore; television cameras on the beaches were showing its approach. It didn't look that large at first, until the reporters mentioned how far away it was. And as Bud watched, the wave grew and grew, to enormous heights and beyond. Tall as skyscrapers, then taller, nearing half a mile in height and the wave was still not at its peak, it was still growing as it neared the shore. And the sound of it, the roar, drowned out even the reporters' voices; only the screams of panicking people could be heard above it. Finally even that sound was overwhelmed by the sound of the onrushing wave. It was unbearable to watch this, to hear it—

And then, suddenly, it was silent.

Twenty-five hundred feet high, the wall of water had come to a halt. Held up by invisible, unguessable forces, it loomed all along the coastlines of the world, ready to come crashing down, ready to destroy—but for now, waiting. Waiting.

The force that could create the wave was already terrifying to imagine. But the force that could *stop* the wave, keep it in place, build trillions of tons of water into a structure as stable as a stone pyramid—the world looked at the wave, dwarfing all the works of man, and were at once terrified and awed.

The point was made. Their power had been shown. Most of humanity had witnessed it, in person or on television. They would not forget.

The wave soundlessly subsided, its work done; the water was released gently on the seaward side, until the ocean returned to its normal level, and breakers of reasonable size once again rolled in to the undamaged shore. The ships that had reported the wave began to broadcast again; they had fallen silent because all the power on board had been damped, but now they had a story to tell, of a wave the size of a mountain that lifted them up, passed under them, and left them undamaged behind it.

Bud looked at the builders, trying to understand. "Why? You could've done it. Why didn't you?"

The screen went dark. Then letters began to appear on it, slowly printing out, as if someone was clumsily typing them.

> KNEW THIS WAS
> ONE WAY TICKET
> BUT YOU KNOW
> I HAD TO COME

And then:

> LOVE YOU WIFE

Bud didn't understand. How could the words he wrote to Lindsey be the reason why humanity was spared? He looked at them, puzzled, questioning. In answer, the builders bowed their heads before him, just for a moment. A gesture of respect to their teacher.

The crew was still together in the control room. They had sealed off the rest of *Deepcore,* and were running the last of the tetramix into this room only. To conserve oxygen they were holding still, trying to stay at rest. They huddled under blankets to stay warm. Bud had accomplished his mission, but he would never come back. They grieved for him, but they knew now that he would likely precede them in death by only a few hours.

Jammer put a blanket around Schoenick's shoulders—he was still tied, because they didn't know what he might do, but they had no desire to punish him. From time to time the ones who were most affected by the diminishing amount of oxygen in the mix would put a Drager mask over their faces and breathe deeply. Lindsey sat apart from the others, slumped in a chair.

And then the UQC came to life. *"Deepcore,* do you read? This is *Benthic Explorer,* over."* McBride's voice sounded like a heavenly choir to them. Somebody remembered they were there. The *Explorer* had come back for them.

Catfish practically ripped the UQC mike off the wall. "Hell yes, we read. Good of you to join us. How's that storm going up there?"

"Well, it's strange. It just kind of blew itself out all of a sudden. We're up here in a flat sea with no wind. But then a lot of weird things've been happening."

Catfish wasn't terribly interested right now in the weird stuff that might have been going on topside. "Well, hell, son. You better get a line to us, we're in moderately poor shape down here."

The next while was pretty busy, explaining to the *Explorer* exactly what had happened, how much damage they had sustained, what their resources were. The support staff on the *Explorer* had spent the storm jury-rigging a system to get a line down to *Deepcore* as soon as they found them—if there was anything or anyone left to find. So there was hope again; they weren't going to run out of oxygen.

There was another kind of hope, too, as McBride told them about the wave, how it came to the coastlines of the world, hung there, and withdrew. At once the crew of *Deepcore* guessed that the NTIs had something to do with it, and they explained to McBride what they all had seen—the water tentacle that probed *Deepcore,* showing the same kind of astonishing control of water that, on a larger scale, produced the wave.

There were other worries, too. Monk assured DeMarco that Coffey had been suffering from HPNS and was behaving irrationally, but it was clear that DeMarco was extremely upset about the loss of two of his men, and didn't necessarily believe all that he was told about the arming—and then disarming—of the warhead. But there was time enough to argue through all of that when they got air to breathe.

A couple of hours after contact was restored, Catfish was

on the hydrophone, talking through details of the *Explorer*'s plan to get the crew of *Deepcore* back to the surface. It was going to take three weeks of decompression, of course, so they couldn't just send down a submersible and haul them up.

"So how're you guys gonna evacuate us?" asked Catfish.

"They're talking about flying in the DSRV from Norfolk," said McBride.

"OK, OK, I understand, but how long's that gonna take?"

McBride didn't know. While he was finding out, Catfish's attention was drawn to a commotion over by the Deep Suit monitor. Hippy had noticed something coming up on the screen. One Night was the first to dare to say out loud what it had to mean. "Hey! Hey! Look, it's Bud!"

VIRGIL BRIGMAN BACK
ON THE AIR

"That's impossible," said Monk. Nobody could live this long without oxygen.

"No it's not," said Lindsey. Nothing was impossible— she knew that now.

McBride had come back on the UQC with his answer, but Catfish wasn't listening. "Six hours. Catfish? Do you hear? *Deepcore,* do you read?"

Catfish finally realized that the box was chattering at him. "Wait a minute. We've got a message from Bud."

They knew topside, of course, that the crew assumed Bud was dead. They also knew that he had gone down into the abyss where the NTIs lived, that he had reported seeing lights down there. If he was alive and had something to tell them, they wanted to know. "What's it say?"

Lindsey took the mike, sat in front of the screen, and read Bud's message. She probably wasn't the best choice to give a clear, dispassionate reading—but since she was sure as hell going to read it out loud anyway, she might as well say it into the mike.

HAVE SOME NEW
FRIENDS DOWN HERE
GUESS THEYVE BEEN
HERE AWHILE

THEYVE LEFT US
ALONE BUT IT
BOTHERS THEM
TO SEE US
HURTING EACH OTHER

GETTING OUT OF
HAND

THEY SENT A
MESSAGE
HOPE YOU GOT IT

Catfish laughed. "I'd say that's a big ten-four, jack."

THEY WANT US TO
GROW UP A BIT
AND PUT AWAY
CHILDISH THINGS

OF COURSE ITS
JUST A SUGGESTION

Up in the *Explorer,* McBride turned to DeMarco. "Looks like you boys might be out of business." DeMarco didn't look happy about it, but any good military man knows when he's facing an irresistible force.

Down in *Deepcore,* Bud's message was no sooner finished than the whole rig began to vibrate. They braced themselves, but they weren't so much frightened as annoyed "What the hell is this," said Catfish. The last thing they needed was an earthquake or something, what with them perched on the edge of the cliff.

It was Lindsey who got them moving. "One Night, get to sonar."

When she got there, the noise in the passive sonar

headphone nearly blew her out. The screens painted the picture pretty clearly. "Something's coming up the wall."

"What is it?" asked Lindsey.

One Night didn't know—it didn't look like anything she'd ever seen before. "Whatever it is, it's major."

A new message from Bud came on the screen.

KEEP PANTYHOSE ON

YOURE GONNA LOVE
THIS

So whatever it was, he knew about it, and it was going to be OK. The rumbling noise increased, and then a glow appeared from the viewpoint. They ran to look. Outside the viewport, hundreds, perhaps thousands of the NTIs were gathering. Not gliders, not porters, but the builders themselves, in their natural shape. This was the shallowest water in which they could survive, and they glowed brightly with the effort it required to maintain their structure—and to do something else.

They reached into *Deepcore* with ten thousand tendrils, touched and penetrated the bodies of the human beings watching there. Down in the city, they had explored Bud's body, discovered in it the dangers of decompression. Then they made simple but profound changes in every cell of his body—the changes they were making now in the people gathered in the control room. The tendrils were invisible, but their touch was not unfelt this time—there was momentary pain, a deep unease as their bodies were changed from the root outward. Yet there was also perfect trust and joy as the builders whispered silently into their minds.

The light from the builders' bodies got brighter and brighter, until they—*we*—couldn't see at all in that direction. But even when we could no longer see them, we knew we had been changed, though we did not yet understand the physical transformation. We were not the same people who had gone down into the sea days or weeks before. We had grown together, we had grown in understanding—we had grown up.

Deepcore began to move.

Not under its own power. It was like a stiff undersea wind began to blow and picked us and lifted us out over the chasm. We had no fear of falling, though, because directly under us was the most incredible structure we had ever seen. A vast convex surface, but not a smooth one—it was formed of organic-looking strands and tissues, ridges and arches, all alive with light and color. Around the edges of it rose eight enormous spires, twisting, spiraling. It was the center of the NTI city, the place that Bud had visited. Normally it wouldn't rise from the seabed until it was time to set out into space, searching for other worlds to colonize. It was the builders' ark—like Noah's ark, and the ark of the covenant, and the ark of bulrushes that carried Moses to safety on the Nile, it held what was most precious to them, everything they'd need to start again in another place. It contained the core of their memory, the heart of all that they valued about themselves. That's what the city was, and all its structures—their collective memory, their library, their cemetery, their home, the single immortal soul that they all shared.

The builders knew that Bud's word alone might be disregarded. The wave had shown their power; Bud had explained what they expected humanity to do. Now they had to show themselves, unmistakable proof that there really were builders living in the depths of the ocean.

The ark rose up, lifting *Deepcore* with it, straight to the surface. As it rose it also picked up the *Explorer* and lifted it out of the water—and the Navy destroyer *Albany,* and several other ships. The water rushed off the top of the ark like a circular Niagara, flowing out to the edges. And there they rested, high and dry, the ships all dwarfed by the spires of memory that ringed the ark.

For the second time, we opened the lockout hatch of trimodule-C. This time, though, it didn't lead into the frozen water of the deep. This time it was air, with a stiff drop down to the hard dry surface of the ark. Catfish went first, but soon we all joined him, standing there in daylight, released at last from the darkness of the bottom of the sea.

"We should be dead," said Lindsey. "We didn't decompress."

"Our blood oughta be fizzin' like a warm shook-up Coke," said Catfish.

"They must've done something to us," said Hippy.

"Oh, yes," said Lindsey. "I think you could say that."

Done something to us? We have all been touched by them, and changed in more ways than I can name. Those of us who stayed with them have been changed the most of all. They can take us from our atmosphere into the deep and back again without harm to our bodies. We can breathe in their underwater city without equipment of any kind. But these are commonplace miracles to us now. The one that always astonishes me is the gift of memory. They've taught us how to sense the difference between our own thoughts and the ones they give to us; we can understand their speech. And they've given us the memories of the people that they scanned, the living and the dead. I've been filled with them, I've lived out their lives from the inside, I've known all their desires, all their fears—Barnes and Kretschmer from the *Montana,* Russian sailors who drowned in the storm, the crewmen who died on *Deepcore,* and all the ones who lived, as well. I have *been* Bud as he slipped down the cliff, I have *been* Lindsey as she drowned, I have felt their love for each other, and they have seen every secret in my heart. One Night, Jammer, Catfish, Hippy, Sonny—I know them as no other human beings have ever known each other, and they know me. And I hold within me the members of my team—Wilhite, Schoenick, Coffey. Men that I thought I knew, thought I loved before. I know them even better now, and though some of the memories are bitter—the hatred Schoenick and Coffey felt for me when they believed that I betrayed them; the agony of Coffey's death in madness—yet still I can say that knowing them is better than remaining strangers.

Not everyone wanted to receive these memories. Schoenick refused—he only wanted to get away. Sonny wanted to go home to his family. But all the rest of us who spent those days together in *Deepcore* are still together; we pass back and forth between the world of air and the deep city of the builders at the bottom of the sea. The builders have changed us, because they had to have ambassadors between our worlds, but they won't change any others—they want humanity to remain human, as much as possible. And you don't want to go through all that we've experienced. Sometimes I wake up so full of other men's and women's dreams that I have to struggle to remember who I am. Sometimes the dead are so present in me that I feel possessed by other people's souls.

And yet I wouldn't lose those memories even if I could. They are alive in me; I wouldn't wish them dead again. I wouldn't wish them lost to me, because I have learned from them what it means to be alive and human, I've learned why it is that people do the things we do, I've learned how other lives are from the inside. And now I've tried to pass it on to you. Not in the purity with which the builders share memory—that isn't the human way. Still, in these pages I've done my best to give you those memories that will show you what we did and why we did it, we who were down there when builders and humans met and changed each other for all time.

So it was that I stood there on the surface of the builders' ark when Lindsey saw Bud stride out of the mouthlike portal in a ridge along the surface of the ark. He dropped his helmet, yelled, waved. Lindsey started toward him, then stopped a few feet away. They had said things to each other at the verge of death—would they still be true in daylight, in safety?

He smiled at her, and took the last few steps to close the gap. She touched him, lightly, a caress and a confirmation—

is he real? Is he mine? Then, sure of each other, they laughed.

"Hello, Brigman," Lindsey said.

"Hello, Mrs. Brigman," he answered.

Two candles, always separate, but living always in each other's light.

Afterword

James Cameron

A *novel* based on a screenplay? The term seems precious in our jaded business.

There are screenplays based on novels, certainly. Our vampiric industry drains much of its unholy creative sustenance from pure literature.

And there are *novelizations* of screenplays. The studios encourage these literary endeavors.

The pages provide filler behind the covers, and the imperative is to display those flashy covers at supermarkets and newsstands throughout the land.

In the critical days before a film's release, the ubiquitous paperbacks create interest, promote title recognition, increase market penetration, and in general add to the potential box office gross on opening weekend.

The fact that someone might actually *read* these novelizations seem to be of little concern.

Well, people do read them.

I read them.

More to the point, I have read certain novelizations of my own films and found them to be cursory, mediocre, often inaccurate, and sometimes downright reprehensible.

I determined that there would be no *novelization* of this film.

There would be a *novel*.

I sought out Orson Scott Card with little knowledge of his award-winning status and current esteem as an SF writer. I remembered his earlier short stories as works of stunning human compassion and sensitivity coupled with an assured style. I hoped he might be a writer who would not be seduced by the hardware, who would tell the story in human terms.

I was not disappointed.

Somehow, while being steadfastly true to the film, Scott managed to weave in his beautiful elaborations and illuminations . . . never altering dialogue, only adding to it . . . never contradicting the intent or tone of a scene, but instead adding a fourth dimension of clarity and emotion.

His intricately worked-out city of the builders and the rationale for their behavior goes far beyond the enigmatic images of the film, in ways that can only be explored in the written word.

Film into novel.

A new form.

The book illuminates the film and vice versa, symbiotic partners in a single, multi-faceted dramatic work.

Scott worked from videotapes of the film as the editing progressed, constantly updating his manuscript as scenes were changed, added, or deleted. And yet despite his great sense of responsibility to the film, he was never enslaved by it. His early chapters capture the characters perfectly and give them great emotional credibility and yet the incidents are entirely his own creation. Perhaps these chapters were his way of making the characters his own, giving himself the necessary creative credential to tell another writer's story in his own words.

I can only speculate as to Scott's thought processes in this creative matrix.

I found the resultant manuscript to be a fascinating

refraction of the story, from which I gained valuable insight into the film as my own work progressed.

An interesting ellipse in the creative process: I gave the respective chapters on the characters' childhoods to Mary Elizabeth Mastrantonio and Ed Harris before filming began. They accepted Scott's interpretation as plausible backstory and incorporated it into their preparation for the film.

In these ways, the novel has fed into the film, just as the film has nourished the novel.

The collaboration has been satisfying.

The resultant book is a damn good read, and should be read as a *book*, not as a roadmap to a movie. It has its own life.

But don't forget . . . you still have to *see* it to believe it.

—James Cameron
Spring 1989

Afterword

Orson Scott Card

My agent, Barbara Bova, called me and said, "Pocket Books has approached me about you doing a novelization."

"Barbara," I said, "you know I don't do novelizations."

Then she mentioned that the director was James Cameron.

I knew who he was. Director of *Terminator* and *Aliens*. Films that could have been run-of-the-mill sci-fi—but weren't, because the filmmaker had taken the time and trouble to create real characters. And now I was being offered a chance to write a narrative adaptation of Cameron's newest film.

"Send me the script," I said.

"First you have to sign a non-disclosure agreement," said Barbara.

Ah, Hollywood. The non-disclosure agreement forbade me to show the script to any unauthorized person or even to let said unauthorized person's shadow fall across the script; furthermore I was enjoined not to speak about the story in the presence of unauthorized persons, or to think about the screenplay while using a public restroom; if I violated these rules, I would immediately be fired, would have to give back any money they had already paid me, and would be tattooed on the forehead with the letters F-I-N-K.

I signed it. The script arrived. I skimmed through it.

The story was wonderful—just what I'd expect from Cameron. While there were plenty of special-effects wonders and virtually non-stop action, the heart of the story was the relationship between two real human beings, Bud and Lindsey Brigman.

But was I the one to write the novelization? I could handle the characters—but there's a lot more to a novelization than that. I had already seen the problem when I reviewed *Willow*. Let me paraphrase some passages from that review:

"The dilemma of the film novelist is that the story already exists. Somebody else wrote it. The novelist is, therefore, merely a translator. Not a translator from one language to another, however—he is translating from one medium to another, and the sad truth is that it's damned hard to do it well.

"You know the problem, because you've seen it time after time going the other way. A good movie generally contains as much story as a long novelet or a short novella. So to translate a novel to the screen means leaving out a lot of stuff—including the entire inner life of the characters. Working in reverse, the novelist finds he must fill up a novel's-worth of pages with only a novelet's-worth of story. Yet he cannot fill it with his own invention—he must, like any good translator, slavishly try to reproduce someone else's world, characters, and events. Worse yet, few novelizers get to see the final cut of the movie—their manuscript must be turned in while the film is still being filmed.

"Can a novelization ever be a really good novel, in novelistic terms? I imagine that it would be possible—if the filmmaker had enough respect for the written word to bring the novelist into his confidence and make him a collaborator. But when has any science fiction or fantasy filmmaker ever shown any evidence of knowing how to read a whole book? There are a few. John Boorman, James Cameron. Maybe some others I've missed. But to most of them, the novelization is exactly as important as the board game, the T-shirts, the action figures, and the coloring books."

How important was the novelization of this film to James Cameron? How much access would I have to the set and to the film itself? How much freedom would he give me to make the book partly my own, to flesh out the story, invent and rationalize in the areas that the film did not fully develop? If I didn't believe that I could make the novelization utterly faithful to the movie *as filmed* and yet at the same time make it a novel to be proud of, then I wasn't interested.

Cameron called me. His answers to my questions were reassuring. As I had suspected, he loved books as well as movies, and this time he was determined that the book would be as effective in its way as the movie. Furthermore, he wanted the book to include facts and explanations that were impossible to put into the movie.

His research on the film had been extraordinary—all of that information was going to be available to me. I was grateful, since I knew nothing about deep-sea diving and had no desire to spend months duplicating his research. I would also have access to the set during the filming, and we envisioned many meetings between Jim and me as I wrote chapters and he read and responded to them.

Everything sounded right. I wanted to do it, partly because the story was so good that I wanted to play around in it for a while, and partly because I wanted to see if a novelization could be as valid a work of art as the film itself. Jim made both goals seem possible.

There were potential barriers. The first was an exclusivity clause in my contract with TOR Books; but Tom Doherty, the founder and publisher, was kind enough to allow me to proceed for no other reason than the fact that I wanted to.

The second barrier was scheduling. Pocket Books, the publisher of the novelization, wanted the finished manuscript in September 1988. Since filming would barely be under way at that time, it was an absurd date for the kind of work I wanted to do. How could I be at all *specific* in my writing, if I didn't know exactly how the actors were going to interpret the dialogue, or how they would move through the set, or what the mood was at any moment in the film? Novelizers who work from the screenplay alone either have to remain vague about physical details, or, in being specific, they will inevitably contradict the film at a thousand points. It was vital both to Jim and to me that the novel be quite specific and yet utterly faithful to the film. So if we couldn't get a due date later than the end of filming, there was no point in proceeding.

Pocket pushed the date back to December. A contract was written. I signed.

For long months, nothing happened. Then, late in August, I got a call from Christa, Jim's secretary. Could I come down to Gaffney, South Carolina? It was time to start.

Why Gaffney? The Earl Owensby Studios were built on the site of an unfinished nuclear reactor. The huge containment tower was watertight—exactly what was needed for the underwater filming. It was important to Jim that the light be just right—which meant working in forty feet of water instead of the normal ten feet.

I got down to Gaffney and began to realize exactly what working on this film meant to the cast and crew. First of all, Gaffney isn't exactly a city. It's barely a *town*. Now, I live in the Carolinas myself, by choice, because I love these small towns and the people who live in them. But for people used to L.A., Gaffney could very quickly start to feel like limbo, if not hell itself. It was a half-hour drive from the studio to the freeway, and another half-hour after that to get to Spartanburg, the nearest town with a mall or a moviehouse.

What impressed me even more, however, was the fact that everybody in the cast was going underwater. Forty feet is no joke—more than once Jim, the actors, and the camera operators were working so deep and so long that they had to spend time decompressing. And while a few effects were done using stuntpeople—Bud's tumble down the wall, for instance—most of the time when you see Bud or Lindsey or Catfish out there in the water, it really is Ed Harris or Mary Elizabeth Mastrantonio or Leo Burmester. Ed Harris had to sit there while his helmet filled with fluid, holding his breath while seeming not to, during some pretty long takes. Mary Elizabeth Mastrantonio really was dragged along underwater, without breathing gear, during long takes. Of course, the process was made as safe as possible—divers with breathing gear were always just out of frame. But as I imagined myself doing some of the things these actors did, I realized that being in this film required raw physical courage.

They offered to let me put on a suit and get into the water. Instead, I fled to my motel room and put down on paper the first two chapters of the book. I had been developing Bud and Lindsey in my mind—who they were, how they came to be involved in undersea work, and why they would be on the verge of divorce when they mattered so much to each other. I turned in the chapters to Jim Cameron. He read them. So did Gale Anne Hurd, the producer; so did Van Ling, Jim's research assistant. All three of them responded, and the verdict was clear: I was going to be able to write the novel I wanted to write.

All three of them became advisers and collaborators in the book. Jim was impossibly busy—our meetings were rare, culminating at last in a midnight phone call on 28 March 1989. I daresay that in person and on the telephone, we spent no more than eight hours working directly together. But that does not give a true picture of the degree of collaboration: Jim and Gale both understand exactly what makes a story work, and so do I, so that we didn't have to waste time trying to teach each other how to read and write a novel.

Van Ling, who was constantly with Jim through every step of the production, was able to respond to my questions and provide hundreds of bits of information, correcting or elaborating on my assumptions. It was Van who read through every chapter within hours of receiving it, sending me notes explaining what was going on in the scenes I was studying. Since he and Jim had discussed everything from character motivations to the function of every piece of equipment in *Deepcore*, the hours I spent consulting with Van were as vital to the collaborative process as the time I spent with Jim.

It's worth noting that almost everything shown in this film except for the builders themselves is either presently feasible or will soon be within reach of current technology. Everything from SEAL training to the ROVs reflects Van's and Jim's deep research and invaluable help from knowledgeable consultants. In particular, you should know that the fluid breathing technique used in Deep Suit has actually been done by the researchers mentioned in chapter seven. When you see Beany breathe underwater, that's not a special effect—it's a real rat breathing fluid and coming out alive.

My most important source, the clearest possible explanation of what Jim wanted the story to be, was the film itself. Starting with a trickle early in January and culminating with most of the edited film in late March, I had stacks of videotape that *showed* me exactly what was happening from moment to moment in the story. The film was so valuable that I ended up throwing out everything I had done from the script itself. Only the first three chapters of my first draft survived in substantially their original form, and that's only because they take place before the movie actually begins. I learned for a fact what I had suspected from the start—that a novelization written from the screenplay is worthless compared to a novelization written from the film itself.

Which brings me to another group of collaborators: the actors. I'm not a starstruck film-lover; I don't get all tingly when in the presence of stars. But I did work for many years as a playwright and stage director, and I *do* get excited when I see a brilliant performance. The whole ensemble in *Deepcore* gave virtually flawless performances. Part of this came from the fact that they really *were* a cohesive group—living in or near Gaffney for six months and working long hours underwater and acting the roles Jim wrote gave them the kind of smoothness together that the *Deepcore* crew would really have. Whether they loved each other every minute is immaterial—neither do the characters. What matters is they played off each other with astonishing sensitivity, and in the climactic ensemble scenes—in conflict with Coffey, reviving Lindsey, talking Bud down the cliff—they worked with such reality that all I had to do was report what I saw and the scenes would work.

Every one of the actors brought details of attitude and interpretation that opened up their characters to me, allowing me to make them more real in the novel than they would ever have been from the script alone. Leo Burmester's Catfish became a father-figure, an anchor in the novel, largely because of the way he played the part; Todd Graff's jumpiness and sense of semi-malicious fun as Hippy, Kimberly Scott's quietly seething One Night, John Bedford Lloyd's sweetly dumb Jammer—all of them opened up their characters for me, and are to some degree co-inventors of the novel.

Coffey and Lindsey were extraordinarily difficult roles to play. Michael Biehn had to play a man who was on the edge of madness—but both he and Jim wanted to avoid letting Coffey be a stock villain. When you think of all the movies where the military bad guy mindlessly runs roughshod over the good guys, you can see how easily Coffey might have been played that way. Biehn never crossed the line into caricature. He made Coffey dangerous, yet without a hint of malice. The result was that I could write Coffey as an interesting and in many ways admirable human being, knowing that Biehn's performance would make Coffey seem as complex as I was making him.

Lindsey Brigman offers a different challenge. In most films, the woman unexpectedly aboard ship would be there solely to be lusted after, rescued, and laid at regular intervals. Jim Cameron already proved in *Terminator* and *Aliens* that he isn't interested in such shallow female characters. Instead, Mary Elizabeth Mastrantonio had to create a character who was at once arrogant and intelligent and impulsive—and also sympathetic. I take nothing away from the Academy-Award-winning performances of Cliff Robertson in *Charly* and Dustin Hoffman in *Rain Man* when I say that it is far easier to play a character who is mentally limited than it is to play one who is intellectually brilliant. Most actors who attempt it merely embarrass themselves. Mastrantonio, on the contrary, made me believe that her

Lindsey Brigman actually designed *Deepcore,* and I believed that when her Lindsey said "jump," she was used to seeing people move up and down. But Mastrantonio also showed me the one thing I hadn't been able to discover in the script: why Bud loved her.

In particular, though, I must single out Ed Harris as one of the co-authors of this book. He has long been an actor's actor, one who has the respect of his peers even though he has not yet achieved the public prominence he deserves. I don't know whether casual audiences in the theater will realize what an extraordinary achievement his performance as Bud Brigman is. Every moment he's on screen, Harris's Bud is alert and alive. He gave Bud gestures, habits, mannerisms, turns of phrase that couldn't be written into a script—but because of Harris's performance, they're in the book. He gave a spin to his dialogue that enriched it. Dozens of times as I watched him work, I laughed aloud in delight as I realized, That's why Bud says that! Harris opened up Bud's soul for me—and yet not once did I detect him playing for the camera. Many of the most-honored actors in film today annoy me beyond endurance because I constantly catch them performing, showing off, strutting, as if they were tugging on the audience's lapels, trying to draw us closer, making sure we see them acting. By contrast, Harris made me believe that he *was* that simple, sometimes-confused, humble yet deeply noble man named Bud Brigman. If I hadn't had a few glimpses of Harris *out* of character in the uncut scenes, I would have believed that he wasn't acting at all, that he was just being himself. Not so. He was being Bud Brigman, and because of that, the Bud Brigman in this book is richer than he would otherwise have been.

There are other people who contributed to this novel. Sally Peters, my editor at Pocket, was heroic in her restraint, as we passed all the deadlines that normally apply to books. At any point she could have said, "Turn the book in *now* or refund the advance"—my contract allowed that—but instead she helped me hold off until the absolutely last possible moment so that I could see almost the entire film before turning in the book. The pressure on her was enormous, but she was careful to make sure that I felt as little of it as possible. As a result, the book is far better as I turn in the final version on 3 April 1989 than it would have been a month or two months or—I shudder—the *four* months earlier that the contract required.

Peter Weissman, Pocket's copy editor, did a thorough and helpful job under very tight deadlines. My noble assistant, Julie Hamilton, got sore feet from standing for hours at the copy machine. Gale Hurd rescued me from last-minute interference by meddlers who wanted to get their fingers into the project. Christa Vausbinder was always helpful and patient as she helped keep lines of communication open. And Van Ling long ago passed from being a resource to being a friend.

My own resident editor, my wife, Kristine, read and responded to every word of the book, and with her clear vision has helped shape this novel as she has everything I write. She also worked impossible hours, including getting up at six in the morning to send manuscripts off on Piedmont Airlines' courier service—just as I was going to bed after printing out and duplicating it. Through all this she went through a pregnancy, a miscarriage, a five-year-old in a body cast, an eight-year-old with chicken pox, and a husband alternately on the verge of madness and exhaustion. Together we are trying to create both a family and a contribution to literature; I can't imagine myself doing either without her.

You have probably already read this novel, and if you haven't yet seen the movie, I hope you will. Then you'll be in a position to judge whether Jim and I succeeded in our goal of making this book, not a novelization as the term is usually understood, but a novel that stands on its own and yet complements, illuminates, and fulfills the movie. Though the story is and always has been, at its roots, Jim Cameron's, it has long since ceased to be possible to go through this book picking out which idea, which nuance, which phrase came from Jim, which from me, and which from the actors. For good or ill, this novel is as close a collaboration between filmmaker and novelist as any other since the collaboration between Kubrick and Clarke in creating *2001: A Space Odyssey*—and I hope you will forgive our ambition in hoping that you will find that both book and movie compare well with that watershed of science fiction film.

Because this book is a far more solid artifact than the ephemeral credits that roll past at the end of the film, I am including a cast list; the names of all the actors belong here, because they are co-creators of both the book and the film.

Bud Brigman	Ed Harris
Lindsey Brigman	Mary Elizabeth Mastrantonio
Lt. Hiram Coffey	Michael Biehn
"Catfish" DeVries	Leo Burmester
Allen "Hippy" Carnes	Todd Graff
"Jammer" Willis	John Bedford Lloyd
Arliss "Sonny" Dawson	J.C. Quinn
Lisa "One Night" Standing	Kimberly Scott
Lew "Bird Dog" Finler	Capt. Kidd Brewer, Jr.
Wilhite	George Robert Klek
Schoenick	Christopher Murphy
Ensign Monk	Adam Nelson
Dwight Perry	Richard Warlock
Lupton McWhirter	Mike DeLuna
Tommy Ray Dietz	Robert Searle
Captain Kretschmer	Peter Ratray
Aaron Barnes	Michael Beach
Executive Officer Everton	Brad Sullivan
Navigator	Frank Lloyd
McBride	Jimmie Ray Weeks
Commodore DeMarco	J. Kenneth Campbell
Kirkhill	Ken Jenkins
Bendix	Chris Elliott
Reporter	Chris Anastasio

Construction Worker	Thomas F. Duffy
Anchorman	Joe Farago
Newscasters	Wendy Gordon
	Marcus Makai
Reporter #1	Gale Anne Hurd
Reporter #2	Emily Yancy
Dr. Berg	Michael Chapman
Older Woman	Robin Montgomery
Young Woman	Polly Cross
The Guy	Patrick Malone
Irate Man	Charles Stewart
News Helicopter Pilot	David Hicks
Crew Members	Phillip Darlington
	Joseph Nemec III

This book was written on a Toshiba 3100 and edited on an ALR-386, using WordPerfect 5.0 software. It was printed out on an Epson GQ-3500 in HP-emulation mode. Manuscript copies were made on a Canon NP-3525-EF.